Palgrave Gothic

Series Editor
Clive Bloom
Professor Emeritus
Middlesex University
London, UK

This series of Gothic books is the first to treat the genre in its many interrelated, global and 'extended' cultural aspects to show how the taste for the medieval and the sublime gave rise to a perverse taste for terror and horror and how that taste became not only international (with a huge fan base in places such as South Korea and Japan) but also the sensibility of the modern age, changing our attitudes to such diverse areas as the nature of the artist, the meaning of drug abuse and the concept of the self. The series is accessible but scholarly, with referencing kept to a minimum and theory contextualised where possible. All the books are readable by an intelligent student or a knowledgeable general reader interested in the subject.

Editorial Board:
Dr Ian Conrich, University of South Australia
Barry Forshaw, author/journalist, UK
Professor Gregg Kucich, University of Notre Dame, USA
Professor Gina Wisker, University of Brighton, UK
Dr Catherine Wynne, University of Hull, UK
Dr Alison Peirse, University of Yorkshire, UK
Dr Sorcha Ní Fhlainn, Manchester Metropolitan University, UK
Professor William Hughes, Bath Spa University, UK

More information about this series at
http://www.palgrave.com/gp/series/14698

James Machin

Weird Fiction in Britain 1880–1939

palgrave
macmillan

James Machin
Royal College of Art
London, UK

Palgrave Gothic
ISBN 978-3-030-08036-5   ISBN 978-3-319-90527-3 (eBook)
https://doi.org/10.1007/978-3-319-90527-3

© The Editor(s) (if applicable) and The Author(s) 2018
Softcover re-print of the Hardcover 1st edition 2018
This work is subject to copyright. All rights are solely and exclusively licensed by the Publisher, whether the whole or part of the material is concerned, specifically the rights of translation, reprinting, reuse of illustrations, recitation, broadcasting, reproduction on microfilms or in any other physical way, and transmission or information storage and retrieval, electronic adaptation, computer software, or by similar or dissimilar methodology now known or hereafter developed.
The use of general descriptive names, registered names, trademarks, service marks, etc. in this publication does not imply, even in the absence of a specific statement, that such names are exempt from the relevant protective laws and regulations and therefore free for general use.
The publisher, the authors and the editors are safe to assume that the advice and information in this book are believed to be true and accurate at the date of publication. Neither the publisher nor the authors or the editors give a warranty, express or implied, with respect to the material contained herein or for any errors or omissions that may have been made. The publisher remains neutral with regard to jurisdictional claims in published maps and institutional affiliations.

Cover illustration: PAINTING / Alamy Stock Photo

Printed on acid-free paper

This Palgrave Macmillan imprint is published by the registered company Springer Nature Switzerland AG
The registered company address is: Gewerbestrasse 11, 6330 Cham, Switzerland

ACKNOWLEDGEMENTS

In researching and writing this book I've relied on the expertise and generous support of numerous people who are nevertheless not responsible for any of its defects. I am particularly grateful to Roger Luckhurst for supervising the PhD thesis from which this book has emerged. The wellsprings of his insight, knowledge, and benevolence seem bafflingly inexhaustible. Thanks to the Birkbeck School of Arts for sustaining such an inspiring and supportive research community. The feedback, encouragement, and guidance offered by Nick Freeman and Adam Roberts, who examined the thesis, has doubtless improved the resulting book no end. I am also very grateful to the readers of the MS for Palgrave, who gave me valuable pushes and nudges in various directions. Thanks of course to Timothy J. Jarvis for the ongoing conversation on all things weird, a conversation that has shaped this book immeasurably. My sincerest appreciation to Clive Bloom for green-lighting the book for the Palgrave Gothic series and steering it into existence. Myriad and diverse thanks also owed to: Michael J. Abolafia, the late great Harold Billings, Godfrey Brangham, John Clute, Douglas Cowie, Stefan Dziemianowicz, Robert Eaglestone, Emily Fergus, Christine Ferguson, Gwilym Games, Sebastian Groes, Matthew Harle, Hallvard Haug, Kenneth Hillier, James D. Jenkins, Michael Jonik, S. T. Joshi, Rob Latham, Kate Macdonald, Johnny Mains, Cato Marks, David McAllister, Rosalie Parker, Mark Pilkington, Jon Preece, Michael Redley, Ray Russell, Brian J. Showers, Andrew Smith, David Tibet, Mark Valentine, Jeff VanderMeer, Sherryl Vint, Rick Watson, and Aaron Worth. Sincere apologies if you're one of the countless people I've pestered on this subject over the last few years and I've omitted you from this list. Thank you to Lina Aboujieb and Ellie Freedman at Palgrave for guiding me through the publication process with such kind efficiency.

This book was made possible by grants awarded by the Robert Gavron Charitable Trust and Birkbeck School of Arts, so I would particularly like to thank Kate Gavron and Carol Watts respectively. It greatly saddens me that due to Lord Gavron's death in 2015 I am unable to write to him to inform him of the publication of this book and thank him again for his incredible generosity. I am very grateful to both the Harry Ransom Center and *Science Fiction Studies* (R. D. Mullen Fellowship) for research grants that enabled travel to archives in Texas and California, and also to the staff at the Ransom Center and the Eaton Collection, University of California Riverside, for being uniformly generous with their expertise and hospitality.

I owe a huge debt of gratitude to my mother Carole, my sisters Becca, Miriam, and Katie, to John Hamilton-Brown, and to Adrian and Judith Jones. I would like to offer innumerable thanks to my wife Lucy Jones. Although she has never troubled to disguise her disdain for my 'goblin books', there is no conceivable way I could have undertaken this work without her unstinting patience and support. For this and much else besides, I will be ever grateful. Finally, I would like to thank my son, Arthur, whose birth in 2014 didn't in the end derail my research too much, and who has been a source of boundless joy ever since. This book is dedicated to the memory of my father, Noel Machin.

Chapter 3 of this book is derived in part from an article published in *Textual Practice*, Volume 31, 2017, copyright Taylor & Francis, available online: https://doi.org/10.1080/0950236X.2017.1358692

Previous versions of some of the material in Chapter 4 have appeared in an article published in *Wormwood* 24, Spring 2015 ('A Surge of Daemonic Energy: John Buchan and *The Dancing Floor*'), and my introduction to the Valancourt 2017 edition of C. F. Keary's *'Twixt Dog and Wolf*. The extracts from holdings of the Harry Ransom Center at the University of Texas, Austin, are used with its kind permission. I am very grateful to the Center, as well as the Creekmore and Adele Fath Charitable Foundation and the University of Texas at Austin Office of Graduate Studies for supporting my visiting fellowship there in 2014.

CONTENTS

1 Introduction   1

2 The Weird Fin-De-Siècle and After   47

3 Shiel, Stenbock, Gilchrist, and Machen   93

4 Buchan   163

5 *Weird Tales* and Pulp Decadence   221

Afterword   249

Index   251

LIST OF FIGURES

Fig. 1.1 Illustration for Arthur Machen's *The House of Souls* (1906) by Sidney Sime (image courtesy of Ray Russell)   15
Fig. 2.1 Advert for the 'Keynotes' series, designed by Aubrey Beardsley (image courtesy of Alamy)   61
Fig. 3.1 Portrait of Eric, Count Stenbock, circa 1886   110
Fig. 4.1 Cover design for John Buchan's *Scholar Gipsies* (1896a) (image courtesy of Kenneth Hillier)   179
Fig. 5.1 July 1928 edition of *Weird Tales*, featuring 'The Bowmen' by Arthur Machen (image courtesy of Alamy)   223

CHAPTER 1

Introduction

This study is, in part, a reaction to the view that the story of weird fiction is 'the story of the rise of the tentacle' and 'the group of writers surrounding Lovecraft' that 'represented a revolution of sorts against old ideas about supernatural fiction' (A. VanderMeer and VanderMeer 2012a, xvi). This account effectively puts the output of the pulp magazine *Weird Tales* during the 1920s and 1930s—especially the work of H. P. Lovecraft (1890–1937), Clark Ashton Smith (1893–1961), and Robert E. Howard (1906–1936)—at the centre of our understanding of the mode and its history. The following discussion is not meant to rebut this account, but rather blur the periodic boundaries put in place that serve to co-opt weird fiction for a 'modern' era and imbue it with a sheen of modernist respectability. Since the term 'pulp modernism' was coined by Paula Rabinowitz (in relation to Noir), refracting popular culture through the prism of Modernism has been a source of productive and insightful scholarship (Rabinowitz 2012). However, making such associations with what is understood as high culture inevitably, even if only inadvertently, involves some animus to legitimize texts that have traditionally been seen as outside the purview of scholarship. China Miéville, for example, achieves both with his comment that weird fiction and high Modernism are 'exactly linked' and are 'a differently inflected statement of the same concerns, the same anxieties, the same attempted solutions' (Venezia 2010, 5).

In their introduction to *The Weird: A Compendium of Strange and Dark Stories* (2012a, b), Ann VanderMeer and Jeff VanderMeer contrast this 'modern era' of weird fiction to 'prior eras' and aver that a break took place: 'The best and most unique supernatural writers from prior eras, like Arthur Machen (his best short fiction written before 1910), would leave their mark on this newer weird, but not a boot print' (xvi). The parenthetical remark is a necessary one to the argument: Machen (1863–1947) outlived Lovecraft by a decade. It is also indicative of the refusal of lives and texts to conform to our desire to retroactively impose order on, and identify process in, the teeming jumble and babel of culture and history.

However, the point of disagreement elaborated upon in what follows is the specific claim that Machen, and his generation of writers, did not leave a 'boot print' on ensuing weird fiction. It is my attempt to reinsert weird fiction back into its wider continuum, taking as my starting point the nineteenth century, and as my end point the iterations of the nineteenth century still very much present and persistent in the 'modernist' *Weird Tales* of the 1920s and 1930s. Reviewing Machen's 1895 novel *The Three Impostors*, H. G. Wells lamented that Machen had 'determined to be weird' (Wells 1896, 48).[1] My argument in this book is that Machen was not alone in this endeavour.

In Lovecraft's influential survey, *Supernatural Horror in Literature* (1927), he defined the weird tale as one consisting of

> something more than secret murder, bloody bones, or a sheeted form clanking chains according to rule. A certain atmosphere of breathlessness and unexplainable dread of outer, unknown forces must be present; and there must be a hint, expressed with a seriousness and portentousness becoming its subject, of that most terrible conception of the human brain—a malign and particular suspension or defeat of those fixed laws of Nature which are our only safeguard against the assaults of chaos and the dæmons of unplumbed space. (Lovecraft 1985, 426)

The ongoing durability of this delineation is perhaps as indicative of Lovecraft's impact on the mode as it is on the perspicacity of his analysis. It seems doubtful that there is any credible definition of weird fiction which is not in some respects a permutation or elaboration of Lovecraft's conceit here. It has certainly been reiterated regularly ever since, and has

---

[1] For the attribution to Wells, see (Philmus 1977, 172).

become (as here) a formula from which most if not all discussions of weird fiction ensue, and with good reason: it manages to limn the mode while deftly avoiding any inaccurately reductive rendering of weird fiction as a rigidly prescribed genre.[2] As Roger Luckhurst observes, the Weird was 'never tied to a fixed typology and continually slipped category', due in no small part to Lovecraft's largesse in his own application of the term (Luckhurst 2017, 1043). Attempting a category fix for weird fiction, therefore, seems tautologically self-defeating when dealing with a mode of writing that is so determined to resist just such ossification into formula.

An ensuing challenge of undertaking a study such as this is, therefore, to resist overstating the case. The following should not be construed as either any particular advocacy of the term 'weird fiction' or a promotion of its use, or an implied criticism of related terms such as Gothic, uncanny, supernatural, horror, strange, and so on. In what follows I will discuss 'weird fiction' in relation to some of these terms but the objective is simply to understand why people use the word 'weird' in relation to fiction at all, and if its deployment can implicitly tell us something about the sort of fiction that provokes such use. I hope, therefore, that (subsequent to this Introduction) repeated use of the term 'weird fiction' (and 'the Weird' more generally) without cautiously reiterating acknowledgements of its difficulties will be tolerated. Writing critically on weird fiction obviously necessitates use of the term, and any such use below should not imply an un-interrogated or complacent assumption of what the term means (the discussion of which is, in part, one of the tasks of the study as a whole) and how it is used.

These difficulties may in part also explain the term's persistence and its provocation; its slipperiness and its suggestion of generically interstitial writing that willfully evades and complicates procrustean critical readings. It also makes it difficult to position any particular author as definitively a writer of weird fiction (even Lovecraft's fiction has a variety of other adumbrations: 'cosmic horror', science fiction, Dunsanian fantasy, etc.). Whenever a particular writer is adduced to my argument, I have attempted to present at least some documentary evidence that their work has been described as 'weird fiction' either by their contemporaries or in subsequent criticism, preferably presenting examples of both. I have sought to avoid getting sidetracked into extensive justifications for considering a

---

[2] Examples from myriad include Joshi 2003, 6; DiBiasio 2009, 88; A. VanderMeer and VanderMeer 2012, xv; Luckhurst 2015, 195; Thacker 2015c, 119.

particular writer to be admissible as this would become an ultimately tedious and repetitive diversion from, rather than a contribution to, the discussion. Rather, I have attempted to imbricate documentary justification for a particular author's inclusion within the discussion itself.

My choices are also informed by the 'connoisseur culture' I delineate in Chap. 3, but which informs much of the discussion throughout: the notion that weird fiction is a mode defined, at least in part, by a process of distinction whereby connoisseurs use the term as an imprimatur for identifying texts of variegated genres deemed to achieve the requisite aesthetic qualities to differentiate them from formulaic genre writing. This is particularly applied to horror texts and often specifically used to differentiate between what John Buchan described as 'mere horror [… and …] legitimate art' (see Chap. 4). Indeed, the issue of the relationship between literariness, artistic legitimacy, and genre, is—as I will argue—intrinsic to the function of the term 'weird fiction', and as such is revisited repeatedly throughout what follows.

For Benjamin Noys and Timothy S. Murphy, the weird can be 'inflationary' (after Carl Freedman)—exposing the reader to the omniferous universe (see Chap. 3)—or deal in 'impoverishment' (after Samuel Beckett), offering harrowing glimpses of the 'shivering void' at the heart of things (Noys and Murphy 2016, 118). Noys and Murphy also observe that both effects can be accommodated within S. T. Joshi's claim that the weird fiction has a capacity for 'refashioning of the reader's view of the world' (Joshi 2003, 118). The British weird fiction discussed in this book certainly tilts to the former, the 'inflationary', rather than the latter, which reflects the post-Lovecraftian nihilism of writers like Thomas Ligotti (1953–). According to Freedman, this 'inflationary' valence of weird fiction (or, specifically, 'the genres that compose weird fiction') inclines 'in various ways, to suggest reality to be richer, larger, stranger, more complex, more surprising—and, indeed, "weirder"—than common sense would suppose' (Freedman 2013, 15). This iteration of the Weird resonates with Machen's own thesis on literary theory, *Hieroglyphics: A Note upon Ecstasy in Literature* (written 1899; published 1902), in which he argues that good literature is an exercise in ecstatic revelation of the numinous with a concomitant imperative for a 'withdrawal from the common life and the common consciousness' (Machen 1923b, 18–19). The 'inflationary' Weird explains how it can appear, on occasion, in texts that cannot be accommodated into the horror genre usually associated with the mode. Moreover, Machen suggests that horror is a *failure* to achieve what he calls the 'ecstatic', when, discussing his early work, he complains: 'I translated awe, at worst awfulness, into evil; again, I say, one dreams in fire and works in clay' (Machen 1923a, 127). A counterexample is Machen's own late tale, 'N' (1936), which he wrote when he was in his seventies, and is a multifaceted account of visionary geographical and temporal 'interpenetrations' in Stoke Newington, an area of northeast London (Machen also co-opts the theological term 'perichoresis', the metaphysical interrelationship between the Trinity). Miéville associates this calibration of the weird mode with 'those religious visionaries and ecstatics who perceive an unmediated relationship with numinosity', that is, the Gnostic mysticism of (for example) William Blake (Miéville 2009, 511). According to Miéville, 'the Weird [...] punctures the supposed membrane separating off the sublime, and allows swillage of that awe and horror from "beyond" back into the everyday. [...] The Weird is a radicalized sublime backwash' (511). The tendency of the writers I discuss in what follows—Vernon Lee, John Buchan, for example, as well as Machen—is to use this numinous (or perichoretic, or inflationary) weird to achieve a register distinct from (or at least not entirely predicated on) horror. This distinguishes them from writers of the *Weird Tales* era, which is more closely and consistently associated with horror and its affect.

WEIRDS OLD AND NEW

The initial work for this book began in 2012, at a time when weird fiction seemed to be making its presence felt across scholarship, publishing, and wider culture to an unprecedented degree. The anthologies *The Weird: A Compendium of Strange and Dark Stories* (mentioned above) and *The New Weird* (2008), both edited by Ann VanderMeer and Jeff VanderMeer, were significant and influential contributions to canon formation (the former particularly). Miéville had recently contributed an essay on 'Weird Fiction' to the *Routledge Companion to Science Fiction* (2009), consolidating and validating its identity within this genre (A. VanderMeer and VanderMeer 2012b, 2008; Miéville 2009). Vintage Classics had published a Lovecraft anthology in 2011, and an Oxford University Press one was in preparation, underwriting the status already afforded Lovecraft by his Penguin Classics editions (see below) (Lovecraft 2011, 2013).

Online, the VanderMeers established the Weird Fiction Review in 2011, and tasked it with being an 'ongoing exploration into all facets of the weird' ("About" n.d.). In his keynote address on 'the future of the novel' at the August 2012 Edinburgh World Writers' Conference, Miéville singled out the Weird Fiction Review for praise as 'a fabulous site that emerges, with brilliance and polymath gusto, out of genre traditions', suggesting that its approach was a route out of paralysis-inducing anxieties concerning literary fiction and genre ('China Miéville—Will the Novel Remain Writers' Favourite Narrative Form? | Edinburgh World Writers' Conference' 2016). In 2012, an academic conference on Miéville held at Senate House, London, styled itself a 'Weird Council' and included contributions from Miéville himself. This was followed the next year by a conference on weird fiction, also at Senate House and convened under the auspices of Birkbeck's Centre for Contemporary Literature.

This book was, therefore, originally galvanized by a peculiar moment of an incursion of the Weird, as critical discourse, into academic and mainstream culture (coeval in some respects with the ever-increasing and often controversial presence of Lovecraft in popular culture). This was, however, itself partly the culmination of a discussion initiated a decade earlier, reflexive of a turn in genre writing occurring at some indefinable point perhaps in the 1990s which became known as 'The New Weird':

> The 'new weird' existed long before 2003, when M. John Harrison started a message board thread with the words: 'The New Weird. Who does it? What is it? Is it even anything?' [...] By the time Harrison posited his question [...] it had become clear that a number of other writers had developed at the same time as Miéville, using similar stimuli. My *City of Saints & Madmen*, K. J. Bishop's *The Etched City*, and Paul Di Filippo's *A Year in the Linear City*, among others, appeared in the period from 2001 to 2003, with Steph Swainston's *The Year of Our War* published in 2004. It seemed that something had Risen Spontaneous—even though in almost every case, the work itself had been written in the 1990s and either needed time to gestate or had been rejected by publishers—and thus there was a need to explain or name the beast. The resulting conversation on the *Third Alternative* public message boards consisted of many thousands of words, used in the struggle to name, define, analyze, spin, explore, and quantify the term 'New Weird'. The debate involved more than fifty writers, reviewers, and critics, all with their own questions, agendas, and concerns. (J. VanderMeer 2008, ix)

Introducing the 2008 anthology *The New Weird*, Jeff VanderMeer in part defined the New Weird by contrasting it against existing understandings of 'weird fiction', or what he called the '"Old" Weird', observing that the latter could often be paraliterary in its pulp iterations:

> Weird fiction—typified by magazines like *Weird Tales* and writers like H. P. Lovecraft or Clark Ashton Smith back in the glory days of the pulps—eventually morphed into modern-day traditional Horror. 'Weird' refers to the sometimes supernatural or fantastical element of unease in many of these stories—an element that could take a blunt, literal form or more subtle and symbolic form and which was, as in the best of Lovecraft's work, combined with a visionary sensibility. These types of stories also often rose above their pulp or self-taught origins through the strength of the writer's imagination. (There are definite parallels to be drawn between certain kinds of pulp fiction and so-called 'Outsider Art'.) (ix)

The New Weird is then partially defined by its appropriation of the science fiction New Wave's habit of 'deliriously mix[ing] genres [and] high and low art': the traditions and tropes of 'low art' legitimized in this context (and in implicit contrast to the 'Old' weird) when deployed with artistic intentionality.

Also involved in this discourse was Miéville, both in his practice as a writer and as a critic. His 2003 guest editorial for *The Third Alternative* magazine bore the proclamatory title 'Long Live the New Weird' (Miéville 2003). At some point before 2005, however, when 'the term "New Weird" was being used with some regularity by readers, writers, and critics', Miéville 'began to disown [the "New Weird"] claiming it had become a marketing category and was therefore of no further interest to him' (xiii). However, in 2002 at least, he was still publicly embracing the less specific term 'weird fiction':

> I don't think you can distinguish science fiction, fantasy and horror with any rigour, as the writers around the magazine *Weird Tales* early in the last century (Lovecraft in particular) illustrated most sharply. So I use the term 'weird fiction' for all fantastic literature—fantasy, SF, horror and all the stuff that won't fit neatly into slots. (*Guardian* 2002)

As mentioned above, Miéville endorsed the Weird Fiction Review website's approach in this respect. The Weird Fiction Review also, however, has influenced and nurtured a more traditional interpretation of weird fiction more in line with Lovecraft's definition: a mode of writing with closer ties to the horror and Gothic lineage than (though not precluding) those of fantasy and science fiction, and commensurate to Miéville's 2009 delineation of weird fiction as 'generically slippery macabre fiction, a dark fantastic [… with a …] focus on *awe*, and its undermining of the quotidian' (Miéville 2009, 510). Likewise jettisoning the science-fictional connotations of New Weird, after 2005 *The Third Alternative* was 'reborn as the dark fantasy and horror magazine *Black Static*' (Ashley 2016).

Similarly, the recently launched *Year's Best Weird Fiction* series defines weird fiction in its publicity material as follows (Baron 2014; Koja 2015):

> No longer the purview of esoteric readers, weird fiction is enjoying wide popularity. Chiefly derived from early 20th-century pulp fiction, its remit includes ghost stories, the strange and macabre, the supernatural, fantasy, myth, philosophical ontology, ambiguity, and a healthy helping of the outré. ("Year's Best Weird Fiction Volume 1" 2014)

Inevitably, the proliferation of the term's application to texts that previously may have blithely presented themselves as horror fiction has been the cause of unease for some. Simon Strantzas, for example, has in a podcast interview expressed his own doubts about the term, despite being positioned by his publisher as 'one of the most dynamic figures in contemporary weird fiction' and serving as guest editor of *The Year's Best Weird Fiction, Vol. 3* ("Burnt Black Suns by Simon Strantzas: Hippocampus Press, Specializes in Classic Horror and Science Fiction" n.d.):

> I definitely hear the term 'weird fiction' being bandied around a lot more now than I used to … for me it's all horror fiction. I've always subscribed to Ramsey Campbell's view that horror is an expansive and never-ending genre and you can classify anything as horror. To me, weird fiction just seems like another term, to some degree, to avoid calling horror what it is. But if your argument is that there is a lot more fiction that strays from the example of Stephen King with the small-town horrors and where good ends up triumphing over evil in the end then, yes, I'd agree we see a lot more horror and weird fiction where the focus is on existence and how things don't necessarily turn out for the best. ("TIH 074: Simon Strantzas on Weird vs. Strange Fiction, Writing Routine and Thinking Horror » This Is Horror" 2016)

Here, Strantzas's reluctance to embrace the term is in keeping with the argument of this study; that one use of the term 'weird fiction' is as a mark of distinction or an imprimatur; a 'stamp of approval' on texts with the aim of emancipating them from 'low' genres, or to reassure commentators and readers that certain texts are not too déclassé to merit attention. This process is analogous (though not identical) to that described by John Rieder regarding 'the most influential members of the first generation of scholars of SF', his argument being that 'legitimizing the study of the genre entailed separating the best, most literary examples of SF from the more familiar, popular, and supposedly inferior versions of it that predominated in mass culture' (Rieder 2017, 1). Regarding weird fiction, this raises the problem that, as David Langford writes of the New Weird, weird fiction may ultimately 'mean little more than "stories we like"', despite or incidental to, rather than because of, their genre (Langford 2012). In 'Supernatural Horror in Literature', Lovecraft in fact defines 'the weird in fiction' in such a way that it allows him to use it as just such a mark of distinction. He explicitly resists ossifying weird fiction into a genre proper, identifiable through any specific tropes, structures, or appurtenances:

> Naturally we cannot expect all weird tales to conform absolutely to any theoretical model. Creative minds are uneven, and the best of fabrics have their dull spots. Moreover, much of the choicest weird work is unconscious; appearing in memorable fragments scattered through material whose massed effect may be of a very different cast. [… I]t remains a fact that such narratives often possess, in isolated sections, atmospheric touches which fulfil every condition of true supernatural horror-literature. Therefore we must judge a weird tale not by the author's intent, or by the mere mechanics of the plot; but by the emotional level which it attains at its least mundane point. If the proper sensations are excited, such a 'high spot' must be admitted on its own merits as weird literature, no matter how prosaically it is later dragged down. (Lovecraft 1985, 426–427)

By so attenuating the weird in fiction to an imprecisely delineated 'high spot', Lovecraft frees himself from Linnean concerns of genre categorization for his subsequent analysis: he can and does identify and valorize entire short stories or novels as laudably 'weird'—regardless of authorial intentionality ('much of the choicest weird work is unconscious')—but he also has free rein to identify 'weird elements' in other works that could never convincingly be wholly appropriated as weird fiction, were it a genre rather than a mode (*Wuthering Heights*, for example).

The above mention of 'philosophical ontology' in the context of promotional material for a trade paperback anthology of weird fiction might at first glance seem surprising, although Strantzas's reference above to weird fiction's 'focus on existence' at least hints at an explanation.

Tangentially to, and occasionally imbricating with, the recrudescence of weird fiction and the naissance of the 'New Weird' was a philosophical vogue which enthusiastically used Lovecraft as a literary springboard for the development of—particularly—phenomenological discourse. Considering Lovecraft's fiction was always concerned primarily with ideas rather than diegesis, with the benefit of hindsight this application of his texts now seems inevitable. There were certainly already precedents: in the francophone world, Lovecraft served as a touchstone in Tzvetan Todorov's structural study of *The Fantastic* (1970) had been discussed several times in Deleuze and Guattari's *A Thousand Plateaus* (1980), and was also the subject of Michel Houellebecq's less recondite study *H. P. Lovecraft: Against the World, Against Life* (1991) (Todorov 1975, 34–35; Deleuze and Guattari 2004, 264, 270, 274, 277, 575; Houellebecq 2005).[3] Lovecraft's advance critical acceptance in France perhaps suggests that his notoriously prolific use of Latinate adjectives lends itself particularly well to translation into French, and renders his writing less at odds with the sort of stylistic dogmas he is exposed to in the anglophone world. Certainly, although an object of critical derision for Edmund Wilson in the 1940s, by the 1960s Lovecraft was already the subject of a doctoral dissertation at the Sorbonne undertaken by Maurice Lévy (subsequently a professor of English literature at the University of Toulouse-Le Mirail), published as a monograph in 1972 and translated into English in 1988 by S. T. Joshi (Luckhurst 2013a, xix; Lévy 1988). Lévy's work anticipated subsequent interest in and enthusiasm for the philosophical implications of Lovecraft's fictions.

In the United Kingdom, an early appropriation of Lovecraft's texts as a catalyst for outré theoretical discourse was undertaken by Nick Land in the 1990s during his tenure at the University of Warwick and involvement in the occasionally controversial Cybernetic Culture Research Unit (Ccru) (Luckhurst 2013b; Land 2011). The conference at Goldsmith's University in 2007 titled 'Weird Realism: Lovecraft and Theory' included contributions from Miéville, as well as critical theorists such as Benjamin Noys and Mark Fisher ("K-Punk: Weird Realism" 2007). The latter's imprint Zero Books published Graham Harman's *Weird Realism: Lovecraft and*

---

[3] In the original French text of Todorov's *Introduction à la littérature fantastique* (1970), he translates Lovecraft's 'weird' as *fantastique*. Confusingly, the Cornell edition's English translation renders Todorov's use of *fantastique* here into 'fantastic', thereby losing Lovecraft's original 'weird'.

Philosophy in 2012, in which Harman describes Lovecraft as a 'tacit philosopher' who is uniquely 'perplexed by the gap between objects and the power of language to describe them, or between objects and the qualities they possess' (Harman 2012, 3). Zero Books also produced a series of well-received theoretical works by Eugene Thacker on the 'horror of philosophy', where he has argued that as far as weird fiction is 'part of the horror genre' it 'presents horror less as a stimulus-response system, in which a threat elicits an emotional response to fear, and more as a kind of freezing of all affect, resulting in a combined state of dread and fascination' (Harman 2012; Thacker 2011, 2015a, b, c, 113). Miéville perhaps acts as the nexus between these two streams, as comfortable contributing to rarefied theoretical discourses as he is participating in more accessible fora in his capacities as an author and critic (Miéville 2008). Mark Fisher's *The Weird and the Eerie* (2017), while very much emerging from his theoretical background is a lucid and accessible essay on manifestations of the Weird across a range of media. Fisher argues that the mode can be identified in the post-punk records of The Fall or the hallucinatory science fiction of Philip K. Dick, as much as the classic weird tales of M. R. James. Overall, *The Weird and the Eerie* is a demonstration and reinforcement of Lovecraft's argument that 'memorable fragments' of the Weird are to be found everywhere (Fisher 2016).

Negotiating Genres

The present study is commensurate with Joshi's and Miéville's argument that the *Weird Tales* iteration of weird fiction in the 1920s and 1930s was only the conclusion of a 'high phase' of such writing which began in the 1880s (Miéville 2009, 510). In 2010, Miéville was teaching

> a course at the University of Warwick on early twentieth-century weird fiction, in which he has theorised a 'para-canon' of the weird in which certain key names recur, notably William Hope Hodgson, Algernon Blackwood, Arthur Machen, and of course, Lovecraft. This is the *locus classicus* of the 'haute weird', roughly spanning the period 1880–1940 and particularly associated with the journal *Weird Tales* (1923–1954). (Venezia 2010, 4)

Also giving credence to this notion of an '*haute* Weird', Penguin has used the demarcation 'weird' when titling its 'Classics' and 'Modern Classics' editions of some of the writers associated with and spanning this 'high phase', including Lovecraft, Algernon Blackwood, and Arthur Machen, all edited by Joshi, and all bearing the subtitle "[...] *and Other Weird Stories*" (H. P. Lovecraft 1999, 2001; Blackwood 2002a; Machen 2011). Noys and Murphy posit a nearly identical periodization, though they opt for the simpler 'Old Weird' rather than Miéville's '*haute* Weird': 'The Old Weird can be dated between 1880 and 1940, and the term is explicitly articulated with the founding of the pulp magazine *Weird Tales* in March 1923' (Noys and Murphy 2016, 118).

Joshi's *The Evolution of the Weird Tale* (2004b) is a survey of the work of a selection of relevant writers from the long nineteenth century rather than an actual exploration of the development of the mode itself, or an attempt to define the early history of the use and meaning of the term 'weird tale' (which I gesture towards in this chapter) (Joshi 2004b). In fact, Joshi explicitly states in his introduction to *The Weird Tale* (1990) that 'the weird tale [...] did not (and perhaps does not now) exist as a genre' (Joshi 2003, 1). The possible contradiction in positing a 'high phase' of weird fiction and then denying its existence as a genre is made resolvable by looking at genre not as 'the permanent product of a singular origin, but the temporary by-product of an ongoing process' (Altman 1999, 54). If it is the case that 'to talk about genre is to talk about type, kind, sort', there is a corollary that one is not talking about specific things, but a 'kind' of thing: in all discussion of genre there exists that vagueness necessary for accommodating different individual texts into 'different sets of sets, which partially overlap' (Brooker 2010, 1). Any and every putative genre, therefore, has an inbuilt, tautological, dilatability; a necessary capaciousness which can also destabilize and derail their discussion.

Accordingly, Rick Altman has argued that attempting to stabilize genre by subjecting it to a Linnaean system of categorization unhelpfully ossifies something that is in actuality dynamic and constantly shifting; a continually contested and renegotiated quantity (Altman 1999, 63–65). Following Altman's thinking, Rieder has argued that such a historical (as opposed to formal) approach to genre theory is 'to be preferred because it challenges its students to understand genre in a richer and more complex way, within parameters that are social rather than just literary' (Rieder 2017, 17). The use of 'weird' as a critical and literary term in the nineteenth century as outlined below certainly fits with Altman's suggestion that the genre process operates through a dialectic based on 'attaching a new adjective to an existing noun genre' (65). However, the reticence suggested by its predominantly *adjectival* use is also commensurate with the VanderMeers' claim that weird fiction is a 'mode of writing' and as such vexatious to 'more rigid taxonomists' (A. VanderMeer and VanderMeer 2012a, xvi). This of course accords with Joshi's objections to weird fiction being considered a genre proper, as well as Lovecraft's caution that one 'cannot expect all weird tales to conform absolutely to any theoretical model' (Lovecraft 1985, 426).

The term 'mode' in a literary context suggests 'a broad but identifiable kind of literary method, mood, or manner that is not tied exclusively to a particular form or genre' (Baldick 2008, 213). Problematizing the durability of considerations of science fiction as the latter, Veronica Hollinger has differentiated mode from genre by delineating it as signifying 'something more than a particular kind of narrative complex—generally understood to be an archive of stories with particular themes, motifs, and figures' (Hollinger 2014, 139–140). Weird fiction has arguably never been considered to be a genre proper, but is still significantly limned by explicitly regarding it as a mode, 'which [as Istvan Csicsery-Ronay Jr writes in relation to science fiction] is neither a belief nor a model, but rather a mood or attitude' and irreducible to 'a programlike set of exclusive rules and required devices' (Csicsery-Ronay Jr 2008, 3, 5). Such formulations fit seamlessly with Lovecraft's claim that the genre of a text can in no way preclude instances of the weird 'mood' manifesting itself, regardless of the overall tone of the work.

Weird fiction, then, is intrinsically problematic for critical discourse: if weird fiction is accepted as a mercurial and 'generically slippery' mode, how is the critic to approach it? One possibility, explored below, involves putting aside the nature of the texts themselves and considering how the mode is used as a process of distinction, whereby 'connoisseurs' deploy the term as an imprimatur for identifying texts of variegated genres deemed to achieve the requisite aesthetic qualities to differentiate them from formulaic genre writing. The term then has an implication of restlessness; or at least signals the author's intent to avoid simple rehearsals of standard generic tropes. This process is particularly applied to horror texts and often specifically used to differentiate between what John Buchan, writing in 1896, demarcates as 'mere horror [… and, conversely …] legitimate art'.[4] Indeed, the issue of the relationship between literariness, artistic legitimacy, and genre is intrinsic to the function of the term 'weird fiction'.

[4] Austin, HRC, John Lane Company Records, Box 64, Reader's reports 1894–1899, 2 July 1896.

As such, recourse to the theoretical work of Pierre Bourdieu can help explicate the operation and function of the term. Bourdieu's analysis of cultural practice addresses similar questions of 'aesthetic value' as well as 'the role of intellectuals and artists and the relationship between high culture and popular culture', and will be occasionally adduced in my discussion below (Johnson 1993, 1).

'Weird' becomes an adjective applied to literature at some point in the nineteenth century after losing (although not altogether) its original meaning as a noun, and I will later investigate this etymological provenance in more detail. In the visual arts, Aubrey Beardsley was parodied by *Punch* as 'Daubaway Weirdsley' and his *Times* obituary referred to 'the weird perversity of his fancy'. Sidney Sime (1865–1941) was the artist who, more so than Beardsley even, created a visual lexicon for weird fiction through his illustrations for Arthur Machen (*The Hill of Dreams* and *The House of Souls*), William Hope Hodgson (*The Ghost Pirates*), and myriad works by Lord Dunsany; Lovecraft honoured him with references to his work in 'The Call of Cthulhu' and 'Pickman's Model'. In an 1899 interview in the *Idler*, the journalist Arthur H. Lawrence refers to Sime's 'weird effects' and his interest in 'the weird and grotesque' before coining the plural 'weirds' to describe Sime's creations in this vein (Lawrence 1898, 764, 766) (Fig. 1.1).

The frequency of the adjectival use of 'weird' does at least give it a claim ahead of the Gothic in terms of its use in relation to literature in the nineteenth century, due to its application where 'Gothic' might be used now. Hence Robert Louis Stevenson's *Strange Case of Dr Jekyll and Mr Hyde* (1886) was described in contemporaneous discourse as a 'weird story' and a 'weird novelette' with a 'weird hero', but not a Gothic novelette (*Era* 1890, 12; *Graphic* 1888, 122; *Glasgow Herald* 1889, 10). Kipling's anthology *Plain Tales from the Hills* (1888) had elements of the 'weird', but not the Gothic (*Murray's Magazine* 1890, 285). Bram Stoker's *Dracula* (1897) was 'wild and weird' but not Gothic (*Freeman's Journal and Daily Commercial Advertiser* 1898, 2). Indeed, after the publication of Sir Walter Scott's *Waverley* (1814), it is difficult to find examples of the latter's use as a literary term until the early twentieth century, with the rare literary applications before this time being explicitly retrospective; after the initial heyday of the Gothic romance, the Gothic, as a literary term, was for most of the nineteenth century deployed only with reference to that specific episode in literary history. This remained the case until it gained its more capacious, critical application in the twentieth century, as

Fig. 1.1 Illustration for Arthur Machen's *The House of Souls* (1906) by Sidney Sime (image courtesy of Ray Russell)

a genre that can now comfortably accommodate most horror media from any and every time period.

Acknowledging that 'weird' is a suggestive adjective and a mode rather than a genre also entails accepting that its subsequent slipperiness means that any attempt at rigidly differentiating it from what is now discussed as the Gothic would be both self-contradictory and counterproductive. It would also require a far more reductive understanding of the Gothic than is evident in contemporary criticism, where the survival and vigour of the genre has been attributed to its very ability to 'invert or split' in a continuum of modes with 'many different shadings and patterns of emphasis' (Luckhurst 2005a, xii). It is, therefore, not remotely my intention to define the Weird and the Gothic as discrete entities. Rather, the Weird is a *mode* closely identified with the Gothic *genre*. It would also contradict the previous suggestion that 'weird' in the nineteenth century is intrinsically slippery because of its determinedly and indeterminately adjectival status, which enables it to surreptitiously (and not so surreptitiously) attach itself to the corpus of many writers who (as Joshi suggests above) would not define themselves as writers of weird fiction; writers whose reputations now largely rest on different aspects of their writing—for example, Arthur Conan Doyle (1859–1930), Rudyard Kipling (1865–1936), and John Buchan (1875–1940)—with weird fiction being the overriding focus of a very few.

Out of the writers discussed in detail below, active before Lovecraft, it is perhaps only Machen who is now specifically remembered as a writer of weird fiction, which was in fact only one facet of a long life in letters. As Joshi noted regarding the subjects of his study *The Weird Tale*, 'only Lovecraft appears to have been conscious of working in a weird tradition [...] the others [...] regarded themselves (and were regarded by contemporary reviewers) as not intrinsically different from their fellow novelists and short-story writers' (Joshi 2003, 1). The same certainly applies to the main subjects of this study, though (and as I will detail) this lack of being perceived as 'intrinsically different' did not mean that their work was never discussed without recourse to consideration of the weird tradition; rather that such generic distinctions were not much used and moreover were only then in the process of coming into existence.

The psychological horror of Edgar Allan Poe (1809–1849) is cited by many of the authors discussed as being the midwife to their own literary nightmares, rather than the action-led melodrama of the Gothic romance, the 'bogle wark' of the 'penny dreadfuls', or the early nineteenth-century proto-sensation fiction of *Blackwood's* tales of terror (although Poe's innovations were certainly shaped by the latter) (Birkenhead 1921, 228; Baldick and Morrison 1995, xiii). British writers after Poe whose writing attracted the adjective 'weird' included Sheridan Le Fanu (1814–1873, 'one of the greatest masters of the weird and the terrible amongst our modern novelists' with a posthumous collection published in 1894 under the title *The Watcher and Other Weird Stories*), Charlotte Riddell ('a decided air of weirdness'), Robert Louis Stevenson ('weird, mysterious'), H. Rider Haggard (1856–1925, 'of weird and grandiose fancy'), Rudyard Kipling ('sometimes the stories are weird, often thrilling'), Arthur Conan Doyle (whose 'Lot No. 249' is reviewed under the subheading 'The Weird in Fiction' in the *Review of Reviews*), and many others, as well as those that serve as the main foci of this thesis (*Temple Bar* 1877, 504; *Saturday Review* 1883; MacCulloch 1898, 644; Sharp 1889, 100; *Scottish Review* 1899, 307; *Review of Reviews* 1892).

To make sense of this proliferation of this literary use of the term 'weird', we must differentiate it somehow from many of the genres that, as a mode, it inflects. It may be helpful to consider the Weird as a line (or tentacle!) weaving through and across various circles in a Venn diagram of genre. Nestling within the wider, intersecting circles of Realism and the Fantastic are Science Fiction (or Scientific Romance), the Gothic, and Horror, and smaller still, perhaps the Ghost Story, and myriad other, seemingly inexhaustible subdivisions. The Weird can inveigle its way into all. For the purposes of this book, however, it is necessary for me to select the type of Weird I want to focus on; the type of weird fiction from which we can glean most about what weird fiction is.

For example, weird fiction tends (and we can only talk about tendencies rather than rules) not to concern itself with the moral didacticism of what I will call the Victorian Ghost Story (referring both to the template established in the nineteenth century and also its later iterations). More fundamentally, the Victorian Ghost Story is exclusively concerned with the notion of life after death, or is, more succinctly, 'a story with a ghost in it' (Joshi 2012, 1:246). Tales such as Margaret Oliphant's 'The Open Door' (1882) are typically predicated on, and invested in, the notion of the posthumous survival of an individual personality, in spirit form. This may seem self-evident, tautological even, though—as Miéville has pointed out—there is a history of critics 'playing fast and loose with categories of ghosthood', confusing and attenuating our understanding of the relevant texts (Miéville 2008, 114). In other words, the alien entity Cthulhu and the spirit of Jemima Jackson's maiden aunt (see below) are obviously not equivalent, though, despite this, might be treated by some critics as comparably 'apparitional'. In a Victorian Ghost Story, the revenant will usually haunt the locale of a historical injustice, and the story will conclude with the protagonist/s investigating the haunting, and so discovering the historical injustice, righting it. Discussing 'The Open Door', for example, Melissa Edmundson Makala has argued that the haunting represents 'some past trauma for the former inhabitants', going to say that:

> this past trauma leads to reconciliation and a greater understanding between the living and the dead. [Such stories] highlight the interest of the authors not simply to scare, but to teach readers lessons of compassion and empathy that go beyond the narrative. (Edmundson Makala 2013, 99)

Typically, through this restoration of justice, the ghost will be laid to rest, and the quotidian order of things resumed. This narrative can often be freighted with many other discourses, concerning, for example, class mobility, capital, trauma, gender, inheritance, and so on. The focus is, in other words, firmly on the network of human social relations. Zoë Lehman Imfeld has argued that, in recent scholarship, this has been the overriding frame for interrogation of the form. Lehman notes a critical 'move away from inwardly directed readings of the ghost story, heavily influenced by psychoanalysis, to refreshed social contextualisation of the texts' (Imfeld 2016, 1). This claim is borne out by studies such as Andrew Smith's *The Ghost Story 1840–1920: A Cultural History* (2010), Simon Hay's *A History of the Modern British Ghost Story* (2011), and Susan Owens's *The Ghost: A Cultural History* (2017)—where the intersections of capital and gender in the texts complement the identical concerns of much wider contemporary critical discourse. Smith argues that 'during the nineteenth century the ghost story became *the* form in which conventional cultural assumptions about identity politics were challenged', challenging 'social narratives relating to class, gender, and national identity', the disembodied ghosts in the texts facilitating an abstract 're-evaluation' of these social constructions (A. Smith 2012, 4). The Victorian Ghost Story and its criticism not only engage with questions of female agency within the texts themselves, but also with the perception that a historical predominance of female authors has been occluded by the valorization of male writers such as Charles Dickens, Henry James, and M. R. James. Moreover, although the predominant concerns of the Victorian Ghost Story tend to be social, relating to the interworking of class, gender, justice, inheritance, and so on, this engagement with the social realm results in ambiguity in relation to critical reception. On the one hand, a status and value are afforded certain texts because of the insight they provide into social conditions in the nineteenth century; as Imfeld has it, 'for the rereading of supernatural tales as social documents, the supernatural fiction of women writers in particular is a gold mine' (Imfeld 2016, 4). On the other, this observation creates its own concomitant anxieties: Lynda E. Rucker argues that 'there is a sense that [… when women writers …] tackle horror, they tackle "women's"—read "lesser"—concerns: the realm of domesticity, the female body, relationships' (Rucker 2017, 12). Her concern is that such readings are coeval with 'the old assumption that men's themes are universal while women's themes are specific to their gender' (12).

At its crudest, the Victorian Ghost Story can be a blunt, didactical moral lesson, with the supernatural element employed solely to instil ethical instruction, just as Marley's ghost terrifies Scrooge into mending his ways in Dickens's *A Christmas Carol* (1843). The Weird, in contrast, tilts towards the existential, the ontological, and the epistemological. Simon Hay has recognized this difference in his discussion of Algernon Blackwood's 'The Willows' (1907), when he says that '[t]he story is an unusual ghost story in that it has no interest in questions for the past and how we inherit it; no interest in *history*, understood as such' (Hay 2011, 119). 'The Willows' is an account of a gradual, cumulative experience in which the two protagonists, in tandem with the shifting wetlands of the Danube delta slowly disintegrating beneath their feet, witness the fabric of reality being relentlessly tested by a vague and oppressively hostile outer force. The liminal antagonists in 'The Willows' are tenebrous and obscure; even when directly witnessed by the narrator, we are given little more information than that they are vague 'shapes' or 'presences', manifestations of the protective *genius loci* of an ancient sacred grove, or *temenos*. For the most part they are detected by implication alone; in the unaccountable stirrings of the foliage with which they are in sinister allegiance, in the inexplicable rent in the canoe that otherwise might provide a means of escape, and in 'deep hollows formed in the sand […] basin-shaped and of various depths and sizes, varying from that of a tea-cup to a large bowl' (Blackwood 2002a, b, 41).

Despite still classing it as a ghost story, Hay's differentiation between Blackwood's engagement with 'the horror of approaching the limits of history, of approaching those aspects of the natural world which resist human control and authority' (Hay 2011, 119) in 'The Willows' and, for example, Charlotte Riddell's 'key concern' in 'The Open Door' (1882, the same year Oliphant published her story of the same name) being 'class mobility' is a very clear one. Discussing the work of E. F. Benson, Joshi notes that his 'most successful tales are not ghost stories at all […] but pure "weird tales" where the phenomena are of a much more unclassifiable sort', a distinction elaborated upon in the present study (Joshi 2012, 2:410). Reviewing Oliver Onions's 1911 collection *Widdershins*, the *Review of Reviews* made a similar distinction, positioning it 'midway between real ghost stories and Mr. Algernon Blackwood's weird tales' (*Review of Reviews* 1911) (not that Blackwood did not also write 'real ghost stories', 'The Empty House' (1906) and 'The Kit-Bag' (1908) being examples).

Vernon Lee uses her preface to her 1896 collection, *Hauntings*, as an opportunity to place the stories therein, if not in direct opposition to, then at least at some remove from, the Victorian Ghost Story. Like Machen, she valorizes mystery ('this vague we know not what' (Lee 1896, vii)) above quotidian accounts of spiritual postmortem survival, which she satirizes as 'culled from the experience of some Jemima Jackson, who fifty years ago, being nine years of age, saw her maiden aunt appear six months after decease', complaining that 'one is struck by the extreme uninterestingness of this lady's appearance in the spirit, corresponding perhaps to her want of charm while in the flesh' (viii). Rather than 'hauntings such as could be contributed by the Society for Psychical Research' (xi), Lee argues that the 'genuine' ghost is the 'one born of ourselves, of the weird places we have seen, the strange stories we have heard', and, most of all, of 'the Past, the more or less remote Past, of which the prose is clean obliterated by distance' (x). Aaron Worth has similarly identified this engagement with 'deep time' as a hallmark of Machen's weird fiction, situating it within the wider context of nineteenth-century advances in understanding of geological and historical chronology, particularly within the fields of 'evolutionary biology and paleoarchaeology' (Worth 2018, xxiii). Lee's suggestion is that Jemima Jackson's aunt and her literary analogues are too much of the present to be anything other than prosaic. The constituent stories of *Hauntings* hit various registers; while 'Oke of Okehurst', which concerns 'the tragic unwinding of a family curse rooted in ancestral adultery' (Stableford 2017, 542), bears many of the hallmarks of the Victorian Ghost Story, others (such as 'Dionea'—see Chap. 3) are, like Blackwood's 'The Willows', closely engaged with 'deep time', the premodern, the Classical past, and landscape ('the weird places'), themes looked at in more detail elsewhere in this book.

By the 1890s, therefore, the Ghost Story was a form some considered clichéd. By the 1920s, it was a form *Weird Tales* magazine was actively defining itself against:

> Certain basic ghost-story themes have been used again and again, until they have lost their savor. The ghosts of fiction derive their interest and fascination from their strangeness; and if ghosts do the same things, in slightly different fashion, through story after story, then they become as humdrum and uninteresting as the sight of a milk wagon to a night-owl. The ghost stories in *Weird Tales* are different. (*Weird Tales* 1927, 580)

Besides this, and perhaps more importantly, it is—as I have stated above—difficult to find even a single work that fits neatly into any of these post hoc generic distinctions. With regards to the Weird and the Victorian Ghost Story, the work of M. R. James, though usually associated with the latter, repeatedly resists this classification and James is duly honoured by Lovecraft as a 'Modern Master' of the weird tale:

> James is regularly cited as a—or *the*—founder of the 'tradition' of English ghost stories. It is commonplace to then wryly point out that James's ghosts are in fact often not ghosts, but inhuman 'demons' of one sort or another. (Miéville 2008, 120)

Peter Keating, for example, regards James's stories as 'exercises in horror rather than supernatural explorations', but also acknowledges that 'for many modern readers' they achieve 'the very type of "English" ghost story' (Keating 1989, 363). Miéville goes on to argue that 'the adversaries of James's stories are disproportionately and emphatically *Weird*' (Miéville 2008, 120, emphasis in original). According to Joshi, the latter half of the nineteenth century saw a proliferation of ghost stories written in an 'unimaginative and rote manner' so that the genre 'gradually doomed itself to aesthetic oblivion in the following generation' (Joshi 2012, 1:246). He goes on to say that 'M. R. James simultaneously raised it to its aesthetic heights and, by that very act, impelled a very different type of ghost story from his successors' (246). This disorientation is not unique to James's *haute* Weird texts, and can occur whenever the Victorian Ghost Story strains against its generic template. For example, in E. Nesbit's 'Man-Size in Marble' (1887), a happily married couple move to a cottage in a village haunted by a legend concerning the medieval statues in the local church, which are rumoured to become animated on All Saint's Eve. Their maid informs them, when pressed, that the house they occupy is under supernatural threat due to the fact that 'in Catholic times, [...] there was a many deeds done here' (Nesbit 1893, 124). Dismissing this as local superstition, the husband inadvertently leads one of the stone monsters back to his house, where the wife, catching a glimpse, is frightened to death. There is a perfectly legitimate reading here of the Gothic past returning to disturb the complacent bourgeois gentility of the middle classes. However, this would only be a partial reading, and still leaves many fundamental aspects of the tale completely unexplained. The animated statue remains 'off screen' for the duration of the story: we only perceive its presence indirectly. The narrator remarks that his maid's description of the statues as 'drawed out man-size in marble' has 'a certain weird force and uncanniness' about it, in itself (125). Is this golem-like apparition possessed of intelligence or personality? Is it an automaton without any agency? What is the specific purpose of its midnight ambulation? These questions remain unresolved, and the implications disturb, despite the rather cloying sentimental tone of the writing.

This critical distinction between the Weird and the Ghost Story is not new: it has a provenance dating from at least the middle of the nineteenth century. In a survey of contemporary literature in the *Scottish Revue* in 1859, the 'power of weird imagination' at work in 'novelists in the past age' is lavished with considerable praise while the lack of its presence in 'recent fictitious literature' is roundly lambasted as 'deplorable' (*Scottish Review* 1859a). Hoffmann, Poe, Shelley, and Scott are cited as exemplars of the past, and Bulwer Lytton's *Zanoni* is posited as a recent exception to prove the rule. Special negative attention is paid to the ghost stories of Dickens, lambasted as 'poor forced factitious things', and Catherine Crowe's *The Night Side of Nature* 'with its cold, stupid, disenchanting lies, and the records of "Modern Spiritualism", the most lamentable exhibitions of human folly and hallucination the annals of the world contain.' The distinction being made between fiction resulting from the 'power of the weird imagination' and the 'poor forced factitious' ghost story is a useful one. Crowe's *The Night Side of Nature*, a best seller published in 1848, is a catalogue of anecdotal 'evidence' for spiritual survival after death, testimonies suggestive not only of life after death, but of the dead intervening at opportune moments to warn or console the living (Wilkes 2008). The use of the supernatural to provide reassurance, moral instruction, and resolution is particularly evident in the Ghost Story and many examples can be found of somewhat insipid revenants exposing 'hidden shames of domestic life' and resolving past injustices 'within the bounded space of the home' (Lynch 2004, 67, 69). The *Scottish Review* article makes a convincing case that this type of 'poor forced factitious' tale falls far short of producing the 'romantic power' of the weird; the ability of the 'terrible things of fancy' to both 'stagger the faith' and slip beyond the power of 'Science and cold-blooded Scepticism' to explain away (*Scottish Review* 1859b, 249).

This distinction is again articulated in—and perhaps explains the ambivalence of—a *Daily News* review of Anglo-Irish writer Charlotte Riddell's anthology *Weird Stories* (1882, as Mrs. J. H. Riddell):

> Mrs. J.H. Riddell's 'Weird Stories' […] are just about as weird as Christmas stories need to be. They have enough of the supernatural, and that of the real not explained-away supernatural, to be fearsome; but their tendency is on the whole to end genially. The ghostly appearances may be described in Mr. Matthew Arnold's words as beings 'not ourselves, which work for righteousness', for as soon as their demands for justice are complied with they vanish, which is what ghosts of good feeling might be naturally expected to do. Only one of the six stories leaves a deeper impression, that is, 'Sandy the Tinker', which recalls some of the reasonless, causeless terrors of nervous derangement. (*Daily News* 1882)

Contrastingly, the *Saturday Review* argues that Riddell's *Weird Stories* 'more than fairly deserves its title', although implicit in this judgement is the suggestion that it does fall someway short of fulfilling the promise of that title (*Saturday Review* 1883). The reviewer goes on to say that all the stories in the collection 'have a decided air of weirdness, and are well above the mark of the ordinary ghost story which turns up in Christmas numbers of magazines'. Here again, a firm distinction is being made between 'the weird' and the 'ordinary ghost story' (Ibid.). The *Saturday Review* also selects 'Sandy the Tinker' for special praise and attention, as 'far superior to the rest in originality and power', perhaps also because of its effective evocation of 'the reasonless, causeless terrors of nervous derangement' rather than the reassurance supplied by the 'ghost of good feeling' evident in other stories in the collection (Ibid.).

'Sandy the Tinker', originally published anonymously in *London Society* in 1880, is a tale told by a minister, Morison (the represented narrator), to a group of travellers sheltering from bad weather in a manse in Scotland

(*London Society* 1880). He relates a crisis experienced 30 years earlier by Crawley, a minister from a neighbouring parish, who was convinced that he had encountered the Devil on an afternoon walk, and, ushered through a gateway accessible by knocking on a particular rock, had been given a tour of the underworld. The Devil agrees to let Crawley go on the condition that he provides a substitute for damnation by the same time the following week. Crawley nominates Sandy the Tinker to serve this purpose, since he is 'Godless' and 'believed in nothing', reasoning that for this rogue Sandy, damnation is inevitable anyway (27). Crawley is released by the Devil, but horrified to see, from his pulpit during his Sunday sermon, Sandy among the congregation, newly repentant. Morison, with medical help, induces unconsciousness in Crawley, and is relieved when, past the hour of his due appointment, Crawley awakes peacefully. They receive news, however, that at the exact moment of Crawley's Satanic assignation, Sandy met with an awful accident and died.

Although it employs the standard folkloric trope of the 'devil in disguise' and the cautionary visit to hell, it lacks the pat resolution of the other tales in the anthology, resulting as it does in the unfair death (and presumably damnation) of the newly devout Sandy, as well as the moral problem presented by Crawley's decision to proxy his own damnation with that of Sandy. There is also a distinct oppositional pairing established between Morison's scepticism (he refers to Crawley's diabolical encounter simply as 'my friend's dream') and Crawley's apparently sincere belief that he was literally kidnapped by the Devil and given a tour of Hell (27). The considerable complications bound up in the narrative are indicated from the beginning, where there is a declaration of the truthfulness of the account by the (as it turns out sceptical) Morison, immediately followed by a listener sarcastically undermining the veracity of not only Morison's story, but that of any type of tale which necessitates an introduction pleading for its veracity (in itself a standard trope of the fantastic or supernatural narrative):

> 'Before commencing my story, I wish to state it is perfectly true in every particular.'
> 'We quite understand that,' said the sceptic of our party, who was wont, in the security of friendly intercourse, to characterise all such prefaces as mere introductions to some tremendously exaggerated tale. (21)

There are disorienting cross-currents of belief, scepticism, credulousness, and resistance to credulousness at work throughout story, as well as anxiety about the potential manipulation of the listener by the apparent sincerity of the narrator, who, despite his explicit scepticism, also asks that his listeners decide for themselves on the actual nature of the narrative they're hearing: 'I can't explain it. I cannot even try to explain it. I will tell you the story exactly as it occurred, however, and leave you to draw your own deductions from it' (21). The first-person narrator of the story (as opposed to the represented narrator Morison)—a member of the traveling party listening to the tale—further complicates the issue by emphasizing the atmospheric circumstances in which the tale is being told:

> The minister paused in his narrative. At that moment there came a tremendous blast of wind which shook the windows of the manse, and burst open the hall door, and caused the candles to flicker and the fire to go roaring up the chimney. It is not too much to say that, what with the uncanny story, and the howling storm, we all felt that creeping sort of uneasiness which so often seems like the touch of something from another world—a hand stretched across the boundaryline of time and eternity, the coldness and mystery of which make the stoutest heart tremble. (26)

There is here an acknowledgement that an appropriate staging for the telling of a weird tale can considerably enhance its potency, as well as of the possibility that an 'authentic' supernatural agency is at work while they are listening. There are unresolved oppositions of authenticity/affect, belief/scepticism, truth/falsehood operating throughout the narrative, constantly undermining the reader's grasp of what exactly is being told and why. The conclusion only deepens the gulf between these oppositions:

> The next day we all stood looking at the frowning cliff and at the Deldy, swollen by recent rains, rushing on its way.
> The youngest of the party went up to the rock and knocked upon it loudly with his cane.
> 'Oh, don't do that, pray!' cried both the ladies nervously—the spirit of the weird story still brooded over us.
> 'What do you think of the coincidence [of Crawley's vision and Sandy's death], Jack?' I inquired of my friend, as we talked apart from the others.
> 'Ask me when we get back to Fleet-street,' he answered. (29)

Instead of the formulaic resolutions of the other stories in the anthology, where 'the troubling histories of the unquiet ghosts [are] revealed and their spirits laid to rest', in 'Sandy the Tinker' the lines between truth and fiction, real and unreal, are still perilously blurred; the 'ladies' are nervous at the possibility that the rock might split and hell might literally break loose. Like the 'great horror of darkness' that 'walled round' Crawley during his encounter with the Evil One near the mountain pool known as 'Witches' Cauldron', the 'weird story still brooded' and still broods, unresolved and—the narrative as convoluted as it is— unresolvable.

The conception of the Victorian Ghost Story presented here has informed my selection of writers in this study. Unlike Vernon Lee, E. F. Benson, Oliver Onions, Henry James, and M. R. James (and other of their contemporaries), John Buchan, Arthur Machen, Robert Murray Gilchrist, M. P. Shiel, and Count Stenbock did not write anything that could sensibly be described as a Victorian Ghost Story (according to my present definition). By filtering out the Victorian Ghost Story from the Weird, I hope to shed clearer light on the latter, or at least that aspect of the Weird which is associated most closely with British weird fiction during the period under discussion. However, I also need to acknowledge two further terms associated with weird fiction, before (and for the same reason) removing them from the specific purview of the present study: Cosmic Horror and Fantasy.

In the 1773 poem 'A Summer Evening's Meditation' by Anna Laetitia Barbauld (1743–1825), the speaker journeys on 'fancy's wild and roving wing' beyond 'the green borders of the peopled earth' to the outer reaches of the cosmos. Beyond the solar system, we encounter 'the trackless deeps of space' beyond 'habitable nature' (Barbauld 1825, 1:126–127):

> To the dread confines of eternal night,
> To solitudes of vast unpeopled space,
> The desarts of creation, wide and wild;
> Where embryo systems and unkindled suns
> Sleep in the womb of chaos

Barbauld's poem is in part a response to contemporaneous advances in cosmological knowledge, notably Kant's claim (in his *Universal Natural History and Theory of the Heavens*, 1755) that 'the Milky Way is merely one lenticular aggregation of stars among a sequence of "island universes"' (Stableford 2007, 68). 'A Summer Evening's Meditation' is a beguiling articulation of the intersecting anxieties provoked by the simultaneous triumph of the empirical, scientific method in revealing the universe to us, and the ensuing displacement of the human subject within that larger, potentially hostile, universe. Barbauld communicates these anxieties through the use of a proto-Gothic lexis: 'dread', 'solitude', 'eternal night', 'womb of chaos', and so on.

Brian Stableford locates the roots of Lovecraftian cosmic horror in this period's intersections of empiricism, romanticism, the Gothic, and the sublime (Stableford 2007, 67–71). The notion of the 'Picturesque' had, towards the end of the eighteenth century, privileged the depopulated, natural landscape over the human figure, from an aesthetic point of view. The sublime landscapes of the Picturesque fed directly into the Gothic novels of, notably, Ann Radcliffe, which intensified this affect by calibrating the sublime to produce horror as well as awe, and engaging with the intermingling of the two discussed by Edmund Burke in his *Philosophical Enquiry into the Origin of Our Ideas of the Sublime and Beautiful* (1757). Both Burke and Kant investigated the philosophical implications of the sublime in various ways that resonated through the subsequent literature:

> The sublime was held to be satisfying either, as for Edmund Burke, in virtue of the pleasurable nature of the terror that it arouses, or, as for Kant [in his *Critique of the Power of Judgment* (1790)], in virtue of its intimation of a capacity of the mind to apprehend the limitless or indeterminable. (Speake 1984, 344)

The horror aesthetic derived from this admixture of terror and the epistemology informed not only the Gothic, but also the late nineteenth-century science fiction of H. G. Wells. Cosmic horror has an inbuilt tilt towards the science-fictional: in order to discuss the cosmic perspective in a narrative, it helps to have some narrative mechanism or putative technology whereby one can achieve this cosmic perspective. There is a natural segue here into the science-romance of Jules Verne and H. G. Wells, and the final chapter of the latter's *The Time Machine* is a good example of this conceit. However, within the demesne of the weird, such technologies are notable by their absence: as in Barbauld's poem, hypothetical contemplation of the cosmos becomes actual, without scientific explanation beyond reference to some sort of psychic projection. Hodgson makes no serious attempt at a rational explanation for his character's travels across vast gulfs of time in either *The Night Land* or *The House on the Borderland*, and both novels are more effective because they avoid such explanations, therefore maintaining and intensifying their central mysteries. Lovecraft, in stories such as 'The Shadow Out of Time' and 'The Whisperer in Darkness', relies on the notion of the disembodied mind to facilitate human access to distant reaches of the cosmos.[5] Regardless, Luckhurst has argued that the 'technocratic', 'scientific' fiction advocated by the influential editor and publisher Hugo Gernsback (1884–1967), from which science fiction emerged as a distinct genre, was always in 'intimate dialectical relation with Lovecraftian "cosmic horror"', a 'symbiotic coupling [which] persists to the present day' (Luckhurst 2005b, 64–65).

If one were to dichotomize between the engagement of weird fiction with the cosmic, or macrocosmic, and that of science fiction, one might argue that science fiction is predicated on the enlightenment confidence in the *knowability* of the material, mechanical, measurable universe, whereas the concern of Hodgson and Lovecraft is its *unknowability*. In Barbauld's poem, the speaker is similarly confronted with the limits of human thought: 'fancy droops, | And thought astonish'd stops her bold career' (Barbauld 1825, 1:127). Barbauld ends her poem hopeful for the possibility of further (posthumous?) revelations:

> Let me here
> Content and grateful, wait th' appointed time
> And ripen for the skies: the hour will come
> When all these splendours bursting on my sight
> Shall stand unveil'd, and to my ravish'd sense
> Unlock the glories of the world unknown.

Contrastingly, Lovecraft, in his pessimism, insists that this veil, this delimitation of human knowledge, is an epistemological safety harness:

> The most merciful thing in the world, I think, is the inability of the human mind to correlate all its contents. We live on a placid island of ignorance in the midst of black seas of infinity, and it was not meant that we should voyage far. The sciences, each straining in its own direction, have hitherto harmed us little; but some day the piecing together of dissociated knowledge will open up such terrifying vistas of reality, and of our frightful position therein, that we shall either go mad from the revelation or flee from the deadly light into the peace and safety of a new dark age.

---

[5] It should be noted that non-technological non-explanations for travel in time and space can also be encountered in texts usually regarded as science fiction, for example Edgar Rice Burroughs's *A Princess of Mars* (1912) and Olaf Stapledon's *Star Maker* (1937).

Eugene Thacker has argued that supernatural horror texts provide 'a way of thinking about the unthinkable world', presumably without actually going insane or rejecting modernity. However, and despite his own practice as a writer, Lovecraft as a theorist rightly emphasized in his oft-repeated formula that what was crucial to the effectiveness weird fiction was the 'atmosphere [...] the *hint*' (emphasis mine) of these 'assaults of chaos'. The British weird tradition, as I present it in this study, is far more engaged in atmosphere and hints than with direct representations of 'unplumbed space'. Wells and Hodgson aside, the direct representation of the macrocosm is the explicit concern of science fiction. In order to avoid unnecessary pettifogging in this regard, for the purposes of this book, I (again) regard it as outside its immediate purview, despite acknowledging the British tradition of cosmic horror and its significant influence on Lovecraftian weird fiction.

As might be inferred from my privileging of the *hint*, above, what I will also regard as beyond the scope of this study is what Farah Mendelsohn describes as 'the immersive fantasy': 'a fantasy set in a world built so that it functions on all levels as a complete world' (Mendlesohn 2008, 59). Again, in the context of weird fiction, this is a distinction made in the service of my specific argument rather than reflective of any definitive historical understanding of what weird fiction is. Indeed, disregarding fantasy on such a basis would be impossible, since some of the writers pre-eminently associated with the mode were also purveyors of immersive fantasy, Lord Dunsany, Robert E. Howard, and Clark Ashton Smith being obvious examples.

Edward John Moreton Drax Plunkett, 18th Baron of Dunsany (1878–1957)—a member of the Anglo-Irish ascendency—was a writer of novels and stories across a range of genres, and 'an immensely popular playwright on both sides of the Atlantic' (Kemp, Mitchell, and Trotter 2002, 110). He was also one of Lovecraft's 'Modern Masters' of the weird tale, and the author of fantasies that had a significant impact on subsequent writing in that genre. Joshi identifies this legacy in the work of not only Lovecraft but 'J. R. R. Tolkien, Fritz Lieber, Ursula K. Le Guin', and C. L. Moore (Joshi 2004a, ix). In his first book, *The Gods of Pegāna* (1905), Dunsany established a unique combination of a fictional legendarium of mythology and cosmology, the declamatory style of the Penateuch, tempered with sardonic wit and a keen sense of irony. Joshi argues that Dunsany's reading of Nietzsche's *Thus Spake Zarathustra* was significant in the regard, and how the sense of wonder in Dunsany's fantasies is shaded with a 'modern sensibility that recognized the insignificance of mankind amidst whose incalculable vortices of space and time that modern science had uncovered' (Joshi 2004a, xi). It is obvious that this comingling was important to Lovecraft's subsequent iterations of cosmic horror, and indeed Lovecraft at one stage lamented: 'There are my "Poe" pieces & my "Dunsany" pieces—but alas—where are any *Lovecraft* pieces?' (Joshi 2005, vii).

However, although Dunsany's gods are certainly wonton and selfish, their vagaries and foibles are more comparable to the Greek pantheon than Lovecraft's Cthulhu mythos, which intensified the conceit of powerful entities indifferent to humanity and made it explicitly horrific rather than simply disconcerting. Lovecraft identified the frisson of scale employed by Dunsany for specific praise in his account of the potency of Dunsany's writing: 'Dunsany loves to hint slyly and adroitly of monstrous things and incredible dooms [… for example …] the vast gate of Perdóndaris, that was carved from a *single piece* of ivory' [emphasis in original] (Lovecraft 1985, 505). This sense of scale—both spatial and temporal, explicit and implied—underwrites not only the cosmicism of Lovecraft and Dunsany but much of weird fiction discussed below, for example the recrudescent paganism of Machen and Buchan, and in its affect is linked to Kant's notion of the aesthetic sublime as something (an idea, an impression) overwhelming: the weird conveys this dizzying, disorienting, and alienating sense of being overwhelmed by deep time and/or deep space, even to the detriment of any other concerns. The frequent criticism of Lovecraft that his fiction contains poor characterization, therefore, misses the point. As Mark Fisher puts it, 'Lovecraft needs the human world, for much the same reason that a painter of a vast edifice might insert a standard human figure standing before it: to provide a sense of scale' (Fisher 2016, 20–21). Houellebecq neatly conveys the temporal and spatial scale underpinning the weird's affect of psychic vertigo as the 'unnameable architecture of time' (Houellebecq 2005, 79).

Here then is the main expression of the weird mode in fantasy writing. Once again, as a mode, weird operates within and across the fantasy genre but should not be misunderstood as identifiable or interchangeable with it. The characters in Tolkien's *The Lord of the Rings* (1954–55), for example, might experience the weird, but the fictional immersive universe within which they operate is not weird in and of itself. Writing contemporaneously to Lovecraft, and in the same pulp milieu, Robert

E. Howard pioneered a subgenre of fantasy that can be described as 'low fantasy' or 'sword and sorcery', in which—in contrast to Tolkien's epic sweep—the stakes are smaller and more personal; Howard's iconic protagonist Conan the Barbarian may concern himself with getting his hands on a particular treasure or rescuing a specific princess, but does not typically deal with expansive, existential conflicts between good and evil in which, for instance, the fate of a people or civilization hangs in the balance. A story such as 'The Tower of the Elephant' (1933) is a good example, however, of Howard's habit of switching to the weird mode to add frisson or an element of supernatural horror to his fantasy realms. In this story, Conan does not inhabit a 'weird' universe, but encounters an irruption of the weird into Howard's fantasy realm—'Yag-kosha', the alien occupant of the eponymous tower—just as Lovecraft might describe such an irruption into the 'real' world. After escaping the tower, Conan doubts the veracity of what he has experienced, wondering if he has been 'bewitched and enchanted' or 'dreamed all that had seemed to have passed' (Howard 2000, 50). In other words, after experiencing the weird episode of his encounter with Yag Kosha, he returns to his 'normal' world: Robert E. Howard's fictional Hyborian Age. The weird, cosmic horror in 'The Tower of the Elephant' does not ensue directly from its fantasy setting, and the tale could easily be transposed to a 'real', mimetic, or contemporary setting (a modern explorer investigating a ruinous tower in an obscure jungle, for example) with a similar intensity of effect. Comparable expressions of the weird mode in a fantasy setting can be found in Clark Ashton Smith's fiction, 'The Tale of Satampra Zeiros' (1929) and 'The Weird of Avoosl Wuthoqquan' (1932) being good examples.

As suggested by the above, weird writing within the wider fantasy genre is more frequently encountered in the American pulp tradition, and the type of fiction it went on to influence, rather than British weird fiction in the period under discussion in this study. A considerable number of Dunsany's works, as well as Hodgson's *The Night Land*, are significant counterexamples, but an in-depth account of both would necessitate detailed analysis of their position within wider fantasy and science fiction genres, which would be both beyond the scope of this study and less illuminating to my central argument than the work of the other writers under discussion.[6] It might be noted, however, that the original resonances of

[6] For detailed analysis of Hodgson's fiction, see (Alder 2009).

the word 'weird', suggestive of a general doom, curse, or a specific fate, continue to be identifiable in a certain strain of gloomy fantasy writing, for example, Poul Anderson's *The Broken Sword* (1954) or more recently George R. R. Martin's *A Song of Ice and Fire* series (1991–) (with its mysterious 'weirwood' trees), in which prophecy and fate have a structural significance in the narrative.

The Wyrd, the Weird-Like, and the Weird

The German-born political refugee and author Karl Blind, writing in the *Academy* in 1879, provides the following provenance for Shakespeare's use of the word (Fryer 2004):

> This name 'Weird' is derived from the Anglo-Saxon Norn Wyrd (Saxon: Wurth; Old High German: Wurd; Norse: Urd), who represents the Past, as her very name shows. Wurd is *die Gewordene*—the 'Has Been,' or rather the 'Has Become,' if one could say so in English.[7] From various passages in the *Edda* it can be proved that Urd was often taken as the typical figure of fate. […] The same use of Wyrd, or Wurd, for Fate in general is proveable from an Old High German translation of the Latin *Fatum*, as well as from Old High German and Saxion locutions referring to fate (Blind 1879).

Here we have a reading of the Weird Sisters in *Macbeth* as personifications of the inexorable; the noun of the 'Has Become' rather than the adjectival 'weird'. Moreover, Blind goes on to suggest that the 'Has Become' does not, in this context, have positive connotations:

> In German folk-lore, three Sisters of Fate bear the names of Wilbert, Worbet, and Ainbet. Etymologically these names seem to refer to the well-disposed nature of a fay representing the Past; to the warring and worrying troubles of the Present; and to the terrors (*Ain* = *Agin*) of the Future (191).

Although Blind claims that the 'Has Become' has no exact English analogue, implicit in his analysis is the suggestion that—at least in a literary context—'Weird' serves this function particularly well. With his analysis,

---

[7] The *Oxford English Dictionary* now provides the following etymological provenance for the noun 'weird': 'Old English *wyrd* (feminine), = Old Saxon *wurd* (plural *wurdi*), Old High German *wurt*, Old Norse *urð-r*, from the weak grade of the stem *werþ-*, *warþ-*, *wurþ-* to become'.

Blind has provided a folkloric and linguistic template for weird fiction: a secure 'normal' (the Past), a troubling irruption or a disruptive inciting incident (the Present) and a lack of resolution (the Future), and all these subsumed as 'fate' or—more precisely—the 'Has Become' or the Wyrd. 'Has Become' is the present perfect, but the implications of 'become' negate the idea of completion in the tense. The process 'Has Become' seems both a foregone conclusion and a process still in operation; in other words, a 'Weird'.

However, discussing *Beowulf*, C. L. Wrenn associates the *wyrd* with 'pre-Christian modes of feeling and thought' and pagan 'fatalism':

> In II. 572–573 the poet expresses what to us moderns may seem a curious blend of the pagan Germanic notion of fate or *wyrd*, and the Christian belief in a God who treats men justly. If, he says, a man is not predestined or doomed already, then often Fate will save him:
>
> *Wyrd oft nereð*
> *unfǣgne eorl, þonne his ellen dēah*
> [Wyrd oft protects the non-doomed earl when he is of courageous hue]
>
> But only, we are told, if his valour is strong: and he must be *unfǣge*, 'undoomed'. Here Catholic Christianity and Germanic paganism have met. (Wrenn 1958, 42–43)

Tolkien, in his commentary on *Beowulf*, cautions against any reductive parsing of the word *wyrd*, which is 'grammatically simply the verbal noun to *weorðan*, "turn out, become, happen"'. He argues that it can mean anything from a 'substitute for the passive, with "unnamed" agent' to a 'happening' or event, to 'Death [… or …] a power or an ordinance in itself,' possibly synonymous with God (Tolkien 2014, 244–5). There is also a long folkloric tradition in the Celtic fringe of doomed heroes having 'weirds' or—in Irish mythology—a 'geis' placed on them by supernatural agency, the latter having connotations of 'a solemn injunction, prohibition, or taboo; a moral obligation' and used by Clark Ashton Smith for the title of his 1934 story for *Weird Tales*, 'The Seven Geases [sic]' ("Geis, N." n.d.; C. A. Smith 1934b). These dooms are usually brought upon the hero by his violation of some prohibition (for example, Ulster hero Cú Chulainn incurring a fatal geis because of his ingestion of dog meat), or—as in the Greek tradition—simple acts of hubris or curiosity (Kotch 2012, 232).

It is evident that in the early nineteenth century, the word 'weird' was still obscure enough to merit clarification when used. Scott's poem *The Bridal of Triermain* (1814) contains the following lines:

> Thou shalt bear thy penance lone,
> In the Valley of St. John,
> And this weird shall overtake thee;—
> Sleep, until a knight shall wake thee. (Scott 1817, 97)

By way of explanation (perhaps for the English readership), Scott (or his editor) goes to the trouble of asterisking the word 'weird' and provides the explanatory synonym 'doom'.

This noun 'weird' seems to have been initially adapted for use as an adjective by appending a qualifying '-like'. Hence, in a review of an 1832 translation of the *Agamemnon* of Aeschylus, Cassandra is described as 'chanting weird-like strains over the dark fate which is connected with the house of Atreus' (*Literary Gazette* 1832). Cassandra's predictions are of course unheeded and disaster not averted. The writer suggests through the use of the term 'weird-like' that Cassandra somehow colludes in the dooms she scryes. The Shakespearean connection is invoked once again in the poem 'The Gray [sic] Old Ash Tree' (1845) by Thomas Miller (1807–1874), who opens his gloomy, doom-laden evocation of rural desolation with a quote from *Macbeth* ('Blood hath been shed ere now i' the olden time'), and sets the following scene:

> [...] There's a raven keeps watch near the gray old ash tree. [...]
> For the place hath a weird-like and eèiry [sic] look.
>   As if Murder lurked anywhere, there it would be;
> 'Tis ruinous, shadowy, fearsome, and lone,
> Abounding with whispers that seem not his own;
>   There are sounds—not of earth—round the gray old ash tree. (Miller 1845)

Like Poe's more celebrated poem about a raven (first published in America earlier that same year), it successfully creates an oppressive atmosphere and a distinct sense of the 'weird-like' as it can be applied to a place instead of a person; the scene of the poem is associated not only with 'Murder', but also with the supernatural—the 'sounds' heard near the tree are 'not of earth'. In 1848, Edward Kenealy (1819–1880) uses the expression 'weird-like' to similar effect in his 'Ballad of Gunhild, or the Phantom Ship':

> Then, from the depths of the ocean, rose
> A wild and shadowy ship,
> And slow, and weird-like, over the waves
> She saw the strange thing skip. (Kenealy 1848)

This use of 'weird-like' here accords again with Blind's positioning of the word as signifying notions of inexorability and predetermination. The ship is travelling under an unaccountable volition, rather than that of human agency; it is beyond human control and hence 'weird-like'.

George W. M. Reynolds (1814–1879) uses the term in *The Necromancer: A Romance* (1852) to describe the icy detachment of the heroine Musidora when, under the baleful influence of occult forces, 'naught was revealed in the icy depths of her weird-like haunting eyes' (Reynolds 1852, 148). Her eyes are 'weird-like' on account of their otherness and their suggestion of an external control influencing Musidora's fate. An article entitled 'Ghost Stories of the North' in *Ainsworth's Magazine* in 1853 includes a similar application of the term, this time to describe a nonhuman entity: '[the apparition was] wearing a certain weird-like, conscious look, that was sufficient to strike terror to the stoutest heart' (*Ainsworth's Magazine* 1853, 89). Like Reynolds's and Kenealy's use, this one also seems to connote a trance-like state and a lack of agency.

By the 1850s, there are examples in both fiction and nonfiction of the use of the 'weird' (now without the pendant '-like') as an adjective. For example, Elizabeth Gaskell's 'The Old Nurse's Story' (1853), originally published in Dickens's *Household Words*, evokes the weird in order to furnish the tale with an unsettling other-worldly ambience: 'I got not to care for that weird rolling music, which did one no harm, if we did not know where it came from', and 'my little lady still heard the weird child crying and mourning' (Gaskell 1853, 14). An investigation into spiritualist phenomena for the *New Monthly Magazine* in 1853 includes the following account of the reporter's arrival at a scene of 'mysterious rappings':

> A cold, grey, leaden London sky, murky and comfortless. Our blood runs shivering through our veins as we stand at the portal of the 'weird mansion', till a very heavy matter-of-fact looking girl relieves our anxiety, and ushers us in through a small dingy floor-clothed hall, up a faded staircase, into the very chamber of mysteries itself. We are astonished to find it so like the common run of furnished lodgings in London. (*New Monthly Magazine* 1853, 486)

The author uses the traditional language of the ghost story to crank up the reader's expectations, in order to more effectively deflate them with the mundane ordinariness of the site of the alleged ghostly manifestations. To do this the term 'weird mansion' is used in parentheses, suggesting that it is already a recognizable trope of either supernatural fiction or 'true' accounts of the supernatural.

The term 'weird story' is used in *Household Words* in October 1853, though in allusion to a poem; Coleridge's *The Rime of the Ancient Mariner* (1798): 'The visitor, like the old mariner in the weird story, held her with her eye' (*Household Words* 1853, 175). It is possible that the author is still using the noun 'weird' rather than the adjectival 'weird' or 'weird-like'; *The Rime of the Ancient Mariner* is, after all, a narrative of a particular doom incurred through a transgression. In a review of Howitt's *Visits to Remarkable Places* in the *John Bull*, its author remarks upon Howitt's enthusiasm for the 'weird tale of the goblin world' (*John Bull and Britannia* 1856). The word 'goblin' was a more ambiguous one at the time than it is now, and was not restricted to signifying solely the wizened creature of folklore, but rather any unexplained or supernatural entity, or disembodied spirit ("Goblin, n.1" n.d.). In his *Minstrelsy of the Scottish Border*, Scott concludes an account of a 'factual' haunting by saying that steps were taken 'to confine the goblin to the Massy More of the castle, where its shrieks and cries are still heard' (Scott 1902, 145). The 'goblin world' therefore is perhaps meant to suggest a generalized adumbral supernatural region rather than relate to a specific folkloric trope.

By the end of the 1850s, the notion of a 'weird' style of fiction becomes particularly associated with Edgar Allan Poe. The *New Monthly Magazine* in 1857 alludes to 'Edgar Poe's weird sketches', the *New Quarterly Review* describes a 'doctor's story' as a highlight of an otherwise disappointing novel due to it being a 'tale worthy of Edgar Poe for weird horror and thrilling interest' and in the *Scottish Review* the 'Marginalia' of Poe are defined as 'distinct from the weird tales altogether' (*New Monthly Magazine*, 385; *New Quarterly Review*, 216; *Scottish Review*, 376). As detailed in the Conclusion, Lafcadio Hearn attributes the word's shift into adjectival use entirely to Poe, who used the word in this manner in prose, poetry, and criticism. Hearn may have been overstating the case, however: the same exercise undertaken with the complete works of Nathanial Hawthorne reveals comparable usage, suggesting that the adjectival use of 'weird' may have been a more general American phenomenon (Hawthorne 2011).

Writing in the *Fantasy Fan* (see Chap. 5), Clark Ashton Smith also identifies Poe as the instigator or at least popularizer of this shift:

> I believe that Poe was perhaps the first to employ this adjective in the modern sense of eerie or uncanny or bizarre; but you will find it used in older writers, such as Shakespeare, with a special application to witchcraft or sorcery. The Fates of classic mythology were spoken of as 'the weird sisters,' and the root-meaning of the word has reference to fate or destiny. As a noun, it is still sometimes used in the latter sense; and it also means a prediction of prophecy. The word itself is of Anglo-Saxon origin, and is related to the old German *wurt* and Icelandic *urdhr*. (C. A. Smith 1934a)

Poe's innovations in horrific, imaginative, and supernatural fiction were a shift away from an emphasis on the multicharacter narratives of the Gothic, to a tighter, finely honed focus on the psychological effects of unusual experiences on the individual, and his employment of the short story as the ideal form to facilitate this. Fred Botting differentiates Poe's tales from the Gothic by arguing that they leave 'boundaries between reality, illusion and madness *unresolved* rather than, in the manner of his contemporaries, domesticating Gothic motifs or rationalising mysteries' (emphasis mine) (Botting 1995, 120).

Poe's unparalleled influence on the weird fiction of late nineteenth-century writers was regularly acknowledged by both critics and authors. Doyle described Poe as 'master of all' at producing 'a single vivid impression', in whose work the 'weirdness of the idea [is] intensified by the coolness of the narrator' (Doyle 1907, 114). Doyle cites Maupassant as Poe's only close rival: 'When Maupassant chose he could run Poe close in that domain of the strange and the weird' (122). The influence of Poe is certainly clear on Doyle's own weird short fiction; for instance, his immurement-based *conte cruel* 'The New Catacomb' (1898) lifts its plot almost entirely from Poe's 'Cask of Amontillado' (1846) (Doyle 2000). In Kipling's 'In the House of Suddhoo' (1886), there seems to be an implicit acknowledgement that attempting to compete with Poe's mastery at evoking weird horror is only possible through simple (albeit perhaps lazy) appropriation: 'Read Poe's account of the voice that came from the mesmerized dying man, and you will realize less than one half of the horror of that [disembodied] head's voice' (Kipling 2006, 81). Both contemporaneous critical reaction and Poe's enduring influence on the weird output of writers later in the century seem to fully support Joshi's assertion that Poe 'will always remain the grandfather of the field

[… through …] his pioneering work in advancing the weird tale beyond the stale conventions of the Gothic' (Joshi 1999, v). The scope and specific periodic focus of this study preclude detailed consideration of Poe's work and his contribution to weird fiction beyond the above acknowledgement of his prominence in its history and development. Nevertheless, his influence is such that his name will be evoked numerous timesbelow, not only with regard to weird fiction, but also literary Decadence and the development of the short story, both of which seem ineluctably associated with his legacy; and with the final decade of the nineteenth century.

Soon after embarking on this project it became clear to me that I faced a problem. The Weird is at once capacious and specific. Its historical application, as regards literature, gave me sufficient scope to write a book on, for example, science fiction, or horror, or fantasy, or magical realism, or any of their myriad intersections. The historical application of the word 'weird' has been restive and labile enough for the entirety of genre writing, together with its interactions with literary realism, to be at my disposal. However, I also realized that I did not hold that the term weird fiction was interchangeable with the entire history of genre writing. The task I set myself was to argue for a particular weird aesthetic, and to do so, I would need to present the relevant evidence, evidence that could only be found by making the relevant aesthetic distinctions. At some point, it occurred to me that these aesthetic distinctions were at the root of what weird fiction is; at least my conception of it, as presented here. I was also determined to focus my research on the weird mode itself rather than devote space to writers simply according to their prominence. Any reader familiar with the weird fiction of the period under discussion might have reasonably expected to find individual chapters on each of Lovecraft's 'Modern Masters' of the weird tale; on Blackwood, M. R. James, Lord Dunsany, and Machen, along the lines of Joshi's existing book-length study *The Weird Tale*. While they do all have at least walk-on parts in what follows (with Machen taking a more central role), I followed my research where it took me, and it took me to John Buchan, Charlotte Riddell, Count Stenbock, and others, who served my central thesis rather than ticked the more obvious boxes. I was drawn towards the recondite, the obscure, the surprising. And so, making a conveniently circular argument, I find myself wondering if this process of distinction is not in itself a demonstration of my central thesis.

The first part of the book focuses on the late nineteenth century and its immediate aftermath. In Chap. 2, I explore the wider literary field of the period and the emergence of the 'high phase' of weird fiction, before focusing on two critical frames which one must consider in order to understand this emergence: the development of the short story and the literary Decadence of the fin de siècle. I also introduce some of the ideas of Pierre Bourdieu, specifically the application of his notions of distinction to fields of cultural production, which serves throughout the project as a theoretical tool used to approach issues relating to high and low art, literariness, and canonicity which underpin and shape much of the discussion in this and subsequent chapters. Finally, I consider the notion of an Edwardian weird, looking primarily at the work of Walter de la Mare and Oliver Onions.

In Chap. 3, I argue that minority or obscurity, and the concomitant amenity to the mythologization of minor or obscure writers and their lives, is central to contemporary understanding and valorization of the *haute* Weird. My focus is on four writers identified by Brian Stableford as 'definitive products of English Decadence', but who are also regarded, to varying degrees, as influential writers of weird fiction: M. P. Shiel, R. Murray Gilchrist, Count Stenbock, and (especially) Arthur Machen. I argue that the privileging of obscure authors over canonical or popular ones typical of weird fiction fits almost seamlessly (and is coeval with) Decadence and its reputation for producing and valorizing lost, prematurely dead, and failed writers, the posthumous mythologization of the author enhancing the reputation of the work. In this context, I posit the notion of a 'connoisseur culture' firmly imbricated with weird fiction, and (referring to the ideas of Bourdieu) the corollary distinctions still being made that, in some instances, can lead to weird fiction being a conscious attempt at achieving a literary authenticity unencumbered by the (to some) problematically déclassé implications of popular genres such as horror. I also identify and discuss some other key contexts to the weird fiction of this period, including orientalism and the arabesque.

Contrasting with Chap. 3, the specific focus of Chap. 4 is a popular and well-known writer whose reputation as a writer of weird fiction has been obscured by his celebrated contributions to the thriller genre: John Buchan. Aside from the wish to redress the critical neglect of the former aspect of his writing, my discussion of Buchan's work seeks to complement the previous chapter's focus on 'lost' writers by considering the intersection of weird and popular fiction during its 'high phase', positioning

Buchan as a transitional figure between the literary Decadence of the 1890s and the pulp magazine market emergent in the early twentieth century. John Buchan began his career operating in the same literary field as the writers discussed in Chap. 3 (some of his earliest fiction appearing in the *Yellow Book*), but I argue that the greater contemporary status afforded to the weird fiction of those writers is—to at least some degree—demonstrably due to their 'failure' as writers and the posthumous mythologization ensuing from their obscurity. Using archival material, I also present some of Buchan's own analysis and discussion of weird fiction, produced in his capacity as a reader for John Lane, a publisher firmly associated with the Decadent 1890s. My discussion of Buchan's own weird fiction also takes in some wider contexts of the mode; its intersections with colonial adventure fiction, with paganism, and its demonstration of modernist anxieties regarding the resilience of civilization.

Finally, in Chap. 5, I turn to what is regarded as both the culmination of the 'high phase' of weird fiction, and one of its definitive iterations: the 1920s and 1930s run of *Weird Tales* magazine. I specifically look at this period of *Weird Tales* through the lens of my previous investigation of fin-de-siècle British weird fiction, and argue that, contrary to some claims, *Weird Tales* was part of an existing tradition and can be credibly seen as a continuation of fin-de-siècle literary Decadence in the age of Modernism. Underlying this discussion, and continuing a structural theme of the entire thesis, is a consideration of canonicity, and of the polluting of neat boundaries between notions of high and low culture.

Works Cited

"About." n.d. Weird Fiction Review. http://weirdfictionreview.com/about/. Accessed 2 Mar 2016.

Ainsworth's Magazine. 1853. Ghost Stories of the North. January.

Alder, Emily. 2009. William Hope Hodgson's borderlands: Monstrosity, Other Worlds, and the Future at the finde siècle. Thesis. Edinburgh Napier University. Retrieved from http://researchrepository.napier.ac.uk/id/eprint/3597.

Altman, Rick. 1999. *Film/Genre*. London: BFI.

Ashley, Mike. 2016. Culture: Third Alternative, the: SFE: Science Fiction Encyclopedia. http://www.sf-encyclopedia.com/entry/third_alternative_the. Accessed 1 May 2016.

Baldick, Chris. 2008. *The Oxford Dictionary of Literary Terms*. Oxford: Oxford University Press.

Baldick, Chris, and Robert Morrison. 1995. Introduction. In *Tales of Terror from 'Blackwood's Magazine*, vii–xviii. Oxford: Oxford University Press.
Barbauld, Anna Lætitia. 1825. *The Works of Anna Lætitia Barbauld*. Vol. 1. 2 Vols. London: Longman.
Baron, Laird, ed. 2014. *The Year's Best Weird Fiction Volume 1*. Toronto: ChiZine.
Birkenhead, Edith. 1921. *The Tale of Terror*. London: Constable.
Blackwood, Algernon. 2002a. *Ancient Sorceries and Other Weird Stories*. Ed. S. T. Joshi. London: Penguin.
———. 2002b. The Willows. In *Ancient Sorceries and Other Weird Stories*, ed. S.T. Joshi, 17–62. London: Penguin.
Blind, Karl. 1879. Correspondence. *Academy*, March 1.
Botting, Fred. 1995. *Gothic*. London: Routledge.
Brooker, Joseph. 2010. Valley of the Genres. *Dandelion* 1 (1): 1–4.
"Burnt Black Suns by Simon Strantzas: Hippocampus Press, Specializes in Classic Horror and Science Fiction." n.d. http://www.hippocampuspress.com/mythos-and-other-authors/fiction/burnt-black-suns-by-simon-strantzas. Accessed 24 Apr 2016.
"China Miéville—Will the Novel Remain Writers' Favourite Narrative Form? | Edinburgh World Writers' Conference." n.d. http://www.edinburghworldwritersconference.org/the-future-of-the-novel/china-mieville/. Accessed 2 Mar 2016.
Csicsery-Ronay, Istvan, Jr. 2008. *The Seven Beauties of Science Fiction*. Middletown: Wesleyan University Press.
Daily News. 1882. Recent Novels. December 25.
Deleuze, Gilles, and Félix Guattari. 2004. *A Thousand Plateaus*. Trans. Brian Massumi. London: Continuum.
DiBiasio, Becky. 2009. The British and Irish Ghost Story and Tale of the Supernatural. In *A Companion to the British and Irish Short Story*, ed. David Malcolm and Cheryl Alexander Malcolm, 81–95. Chichester: John Wiley & Sons.
Doyle, Arthur Conan. 1907. *Through the Magic Door*. London: Smith Elder.
———. 2000. The New Catacomb. In *Tales of Unease*, 29–41. Ware: Wordsworth.
Edmundson Makala, Melissa. 2013. *Women's Ghost Literature in Nineteenth-Century Britain*. Cardiff: University of Wales Press.
Era. 1890. The Drama in America. October 25.
Fisher, Mark. 2016. *The Weird and the Eerie*. London: Repeater.
Freedman, Carl. 2013. From Genre to Political Economy: Miéville's the City & the City and Uneven Development. *CR: The New Centennial Review* 13 (2): 13–30. https://doi.org/10.1353/ncr.2013.0013.
Freeman's Journal and Daily Commercial Advertiser. 1898. Literature. February 25.

Fryer, S. E. 2004. *Karl Blind*. Oxford Dictionary of National Biography. https://doi.org/10.1093/ref:odnb/31927. Accessed 10 Sept 2012.
Gaskell, Elizabeth. 1853. The Old Nurse's Story. *Household Words*, February 26.
"Geis, N." n.d. *OED Online*. Oxford University Press. http://www.oed.com/view/entry/77336. Accessed 2 May 2016.
Glasgow Herald. 1889. Literature. December 19.
———. 1893. Literature. December 21.
"Goblin, n.1." n.d. *OED Online*. Oxford University Press. http://www.oed.com/view/entry/79613. Accessed 2 May 2016.
Graphic. 1888. Theatres. August 4.
Guardian. 2002. China Miéville's Top 10 Weird Fiction Books. May 16, sec. Books.http://www.theguardian.com/books/2002/may/16/fiction.bestbooks.
Harman, Graham. 2012. *Weird Realism: Lovecraft and Philosophy*. Arlesford: Zero Books.
Hawthorne, Nathanial. 2011. *Delphi Complete Works of Nathaniel Hawthorne*. Bexhill-on-Sea: Delphi Classics.
Hay, Simon. 2011. *A History of the Modern British Ghost Story*. Basingstoke: Palgrave Macmillan.
Hollinger, Veronica. 2014. Genre vs. Mode. In *The Oxford Handbook of Science Fiction*, ed. Rob Latham, 139–151. Oxford: Oxford University Press.
Houellebecq, Michel. 2005. *H. P. Lovecraft: Against the World, Against Life*. Trans. Dorna Khazeni. San Francisco: Believer Books.
Household Words. 1853. The Eve of a Journey. October 22.
Howard, Robert E. 2000. The Tower of the Elephant. In *The Conan Chronicles Volume 1: The People of the Black Circle*, 25–50. London: Gollancz.
Imfeld, Zoë Lehmann. 2016. *The Victorian Ghost Story and Theology: From Le Fanu to James*. New York: Palgrave Macmillan.
John Bull and Britannia. 1856. Literature. December 13.
Johnson, Randal. 1993. 'Editor's Introduction: Pierre Bourdieu on Art, Literature and Culture.' In *The Field of Cultural Production*, by Pierre Bourdieu, 1–25. Cambridge: Polity.
Joshi, S.T. 1999. Introduction. In *Great Weird Tales*, v–xi. Mineola: Dover.
———. 2003. *The Weird Tale*. Holicong: Wildside Press.
———. 2004a. Introduction. In *In the Land of Time, and Other Fantasy Tales*, ed. Lord Dunsany and S.T. Joshi, ix–xxiii. London: Penguin Classics.
———. 2004b. *The Evolution of the Weird Tale*. New York: Hippocampus.
———. 2005. Introduction. In *The Dreams in the Witch House and Other Weird Stories*, ed. H.P. Lovecraft, vii–xvi. London: Penguin.
———. 2012. *Unutterable Horror*. Vol. 1. 2 vols. Hornsea: PS Publishing.
Keating, Peter. 1989. *The Haunted Study: A Social History of the English Novel, 1875–1914*. London: Secker & Warburg.

Kemp, Sandra, Charlotte Mitchell, and David Trotter, eds. 2002. *Oxford Companion to Edwardian Fiction 1900–14: New Voices in the Age of Uncertainty.* Oxford: Oxford University Press.
Kenealy, Edward. 1848. The Ballad of Gunhild, or the Phantom Ship. *Dublin University Magazine*, January.
Kipling, Rudyard. 2006. In the House of Suddhoo. In *The Mark of the Beast and Other Fantastic Tales*, 76–83. London: Gollancz.
Koja, Kathe, ed. 2015. *The Year's Best Weird Fiction Volume 2.* Toronto: ChiZine.
Kotch, John T., ed. 2012. *The Celts: History, Life and Culture.* Santa Barbara: ABC-CLIO.
"K-Punk: Weird Realism." 2007. http://k-punk.abstractdynamics.org/archives/009048.html. Accessed 10 Apr 2016.
Land, Nick. 2011. In *Fanged Noumena: Collected Writings 1987–2007*, ed. Ray Brassier and Robin Mackay. New York: Urbanomic.
Langford, David. 2012. Themes: New Weird: SFE: Science Fiction Encyclopedia. http://www.sf-encyclopedia.com/entry/new_weird. Accessed 25 Apr 2016.
Lawrence, Arthur H. 1898. The Apotheosis of the Grotesque. *The Idler*, January.
Lee, Vernon. 1896. Preface. In *Hauntings*, vii–vxi. London: John Lane/The Bodley Head.
Lévy, Maurice. 1988. *Lovecraft, A Study in the Fantastic.* Trans. S.T. Joshi. Detroit: Wayne State University Press.
Literary Gazette. 1832. The Agamemnon of Aeschylus, Translated from the Greek; Illustrated by a Dissertation on Grecian Tragedy, & c. May 26.
London Society. 1880. Sandy the Tinker. December.
Lovecraft, H.P. 1985. Supernatural Horror in Literature. In *Dagon and Other Macabre Tales*, 421–512. London: Panther.
———. 1999. *The Call of Cthulhu and Other Weird Stories.* Ed. S.T. Joshi. London: Penguin.
———. 2001. *The Thing on the Doorstep and Other Weird Stories.* Ed. S.T. Joshi. London: Penguin.
———. 2005. *The Dreams in the Witch House and Other Weird Stories.* Ed. S.T. Joshi. London: Penguin.
———. 2011. *The Call of Cthulhu and Other Weird Tales.* London: Vintage Classics.
———. 2013. *The Classic Horror Stories.* Ed. Roger Luckhurst. Oxford: Oxford University Press.
Luckhurst, Roger, ed. 2005a. Introduction. In *Late Victorian Gothic Tales*, ix–xxxi Oxford: Oxford University Press.
———, ed. 2005b. *Science Fiction.* Cambridge: Polity.
———, ed. 2013a. 'Introduction.' In *The Classic Horror Stories*, by H.P. Lovecraft, vii–xxviii. Oxford: Oxford University Press.
———, ed. 2013b. Lovecraft Resurgent. *Fortean Times*, August.

———. 2015. American Weird. In *The Cambridge Companion to American Science Fiction*, ed. Gerry Canavan and Eric Carl Link, 194–205. Cambridge: Cambridge University Press.

———, ed. 2017. The Weird: A Dis/Orientation. *Textual Practice* 31 (6): 1041–1061.

Lynch, Eve M. 2004. Spectral Politics: To the Ghost Story and the Domestic Servant. In *The Victorian Supernatural*, ed. Nicola Bown, Carolyn Burdett, and Pamela Thurschwell, 67–86. Cambridge: Cambridge University Press.

MacCulloch, J.A. 1898. R. L. Stevenson: *Westminster Review*, June.

Machen, Arthur. 1923a. *Far Off Things*. London: Martin Secker.

———. 1923b. *Hieroglyphics*. London: Martin Secker.

———. 2011. *The White People and Other Weird Stories*. Ed. S.T. Joshi. London: Penguin.

Mendlesohn, Farah. 2008. *Rhetorics of Fantasy*. Middletown: Wesleyan University Press.

Miéville, China. 2003. Long Live the New Weird. *The Third Alternative* 35: 3.

———. 2008. M.R. James and the Quantum Vampire. *COLLAPSE* IV (May): 105–128.

———. 2009. Weird Fiction. In *The Routledge Companion to Science Fiction*, ed. Mark Bould, Adam Roberts, Andrew M. Butler, and Sherryl Vint, 510–515. London: Routledge.

Miller, Thomas. 1845. The Gray Old Ash Tree. *New Monthly Magazine*, July.

Murray's Magazine. 1890. Book Review. February.

Nesbit, Edith. 1893. Man-Size in Marble. In *Grim Tales*, 111–143. London: A. D. Innes.

New Monthly Magazine. 1853. My Visit to the 'Mysterious Rappings', and What They Brought Me. April.

New Quarterly Review. 1858. Retrospect of the Literature of the Quarter. August.

Noys, Benjamin, and Timothy S. Murphy. 2016. Introduction: Old and New Weird. *Genre* 49 (2): 117–134.

Philmus, Robert M. 1977. H. G. Wells as Literary Critic for the Saturday Review. *Science Fiction Studies* 4 (2): 166–193.

Rabinowitz, Paula. 2012. *Black & White & Noir: America's Pulp Modernism*. New York: Columbia University Press.

Review of Reviews. 1892. The Weird in Fiction. September.

———. 1911. The Review's Bookshop. February.

Reynolds, George W.M. 1852. The Necromancer: A Romance, Chapter XXVII. *Reynold's Miscellany*, March 27.

Rieder, John. 2017. *Science Fiction and the Mass Cultural Genre System*. Middletown: Wesleyan University Press.

Rucker, Lynda E. 2017. Introduction. In *A Suggestion of Ghosts*, ed. Johnny Mains, 11–16. Kent: Black Shuck Books.

Saturday Review. 1883. Minor Notices. January 13.
Scott, Sir Walter. 1817. *The Bridal of Triermain*. Edinburgh: Ballantyne.
———. 1902. *Minstrelsy of the Scottish Border*. London: Blackwood.
Scottish Review. 1859a. Novels, Novel Readers, and Novel Writers. July.
———. 1859b. Novels, Novel Readers, and Novel Writers. July.
———. 1899. Mr Rudyard Kipling's Prose Writings. October.
Sharp, William. 1889. New Novels. *Academy*, August 17.
"Sir Nathaniel." 1857. Notes on Note-Worthies, of Divers Orders, Either Sex, and Every Age. *New Monthly Magazine*, April.
Smith, Clark Ashton. 1934a. Letter. *Fantasy Fan*, January.
———. 1934b. The Seven Geases. *Weird Tales*, October.
Smith, Andrew. 2012. *The Ghost Story 1840–1920: A Cultural History*. Reprint. Manchester: Manchester University Press.
Speake, Jennifer, ed. 1984. *A Dictionary of Philosophy*. London: Pan.
Stableford, Brian. 2007. The Cosmic Horror. In *Icons of Horror and the Supernatural*, ed. S.T. Joshi, 65–96. Westport: Greenwood Press.
———. 2017. Vernon Lee. In *Horror Literature Through History*, ed. Matt Cardin, vol. 2, 542–543. Santa Barbara: ABC-CLIO.
Stoker, Bram. 2006. *Dracula's Guest and Other Weird Stories*. Ed. Kate Hebblethwaite. London: Penguin.
Temple Bar. 1877. An Irish Poet and Novelist: Joseph Sheridan Le Fanu. August.
Thacker, Eugene. 2011. *In the Dust of This Planet: Horror of Philosophy Vol. 1*. Winchester: Zero Books.
———. 2015a. Meditations on the Weird. In *Tentacles Longer Than Night: Horror of Philosophy Vol. 3*, 110–168. Winchester: Zero Books.
———. 2015b. *Starry Speculative Corpse: Horror of Philosophy Vol. 2*. Winchester: Zero Books.
———. 2015c. *Tentacles Longer Than Night: Horror of Philosophy Vol. 3*. Winchester: Zero Books.
"TIH 074: Simon Strantzas on Weird vs. Strange Fiction, Writing Routine and Thinking Horror This Is Horror." 2016. http://www.thisishorror.co.uk/tih-074-simon-strantzas-on-weird-vs-strange-fiction-writing-routine-and-thinking-horror/. Accessed 26 Jan 2016.
Todorov, Tsvetan. 1975. *The Fantastic: A Structural Approach to a Literary Genre*. Trans. Richard Howard and Robert Scholes. Ithaca: Cornell University Press.
Tolkien, J.R.R. 2014. *Beowulf: A Translation and Commentary*. Boston: Houghton Mifflin Harcourt.
VanderMeer, Jeff. 2008. Introduction. In *The New Weird*, ed. Ann VanderMeer and Jeff VanderMeer, ix–xviii. San Francisco: Tachyon Publications.
VanderMeer, Ann, and Jeff VanderMeer, eds. 2008. *New Weird, The*. San Francisco: Tachyon Publications.

———, eds. 2012a. *The Weird: A Compendium of Strange and Dark Stories*. London: Tor.
——— 2012b. Introduction. In *The Weird: A Compendium of Strange and Dark Stories*, xv–xx. London: Tor.
Venezia, Tony. 2010. Weird Fiction: Dandelion Meets China Miéville. *Dandelion* 1 (1): 1–9.
Weird Tales. 1927. The Eyrie. November.
Wells, H.G. 1896. The Three Impostors. *Saturday Review*, January 11.
"What Books to Read, and How to Read Them." 1859. *The Scottish Review*, October, pp. 368–80.
Wilkes, Joanne. 2008. *Crowe [Née Stevens], Catherine Ann (1790–1872)*. Oxford Dictionary of National Biography. https://doi.org/10.1093/ref:odnb/6822.
Worth, Aaron. 2018. Introduction. In *The Great God Pan and Other Horror Stories*, by Arthur Machen, ix–xxx. Oxford: Oxford University Press.
Wrenn, C.L. 1958. Introduction. In *Beowulf*, 9–84. London: George G. Harrap.
"Year's Best Weird Fiction Volume 1." 2014. https://www.amazon.co.uk/Years-Best-Weird-Fiction-1/dp/0981317758. Accessed 18 Apr 2016.

CHAPTER 2

The Weird Fin-De-Siècle and After

I have so far discussed the evolution of 'weird' as a critical and literary term over the course of the nineteenth century and attempted to identify some specificities of use indicative of what might differentiate 'weird fiction' from both general literature as well as cognates like 'supernatural', 'strange', 'horror', 'uncanny', and Gothic fiction. As discussed in the Introduction, there has been something approaching an ongoing consensus (iterated among others by H. P. Lovecraft, S. T. Joshi, and China Miéville) that a 'high phase' of weird fiction was achieved in the fin-de-siècle and Edwardian periods (Miéville's *haute* Weird), and it is to some of the writers who constituted that 'high phase' that I will now turn my attention. The writers I will focus on are ones whose ongoing influence is still felt in contemporary self-identifying weird fiction, and whose relative obscurity has resulted in some critical space remaining within which the commentator can function without being overwhelmed by their critical baggage.

These two parameters are in some ways directly linked: Bram Stoker's *Dracula* is now canonical, and although (as previously discussed) it certainly attracted the epithet 'weird' in early reviews, it can be argued that its basis in Judeo-Christian notions of good and evil and employment of the folkloric staple of the vampire excludes it from being a 'true' weird fiction. There is certainly a desire, explicitly expressed, to put clear blue water between, for example, the anthropomorphic undead of the vastly popular and populist *Twilight* series and the notion of weird fiction promoted by the Weird Fiction Review website and self-identifying publishers of weird fiction such as Kraken Press. In its 'Dogme 2011 for Weird Fiction' the former explicitly forbids use of 'stock anthropomorphic monsters: no vampires, no zombies, no werewolves, no mummies, no ghouls' (Nicolay 2011). In its submission guidelines, Kraken Press cautions that it is 'not likely to publish anything with vampires, werewolves, or zombies' ("Kraken Press Submission Manager" n.d.). One subtextual implication here is that weird fiction is a more literary mode, which values originality and subtlety rather than the standard anthropomorphic (and, importantly, anthropocentric) tropes of the Gothic and horror genres. This is not a novel development in weird fiction; a satire in a 1934 edition of *The Fantasy Fan* includes the following complaint:

> [I]f more people could only appreciate and understand the significance of the weird tale! And if scribes could only emulate Smith or Lovecraft or Howard! If they would only strive for originality of beauty! But no! We poor and insignificant readers of the weird tale must continue to be plagued with time-worn vampires, witches, rituals, and other weird senilities. (Nelson 1934)

The ensuing claim for cultural value above that normally afforded 'genre' fiction has been discussed in the Introduction and will be discussed in further detail elsewhere in this book. It is, at root, predicated on the same high/low cultural divide precipitated by the fin-de-siècle publishing boom and intensified by Modernism. Also implicit is a distinction between two conceived groups: the consumers of populist lowbrow texts and a more educated cultural elite who can identify and appreciate literature of value.

Ironically, in terms of contemporary cultural impact, only the materialist, extraterrestrial horrors of H. P. Lovecraft can compete with the 'zombies, werewolves, mummies, [and] ghouls' which still overwhelmingly dominate contemporary horror fiction and cinema, and the previously unassailable centrality of Lovecraft to weird fiction is now being lobbied against accordingly from some quarters, Lovecraft increasingly becoming a critical victim of his own posthumous success (VanderMeer 2012). The nebulosity of pre-Lovecraftian weird fiction means that it is far harder to commodify, which has also perhaps resulted in a lack of direct visibility in popular culture. However, the influence of writers like Machen and Shiel is certainly still present albeit filtered through the work of more culturally impactful writers like Lovecraft and Stephen King. Their lack of direct visibility has also resulted in a culture of self-identifying 'connoisseurship', in which networks of collectors, enthusiasts, and writers can wear the obscurity of their enthusiasms as a badge of honour, a mark of authentic understanding and appreciation of weird fiction, particularly of this pre-Lovecraftian period, and, importantly, of what demarcates it from the arguably cruder albeit more popular 'horror' genre, especially from the latter's schlockier manifestations ('the literature of mere physical fear and the mundanely gruesome') (Lovecraft 1985, 426).

It is this tendency that has resulted in small but dedicated and passionate coteries of 'collector-fans' (so described by Kirsten MacLeod) or 'connoisseurs', who Baudrillard distinguishes as those who respond to 'singularity and differentness', keeping alive the names of otherwise almost entirely forgotten writers such as Count Eric Stenbock, discussed below (MacLeod 2004, 121; Baudrillard 1994, 10). Although most often associated with small presses and amateur societies, this culture of 'connoisseurship' is also participated in by, for example, Stephen King and director Guillermo del Toro, who—hugely successful and popular—perhaps also harbour a desire to demonstrate and reinforce to the cognoscenti (i.e., their fellow connoisseurs rather than their wider audience) their cultural capital, where their economic capital is self-evident to the population at large. Both King and del Toro, for example, are effusive and unequivocal in their enthusiasm for Machen, an otherwise little-read 'minor' writer whose brief periods of commercial success were limited to the 1890s in Britain and a brief revival in America in the 1920s, but who King, particularly, imbues with an artistic value even to the detriment of his own work ("StephenKing.Com – Messages from Stephen" 2008; del Toro 2011).

One anomalously dependable demarcation of weird fiction is its tendency towards the short form. There are of course always exceptions to prove the rule, but the multicharacter narrative usually necessitated by the long form normally results in a novel that might incorporate weird elements but not be purely identifiable as weird in and of itself. Or, as Lovecraft puts it, the weird can appear 'in memorable fragments scattered through material whose massed effect may be of a very different cast' (Lovecraft 1985, 427). Machen's novel *The Three Impostors* could perhaps be cited here but only if one were to ignore the fact that it is a portmanteau assembly of short stories, some of which had seen print before.

In what follows I will examine how the publishing field of the 1880s and 1890s created optimal conditions for the short story form. I will argue that the demand for short fiction led to an ascendancy of the influence of Edgar Allan Poe and Robert Louis Stevenson as masters and innovators of the form, which (even if contingently) may have led to an imitation of the former's subject matter as well as his technical expertise. I will also argue that both Poe and Stevenson had the perhaps unique position of being equally influential both to writers of accessible, middle-brow 'healthy' fiction and, through the status accorded to both writers by the French avant-garde, to the contributors to the brief flowering of British Decadence in the 'yellow nineties'. It was from this confluence and the resulting complicated yet vibrant field of literary production that weird fiction found the fertile soil in which to plant its roots and thence spread its strange tendrils. Inevitably, and where relevant, I will also need to draw upon the cultural and, to a lesser extent, philosophical, scientific, and social discourses of the fin de siècle in order to properly situate and ascertain the place of weird fiction within it. I will begin by looking at the publishing field of the period.

The Literary and Publishing Field of the 1890s

Pierre Bourdieu has argued that 'to be fully understood, literary production has to be approached in relational terms, by constructing the literary field, i.e. the space of literary *prises de position* that are possible in a given period in a given society' (Bourdieu 1983, 311). In *British Literary Culture and Publishing Practice, 1880–1914* (2002), Peter D. McDonald has ably demonstrated the efficacy of applying Bourdieu's ideas—which are in effect a methodology of cultural history, countering discourse in which 'ignorance of everything which goes to make up the "mood of the age" produces a derealization of works'—to the same period as I will investigate below, albeit with a different emphasis (314). At least partly as a result of the publishing boom and increased literacy rates of the fin de siècle, it was a moment of intense self-consciousness and anxiety regarding these *prises de position*. Bourdieu encourages an emphasis on the field as opposed to the work itself, which on its own fails to take into account that the 'essential explanation of each work lies outside each of them, in the objective relations which constitute this field' (312). I will therefore provide an account of this particular field, also paying attention to Bourdieu's caution that:

> It is difficult to conceive the vast amount of information which is linked to membership of a field and which all contemporaries immediately invest in their reading of works: information about institutions—e.g. academies,

journals, magazines, galleries, publishers, etc.—and about persons, their relationships, liaisons and quarrels. Information about the ideas and problems which are 'in the air' and circulate orally in gossip and rumour. (314)

The digitization of archives which has taken place since Bourdieu wrote these words in 1983 has arguably made at least some of this information more easily accessible than ever before. Although a comprehensive account is of course impossible, what can be gleaned from the information that is available does at least allow a discussion on where to situate weird fiction during the opening years of its high phase within the wider literary and cultural contexts. Implicit in this is the hope that such an understanding will shed some light in its subsequent and continuing impact in the twentieth and twenty-first centuries.

Several convergent factors precipitated a publishing boom in the closing decades of the nineteenth century. One of the most prominent was the 1870 Education Act, which considerably (and not without controversy) increased literacy rates and led to the creation of a far larger potential reading audience, from a far wider social demographic, than ever before. Peter Keating argues that of at least as much significance was the accompanying 'growth in numbers of teachers as training colleges and universities expanded to meet the new educational demands'·

> Nothing is more characteristic of the fundamental social changes taking place at the end of the nineteenth century than this new class of meritocrats and the neat, brick buildings in which they worked. As far as the future of literature was concerned, their taste and judgment were to be vital. (Keating 1989, 143)

Another impetus was the gradual repeal of various publishing taxes from the mid-century onwards. The abolition of the advertising tax in 1853, stamp tax in 1855, and of paper duty in 1861, saw production costs fall, cover prices drop, and circulations and profits increase exponentially (Gillies n.d.; Brake 2001, 8). This combination of increased potential revenues from an expanded reading public and the lifting of the tax burden on publishing created an unprecedented demand for new fiction. Traditionally, fiction had been produced and consumed in the form of the serial (with each part issued monthly) and the Victorian 'three-decker', the latter a form promoted by the prominent lending library Mudie's. The three-volume novel was too expensive for the average reader to purchase outright, and therefore accessed through the circulating libraries through which, for a more widely affordable fee, one could keep up with the latest titles.

By the 1880s, however, the circulating libraries were essentially monopolized by Mudie's, and to a lesser extent, W. H. Smith & Son's ('Mudie's only serious national rival'), which, finding themselves in the position of effectively controlling the fiction put before the general reading public, were also therefore in the assumed position of unofficial censors (Smith the younger's austere Protestantism had earned him the soubriquet 'Old Morality') (Keating 1989, 23; Davenport-Hines 2004). It wasn't financially viable for writers and publishers to produce work deemed too morally dubious or adventurous by Mudie's, as they would simply refuse to stock the book, resulting in the publisher being denied the bulk order through which the overwhelming majority of the profit was to be made and a career as an author maintained.

That this situation was not to everyone's satisfaction was made clear in December 1884 when George Moore (1852–1933)—a 'young and then relatively unknown novelist'—questioned the 'power and moral authority of the circulating libraries' in the pages of the *Pall Mall Gazette* (Llewellyn and Heilmann 2007, 372):

> At the head, therefore, of English literature, sits a tradesman, who considers himself qualified to decide the most delicate artistic question that may be raised, and who crushes out of sight any artistic aspiration he may deem pernicious. And yet with this vulture gnawing at their hearts writers gravely discuss the means of producing good work; let them break their bonds first, and it will be time when they are free men to consider the possibilities of formulating a new aestheticism. (Moore 1884, 1)

Mark Llewellyn and Ann Heilmann have observed that while 'from the mid-century onwards writers had waged war on the circulating libraries for placing a stranglehold on the literary marketplace', Moore's attack precipitated 'fierce debate in the *Pall Mall Gazette* that raged over several weeks, drawing not only long-suffering authors but also readers and publishers into the public arena' (Llewellyn and Heilmann 2007, 372–373). Subsequent correspondents argued against Moore, claiming that writing, being a 'trade', was quite rightly dependent on the simple laws of supply and demand that the circulating libraries fulfilled, a view which provoked the novelist George Gissing (1857–1903) to reclaim fiction as an art rather than a trade, lamenting the failure of novelists to take more commercial risks[1]: 'English novels are miserable stuff for a very miserable reason, simply because English novelists fear to do their best lest they should damage their popularity, and consequently their income' (J. W. 1884; Gissing 1884).

That the risk of flouting the circulating library standard of propriety in letters was a genuine one was demonstrated in 1888 when W. T. Stead, in association with the National Vigilance Committee, launched an investigation into Vizetelly & Co.'s distribution of several of Zola's works in 'unmutilated' (and therefore unexpurgated) editions (Llewellyn and Heilmann 2007, 378). An ensuing House of Commons debate on 'the rapid spread of demoralizing literature in this country' called for 'the law against obscene publications and indecent pictures and prints [… to be …] vigorously enforced, and, if necessary, strengthened' and led to a court action, with disastrous consequences for the defendant (378). Vizetelly & Co. continued to distribute expurgated versions of the texts after misinterpreting the verdict of the first trial, leading to a second trial resulting in 'the bankruptcy of Vizetelly & Co., and the six-month imprisonment of the seventy-year-old Henry Vizetelly on 30 May 1889' (379). That the writer in question in the Vizetelly trial was Zola was indicative of the wider francophobic mood of the times and the 'vulgar [British] superstition that French things were naughty', that 'French art, novels, dress, habits, were all alike immoral' (Croft-Cooke 1967, 165).

However, despite such controversies, by the 1890s, the market had been liberated from the pressure of onerous tax burdens and the stultifying effect of the monopoly of the circulating libraries on literature was significantly eased by the appearance of the new magazines, and the newly profitable, affordable one-volume novel, the latter reducing 'the price of much new high and middle zone fiction […] by at least two-thirds' (Brake 2001, 23). Publishers could subsequently afford to take more, albeit significant, risks and one such was taken by John Lane, who, despite the antipathetic mood outlined above, launched the *Yellow Book* in April 1894, a journal through which, according to its detractors at least, Lane had

---

[1] Although the specific context for this controversy was a new one, this fundamental argument over whether literature was an art or a trade was not. John Gross, for example, writes of Thackeray's contempt for Bulwer's and Dickens's Guild of Literature and Art launched in 1851. Thackeray objected that 'a lot of humbug was talked about the special privileges of genius, Grub Street in the old sense had disappeared, literature was a trade like any other, etcetera' (Gross 1973, 32).

given its contributors 'license to talk about ugly things inartistically' and exhorted them to 'be mystic, be weird, be precious, be without value' (Wedmore 1894, 349; "A Yellow Melancholy" 1894, 468). In its prospectus for the title, the Bodley Head announced that the *Yellow Book* would be a departure from the 'bad old traditions of periodical literature' and would 'not tremble at the frown of Mrs Grundy', the apocryphal personification of pompous middle-class censoriousness ("The Yellow Book: Prospectus to Volume 1" 1894).

Although its self-consciously avant-garde choice of material ensured only a minority appeal, it was to become an 'absolute symbol of decadence' and one of the key signifiers of the new cultural turn of the decade (Calloway 1993, 38). Writing in 1911, William Blaikie Murdoch was unequivocal about the impact of the *Yellow Book* and its successors:

> In 1894 there occurred a momentous event in the history of aesthetics generally, this being the founding of the *Yellow Book*. It was followed by the *Savoy*, the *Dome*, and the *Pageant*; and it was the artists who clustered round these periodicals (particularly the two noted first) who formed the fieriest star in the new constellation, and whose output chiefly makes it reasonable to speak of the nineties as marked by upheaval. (Murdoch 1911, 18)

There was a new incentive among writers, editors, and publishers to attract readers with risqué or 'sensational' work that would never have been countenanced by the morally didactic Mudie's. However, there was a fine balancing act to be performed, as fiction which crossed a line—the exact position of which was still being decided—could find itself attracting opprobrium and outrage rather than increased sales, from both the moral guardians of the establishment and a fickle public wanting to be at once entertained yet keen to maintain an aspirational civic respectability. Incidents like the Vizetelly trial would presumably have been at the forefront of the mind of publishers like John Lane—whose 'little magazine' the *Yellow Book* and 'Keynotes' series of novels became almost inextricably identified with the spirit of their time—when they were testing the boundaries of what was acceptable far enough to attract high sales, yet to still operate within the bounds of conscionable taste.

This feat was perhaps exemplarily performed by Annie Sophie Cory (1868–1952, as 'Victoria Crosse') with *The Woman Who Didn't* (1895). Written partly in response to Grant Allen's provocative novel of female emancipation *The Women Who Did* (1895), and also published in the

Keynotes series, Cory's novel has a title that cleverly evokes that book's controversies while avoiding them itself. Its 'title assures us that nothing dishonourable will occur, while the working out of the story keeps us, or kept readers of the Nineties, on a titillating knife-edge' (Lambert and Ratcliffe 1987, 102). In its initial manifestation the *Yellow Book* was 'unique, individual, a little weird, often exotic, demanding a right to *be*—in its own way even to waywardness' (Jackson 1913, 52). However, even a minor misjudgement of what was acceptable could quickly generate commercially disastrous criticism from both reviewers and the reading public.

The newly heterogeneous publishing field sketched above foregrounded debates about not only what constituted appropriate subject matter for literature, but also on what constituted acceptable literature itself, and these cultural issues were of course predicated on the wider social and political discourses of the 1890s. Tensions were considerably heightened by the Wilde scandal of 1895. In January of that year, the Marquess of Queensbury, furious over rumours concerning the nature of Wilde's relationship with his son Lord Alfred ('Bosie') Douglas, sought out Wilde at the Albemarle Club. Failing to find him present, Queensbury left a scribbled visiting card for 'Oscar Wilde posing somdomite [sic]', in effect a public accusation of homosexuality. Queensbury was the subject of an initial suit by Wilde for defamation of character, a suit quickly lost, initiating a counter suit of 'gross indecency', resulting in Wilde's imprisonment and public humiliation. It also precipitated a widespread backlash against the perceived moral threat of all that Wilde represented, particularly the cultural avant-garde who were operating, either voluntarily or under sufferance, within a paradigm that had come to be styled 'Decadence'.

That the latter term, discussed in more detail below, is broad and ill-defined is suggested by the fact that it can be credibly presented on the same page as one of the 'last exotic pendants of a hopelessly frumpish Victorianism' and also 'for the English […] simply shorthand for the 1890s' itself' (Fletcher and Bradbury 1979, 7). In the narrowest sense, it was perhaps a common sympathy between many of the avant-garde cultural producers who, informed by what Holbrook Jackson described as the many 'isms' of the age ('Realism', 'Impressionism', 'Aestheticism', and so on) 'gracefully accepted the pejorative label thrust on them by higher journalism and the progressive critique' (Fletcher and Bradbury 1979, 9). Although there is an account of the period as 'the age of the transition'—precipitated by and participated in by Decadence—drawing a convenient and neatly placed curtain across staid Victorian literary and artistic culture and preparing the ground for the dazzling excitements of Modernism, closer examination of the weird fiction of the period helps further complicate and resist what has already been criticized as a superficial and reductive narrative (Fletcher and Bradbury 1979, 8).

Controversies such as the Wilde trial, as well as the perceived threat of degeneration (with Decadence as its cultural manifestation) to the project and work of Empire, 'healthy' masculinity, and establishment values, led to some of the alleged disciples of Decadence taking pains to dissociate themselves from what was fast becoming a term simply too damaging to reputation and commercial viability. On 5 April 1895, and directly precipitated by a misreporting that Wilde had one day attended court with a copy of the *Yellow Book* under his arm (rather, he was reading *a* yellow book when the police arrested him), John Lane had his office windows in Vigo Street stoned by 'the mob' and 'in panic dismissed [Aubrey] Beardsley', the young artist who had almost single-handedly created the visual iconography of the movement, earning him the soubriquet 'Daubaway Weirdsley' from *Punch* (Freeman 2014, 103; Lambert and Ratcliffe 1987, 80; *Punch* 1895).[2] Lane had also been pressured into making this decision by 'six of the most prominent [writers] of the Bodley Head', who had given him an ultimatum to the effect that 'unless he suppressed Beardsley's work in Volume V of the *Yellow Book* and omitted Oscar Wilde's name from his catalogue, they would withdraw their books' (Lambert and Ratcliffe 1987, 80). And so it was that the fifth volume was described by the *Athenaeum* in May 1895 (the month of Wilde's sentencing) as 'chastened and sobered' and the withering observation made that the inclusion of a portrait of George Egerton only serves 'to remind us […] of the former tendencies of this quarterly' (*Athenaeum* 1895, 608). Writing little over a decade later, Holbrook Jackson still thought it worth reminding his readers that the culture represented by the initial manifestation of the *Yellow Book* was 'really an abnormal minority, and in no sense national' (Jackson 1913, 52). By the time Arthur Symons (1865–1945) expanded his influential essay 'The Decadent Movement in Literature' (1893) into a book in 1899, he deemed it wise to rechristen it with the less contentious title *The Symbolist Movement in Literature* (Symons 1893, 1899).

Symons, wanting to refocus on literary discourse free of contention, was perhaps keen to liberate the 'new style' from both the controversies of

---

[2] The apparent lack of any contemporary newspaper coverage of the incident at Vigo Street raises at least a question mark over the actual size of this 'mob'.

Decadence and its more strident critics and reclaim it for the literary cognoscenti to use in elite discourses safely away from the uncomfortable glare of public scrutiny. As well as the word 'Decadence' itself, all mention of William Ernest Henley's (1849–1903) poetry, originally lauded by Symons as an indicative British expression of the movement, was excised. Henley, a successful editor and critic as well as a practitioner, was initially sympathetic to the formal and stylistic literary experiments associated with Decadence and was evidently neither a philistine nor a prude: he had been one of the early champions of the works of Rodin and at the end of the 1890s was at work on an 'etymologically brilliant' dictionary of slang (including obscenities) with John S. Farmer in an effort to 'compensate for the omissions of the staid *Oxford English Dictionary*' (Mehew 2004; Slade 2001, 758).

In 1895, however, he was, publicly and professionally at least, unequivocal in his damning criticism of all that Wilde represented, remarking as editor of the *National Observer*—a paper whose 'dominant note' was one of 'militant Conservatism and advocacy of imperialism'—that there was 'not a man or woman in the English-speaking world possessed of the treasure of a wholesome mind who is not under a deep debt of gratitude to the Marquis of Queensberry for destroying the High Priest of the Decadents' ("Oxford DNB Article: Henley, William Ernest" n.d.; Henley 1895, 547). Linda K. Hughes has suggested with good reason that Henley—the 'imperial aesthete'—was conflicted in his private and public reactions to the trial, citing W. B. Yeats's comment that 'Henley never wholly lost that first admiration [of Wilde], for after Wilde's downfall he said to me: "Why did he do it? I told my lads to attack him and yet we might have fought under his banner"'(Hughes 2006, 82, 2006, 68).

As well as erstwhile 'fellow travellers' like Henley, those who had long opposed the avant-garde in its earlier manifestations of Aestheticism, Symbolism, and Impressionism and associated themselves with the reactionary 'philistine' wing of cultural criticism, such as the belligerent art critic Harry Quilter, scented blood after the Wilde trial and became increasingly vitriolic in their attacks on contemporary literary trends. Some of Quilter's bitterest rhetoric was aimed at Machen's story 'The Great God Pan', which he lambasted at length in an article in the *Contemporary Review* detailing his objections to 'new departures in the arts' at variance to the 'national character' and its accompanying 'decencies and restrictions of thought and emotion' (Quilter 1895, 3). This specific attack on one of the exemplar texts of weird fiction will be discussed in further detail below.

The impact of the Wilde trial can perhaps be gauged through Jackson's remark that it was the culmination of what he describes as the 'nihilism' of the tendency in much the same way that the Boer War was the culmination of the jingoistic 'Yellow Press' sensationalism of Fleet Street (Jackson 1913, 53). However, regardless of these high-profile scandals and the extremes of vitriol finding their way into print, for many authors attempting to establish literary careers at the time there was no simple bifurcation between establishment-endorsed conservatism in letters and risqué experimentalism.

Those who saw themselves as the stylistic avant-garde could often also assume a role of cultural stewardship and of being a bulwark against the perceived threat to the traditional 'purist' ideals of literariness. Peter McDonald posits Henley and his associated circle (occasionally referred to as the 'Henley Regatta', after a witticism made by Max Beerbohm) as an exemplar of these advocates of 'literary purism' (Mehew 2004). Henley and the periodicals under his editorial control and influence were staunchly pro-establishment and pro-Empire, advocating traditional social and civic values. However, the 'fiercely purist' Henley was also keen to propagate and disseminate an idea of literature and literariness as something executed by an educated elite, not insensible to sophisticated developments on the continent, and sympathetic to hierarchical notions of art commensurate with his reactionary political beliefs (McDonald 2002, 29).

McDonald describes this project in terms of Henley and his circle attempting to maintain 'exclusive control over literary value' at a time when the sheer volume of new fiction being produced made an actual 'gatekeeping' role impossible (McDonald 2002, 30). Already by 1879 Frederic Harrison had fretted, in his literary survey *The Choice of Books*, over 'how a man with only twenty-four hours a day at his disposal can be expected to cope with the unprecedented torrent of modern literature' (Gross 1973, 129). The rapidity and extent of the growth in the literary market was becoming a cause of distinct anxiety for practitioners at every level, from the Henley Regatta down to subsistence scribblers occupying squalid 'New Grub Street' garrets: 'This huge library, growing into unwieldiness, threatening to become a trackless desert of print—how intolerably it weighed upon the spirit!' (Gissing 2007, 143).

Henley's purist stance was also, however, tempered with a political commensurability with advocates of healthy romance and 'manly' adventure, as opposed to the (perceived) over-intellectual, possibly deleterious, effeminate, and morally ambiguous currents in continental letters.

Commentators like Andrew Lang endorsed the notion of fiction as wholesome, straightforward, and improving, and posited the 'romances' of Robert Louis Stevenson and H. Rider Haggard (both writers advocated by Henley) as preferable to the 'misery' to be found in the works of 'M. Dostoieffsky' or (in Lang's view) the unbalanced emphasis on the 'Unpleasant Real' evident in Zola, both writers then exciting the British literary avant-garde with their bold formal and stylistic experiments (Lang 1887). In his study of popular fiction magazines of the period, Mike Ashley follows Roger Lancelyn Green's lead in crediting Stevenson with almost single-handedly ushering in what Green styles the 'age of the Story Tellers'; the period of the proliferation of serial titles catering to a middle-brow family audience and providing them with 'romances and adventure stories in an ever-thickening stream' (Ashley 2006, 1–3).

However, Stevenson was also claimed by the Decadents as one of their own, on both sides of the Channel. For example, the French symbolist Marcel Schwob translated not only Wilde into French but Stevenson too, and was an ardent enough admirer of the latter to undertake a pilgrimage to Samoa in homage of his late literary hero (White 1982, 3–5). Machen's admiration of and stylistic debt to Stevenson—and particularly Stevenson's 'insatiable taste for weird adventure, for *diablerie*, for a strange mixture of metaphysics and romance'—is discussed in more detail below (*Illustrated London News* 1894, 769). Haggard's African romances, as well as being perceived as largely healthy and of sound virility, also attracted the adjective 'weird' and exerted a clear and enduring influence on the development of both weird and pulp fiction in general (Haggard's influence can be tracked in writers including, but certainly not limited to, Doyle, Edgar Rice Burroughs, Lovecraft, and Howard) (Sharp 1889, 100). Machen's debt to Stevenson is considerable and acknowledged in the fiction that first brought his name before the public, but far from being published by one of the adventure or family magazines of the day, Machen was given his platform by John Lane in his Keynotes series, an imprint usually regarded as one of the definitive literary expressions of British Decadence.

Although the two positions are not mutually exclusive, Wendell V. Harris presents John Lane as an opportunist rather than a cultural ideologue: a 'shrewd business man' who knew how to 'exploit literary fashions' (Harris 1968, 1407). This view is in concordance with Rupert Croft-Cooke's blunt appraisal that 'the Decadence of the Nineties was not so much a literary movement as a publishing stunt […] promoted by John

Lane and Richard Le Gallienne, his friend and adviser' (Croft-Cooke 1967, 164). McDonald certainly doesn't contradict this account of Lane's commercial acumen, but he also argues that Lane's stable of writers had much in common with the established 'Henley Regatta' of purist writers, keen to defend their position and keep their ranks free from contamination by parvenus, and worse—populist parvenus. The real battle, then, was for the defence of the cultural high ground: 'Avowedly popular writers and publishers [...] were easy to rule out; more serious pretenders within the republic were another matter' (McDonald 2002, 36). Despite his broader concerns, Harris does concede that the Keynotes series is a 'valuable epitome of the kinds of fiction Lane and his staff thought new and vital at the time' and that several of the Keynotes authors have 'secure if tiny niches in literary history' (Harris 1968, 1407).

Harris also remarks upon the difficulties of assessing a series that while on the one hand is considered representative of the age on the other contains such wildly disparate work. He cites the three best known books of the sequence to be George Egerton's *Keynotes* (1893), Grant Allen's *The Woman Who Did* (1895), and Machen's *The Great God Pan and The Inmost Light* (1894), going on to say that 'three more incommensurate works of fiction it would be hard to find' (1408).[3] More precisely, it might be said that Egerton's 'New Woman' fiction and Grant Allen's *The Woman Who Did*, a social critique of the stifling effect of the institution of marriage on female emancipation described by a contemporary reviewer as no less than an 'assault on the middle classes', are in fact certainly commensurate, with Egerton's 'striking naturalism' working in a similarly mimetic field of contemporary social critique as Allen's realism, both in counterpoint to Machen's weird romances (T. P. G 1893, 609; *Saturday Review* 1895, 319) (Fig. 2.1).

Grant Allen began his literary career as a writer of weird fiction, although he also reveals no sense of a Chinese wall between genres or modes when he makes the following remark about his own early experience as a professional author:

> I drifted into fiction by the sheerest accident. [...] I wanted to write a scientific article on the improbability of knowing one had seen a ghost. For con-

---

[3] Hereafter I shall abbreviate the 1894 Keynotes book *The Great God Pan and The Inmost Light* to *The Great God Pan* (italicized), differentiating it from its constituent story 'The Great God Pan'.

Fig. 2.1 Advert for the 'Keynotes' series, designed by Aubrey Beardsley (image courtesy of Alamy)

science sake, and to make the moral clearer, I threw the argument into narrative form. (Jerome 1894, 47–48)

Allen emphasizes the accidental and impromptu circumstances of his fictional debut, and its basis in an interest in scientific discourse rather than literature. He then claims to have simply responded to a request from his publisher to supply more stories in a similar vein, which resulted in the anthology *Strange Stories* (1884). When asked to produce a novel, however, Allen switched from supernatural fiction to political and social critique (i.e., realism). A shift that would almost certainly be at very least surprising today is deemed unremarkable by Allen, although his publisher expresses concerns that *Philistia* (1884) is too 'socialistic' (Jerome 1894, 51). By 1895, when the Keynotes series had been under way for two years, this new plurality of fiction was remarked upon as a novel one in the *Academy*: 'Now the public appears ready to receive in the same library parcel Rudyard Kipling's jungle epic […] and Mr. George Gissing's latest study in drab' (Sharp 1895, 189). It is worth noting that earlier in the same article Gissing's oeuvre is described as 'the *romance* of "the unclassed"' (italics mine), while the author himself is styled 'the first of our realists, in the commonly restricted sense of that word' (Sharp 1895, 189). The Keynotes series was clearly representative of the permeable and inchoate genre boundaries of the time rather than anomalous to any hypothetical ordered structural taxonomy of modern fiction.

That the weird mode finds an expression in nearly all these competing strains of the publishing field of the 1890s can be explained by its operation as a mode rather than a genre. As discussed in more detail in the Introduction, the term 'mode' in a literary context suggests 'a broad but identifiable kind of literary method, mood, or manner that is not tied exclusively to a particular form or genre' (Baldick 2008, 213). It is as much evident in the *haute*-Decadent 'excesses' of the Keynotes series as it is in Haggard's and Kipling's colonial adventures, despite the ostensible differences between the two genres.

Many writers experimented and shifted authorial identity according to the promise of commercial success or artistic status, sometimes attaining both at once or at different times. McDonald analyses in detail the career of Arnold Bennett, who felt free to produce works of naturalist purism and populist sensation according to his mood and his bank balance, although not without attracting criticism from his more purist peers (McDonald 2002, 68–117). Less popular writers, or those establishing careers in the

1890s, would often struggle to strike the right tone, find their voice, and balance commerce with artistry, a process vividly and starkly portrayed in George Gissing's *New Grub Street* (1891). By 1895, genre was at least on occasion being used specifically as an identifier of literary worth, with the *Academy* criticizing the Irish writer Frankfort Moore (1855–1931) as having 'taken the plunge, and descended to an *impossible* story' (italics mine) despite proving 'he was able to treat his art seriously' with his previous novel, *I Forbid the Banns* (1893). The work concerned, *The Secret of the Court* (1895), tells the story of an archaeologist's discovery of a subterranean sect of immortal priests in Egypt, and although the reviewer is initially disparaging, they happily concede that it is 'skilful, racy and coherent' and 'too ingenious and cleverly written' for them to be 'much annoyed' by Moore's choice of subject matter (Little 1895, 311–312). It is clear that in this instance the novel is guardedly judged a success despite, rather than because of, its weird subject matter.

Also shifting between genres, Machen turned his hand to translation, self-published pseudo-medieval romances, and pieces of whimsy and satire before finding some success with his weird classics *The Great God Pan* and *The Three Impostors* (both published by John Lane in the Keynotes series). Similarly, Machen's friend M. P. Shiel tried his hand at various combinations of weird, Decadent, and detective fiction for Keynotes before turning to many other modes and genres to sustain an uneven but enduring career as a writer. Soon after deciding on writing as a career, Shiel 'discovered that editors were not necessarily interested in the original work of a creative literary stylist' and switched to 'hackwork for the hungry penny papers' (Billings 2005, 131). At the outset of his career, Shiel, like Machen, also found a source of revenue in translation work, an early success being the appearance of his rendering of Villiers de l'Isle-Adam's 'A Torture of Hope' in the February 1891 edition of the *Strand* (131). Shiel's biographer, Harold Billings, suggests that the success of this translation gave Shiel the impetus to switch from 'family-oriented stories' (what Shiel described as 'tea-cup' stories—see below) to attempting his own 'darker work' in the Poe vein: 'Elements of the supernatural would begin to show up in his stories [from this point]' (131).

Arthur Conan Doyle established himself as a writer variously of weird fiction, adventure stories, and humorous pieces before achieving unassailable success with the vastly popular Sherlock Holmes stories, and unsuccessfully attempting to establish serious literary credentials through his historical romances. Haggard's disparate first forays into a writing career covered both South African political history and commentary in *Cetywayo and His White Neighbours* (1882) and a Mudie-friendly melodrama 'published in three fat volumes' (i.e., a Victorian three-decker), *Dawn* (1884) (Jerome 1894, 142). Haggard's subsequent adventure romances like *She* and *King Solomon's Mines* contain utterly weird elements but were also keenly endorsed by advocates of 'healthy' literature like Lang, who unapologetically expressed a preference for Haggard's stirring 'boy's books' over his 'novels' (Lang 1887, 690). Similarly, Rudyard Kipling's colonial reportage and realism was tempered with an almost peerless skill at engaging the weird mode in stories like 'In the House of Suddhoo' and 'The Mark of the Beast' (1890). John Buchan, although now widely remembered as the producer of 'healthy' adventure fiction like his 'shocker' *The Thirty-Nine Steps* (1915), began his literary career at a precociously young age as a reader for John Lane, a contributor of 'literary' pieces to the *Yellow Book*, and also a writer of weird tales like the heavily Machen-indebted 'No-Man's Land', published in *Blackwoods* in 1899.

Henry James, whose purist credentials were exemplary, increasingly turned his hand to supernatural fiction during this period, producing such classics as 'The Turn of the Screw' (1898) and 'The Jolly Corner' (1908), both unarguably literary and arguably weird. James aside, it is possible to identify two distinct (although often interwoven) strands of weird writing evident in the above examples: those, like Machen and Shiel, who engaged with and were identified with (even if they didn't do so themselves) the Decadent movement of the period and those, perhaps typified by Haggard, Kipling, and Doyle, who were claimed by the Lang school of 'healthy' romance. However, as with literary production as a whole, the positioning of a particular author within those two ostensibly opposed schools was rarely neat. Henley straddled both the avant-garde and the reactionary, the 'Decadents' Machen and Shiel both demonstrated unapologetic admiration for Doyle, Doyle was accused by Quilter, quite incorrectly, in the *Contemporary Review* of being a 'morbid, painful, and depressing' Keynotes author, and Buchan's first nonfiction work, *Scholar Gipsies* (1896), was criticized for being 'a great deal too precious' by the *Athenaeum* while praised by the *Bookman* for its 'healthy' sentiment and 'modest' tone (both reactions a reflection, perhaps, of the unevenness of the then 21-year-old Buchan's authorial voice) (Quilter 1895, 772; *Athenaeum* 1896; *Bookman* 1897).

Such blithe genre hopping should be considered in the broader literary context, already touched upon above, of the complicated structures of political, social, and artistic interests jostling for both cultural high ground and commercial success. Writers of an aesthetic or symbolist bent felt besieged and vilified by a philistine middle class, while at the same time seduced by the potential commercial opportunities presented by that same middle-class appetite for sensationally 'dangerous' fiction. It is, of course, difficult now to gauge exactly how these culture wars manifested themselves in practice, and for all the heated rhetoric, the dinner hosted by *Lippincotts* magazine in 1889, during which Wilde was commissioned to write *The Picture of Dorian Gray* (1890) and Doyle *The Sign of Four* (1890), seems to have been a friendly and quotidian business meeting, despite both authors arguably belonging to very different cultural camps (McDonald 2002, 135).

Guilt by association was rife, however. Harry Quilter identified Doyle as a Decadent purely on the basis of the aforementioned misapprehension that Doyle's novella 'The Parasite' had been published in the Keynotes series, while Machen was of the opinion that an inopportune expression of admiration for Doyle's new Holmes collection at a literary dinner in 1895 had 'shocked' Henry Harland, editor of the *Yellow Book*, to the extent that Machen felt he was 'finished' as far as Harland was concerned (and, indeed, Machen never was invited to contribute to the journal) (Gawsworth 2013). Similarly, Billings ascribes Shiel's absence from the pages of the *Yellow Book* to, among other factors, Shiel's failure to present himself among John Lane's 'young men' as a 'dedicated *litterateur*' (Billings 2005, 138). Doyle, on his part, describes his 1889 meeting with Wilde as 'a golden evening' and claimed that Wilde 'towered above' the rest of the company and left 'an indelible' impression on the then fledgling writer (Doyle 1924, 78). Doyle adds that upon meeting Wilde again in later years he questioned Wilde's sanity, and although he expresses regret concerning the 'monstrous development' that ruined Wilde, he demonstrates none of the rancour poured on Wilde by his bitterest critics, including Henley (79). Indeed, Doyle concludes his reminiscence by quoting at length from a letter he received from Wilde in which Wilde expresses considerable appreciation of Doyle's praise for *The Picture of Dorian Gray*. Doyle also states that modesty forbids him quoting the section of the letter in which Wilde lauds Doyle's own *The Sign of Four*, and therefore unambiguously demonstrates an enthusiasm, in 1924 at least, to be aligned with the erstwhile pariah and 'champion of aestheticism' (78–80).

Doyle and Wilde's shared debt to Poe provides one explanation of an otherwise surprising alliance and mutual empathy, as it does the wider commonality between the Decadents and the Lang school of 'healthy' romance. Baudelaire's nascent modernity and Decadence were built on the foundation of Poe's aesthetic and formal innovations, and thence amalgamated into the French influence on British writing. Poe's legacy as a progenitor of the modern short story, the weird tale, and, perhaps most notably in Doyle's case, detective fiction manifested itself in fertile ground in the periodical boom of the 1880s and 1890s. The 'Age of the Storytellers' and the age of Decadence and nascent literary Modernism is one and the same, a fact that has not left subsequent commentators untroubled. For example, Harris, writing in 1968, identifies one of the dangers of investigating the 1890s as being the risk of being steered away from the canon:

> The difficulty is to find approaches to the 1890s which allow us to see its complexity, yet preserve us from being overwhelmed by the great number of minor writers we encounter once we cast our nets beyond Wilde, Beardsley, Beerbohm, and the Rhymers' Club. (Harris 1968, 1407)

Or, to put it in plainer terms, the practice of 'resurrecting forgotten texts and dredging up minor curiosities' means that 'great books' are in 'danger of being smothered by the sheer weight of little ones' (Gross 1973, 129).[4] This concern was not a novel one: John Gross writes of 'powerful voices raised throughout the Victorian age, inveighing against the pursuit of second-rate novelty, exhorting readers not to waste their time on anything less than the best, the very best, that had been thought and said in the world' (211).

Although the animus behind Harris's reasoning is still arguably predicated on this assumption that good literature is morally improving literature, it is also possible of course that he is simply chary of a counterproductive 'tar baby' effect; the risk that, when investigating an age when the printed word increased so exponentially over a short space of time, one will be overwhelmed. However, it is also evidence of a continuing anxiety (commensurable with what Andreas Huyssen describes as Modernism's 'anxiety of contamination'), over half a century after the event, and resulting from a perceived threat to canonical 'literariness' posed by the fin-de-siècle shift in publishing practices, as represented by the move away from the canon-

---

[4] This is an excerpt from a passage in which Gross is sketching Frederic Harrison's 'anxiety of contamination' from the 1870s onwards.

ized, respectable Victorian three-decker to the proliferation of both purist and populist forms whose cultural capital remains as yet unresolved (Huyssen 1988, vii). One of the manifestations associated with this shift, and one which was oppositional to the traditional three-decker in both form and often content, was the rise of a new literary brevity more commensurate with the expanding periodical market: the short story.

The Short Story

Paul March-Russell has described the term 'short story' as a 'neologism [signifying] a redefinition of literature towards the end of the nineteenth century; how it is produced, received and consumed' (March-Russell 2009, 1). Reflecting on 'English Literature in 1893', the *Athenaeum* observed that there 'has been a distinctly new growth in the short story', adding that 'with two or three exceptions, all the best fiction of the year has been in the form of short stories' (*Athenaeum* 1894, 17–18). The phenomenon is identified as being the result of a not altogether respectable continental influence—the author appropriates Tennyson's line 'poisonous honey stol'n from France' to describe the form's provenance—and associated with 'a new license in dealing imaginatively with life' (17–18). Writing in *Cornhill* in July 1899, the American expatriate and popular writer Bret Harte (judged by Doyle to be responsible for 'perhaps [...] three short stories of unsurpassed merit') says of the 'short story' that while a novel form in British letters, it was 'familiar enough [...] in America during the early half of the century' (Doyle 1890, 648; Harte 1899, 1). Although he develops an argument that it is the emphasis on humour which differentiates the American modern short story from the British, he specifically associates the genesis of the form with Poe, Hawthorne, and (to a lesser extent) Longfellow, speculating that the 'proverbial haste of American life was some inducement to [the form's] brevity' (1).

Writing a century later, R. C. Feddersen concurs with Hart's identification of Poe and Hawthorne as the progenitors of the form, but adds the Russian Nikolai Gogol as a third, specifically citing the latter's 'The Overcoat' (1840) as 'the first clear example of the early short story' (Feddersen 2001, xviii). (The considerable influence of *Blackwoods Edinburgh Magazine* on Poe in this respect has been alluded to in the Introduction). Interestingly for our purposes, Feddersen goes on to sketch the unifying characteristics of this triumvirate in terms that could convincingly be applied to the weird tale: 'a single character engaged in a "real" world, but generally, a somewhat unusual conflict and a plot that includes supernatural or dreamlike elements' (Feddersen 2001, xviii). He also notes that 'some German writers of the eighteenth century had been producing *novellae* that often depicted unusual experiences or even the supernatural' (Feddersen 2001, xvii). This implied imbrication of the short story form with the weird tale also usefully acknowledges the weird mode's oneiric and visionary manifestations as well as the more generally acknowledged tropes of the Gothic and monstrous.

As discussed in the Introduction, Poe had been identified as a writer of weird fiction since at least the 1850s. In an overview of his work from 1854, the *Critic* describes Poe as an author of 'tales as weird [...] as those of Hoffman [sic]', before going on to observe that Poe's power lies in his ability to add 'an air of circumstantial verity to incredibilities [... as well as ...] throwing a weird lustre upon commonplace events' (Apollodorus 1854, 120). The *New Monthly Magazine* in 1857 alludes to 'Edgar Poe's weird sketches', the *New Quarterly Review* describes a 'doctor's story' as a highlight of an otherwise disappointing novel due to it being a 'tale worthy of Edgar Poe for weird horror and thrilling interest', and in the *Scottish Review* Poe's 'Marginalia' is described as 'distinct from the weird tales altogether' (Nathaniel 1857, 385; *New Quarterly Review* 1858, 216; "What Books to Read, and How to Read Them" 1859, 376).

By the 1890s, Poe had more directly penetrated the field of British letters through at least two more impactful routes than the indirect influence implied by Harte. First, if Harte was correct in his argument that the short story was an American import, originating with Poe, it had also made inroads to Britain through French Decadence—as recognized by the *Athenaeum* (quoted above)—accompanied by no little controversy. Poe's influence was also a direct one on the weird fiction produced to fill the huge demand precipitated by the boom in periodical publishing discussed above. It was recognized by aspiring writers hoping to exploit the demand for short fiction that the weird tale, as demonstrated by Poe, could provide the 'strength, novelty, compactness, intensity of interest, a single vivid impression' desirable and perhaps necessary to create sellable product (Doyle 1908, 62).

March-Russell remarks that the American critic Brander Matthews's 'dissemination of Poe's theory' in the *Saturday Review* in 1884—to the effect that '"a *true* Short-story differs from the Novel chiefly in its *essential* unity of impression"'—was as influential to periodical editors as it was to individual writers (March-Russell 2009, 35). It is perhaps hardly surprising that subsequent literary culture found a ready place for short fiction that aspired to Poe in its content, as well as its form, and one could speculate that, courtesy of this received wisdom, a piece of fiction exhibiting Poe's influence might automatically be assumed to be of some worth. Jackson also observed that the 'popular magazines had still to deaden down the conception of what a short story might be to the imaginative limitation of the common reader', implying that a consensus—possibly in terms of taste, artistic value, and acceptability, or suitability of subject matter—was yet to be reached that would subsequently stultify a vibrant and fecund experimentalism:

> I do not think the present decade [1910s] can produce any parallel to this list [of exemplary short stories published in the 1890s], or what is more remarkable, that the later achievements in this field of any of the survivors from that time, with the sole exception of Joseph Conrad, can compare with the work they did before 1900. It seems to me this outburst of short stories came not only as a phase in literary development, but also as a phase in the development of the individual writers concerned. (Jackson 1913, 229)

This has proved problematic for critics ever since, who have difficulty accommodating the weird elements of otherwise canonical writers' fiction, often excusing it as ephemeral to the 'serious' work, or conveniently excising it from their analysis of an individual work.

For example, discussing Kipling's 'At the End of the Passage' (1890), John Bayley relegates the weird mode of the text to the position of a 'device from Poe used to give punch and climax' to the story, and argues that its 'reality' is 'exaggerated' or 'overlaid' by this (Bayley 1989, 66). The 'reality' posited by Bayley is that of the 'heat, insomnia and loneliness' of remote colonial life, all unarguably represented to great effect in the story (66). Kipling's unpalatable and subversive critique of Empire is therefore smuggled in front of the reading public within a weird tale in the tradition of Poe; a commercially acceptable quantity. However insightful this reading of 'At the End of the Passage' is, however, it quickly becomes problematic to apply its lessons more broadly. Admittedly, Bayley subsequently observes how the 'two narrative modes act powerfully in combination' in 'The Strange Ride of Morrowbie Jukes', although it should also be noted that although this story has no 'supernatural' element at all, it is still deemed by Bayley to be Poe-esque on account of 'the combination [...] of adventure story with something very like a search for a secret cause, a deep and disconcerting mystery', a description equally fitting of Machen's fiction of the period (67–68).

Bayley identifies 'the mysterious' as one of two 'general ideas' of the literature of the 1890s (the other being 'art for art's sake'), but also hints at the implicit contradiction of discussing literature concerning a 'sense of mystery [… associated …] with the idea of an absolute, external reality, something that art cannot touch but only reveal' (p. 1). If only the mystery is evident in the text, then how is one to discuss the text's relation to 'facts, truths, circumstances outside itself'?' (2). Weird fiction complicates this even further by often representing the 'mystery' as supernatural, analogous not to 'facts, truths, circumstances outside itself' but rather representing the 'mystery' in terms of Lovecraft's 'unexplainable dread of outer, unknown forces' (Lovecraft 1985, 427). Writing about Stevenson in 1893, a commentator makes a similar set of associations, which she argues result in the 'strange weird thrill' of some of Stevenson's fiction:

> Side by side with the artistic realm of much of Mr Stevenson's work runs a vein of pure romance. […] It comes, to use his own phrase […] 'like a kind of dancing madness', and when the fit is on him, this author is a master of fanciful horror, as seen in the fearsome creature Edward Hyde, in 'Olalla', or 'Thrawn Janet', in some of the *New Arabian Nights*, and in passages throughout his works. The secret of this strange weird thrill is perhaps his strong sense of the 'maddening brain-confounding mystery of life'. (Newton-Robinson 1893, 604)

The 'secret cause' and 'mystery' was also much dwelt upon by Machen in his own fiction and critical work and John Gray has recently described Machen as an exponent of what Gray calls 'hermetic doubt'. Gray posits 'hermetic doubt' as a 'recognizable tradition' of writing that shares 'a mistrust of the solidity of everyday things—but without affirming a reality, somewhere beneath the surface, which is any more substantial' (Gray 2013). Although Gray doesn't specifically mention short fiction while making this observation—he is in fact primarily discussing M. John Harrison's trilogy of novels *The Kefahuchi Tract* (2002–2012)—his notion of 'hermetic doubt' neatly dovetails with Bayley's assertion that one of the short form's strengths is its tendency towards fragmentariness and incompleteness, which imbues it (regardless of the valences of its genre) with a structural mimesis lacking in the novel's tendency to unrealistically comprehensive exposition and resolution of narrative.

Similarly, in his observation that 'the possibility of literature is found in the radical impossibility of creating a complete work', Maurice Blanchot is by implication endorsing the short form's explicit engagement with its own incompleteness as grounds for its authenticity of representation: its more accurate mimesis in regard to the fragmentary nature of experience and subjective consciousness (Critchley 2004, 41). Bayley concludes his study of the short story by asserting the following:

> The duality of a really good short story constitutes its expression of our human awareness that everything in life is full of significance, and at the same time that nothing in it has any significance at all. Every situation or event may have a story in it, but the short story's best art will also reveal an absence: the absence of its own meaning. The story's epiphany must also encounter and accept emptiness. To put it like that may sound a bit glib, but the effect is none the less basic to the developed short story. The tradition of the novel is quite different. It solves and settles its narrative, and belongs to an epoch in which solutions and explanations were taken for granted. (Bayley 1989, 182)

It is possible to find some accord between the last sentence and the tendency of fin-de-siècle weird fiction to invoke the mysterious to trouble and disquiet rather than offer resolutions and explanations. Similarly, according to Simon Critchley's reading of Blanchot, the 'nothing or silent solitude that is the source of literature' is largely 'equated by Blanchot—drawing discretely on a whole network of allusions to the theme of dread in Kierkegaard and Heidegger—with dread or anguish', both of which are typically evident in weird fiction (Critchley 2004, 43).

In the above I have attempted to demonstrate that the short story form was, to the point of inevitability, a crucible for the creation of weird fiction: in both its provenance (with Poe and Stevenson), the commercial potential, and platform provided by the fin-de-siècle publishing field (which led to writers having a pecuniary motive for imitating not only the form but the content of Poe and Stevenson) and also—inextricable from these aforementioned—the short form and the weird tale's predication on mystery, dread, and lack of closure, the associated potency of which was also resonant with the uncertain mood of the later nineteenth century. The oft-repeated (and previously quoted) paragraph by Lovecraft, in which he adumbrates his notion of the 'weird tale', concludes with an important but regularly neglected sentence: 'And of course, the more completely and unifiedly a story conveys this atmosphere, the better it is as a work of art in the given medium' (Lovecraft 1985, 427). Implicit in this is an endorsement of Poe's advocacy of the short form's potency in this respect. Taking all these things into account provides an explanation for the rise of a 'high phase' of weird fiction still impacting, directly or otherwise, on popular and literary culture to this day.

Weird Decadence

One word that the reader encounters repeatedly when perusing both *The Weird: A Compendium of Strange and Dark Stories* and *The New Weird* is 'decadence'. Jeff VanderMeer describes the influence of the 'Decadence of the late 1800s' as a constituent part of the 'brain of New Weird', and the 'French/English Decadents' as 'forbears' (J. VanderMeer 2008, x). He identifies the 'unabashed decadence of K. J. Bishop's "The Art of Dying" as one of the 'highlights' of *The New Weird* (p. xvii). In *The Weird: A Compendium of Strange and Dark Stories*, Ann VanderMeer and Jeff VanderMeer identify Decadence as a distinguishing valence of the work of many of the contributors across the chronological span of the anthology, including Hans Heinz Ewers, Alfred Kubin, Gustav Meyrink, Jeffrey Ford, Micaela Morrissette, and (again) K. J. Bishop (A. VanderMeer and VanderMeer 2012, 1, 71, 963, 1075, 1106). This imbrication of weird fiction and Decadence is one that is returned to repeatedly below, and—as I will argue—imperatively so. I will go on to suggest that what came to be regarded in the twentieth and twenty-first centuries as weird fiction can be credibly and revealingly discussed as a persistence of Decadence (rather than the result of a *post facto* influence), without contesting its involvement within the wider Gothic tradition. For example, all three streams recently converged in the first season of the popular HBO television series *True Detective* (2014), which uses tropes from Robert W. Chambers' 1895 anthology of interlinked Decadent weird tales *The King in Yellow*, as well as demonstrates the influence of contemporary weird fiction author Thomas Ligotti (Mariani 2014).

There are two potential difficulties in specifically identifying a weird turn in Decadence. Firstly, the term 'weird' was used liberally but without much reflexivity by contemporary commentators to identify an unspecific mode that could either be evident in an entire piece of work or occasionally intrude in a work and destabilize its apparent verisimilitude, or destabilize the reader's understanding of that which the fiction strives to reflect. Secondly, as discussed in the Introduction, a clear canon of weird fiction is still being constructed and no definitive criteria for inclusion in this weird canon have been forthcoming, perhaps with the happy consequence that the risk of artificially isolating and therefore inadvertently ossifying a dynamic genre process has been avoided. In the 1890s, the use of the word 'weird' in literary discourse was commonly associated with fiction that provoked notions of 'fear', 'perversity', 'unease', 'the uncanny', the 'unhealthy', the 'horrific', the 'supernatural', and sometimes even the 'disgusting'. The Decadent turn in English letters also attracted many of these epithets and it is therefore perhaps sensible to work inwards from this broader frame when thinking about the cultural history of weird fiction.

Decadence was one of the most tendentious and divisive terms of the literary battles of the fin de siècle, and perhaps because of this impact its meaning has often become attenuated to the point of being 'simply shorthand for the 1890s' itself (Fletcher 1980, 7). Sometimes identified as being initiated in the mid-century by the response of Baudelaire to the new post-Industrial metropolis, and the increased speed and anonymity of European modernity, the term has also been interpreted as reflecting 'new moods of uncertainty, bewilderment' ensuing from the increasing destabilization of long-established beliefs by the seemingly ineluctable progress of science and technology (Lester 1968, 11). The threat of scientific materialism, Darwinism, and new Biblical scholarship to old religious certainties facilitated a new relativism: 'To regard all things and principles of things as inconstant modes or fashions has more and more become the tendency of modern thought' (Pater 1902, 243). In his study *The Renaissance: Studies in Art and Poetry* (1873), Walter Pater advocated a new subjective focus in response to the weakening of objective certitudes: to be 'present always at the focus where the greatest number of forces unites in their purest energy' (246). Evidence of this new subjectivity, of dis-unified moments of experience and the intensity of the moment—'the passage and dissolution of impressions, images, sensations' and the 'tremulous wisp constantly reforming itself on the stream, to a single sharp impression, with a sense in it, a relic more or less fleeting, of such moments gone by'—were to be found in impressionist painting and experimental poetry, as well as fiction which abandoned 'the conventional novel in chapters, with its continuous story' and sought to find 'a new way of saying things, to correspond with that new way of seeing things' (245–46).

Before the term Decadence gained currency, these cultural impulses had also found expression through the Aesthetic movement and the notion of 'Art for Art's Sake'. In this, perhaps less contentious guise, the perceived affectations of the avant-garde were tolerated and even indulged in by the middle classes, while its detractors could gently mock and safely dismiss the phenomenon as a harmless if pretentious enthusiasm for over-fussy soft furnishings and William Morris wallpaper. The emerging notion of Decadence seemed more threatening, however, loaded as it was with an implicit threat to social decorum and normative bourgeois values at the very least, and ultimately the very future of civilization if its more excitable critics were to be believed (Symons 1893, 862).

In his 1893 essay 'The Decadent Movement in Literature', the poet and critic Arthur Symons was at pains to point out the term's complications and difficulties, acknowledging its blurred and fractious relationship with the near-synonymous Impressionism and Symbolism before positing the word as a compromise, its somewhat tautological task amounting to no more than conveying 'some notion of that new kind of literature which is perhaps more broadly characterized by the word Decadence' (Lisa Rodensky 2006, xxvii). Wilde, whose *The Picture of Dorian Gray* is now often regarded as an *ur*-text of British Decadence, is entirely absent from Symons's account, and he instead posits Walter Pater and W. E. Henley as the key domestic exponents of Decadence. Stylistically 'over-subtilizing refinement upon refinement', Symons also saw in Decadence evidence of a 'spiritual and moral perversity': 'Healthy we cannot call it, and healthy it does not wish to be considered' (Symons 1893, 859). The term Decadence was therefore not only a literary-critical tool, but had implications of an attitude or a pose beyond words on a page: 'contempt for the usual, the conventional, beyond the point of literary expression' (p. 862). Max Beerbohm, writing in one of the definitive periodicals of the movement, the *Yellow Book*, saw Decadence as having implications of 'marivaudage, lassitude, a love of horror and unusual things, a love of argot and archaism and the mysteries of style' (Beerbohm 1894, 284).

Paradoxically, as well as this turn towards the '*outré* and the bizarre', there was a concurrent 'search after *reality* in literature', not to be necessarily conflated with what is now generally regarded as 'literary realism' (Lester 1968, 12; Symons 1893, 860). The reality being sought after was variegated and often nebulous. It could be the reality of the 'deeper meaning of things' behind the everyday veil of the quotidian, a numinous reality whose fire and ecstasy could be dimly accessed through their symbolic representation in art and literature, a representation striving towards what Machen called the 'quiddity' of things: 'that essence which is present in all things, which indeed makes them to be what they are, which is nevertheless unsearchable and ineffable' (Symons 1893, 860; Machen 1923b, 78). Alternatively, the reality aspired to could, as previously suggested, be the

Paterian mercurial subjectivity of lived experience; the perception that, as Conrad put it, 'we live in the flicker' (Conrad 1899, 195). To some, literary realism revealed the operation of stark existential truths, akin to the notion of the 'Will' in Schopenhauer's notoriously pessimistic worldview and the blind striving of Darwin's evolution, both reflected in the 'Naturalism' of Hardy and Zola, in which the characters are inescapably bound to their biologically determined fates.

There were also experiments in literary realism 'proper' associated with Decadence (possible examples being Grant Allen's and George Egerton's contribution to the Keynotes series) and a subsequent criticism that the realism represented in such fiction was nothing more than drab detail and prosaic verisimilitude at best, as parodied by Gissing in *New Grub Street*, in which one of the characters writes an audaciously soporific and exemplarily quotidian novel titled 'Mr Baily, Grocer'. At its worst, held its critics, it was 'degrading art' representing little more than a salacious, morbid, and possibly pathological interest in sex, adultery, poverty, violence, and foul language (Quilter 1895, 766).

However, these differences in execution aside, Symons—citing the plays of Maeterlinck, the fiction of Huysmans, the poetry of Verlaine, and the paintings of Whistler—identified the unifying theme among the avant-garde artists of his day as being the desire to 'revolt [...] from the bondage of traditional form' and interrogate the 'finer sense of things unseen, the deeper meaning of things evident' (Symons 1893, 859). In its striving for 'further and further extremes of experience' Decadence is certainly commensurable with weird fiction, and even the concept was seen as 'weird' in and of itself: 'a weird word has been invented to explain the whole business. Decadence, decadence: you are all decadent nowadays' (Lester 1968, 12; Crackanthorpe 1894, 266).

If one of the aims of the exponents of Decadence was to mystify and shock the bourgeoisie, they occasionally succeeded beyond what might have otherwise been considered by their co-practitioners to be an acceptable level of notoriety. Writers perceived as Decadent could be conveniently pigeonholed and dismissed in the broadest brush strokes by antipathetic critics. An 1894 review of the minor writer Count Stenbock's (who I will discuss in more detail in Chap. 3) volume of poetry *The Shadow of Death* (1893) condemned it as 'an elaborate and screaming parody of that latterday [sic] literary abortion, the youthful *décadent*':

> The slipshod versification, the maudlin sentiment, the affected preciousness, the sham mysticism and sham aestheticism, the ridiculous medley of Neo-Paganism and Neo-Catholicism, Verlaine and Vulgate—all the nauseating characteristics of the type. (*Pall Mall Gazette* 1894, 4)

If one ignores the disparaging modifiers, this account of Decadence is almost identical to Symons's: whether one was for or against it, there was at least some agreement on what it *was*. Such adverse reactions to the movement were intensified by contemporary discourse on the notion of 'degeneration', which was regularly conflated in haphazard ways with cultural trends of the day, including Decadence. Daniel Pick situates the development of the notion of 'degeneration' in the nineteenth century within the contexts of the criminological and psychiatric discourses of the period, also noting how it reflected how evolutionary theory became 'enmeshed' in 'language, politics [and] culture' (Pick 1989, 6). Pick also acknowledges that degeneration was a 'shifting term produced, inflected, redefined, and re-constituted in the movement between human sciences, fictional narratives and socio-political commentaries' (Pick 1989, 7). For example, in *Degeneration* (1892), the German sociologist Max Nordau made explicit links between Decadent literature and actual social and biological decline, evoking pseudoscientific and garbled Darwinism in his use of the term 'degeneration' and propagating the specious sub-Lamarckian notion that moral recidivism and physical dissolution could be inherited and could fatally weaken a bloodline within generations.

For Nordau, the fin de siècle and Decadence became pejorative synonyms for an amorality, morbidity, and incontinence that threatened not only the social fabric but the future of civilization itself. Atavism was evidenced by physical, cultural, and psychological symptoms, and manifestations of degeneracy were to be found in the 'stigmata' of misshapen physiognomy ('disproportionate growth of particular parts'), the 'inchoate liminal presentations' of degenerate contemporary art, and the 'mental imbalance' of the artist (Nordau 1895, 23, 1895, 61). According to Nordau, some figures, such as Paul Verlaine, had the dubious honour of exhibiting all these symptoms simultaneously (Nordau 1895, 119–120). Over the course of nearly 600 pages, Nordau details a bewildering quantity and variety of symptoms of degeneration, including 'emotionalism', being 'tormented by doubts', the seeking after 'the basis of all phenomena', revolutionary and anarchist activity, political inclination, Buddhism, and pessimism. Even the tendency to 'associate in groups' is included on a charge sheet that seems to encompass the sum of all human activity, and Nordau identifies figures as disparate as Wagner, the children's illustrator Kate Greenaway, furniture-designer Rupert Carabin, and Oscar Wilde as all exhibiting the atavistic neurological disorders of the degenerate mind.

The absurd reach of Nordau's thesis was certainly identified and criticized at the time, although typically with a concession to the ambition of Nordau's vision: Israel Zangwill described it as being 'as brilliant as it is wrong-headed' and the *Review of Reviews* called it a 'bad but interesting book' in which Nordau's 'idea' is 'pressed home unsparingly with manifold examples, and with a continuous vigour of writing' (Zangwill 1895, 160). George Bernard Shaw was moved to write a lengthy riposte for the American journal *Liberty*, and although he would later claim that with his rebuttal of Nordau the '*Degeneration* boom was exhausted', Nordau's treatise still ran into seven editions in the year of its publication alone in Britain. Moreover, his perception that some contemporary cultural trends were predicated upon a 'contempt for traditional views of custom and morality' certainly resonated with more reactionary commentators (Shaw 1919, 12; Nordau 1895, 5). The influence of *Degeneration* was also intensified by the concurrency of its popularity with the Wilde trial, the first British edition being published four days after 'the Marquess of Queensbury left his libellous card at the Albemarle' (Söder 2009, 63).

Given this *milieu*, and the nature of Decadence itself, it was perhaps inevitable that a process of intense mythologization would develop contemporaneously with the movement. Kirsten MacLeod has cogently argued that this has had a direct impact on the subsequent status of Machen's and Shiel's work, primarily through W. B. Yeats's reductive and self-serving (even if unintentionally so) ossification of the notion of British Decadence as the 'Tragic Generation', retroactively delimiting the movement to a particular set of writers who were both poets and perceived martyrs to the Decadent ideal. MacLeod deconstructs the myth of the independently wealthy, aristocratic Decadent writers who in their art and life remained unsullied by the tawdry concerns of the marketplace, and demonstrates that this was a mythology intentionally, although perhaps not cynically, propagated by Yeats in order to privilege the contribution of the Rhymers' Club and by implication the position of poetry in a vertical hierarchy of art. Subsequently, although the art and literary criticism of Walter Pater and Symons is given its due as setting the theoretical framework for the practitioners of Decadence, fiction itself has never entirely been given the prominence it had at the time in subsequent consideration of the period, as far as

Britain is concerned. As MacLeod makes clear, the irony of the essentialist reading of the fin de siècle is that the Rhymers' Club were to a man (and Yeats certainly excludes women writers from his selection) middle-class products of the bourgeoisie whose values they so stridently rejected; through both their aristocratic pose and immersion in the 'low' working-class entertainments of the music hall and its associated vices.

The uncritical acceptance of Yeats's account of British Decadence has, according to MacLeod, resulted in assumptions that prevail to this day. To reiterate the points particularly relevant to this thesis: the privileging of poetry over fiction (with some notable exceptions—for example, Wilde's *The Picture of Dorian Gray* and Pater's *Marius the Epicurean* (1885)); this privileging resulting in the positioning of British Decadence as a purely 'high art' phenomenon; the subsequent neglect of discussion of the impact of decadence in popular culture; and the Decadents' own engagement with the commodification of their work. There is a continuing propagation of the 'class myths' of Decadence as either an aristocratic or bohemian phenomenon, myths eagerly cultivated by its overwhelmingly middle-class exponents, who—despite their actual keen engagement with the publishing market—were at pains to ostensibly reject and distance themselves from the middle-class commodification of culture by repositioning themselves as aristocratic dilettantes, or bohemians wallowing in the working-class milieu of low dives and music halls, or some combination thereof (MacLeod 2006, 22). As Symons himself wryly observed, the desire 'to bewilder the middle-classes is in itself middle-class' (Thornton 1980, 17).

Part of MacLeod's thesis is that as writers of fiction in this period, both Machen and Shiel should reclaim some of the critical space from which they have perhaps unfairly been excluded by Yeats's retroactive adumbration of the movement. This argument also has the side effect of giving weird fiction a more prominent position than it has previously been afforded, an imbrication underpinned by the stylistic crossover between weird fiction and Decadence. Brian Stableford anticipates MacLeod when he writes the following:

> The most intensely lurid products of English Decadence can be found in a small group of short story collections issued between 1893 and 1896: Count Eric Stenbock's *Studies of Death* (1893); R. Murray Gilchrist's *The Stone Dragon and Other Tragic Romances* (1894); the three 'Keynotes' volumes: Arthur Machen's *The Great God Pan and the Inmost Light* (1894), and M. P. Shiel's *Prince Zaleski* (1895) and *Shapes in the Fire* (1896). (Stableford 1993, 60)

Stableford goes on to add that 'the collections named above are remembered today mainly because the supernatural stories in them are sometimes reprinted in collections of horror stories' (Stableford 1993, 61). Considering the fecundity of the fin de siècle in terms of weird fiction, it seems sensible to look at these four writers in further detail, since—as well as being the 'most intensely lurid products of English Decadence'—they also all produced fiction in the weird mode, a perhaps inevitable result of the confluence of factors already discussed.

As mentioned above, Harris, writing in the 1960s, articulated a fear of contamination by accidental engagement with noncanonical literature of the 1890s, predicated on the assumption that such value hierarchies would be shared in by Harris's scholarly readership. In making his argument, he uses language almost entirely in tune with the more hysterical reactions to Keynotes books of the period itself: he excuses himself of any requirement to consider Shiel's and Machen's contributions to the series by claiming that it is 'only from Shiel and Machen that one can draw examples of the perverse disease of the imagination which came to be suggested by the term "decadence"', before attempting to excise them from the record entirely, albeit in a rather desultory fashion: 'it need perhaps hardly be said that this is not what Arthur Symons had meant when he set out to exploit the term' (Harris 1968, 1408). Harris therefore manages both to dismiss Machen and Shiel as 'perverse' examples of Decadence, while also excluding them from the 'respectable' delineation of Decadence he identifies with Symons, thereby neatly absolving himself of any requirement to discuss Machen and Shiel at all. The subtext of this message from Harris is one that is conspiratorial with his reader: both parties, it is assumed, have the good sense and good taste to avoid engagement with noncanonical writers, and it is therefore unfortunate that Harris has to risk contamination by acknowledging Shiel's and Machen's existence when writing about the Keynotes series.

Such positions—underwritten by the presumption of a platonic canon—continue to be assumed. Terry Eagleton, for example, in his review of *The Prose Factory: Literary Life in England since 1918* (2016) by D. J. Taylor, criticizes Taylor for his 'unflagging interest in literary figures nobody else has heard of' and the attention given to 'irredeemably minor members of the scribbling classes' (Eagleton 2016). However, no explanation is given as to why obscurity should axiomatically preclude an author from warranting critical attention, Eagleton assuming it to be self-evident that a specific, finite, and immutable list of figures and works should remain the privileged focus of any respectable discussion. A contrasting view is taken by Malcolm Bradbury and Ian Fetcher who, writing in 1978, argue that the 'commitment to fluidity, that aversion to the canonical, dominant in the [fin-de-siècle] period [...] invites analysis [... and ...] recognition of the role of failed systems, through an attention to minor figures and the nature of their minority' (Fletcher and Bradbury 1979, 9). It is the latter methodology that I shall invoke, alongside Stableford's argument above, as well as MacLeod's advocacy of a reassessment of the contribution of Machen and Shiel's fiction to British Decadence. The discussion of weird fiction in this context will hopefully also be relevant to the broader cultural discourses of the period. In the next chapter, I will therefore discuss Machen, Shiel, Gilchrist, and Stenbock, paying attention to these 'minor figures and the nature of their minority'.

An Edwardian Weird?

The notion of a 'long nineteenth century' has found considerable traction since Eric Hobsbawm discussed the term in his *Age Of Empire: 1875–1914* (1987). However, in that book he was clear that it was an instrumental term, highlighting August 1914 (the beginning of the Great War) as 'one of the most "natural breaks" in history', but also qualifying this claim:

> It was felt to be the end of an era of the time, and it is still felt to be so. It is quite possible to argue this feeling away, and to insist on the continuities and enjambments across the years of the First World War. After all, history is not like a bus-line on which the vehicle changes all its passengers and crew whenever it gets to the point marking its terminus. Nevertheless, if there are dates which are more than conveniences for purposes of periodization, August 1914 is one of them. It was felt to mark the end of the world made by and for the bourgeoisie.

Hobsbawm goes on to note how this periodization has 'attracted historians, amateur and professional, writers on culture, literature and the arts [...] in astonishing numbers'. Discussing weird fiction, Miéville has followed suit, arguing that early twentieth-century weird fiction was, at least in part, a response to the 'shattering' of the 'cruder nostrums of progressive bourgeois rationality', at the heart of which was the First World War (Miéville 2009, 513).

John Buchan's 'The Shut Door' was first published in 1926 in *The Boy's All-round Book* (Buchan 1926, 9–17). It is the first item in this anthology of schoolboy adventure, cricket advice, and imperial reportage. Given this context, the tale is surprisingly bleak and self-reflexive. It is short, but gestures at a much longer narrative cut short, like the central character and so many others, in the pitiless violence of the Great War. In a 'dugout near Gouzeaucourt, the night before the Boche made his counter-attack at Cambrai' (9), several comrades are keeping their 'nerves quiet' by chain-smoking cigarettes and sharing 'yarns'—the Club Story staged in the trenches, in other words (9). The company includes three 'who between them had pretty well covered the globe' and Buchan sketches just enough suggestive detail to delineate three adventurers and polymaths typical of Victorian adventure fiction: 'big exploring expeditions [...] one to the Northern Congo [...] discovery of a special kind of Okapi. [...] He spoke a dozen Oriental tongues. [...] There were some who said he had been to Mecca in disguise' (9). They discuss their post-demob plans, all in a similar vein of colonial adventure and derring-do. A 'very dark horse called Lacon' (appropriately named according to the narrator) has his sights set on a mysterious region in the south-west Amazon, about which nothing is known (9–10):

> The place is far more strongly fenced than Tibet was a hundred years ago. It is a poison land—poison everywhere, in the flowers, in the insects, in the sap of the trees, and on every Indian arrow—deadly poison that makes a man die crazy with pain in three minutes. (13)

In writing approaching Lovecraft's in terms of its sinister evocation of ancient nonhuman agencies persisting in the remote regions of the world, Lacon's description of his lost world becomes increasingly weird and fantastical: giant venomous man-eating foxes and a 'great people', pale and 'hardly human', millennia older than the Incas: '[T]hey were great before people when there was a land bridge to Asia, and before the towers of Atlantis had fallen.' They are 'advanced scientists' who artificially light their vast windowless towers; 'earth-dwellers [...] but their burrows are above the ground' (14–16). They are 'masters of every kind of hellish device, lairing in their great blank castles. Hoar-ancient, you know—so old that the Sphinx is young beside them. Something out of the "dark backward and abysm of time", left untouched by the centuries' (16). Buchan seems to be letting the breaks off his imagination here intentionally, perhaps imitating the excesses of nascent American pulp writing, an emergent culture with which Buchan had by then been engaged for over at least a decade, in order to intensify the reader's disappointment that the promises made of wonders and perilous adventure are irrevocably broken when Lacon 'and half his squad [are] wiped out by some heavy stuff' the following day (17). Buchan skillfully whets the readers' appetite before leaving them bereft. In place of the story is an absence, and an utterly melancholy one at that: 'I couldn't say anything, for I felt, more acutely than I had ever felt it before, the preposterous waste of war.' In 1919, Buchan wrote a short, moving account of several of his close acquaintances who died in the Great War, and published it under the title *These for Remembrance* (Buchan 1919). In 'The Shut Door', Buchan skillfully contrives a sense of narrative bereavement and the withdrawal or abrupt removal of the omniferous universe. The imagery of the open and shut book and the open and shut portal serves similar ends here. Lacon never searches for his weird South American civilization (the 'old Rider Haggard business', as one of his listeners comments (14)) and one gets the impression the door is shutting not only on this particular mystery but on the Victorian age of adventure itself. The industrial scale of modern mechanical slaughter is something against which even Allan Quatermain would never have stood a chance.

Buchan identified this terminus himself: not only, as described above, in 'The Shut Door', but also in *The Dancing Floor* (1926), when Edward Leithen remarks that he has been given a 'distaste for the fantastic' by 'four years' hard campaigning' (Buchan 1946, 82). Here we get a sense of what Clute has described as 'the dessicating [sic] torpor of Aftermath' (Clute 2006, 17). The closed portal of 'The Shut Door' signals not only an 'awareness that the story is done' but a 'world no longer storyable' (17). One side effect of the war for Buchan was a disinterest in literature: 'I found that I could read very little, and that many things which used to charm me seemed meaningless, since they belonged to a dead world' (Buchan 1941, 167). Accordingly, Buchan specifies in the final sentence of 'The Shut Door' that 'a door leading to amazing mysteries had now been shut and bolted' (Buchan 1926, 17). However, Buchan made the world 'storyable' again through his multivolume study of the war itself, written in monthly instalments as it unfolded, in which he recast it as 'a gigantic cosmic drama' (Buchan 1941, 167).

If, as Miéville argues, the First World War is a point at which weird fiction is eclipsed by reality, it is perhaps only a conclusion of a process started two decades previously. John Clute has argued that many fantasies are 'fables of recovery', the attempt to redress a diminishment or shore up the world against the losses imminent in modernity, naming this process of loss 'Thinning'.

Clute cites as a basic example of Thinning the departure of the Elves from Middle Earth at the end of Tolkien's *The Lord of The Rings*, marking the end of an age of myth and the beginning of our own, comparatively quotidian, historical age. Clute also applies the term Thinning to all the 'Pan-worship engaged upon by the many Edwardian fantasists—including J. M. Barrie, E. M. Forster, Kenneth Grahame, Arthur Machen, Barry Pain and Saki— who bemoaned the loss of childhood and the rise of suburbia' (Clute 1997). The 'spoiling of the suburbs' was the 'process by which established and largely green middle-class suburbs were engulfed by new development, with rows of houses being fitted on to adjacent meadow land, and the gardens of old mansions being bought by speculative builders' (Carey 1992, 47). Accordingly, 'the ruined childhood paradise becomes a familiar refrain in writers' biographies and autobiographies' from the period (47). Despite being raised in Border country, Buchan didn't escape early inculcation with this dread of suburban encroachment on the countryside, and a concomitant fear—demographically as well as geographically specific— of what he perceived to be the deadening grind of lower middle-class suburban life:

> As a child I was always in terror of being compelled to earn my bread as a clerk should my father die. This gloomy fate I associated with some kind of English domicile, probably a London suburb. The suburbs of the metropolis, of which I knew nothing, became for me a synonym for a dreadful life of commercial drudgery without daylight or hope. (Buchan 1941, 46)

Machen too admitted that it was the sudden 'irruption of red ranks of brand-new villas' in a previously rural area of Harlesden that he 'clumsily' transliterated into 'The Great God Pan' (Machen 1923a, 126). In Machen's 1906 novella *A Fragment of Life*, Mr and Mrs Darnell, a suburban Edwardian couple (he, a clerk), are emancipated from their 'dreadful life of commercial drudgery' through their reengagement with a secret family heritage involving the transformative power of the story of the Graal, fleeing London for the 'West'.

Such wish fulfilment aside, it hardly seems surprising then that British weird fiction would from 1918 onwards tend towards the quieter melancholy and psychological chill of writers like Oliver Onions, Walter de la Mare, and eventually Robert Aickman. Across the Atlantic, however, the mechanical killing fields of the Western Front were not generally experienced at first hand. Unlike Leithen, many in the United States still had a taste for the fantastic, and the world remained storyable. Weird fiction, Decadence, and the tradition that reached its apotheosis in Britain at the fin de siècle may have fallen out of favour in its homeland, but it was seized upon vigorously by the emerging and cheerfully populist and energetic pulp market in the United States This is something I will return to in detail in Chap. 5, but here I will now look more closely at what I mean by the 'quieter melancholy and psychological chill' of the British weird fiction most closely associated with the opening decades of the twentieth century.

Exemplary in this respect is the short story 'Seaton's Aunt' by Walter de la Mare, first published in the *London Mercury* in 1922. Its narrator, Withers, relates the history of his on/off acquaintance with a man called Arthur Seaton. As schoolmates, Withers agrees to spend a half-term holiday with Seaton, an awkward, unpopular boy, more out of pity and obligation than genuine friendship. Seaton is the ward of his elderly, imposing Aunt, and during this first encounter with the pair, Withers is told by Seaton that he regards his aunt as having some sort of psychic and malignant influence on him. Over an ostentatiously extravagant meal (suggestive of pre-war Edwardian excess), Seaton's aunt intimidates Withers and humiliates Seaton. Several years later, Withers again visits Seaton, after a chance encounter, and is introduced to Seaton's fiancée, Miss Outram. Withers loses track of Seaton and his affairs, until, through guilt, he visits Seaton's aunt's house intending to belatedly congratulate Seaton, assuming he and Miss Outram are by now married. After being admitted by the housekeeper, he finds only Seaton's aunt at home—bewildered, vague, and hostile—and can elicit little information from her on Seaton's whereabouts. He leaves and, inquiring in a local butcher shop, discovers that Seaton has been 'dead and buried these three months or more' (de la Mare 1923, 140).

'Seaton's Aunt' is a disturbing and upsetting inversion of the apocryphal Edwardian idyll, the complacent, indolent 'long summer afternoon' shattered by the Great War (Powell 1996, vii). It shares many of its elements with the world of P. G. Wodehouse, that of public-school life, of 'country houses […], awesome aunts, of bold women […] in pursuit of enfeebled young men' (Kemp et al. 2002b, 423). In 'Seaton's Aunt', however, Wodehousian fantasy is recast as a bleak encroachment of despair; the influence of the aunt is malignant, and the potential marriage upon which (as with many of the 'Jeeves' stories) the narrative hinges ends in the mysterious death of Seaton. Like Jeeves, Seaton is an orphan, but rather than blithe and relentlessly cheerful, Seaton is perennially haunted by some vague existential, possibly supernatural, dread. 'Seaton's Aunt' shares with other of de la Mare's stories a muted, disparaging response to Victorian Spiritualism. Seaton's aunt herself is a superannuated relic of a vanished age, her overbearing disquisitions not only concern unseen presences, but perhaps even engage with them; she is an embodiment of Edwardianism as 'frequently distinguished from Modernism by its supposed assertion of continuity and tradition [... over the ...] "modern" resisting of the past and assertion of a new identity' (Kemp et al. 2002a, xiii). At the end of the story, Withers comments that Seaton, even though only recently deceased, 'had never been much better than "buried" in my mind' (de la Mare 1923, 141)—one could argue that Seaton has been buried in the suffocating crinoline of the Victorian age, unable to shake of its lingering, cloying influence and embrace the twentieth century.

The intimations of drawing-room contact with the spiritual realm in de la Mare's 'A Recluse' (1926) are similarly represented as a stifling, melancholic, detachment from the living—a kind of senescent resignation. The suffocating attentions of the narrator's host, Bloom, exasperate and bore him; he complains of Bloom's 'tedious discourse' (over another meal of Edwardian excess) on 'automatic writing, table-rapping, the hidden state, ectoplasm, and all the other—to me rather disagreeable—paraphernalia of the spiritualistic *séance*' (de la Mare 1930, 19). The narrator associates the subject with 'an elderly female friend', who would occasionally 'bring out the hateful little round Victorian table, and the wine-glass and the cardboard alphabet' (20). He describes the answers to the resulting 'cross-examination' as 'useless and futile' (21). Despite Bloom's hyperbolic claim regarding the existence of 'deeps, and vasty deeps', and the story's dénouement—the suggestion that Bloom is either already dead or in some process of transposition to 'the other side'—the final intimation, and bathos, of the text is that this 'other side' is in itself 'useless and futile', and offers no transcendence of the quotidian. The real horror of 'Seaton's Aunt' and 'A Recluse' is, therefore, the suggestion that what Machen described as the 'squalid [...] back-parlour magic' of Spiritualism (Machen 1899) is simply a foreshadowing of a vacuous afterlife of confused 'groping' and 'querulous protestation'—an eternity of lonely senility in the 'shivering void'.

Another author of weird fiction associated with the Edwardian period is Oliver Onions (1873–1961), an erstwhile illustrator who began writing for the periodicals in the 1890s, publishing his first novel in 1900 (Kemp et al. 2002b, 301). His most well-known story, 'The Beckoning Fair One', is an example of the clear influence of Henry James on his writing, effective as it is in its own right. This, and several other of Onions' stories, is concerned with an artist struggling with the creation of their art, expressed through a supernaturally inflected narrative. Even though Onions was clearly drawn to psychic phenomena and ghost lore—explicitly referencing the Society for Psychical Research in 'Benlian' (1911) for example (Onions 1911, 177)—his oeuvre evades being subsumed within the ghost story genre proper, a fact not lost on contemporary critics:

> The stories are by no means all to be dismissed as 'ghost' stories. They deal rather with various forms of supernaturalism which man does not profess, or is unable, to account for. (*Athenaeum* 1911, 274)

A good example of this weirder valence of his writing is the 1910 story 'Rooum', which concerns an invisible presence stalking the titular character, an itinerant construction engineer. Onions blends the traditional trope of supernatural persecution (a nineteenth-century example being Sheridan Le Fanu's 'The Familiar' (1872)) with contemporary scientific theory. In his attempts at explaining his strange affliction, Rooum speaks vaguely of 'osmosis' and 'molecules', which the narrator, although demonstrating greater scientific education, struggles to parse (Onions 1910, 1118). Typically, Onions never offers a definite explanation in terms of any specific supernatural agency (there is no ghost, as such), and never closes the door on the possibility that what is being described is a purely psychological affliction. Despite its brevity, Onions' execution of the narrative is compellingly suggestive: is Rooum's crisis over his identity, and the alleged threat to it, based on his own ethnicity (he is described by the narrator as mixed race and 'very dark' (1115))? Or is it connected with the liminal spaces of construction, and (again) the metropolitan suburbs in which the story is set (the 'eruption of red-brick houses' (1117))?

As I have discussed, this latter trope was a particular Edwardian hobby horse, but despite this, Onions' work refuses to conform neatly to retroactive periodization. Reviewing *Widdershins*—the collection that included 'Rooum'—the *Saturday Review* objects to Onions' alleged preoccupation with 'decay', leading them to place him with the 'decadent class of writers who, tired of the beautiful, seek only sensations and find them in the study of all that is repulsive' (*Saturday Review* 1911, 214). The reviewer repeatedly criticizes Onions for 'taking the ugly theme of madness for so many of the stories', a preoccupation the reviewer again associates with decadence, 'the flowers of evil', and Charles Baudelaire (214–15). This reading of *Widdershins* as a series of investigations into degenerate psychological maladies sidelines any supernatural element to the work. For instance, 'The Beckoning Fair One' is described as 'a pitiless record of the various stages traversed by a man on his way from perfect sanity to the lunatic asylum,' though 'disguised as a ghost story' (the reviewer here echoing Max Nordau).

Indeed, this fin-de-siècle atmosphere is readily evident throughout the collection: the bohemian studio milieu of '*Hic Jacet*' (1911) for instance, or the Classical Paganism of 'Io' (1911). In this latter story, which the *Saturday Review* concedes to be a 'wonderfully clever piece of writing' (215), a woman is transported from her humdrum middle-class existence into a Bacchic frenzy; whether this is through actual invocation of a divine agency or insanity is unresolved. The *English Review* said of the story that it was 'a masterly and beautiful conjunction of clerkly life and Dionysiac ecstasy', a description that could also apply to several of Machen's works, including 'A Fragment of Life' (*English Review* 1911, 755). Here again there is a through line between torrid fin-de-siècle paganism and what Carey identifies as the Pan-worship provoked by the quotidian suburbs: the quiet external lives of their inhabitants, a stability interrupted, destabilized, and enriched by the resurgence of the romantic imagination.

Although it is certainly possible, as I have demonstrated, to identify various tropes and tendencies in Edwardian weird fiction, it is of course impossible to neatly distinguish fiction written after 1900 from that written before it. Onions in 1911, for example, was clearly being written about as an (unwelcome) outlier from the Yellow Nineties. In Chap. 4, I will discuss in detail the weird fiction of John Buchan, specifically in this context. Having acknowledged the possibility of an Edwardian weird fiction, therefore, I will once again subsume it within the more capacious ambit of the long nineteenth century.

Works Cited

"A Yellow Melancholy." 1894. *The Speaker* 9 (April): 468–469.
Apollodorus. 1854. Authors and Books. *The Critic* 13 (310): 119–121.
Ashley, Michael. 2006. *The Age of the Storytellers: British Popular Fiction Magazines 1880–1950*. London: British Library and Oak Knoll Press.
Athenaeum. 1894. English Literature in 1893. January 6.
———. 1895. Our Library Table. May 11.

———. 1896. Scholar Gipsies. November 14.
———. 1911. Short Stories. March 11.
Baldick, Chris. 2008. *The Oxford Dictionary of Literary Terms*. Oxford: Oxford University Press.
Baudrillard, Jean. 1994. The System of Collecting. In *The Cultures of Collecting*, ed. John Elsner, and Roger Cardinal, Trans. Roger Cardinal, 7–24. London: Reaktion.
Bayley, John. 1989. *The Short Story: Henry James to Elizabeth Bowen*. London: Harvester Wheatsheaf.
Beerbohm, Max. 1894. A Letter to the Editor. *Yellow Book*. July.
Billings, Harold. 2005. *M.P. Shiel: A Biography of His Early Years*. Austin: Roger Beacham.
Blackwood, Algernon. 1911. *The Centaur*. London: Macmillan.
———. 2002. The Wendigo. In *Ancient Sorceries and Other Weird Stories*, ed. S.T. Joshi, 147–191. London: Penguin.
Bookman. 1897. Scholar-Gipsies. January.
Bourdieu, Pierre. 1983. The Field of Cultural Production, or: The Economic World Reversed. *Poetics* 12: 311–356.
Brake, Laurel. 2001. *Print in Transition, 1850–1910*. Basingstoke: Palgrave.
Buchan, John. 1919. *These for Remembrance: Memoirs of Tommy Nelson, Bron Lucas (Auberon Herbert), Cecil Rawling, Basil Blackwood, Jack Stuart-Wortley and Raymond Asquith*. Privately Printed.
———. 1926. The Shut Door. In *The Boy's All-Round Book*, ed. Walter Wood, 9–17. London: Thomas Nelson.
———. 1941. *Memory Hold the Door*. London: Hodder & Stoughton.
———. 1946. *The Dancing Floor*. London: Thomas Nelson.
Calloway, Stephen. 1993. The Colours of a Decade. In *High Art and Low Life: The Studio and the Fin de Siècle*, ed. Michael Spens, 34–38. New Hampshire: Sackler Foundation.
Carey, John. 1992. *The Intellectuals and the Masses*. London: Faber.
Clute, John. 1997. Encyclopedia of Fantasy (1997) – Thinning. http://sf-encyclopedia.uk/fe.php?nm=thinning. Accessed 18 May 2015.
———. 2006. *Darkening Garden: A Short Lexicon of Horror*. Cauheegan: Payseur & Schmidt.
Conrad, Joseph. 1899. The Heart of Darkness. *Blackwood's Edinburgh Magazine*, February.
Crackanthorpe, Hubert. 1894. Reticence in Literature Some Roundabout Remarks. *Yellow Book*, July.
Critchley, Simon. 2004. *Very Little... Almost Nothing: Death, Philosophy and Literature*. London: Routledge.
Croft-Cooke, Rupert. 1967. *Feasting With Panthers: A New Consideration of Some Late Victorian Writers*. London: Allen.

Davenport-Hines, Richard. 2004. Oxford DNB Article: Smith, William Henry. https://doi.org/10.1093/ref:odnb/25938.

de la Mare, Walter. 1923. Seaton's Aunt. In *The Riddle and Other Stories*, 97–141. London: Selwyn & Blount.

———. 1930. A Recluse. In *On the Edge*, 1–42. London: Faber and Faber.

del Toro, Guillermo. 2011. Foreword. In *The White People and Other Weird Stories*, by Arthur Machen, ed. S. T Joshi, vii–ix. New York: Penguin Books.

Doyle, Arthur Conan. 1890. *Mr. Stevenson's Methods in Fiction*. Ed Alfred Austin. *The National Review* 14 (83): 646–57.

———. 1908. *Through the Magic Door*. New York: McClure.

———. 1924. *Memories and Adventures*. London: Hodder & Stoughton.

Eagleton, Terry. 2016. A Toast at the Trocadero. *London Review of Books*, February 18.

English Review. 1911. Book Notices. March.

Feddersen, R.C. 2001. Introduction: A Glance at the History of the Short Story in English. In *A Reader's Companion to the Short Story in English*, ed. Erin Fallon, xv–xxxiv. Chicago: Fitzroy Dearborn.

Fletcher, Ian, ed. 1980. *Decadence and the 1890s*. London: Holmes & Meier.

Fletcher, Ian, and Malcolm Bradbury. 1979. Preface. In *Decadence and the 1890s*, ed. Ian Fletcher, 7–13. London: Holmes & Meier.

Freeman, Nicholas. 2014. *1895: Drama, Disaster and Disgrace in Late Victorian Britain*. Edinburgh: Edinburgh University Press.

Gawsworth, John. 2013. *The Life of Arthur Machen*. Leyburn: Tartarus.

Gilbert, R.A. 2017. Introduction. In *The House of the Hidden Light*, ed. Arthur Machen and A.E. Waite, v–xxv. Leyburn: Tartarus.

Gillies, Steward. n.d. *Concise History of the British Newspaper in the Nineteenth Century*. Text. http://www.bl.uk/reshelp/findhelprestype/news/concisehistbrit news/britnews19th/. Accessed 11 Sept 2013.

Gissing, George. 1884. Correspondence. *Pall Mall Gazette*, December 15.

———. 2007. *New Grub Street*. Ed. by Stephen Arata. Peterborough: Broadview.

Grant, Paul Benedict. 2009. Buchan's Supernatural Fiction. In *Reassessing John Buchan: Beyond the Thirty-Nine Steps*, ed. Kate Macdonald, 183–192. London: Pickering & Chatto.

Gray, John. 2013. The Kefahuchi Tract Trilogy: A Future Without Nostalgia. http://www.newstatesman.com/2013/10/future-without-nostalgia. Accessed 4 Dec 2013.

Gross, John. 1973. *The Rise and Fall of the Man of Letters*. London: Penguin.

Harris, Wendell V. 1968. John Lane's Keynotes Series and the Fiction of the 1890's. *PMLA* 83 (5): 1407–1413.

Harte, Bret. 1899. The Rise of the 'Short Story.' *Cornhill*, July.

Henley, William. 1895. Notes. *National Observer*, April 6.

Hughes, Linda K. 2006. W. E. Henley's Scot's Observer and Fin-de-Siècle Books. In *Bound for the 1890s*, ed. Jonathan Allison, 65–86. High Wycombe: Rivendale Press.
Huyssen, Andreas. 1988. *After the Great Divide: Modernism, Mass Culture and Postmodernism*. Basingstoke: Macmillan.
Illustrated London News. 1894. Robert Louis Stevenson. December 22.
J. W. 1884. Correspondence. *Pall Mall Gazette*, December 13.
Jackson, Holbrook. 1913. *The Eighteen Nineties: A Review of Art and Ideas at the Close of the Nineteenth Century*. London: Grant Richards.
Jerome, Jerome K., ed. 1894. *My First Book*. London: Chatto & Windus.
Keating, Peter. 1989. *The Haunted Study: A Social History of the English Novel, 1875–1914*. London: Secker & Warburg.
Kemp, Sandra, Charlotte Mitchell, and David Trotter. 2002a. Introduction. In *Oxford Companion to Edwardian Fiction*, ix–xviii. Oxford: Oxford University Press.
———, eds. 2002b. *Oxford Companion to Edwardian Fiction 1900–14: New Voices in the Age of Uncertainty*. Oxford: Oxford University Press.
"Kraken Press Submission Manager." n.d. https://kraken.submittable.com/submit. Accessed 25 Nov 2013.
Lambert, J.W., and Michael Ratcliffe. 1987. *The Bodley Head, 1887–1987*. London: Bodley Head.
Lang, Andrew. 1887. Realism and Romance. *Contemporary Review* 52 (November): 683–693.
Lester, John Ashby. 1968. *Journey Through Despair, 1880–1914: Transformations in British Literary Culture*. Princeton: Princeton University Press.
Little, Jas Stanley. 1895. New Novels. *Academy*, April 13.
Llewellyn, Mark, and Ann Heilmann. 2007. George Moore and Literary Censorship: The Textual and Sexual History of 'John Norton' and 'Hugh Monfert. *English Literature in Transition, 1880–1920* 50 (4): 371–392. https://doi.org/10.2487/elt.50.4(2007)0006.
Lovecraft, H.P. 1985. Supernatural Horror in Literature. In *Dagon and Other Macabre Tales*, 421–512. London: Panther.
Machen, Arthur. 1899. The Literature of Occultism. *Literature*, February 18.
———. 1923a. *Far Off Things*. London: Martin Secker.
———. 1923b. *Things Near and Far*. London: Secker.
MacLeod, Kirsten. 2004. Romps with Ransom's King: Fans, Collectors, Academics, and the M. P. Shiel Archives. *ESC: English Studies in Canada* 30 (1): 117–136.
———. 2006. *Fictions of British Decadence: High Art, Popular Writing and the Fin De Siècle*. Basingstoke: Palgrave Macmillan.
March-Russell, Paul. 2009. *The Short Story: An Introduction*. Edinburgh: Edinburgh University Press.

Mariani, Mike. 2014. *Terror Incognita: The Paradoxical History of Cosmic Horror, from Lovecraft to Ligotti*. Los Angeles Review of Books. https://lareviewofbooks. org/article/terror-incognita-paradoxical-history-cosmic-horror-lovecraft-ligotti/. Accessed 25 Apr 2016.
McDonald, Peter D. 2002. *British Literary Culture and Publishing Practice, 1880–1914*. Cambridge: Cambridge University Press.
Mehew, Ernest. 2004. Henley, William Ernest (1849–1903), writer. Oxford Dictionary of National Biography. https://doi.org/10.1093/ref:odnb/33817.
Miéville, China. 2009. Weird Fiction. In *The Routledge Companion to Science Fiction*, ed. Mark Bould, Adam Roberts, Andrew M. Butler, and Sherryl Vint, 510–515. London: Routledge.
Moore, George. 1884. A New Censorship in Literature. *Pall Mall Gazette*, December 10.
Murdoch, William Garden Blaikie. 1911. *The Renaissance of the Nineties*. London: Alexander Moring.
Nathaniel, Sir. 1857. Notes on Note-Worthies, of Divers Orders, Either Sex, and Every Age. *New Monthly Magazine*, April.
Nelson, Robert. 1934. The Weird Tale—A Dialogue. *The Fantasy Fan*, May.
New Quarterly Review. 1858. Retrospect of the Literature of the Quarter. August.
Newton-Robinson, Janetta. 1893. Some Aspects of the Work of Mr Robert Louis Stevenson. *Westminster Review*, January.
Nicolay, Scott. 2011. *Dogme 2011 for Weird Fiction*. Weird Fiction Review. http://weirdfictionreview.com/2011/11/dogme-2011-for-weird-fiction-by-scott-nicolay/. Accessed 25 Nov 2013.
Nordau, Max Simon. 1895. *Degeneration*. New York: Appleton.
Onions, Oliver. 1910. Rooum. *Fortnightly Review*, December.
———. 1911. Benlian. *Fortnightly Review*, January.
Pall Mall Gazette. 1894. Reviews. March 1.
Pater, Walter. 1902. *The Renaissance*. Portland: Mosher.
Pick, Daniel. 1989. *Faces of Degeneration: A European Disorder, c.1848–c.1918*. Cambridge: Cambridge University Press.
Powell, David. 1996. *The Edwardian Crisis: Britain, 1901–14*. British History in Perspective. Houndmills, Basingstoke, Hampshire: Palgrave.
Punch. 1895. From the Queer and Yellow Book. February 2.
Quilter, Harry. 1895. The Gospel of Intensity. *Contemporary Review*, June.
Lisa Rodensky, ed. 2006. *Decadent Poetry from Wilde to Naidu*. London: Penguin Classics.
Saturday Review. 1895. The Woman Who Did. March 9.
———. 1911. Novels. February 18.
Sharp, William. 1889. New Novels. *Academy*, August 17.
———. 1895. New Novels. *Academy*, March 2.
Shaw, George Bernard. 1919. *The Sanity of Art*. New York: Boni & Liveright.

Slade, Joseph W. 2001. *Pornography and Sexual Representation: A Reference Guide*. Westport: Greenwood.
Söder, Hans-Peter. 2009. *That Way Madness Lies: Max Nordau on Fin-de-Siècle Genius*. High Wycombe: Rivendale Press.
Stableford, Brian M. 1993. Introduction. In *The Dedalus Book of Decadence (Moral Ruins)*. Sawtry: Dedalus.
"StephenKing.Com – Messages from Stephen." 2008. http://www.stephenking.com/stephens_messages.html. Accessed 26 Nov 2013.
Symons, Arthur. 1893. The Decadent Movement in Literature. *Harper's New Monthly Magazine*, November, 858–867.
———. 1899. *The Symbolist Movement in Literature*. London: Heinemann.
T. P. G. 1893. A Literary Causerie. *Speaker*, December 2.
"The Yellow Book: Prospectus to Volume 1." 1894. Elkin Matthews & John Lane.
Thornton, R.K.R. 1980. 'Decadence' in Later Nineteenth-Century England. In *Decadence and the 1890s*, ed. Ian Fletcher, 15–30. London: Holmes & Meier.
Turcotte, Gerry. 2009. *Peripheral Fear: Transformations of the Gothic in Canadian and Australian Fiction*. Brussels: P.I.E. Peter Lang.
VanderMeer, Jeff. 2008. Introduction. In *The New Weird*, ed. Ann VanderMeer and Jeff VanderMeer, ix–xviii. San Francisco: Tachyon Publications.
VanderMeer, Jeff. 2012. Moving Past Lovecraft. Weird Fiction Review. http://weirdfictionreview.com/2012/09/moving-past-lovecraft/. Accessed 25 Nov 2013.
VanderMeer, Ann, and Jeff VanderMeer, eds. 2012. *The Weird: A Compendium of Strange and Dark Stories*. London: Tor.
Wedmore, Frederick. 1894. The Yellow Book. *Academy*, April 28.
Wells, H.G. 1896. The Three Impostors. *Saturday Review*, January 11.
"What Books to Read, and How to Read Them." 1859. *The Scottish Review*, October, 368–380.
White, Iain. 1982. Introduction. In *The King in the Golden Mask and Other Writings*, 1–13. Manchester: Carcanet.
Zangwill, I. 1895. Without Prejudice. *Pall Mall Magazine*, May.

CHAPTER 3

Shiel, Stenbock, Gilchrist, and Machen

The list of four 'Intensely lurid products of English Decadence' identified by Stableford provides a functional starting point for the purposes of this chapter, but is by no means exhaustive: for example, one could easily include Vincent O'Sullivan's *A Book of Bargains* (1896), advertised in the *Savoy* as a collection of 'Stories of the Weird and Fantastic [...] with Frontispiece Designed by Aubrey Beardsley', a collection that fell into immediate obscurity with the notable exception that one of the component stories ('When I Was Dead') was included by noted weird fiction writer Robert Aickman (1914–1981) in his *The 4th Fontana Book of Great Ghost Stories* (1967), where he advises his readers to seek out further work by O'Sullivan with the combined caveat and recommendation that 'the quest is difficult, but the product distinctive' (Symons 1896, 95; Aickman 1967, 9). All these works therefore represent a synthesis of Decadent writing with supernatural and/or horrific themes presented in the short story form, and furthermore were recognized by both their contemporaries and later critics as being produced by writers who operated in the weird mode. However, it should also be acknowledged that in the case of Shiel, Gilchrist, and Stenbock, the short stories anthologized in the above collections do not uniformly incorporate the supernatural and yet, despite this, they remain 'weird'.

In an attempt to provide an account of the coalescence of weird fiction in the 1890s, I will examine aspects of the life and work of these writers relevant to the development of weird fiction and its subsequent cultural impact in the twentieth century. Machen is especially relevant in this respect due to his considerable influence on the fiction of Lovecraft in the early twentieth century, and his ongoing influence on the 'New Weird' oeuvre of M. John Harrison, evidenced in both the title and content of his short story 'The Great God Pan' (1988), a work expanded into the novel *The Course of the Heart* (1991), which incorporates references to and appropriations of both Machen's novella *A Fragment of Life* and his final novel *The Green Round* (1933).

As previously demonstrated, Machen is normally discussed in contemporary critical discourse as an exemplar minor Decadent writer, an exponent of 'precious' aesthetic prose who when he turned his hand to horror became a 'flower-tunicked priest of nightmare', impossible to consider without firmly embedding him in the Decadent *mise-en-scène* of the 'Yellow Nineties' (Dobson 1988, 6). Together with Shiel, it is possible to track Machen's fortunes in terms of cultural capital by visual reference to the covers his work has been printed under. From the 1890s heyday of exquisite Beardsley-designed frontispieces, by the mid-twentieth century his work was only seeing print under cover of garish and crude pulp art, normally foregrounding physical gore and horror. From the 1990s onwards, he is repackaged under a Beardsley cover for the Everyman edition of *The Three Impostors*, Tartarus Press's elegant hardcover editions with dust jackets and embossed boards, and most recently the tastefully minimalist yellow buckram of the 2018 Oxford World Classics edition.

I would like to attempt to demonstrate that a closer examination of Machen's life and career problematizes his relationship to the period at almost every turn, creating ensuing complications for a neat and orderly generic delineation of weird fiction. Even the fairly established view that the weird tale in the late nineteenth century was a pre-echo of Lovecraft's more defined paradigm shift away from Judeo-Christian folkloric tropes in supernatural horror, resulting from the neutering of these fears by the advance of scientific materialism, is undermined by many of the relevant writers' failure to demonstrate the necessary crisis of belief upon which the suggested paradigm shift is predicated. In order to do this, I would like to discuss the other almost forgotten writers of the 1890s suggested by Stableford who produced weird fiction, but—unlike Machen—can be embedded in Decadence in a far more convincing way. The life and work of Count Stanislaus Eric Stenbock also reveals some tropes that, used by him and other writers of weird fiction, may help us track its course into the early twentieth century. In the following section I will discuss how notions of a weird mode in literature and notions of Decadence were commingled in the 1890s and how this connection remained an important one in regard to the subsequent development of weird fiction.

M. P. Shiel

With *Prince Zaleski* (1895), Shiel consciously abandoned the style of his earlier magazine stories, which he considered to be 'of the "tea-cup" realistic sort of which [he had] grown to feel a little bit ashamed'.[1] The 'modern "teacup and saucer" drama' was ever a pejorative, a genre one commentator in the 1870s regarded as having been 'elevated and dignified' by Trollope (Hueffer 1878, 445). Hall Caine had in 1890 used this term to criticize the timidity of English literary realism:

> In France it has been nasty, and in England it has been merely trivial. But the innings of realism is over; it has scored badly or not at all, and is going out disgraced. The reign of mere fact in imaginative literature was very short, it is done, and it is making its exit rapidly, with a sorry retinue of […] teacup-and-saucer nonentities […] at its heels. (Caine 1890, 487)

As John Gross writes of Thackeray, this was a style of literature 'bogged down in the minutiae of drawing-room protocol' (Gross 1973, 33). Not that Shiel's early stories were actually particularly 'tea-cup': his story 'The Eagle's Crag' for the *Strand*, for example, is an Italian Apennines-set melodrama replete with a hunch-backed villain (M. P. Shiel 1894). Regardless, as Harold Billings has observed, Shiel consciously changed direction with his writing in the mid-1890s:

> He devoted a great deal of energy [in 1894] to begin his arabesque stories that would *not* appear in the periodicals, but as the complete fictional content of *Prince Zaleski* and, in the next year, *Shapes in the Fire*, those titles in John Lane's 'Keynotes Series', whose initial full-blown decadent book designs by Aubrey Beardsley helped distinguish this series of avant-garde prose as much as their powerful content. (Billings 2010, 17)

Billings goes on to speculate that Shiel may have ascertained a gap in the market to which *Prince Zaleski* was his response:

---

[1] Austin, Harry Ransom Center (hereafter HRC), John Lane Company Records, Box 43, Shiel to John Lane, 9 August 1894.

> Conan Doyle's decision to 'kill' Sherlock Holmes at Reichenbach Falls in *The Strand* in December 1893 may have encouraged Shiel to write the three Zaleski stories (with Poe's Dupin also in mind) to fill the gap of mystery stories that the reading public was demanding. [...] But Zaleski exaggerated anything that Poe had written, filled with as much decadent surroundings and story detail, as much ornate language, as Shiel could then muster. (17–18)

Once again, any notions of the existence of a *cordon sanitaire* between Decadent purism and populism are fallacious. *Prince Zaleski*, a volume of three short stories—each an account of a case solved by the eponymous 'sphinx-like' Decadent detective—contains no explicit or implied supernatural elements and yet provoked the complaint in the *Academy* that the reviewer was 'heartily tired of the weird in fiction: the taint in the blood, the stain on the floor, with the accessories of hanging lamps and Oriental draperies' (Little 1895, 312). These three identifiers—corrupted inheritance, the nebulously sinister, and the 'arabesque'—are indicative ones. The first and second have already been alluded to above and the third will be explored in further detail below.

W. T. Stead's *Review of Reviews* found that 'imagination of the weirdest and the strangest runs rife' in the Prince Zaleski stories, adding that the 'personage of the title is a sort of *dilettante* Sherlock Holmes, but with far weirder problems to unravel than ever were fell to the lot of Dr Doyle's detective' (*Review of Reviews* 1895, 293). Zaleski's 'weirder problems' include (in 'The S.S.') an international conspiracy of assassins undertaking a murderous eugenics programme and (in 'The Stone of the Edmundsbury Monks') a literal assassin ('a person of Eastern origin', discipled to Hassan-i-Sabbah) inveigling himself into an English baronet's household to reclaim a gemstone plundered from his order centuries before during the Crusades. Again, the comparators used to communicate the nature of these stories are familiar ones: they remind 'one now of Poe and now of Stevenson's *New Arabian Nights*' (the latter originally serialized in the Henley-edited periodical *London*) (*Review of Reviews* 1895, 293).

Stead was impressed enough by Shiel's oeuvre that they collaborated on a novel, *The Rajah's Sapphire* (1896), which, according to its subtitle, was written by Shiel 'from a plot given him vivâ voce by W. T. Stead', and with a title that is very nearly a direct lift from 'The Rajah's Diamond' episode of *New Arabian Nights*, both of course likely inspired by Wilkie Collins's *The Moonstone* (1868) (M. P. Shiel 1896b). Shiel repined to John

Lane that it was 'a vile melodramatic kind of novelette (for Mr Stead of all people)' adding that since he 'cannot even do vile things altogether vilely [...] every minute [was] precious bane.'[2] Shiel certainly made no attempt to curtail his own stylistic excesses: reviewing the novel for the *Saturday Review*, H. G. Wells opined that it appeared 'to have been written by a lunatic' (*Saturday Review* 1896, 96). Shiel clearly regarded his Keynotes books as being on an altogether different plane from such hackwork, complaining in a letter to his sister: 'But why do you insist on comparing me with Conan Doyle? Conan Doyle does not pretend to be a poet. I do' (Billings 2010, 18). He also saw Machen as his natural comparator:

> Of course the writing of a great book is the finest thing in the world. What is finer? Only there are so few of them—not ten altogether, since the world began. And of these ten, the Great God Pan and Prince Zaleski are not, *not*, two! Nor yet Bleak House and Pendennis![3]

Although Shiel presumes for comic effect Lane's astonishment that *The Great God Pan* and *Prince Zaleski* are not two of the ten greatest books in the world, it is perhaps based on more than simply his friendship with Machen that he allies himself with Machen when doing so.

Shiel followed up *Prince Zaleski* with another volume of short stories for Keynotes in 1896, *Shapes in the Fire*, some of which were considered by the *Saturday Review* to be 'raving lunacy—absolute frenzied nightmare' (*Saturday Review* 1897, 278). Constituent stories included 'Xélucha' (described by Stableford as being 'as close to a wholehearted celebration of Decadent lifestyle fantasy as Shiel ever came thereafter'), 'Vaila' (later revised, and arguably etiolated, for publication as 'The House of Sounds'), and 'Tulsah', a 'weird romance' which 'exhales an atmosphere of veiled horror' (anomalous praise in a review that dismisses the rest of the book as 'equally ridiculous and repulsive') (B. Stableford 2009, 17; "Fiction" 1896). 'Vaila', anthologized by Roger Luckhurst in *Late Victorian Gothic Tales*, is identified by him as exemplary of the period in its 'fusion of styles, at a time when the distinctions of high and low literature, in their modern conception, were just in the process of being formed' (Luckhurst 2005, xxx–xxxi). Shiel's stylistic excesses may have synchronized perfectly well

---

[2] Austin, Harry Ransom Center (hereafter HRC), John Lane Company Records, Box 43, Shiel to John Lane, 29 February 1895.

[3] Austin, HRC, John Lane Company Records, Box 43, Shiel to John Lane, 16 January 1895.

with Decadence, though his enthusiasm for Thomas Carlyle is as much apparent in his lexical exuberance as any influence from his contemporaries.

Luckhurst also describes Shiel as a 'presiding influence on the American pulp magazine *Weird Tales*' (xxxi). Lovecraft was certainly an admirer, especially of 'The House of Sounds' and the later novel *The Purple Cloud* (1901) (Lovecraft 1985, 484–85). *The Purple Cloud* was adapted (beyond all recognition) for the screen in 1959 as *The World, the Flesh and the Devil* and achieved Penguin Classics status in 2012 (M. P. Shiel 2012). It is impossible yet to tell how the discovery by Kirsten MacLeod in 2008 that Shiel spent a term in jail in 1914 for 'the sexual assault of a minor' will affect long-term interest in his writing (MacLeod 2008, 356). Although he has certainly attracted some dedicated attempts to curate his legacy, from the late 1890s onwards as well as short fiction Shiel produced novels in a variety of genres—including science fiction, invasion thrillers, and melodramas—and this prolificacy has perhaps attenuated his posthumous regard, especially in terms of its appeal to weird fiction's connoisseur culture.[4]

Shiel had considerable commercial success 'on both sides of the Atlantic' with *The Yellow Danger* ('which appeared in eight separate editions between 1898 and 1908'), now regarded as a particularly extreme iteration of the period's hyper-racialized invasion (or 'predictive war') fantasies and as such has done some enduring damage to Shiel's posthumous reputation (Frayling 2014, 259–260). As with much of Shiel's fiction, however, it is difficult to be entirely certain where the line between ludic (or 'lunatic') stylistic and imaginative excess and actual political conviction stands. Christopher Frayling confesses to finding it 'difficult to tell' whether or not *The Yellow Danger* is 'tongue in cheek' (260). Shiel's Montserratian mixed-race heritage, which in Britain he occluded with the claim that he was simply 'an Irish Paddy', opens the 'shrill, obsessive, preposterous performance' of *The Yellow Danger* to the charge of being an exercise in denial. However, Frayling leaves the question 'Where exactly *was* the authorial voice in stories such as *The Yellow Danger*?' as a rhetorical one (262).

Regardless of the dilution of Shiel's weird fiction credentials by the 'preposterous' nature of some of his work in different genres, his two novels for John Lane, *Prince Zaleski* and *Shapes in the Fire*, which placed him

---

[4] For further detail, see (MacLeod 2004).

if only fleetingly among the 'decadents, esoterics, and exquisites', represent an exemplary imbrication of both Decadence and weird fiction, a legacy that persists and is valorized to this day (Sutherland 2012, xvii). The former text also amplifies and informs the discussion of 'Decadent performance' in the sections on Count Stenbock and weird orientalism below.

R. Murray Gilchrist

'Forgotten novelist' Robert Murray Gilchrist (1867–1917) published many of his early stories under the editorship of Henley. One of his readers later remembered that they 'week by week scanned the columns of the *National Observer* for those weird creations which occasionally appeared above [Gilchrist's] name' (Bush 2010, 32; Rogers 1899, 518). Gilchrist's short story 'The Crimson Weaver' appeared in volume six of the *Yellow Book* in July 1895, an edition which also featured short fiction by Henry James and Kenneth Grahame. As discussed above, the journal's reputation was by then already suffering: 'its novelty was wearing off, and the formerly outraged were growing blasé, characterising the journal as the Bodley Head's house magazine' (Freeman 2014, 37).

Possibly reflecting hostility to the venue of the story rather than their former colleague, a reviewer for the *National Observer* expresses indifference to Gilchrist's contribution to the 'dull grey of its prevailing tone', describing 'The Crimson Weaver' as 'weird, but vague, and not up to [Gilchrist's] best' (*National Observer* 1895, 385–386). A contemporary review of the collection *The Stone Dragon* (1894) noted the studied artifice and opulent and macabre bricolage of Gilchrist's work:

> The weird beings who people the pages of [... *The Stone Dragon* ...] are as unnatural as the clothes they wear, the 'long rippling gown of flame-coloured silk, whose lowest hem was wrought round with golden tongues', or the gloves, 'of a claret-coloured semi-transparent skin, made of the skin of a murderess gibbeted in these parts a hundred and twenty years ago'. (*Saturday Review* 1894, 419)

Methuen announced *The Stone Dragon* as 'a volume of stories of power so weird and original as to ensure them a ready welcome', and in 1926 Eden Phillpotts was unequivocal in his evaluation of Gilchrist's writing, remarking that 'no record of the English story would be complete without a study of his contributions', implying that Gilchrist's short stories had some value in the context of the English short story itself rather than within any specific genre ("A List of New Books & Announcements of Methuen and Company Publishers" 1893; Lamb 1977, 43).

In an 1899 profile in the *Academy* it is remarked that Gilchrist has 'established himself as a specialist in fiction', his specialties being 'first, the short story, and, second, the Peak District of Derbyshire' (*Academy* 1899). The following is said of his earlier work:

> It was in 1894 that *The Stone Dragon, and Other Tragic Romances*, first gave his name a vogue among those people who happen to be interested in literary phenomena. [...] It is a collection of stories laid, for the most part, in a conventionalised eighteenth century, but really depending very little upon any sort of local colour. The tales rely for their success upon a fundamental power of imagination moving amid primal passions, and they do not rely in vain. The book is sinister, enveloped in gloom—yes, and decadent (like much fine literature); but it is strong, it has authenticity; the effect sought is the effect won. There is nothing like *The Stone Dragon* in modern English fiction; but in it you may distinctly trace the influence of Poe, and perhaps also of Villiers de l'Isle Adam and Charles Baudelaire. Indeed, if there is a man who could catch and cage the spirit of *Fleurs du Mal* in our Saxon tongue, it is the author of *The Stone Dragon*. (689–90)

Writing in 2011, Laurence Bush argues that Gilchrist's significance can be ascertained by reading

> contemporary reviews, Clarence Daniel's brief book on his regional writing and life; reminiscences by Hugh Walpole; and correspondence Gilchrist received from prominent writers, and editors, including Richard Le Gallienne, Henry Harland, H. G. Wells, W. E. Henley, and William Sharp'. ("Robert Murray Gilchrist (1868–1917): Lost among Genres and Genders" 2011)

Bush goes on to note that 'critics admired [Gilchrist's fiction's] emotive power and originality but decried his penchant for horrid deeds and insanity', an antipathy that perhaps also provides an explanation for Gilchrist's posthumous lapse into obscurity.

Despite this obscurity, Gilchrist's contributions to the literature of the fin de siècle have been occasionally noted in specialist works on Decadence and supernatural fiction. As well as Stableford's brief account mentioned above, Hugh Lamb writing in the 1970s described *The Stone Dragon* as 'one of the most singular volumes of weird tales in English literature' (Lamb 1977, 43). Out of Stableford's four 'intensely lurid products of English Decadence', Gilchrist is the only one who lacks an entry in the Oxford Dictionary of National Biography, although his work does intermittently see print: for example, a Wordsworth collection of his stories was published in 2006 in their budget 'Tales of Mystery & The Supernatural' series (Gilchrist 2006).

Unlike Machen, Shiel, and Stenbock, there is no Gilchrist biography, although there is an archive held in Sheffield. In a brief biographical sketch of Gilchrist, Bush remarks that Gilchrist 'was the only writer of the Decadent Movement who regularly contributed to *The Abstainer's Advocate*, the journal of the British temperance movement' ("Robert Murray Gilchrist (1868–1917): Lost among Genres and Genders" 2011). Gilchrist was a lifelong teetaler and despite an enthusiasm for dressing flamboyantly seems to have led a largely blameless and respectable life, and therefore one unconducive to posthumous mythologization: Gilchrist's biographical details don't 'add value' to his work in the same way that Count Stenbock's unequivocally do.

Eric, Count Stenbock: 'Ideated Degeneracy' and 'Weird Performance'

Eric, Count Stenbock (1860–1895) was 'by far the most enthusiastic decadent in London' and 'one of fin-de-siècle London's most extraordinary characters' (B. M. Stableford 1993, 60; Freeman 2014, 116). He was also exemplary in terms of dedicating his short life to a perhaps unique performance of 'ideated degeneracy' (Reed 1995, 7). According to Symons, Stenbock lived a life that was 'bizarre, fantastic, feverish, eccentric, extravagant, morbid, and perverse' (Symons 1969, 89). His 'weird propensities' were such that 'he was like one of his own characters in that amazing book of his, *Studies of Death*' (90). A later commentator goes a step further, remarking that Stenbock 'chose to become a fiction', an ambition assisted by the subsequent enthusiastic mythologization he has received at the hands of his very few commentators:

> [L]ittle is known about Count Stanislaus Eric Stenbock beyond the facts of his occultism, opium and alcohol addiction, zoöphilia, and tragic death. Even for that era he was bizarre. Only his weird fiction is known. (Reed 1995, 5–6; Eng 1981, 419)

Being the scion of an aristocratic family that were 'among the greatest landowners in Estonia'—inheriting his title and estate in 1885—Stenbock had the financial resources to 'perform' Decadence to a degree that others could only achieve vicariously in their fictions (Adlard 1969, 18).

The self-destructive opposition of his homosexuality and devout Roman Catholicism, which anticipates that of Sebastian Flyte in Evelyn Waugh's *Brideshead Revisited*, equipped him with the necessary inner conflict to function as one of Yeats's 'Hamlets of our age' (27), a term itself coined by Yeats's father when he 'heard his son talking at dinner about the immensely eccentric Count Stenbock' (Bristow 2005, 31–32). Precipitated by the ravages of drug and alcohol abuse, Stenbock's death occurred on 26 April 1895, and 'can be read as an ominous portent' of the impact of the Wilde trial on the decade, the criminal proceedings against Wilde commencing on that same day (Freeman 2014, 116). Joseph Bristow suggests that it was in fact Stenbock who served as the original model for Yeats's 'tragic generation':

> With some license, Yeats took Stenbock, who had died of cirrhosis of the liver in 1895, as the model for the other—far more notable—poets whose personal decline happened to coincide with the fin de siècle. (Bristow 2005, 32)

Stenbock left enough of an impression on Yeats for the latter to fictionalize him as a character ('Count Sobrinski') in his unfinished autobiographical novel *The Speckled Bird*. However, Yeats's admiration for Stenbock's poetry clearly fell short of including him in his *Oxford Book of Modern Verse* (1936), despite mentioning Stenbock in the introduction as a 'scholar, connoisseur, drunkard, poet, pervert, most charming of men'— again, it is the character of Stenbock himself that is present as a cipher for the 1890s, rather than his work (W. B. Yeats 1936, ix–x).

Raised a protestant, Stenbock converted to Rome while at Balliol and although he practised his religion with as much eccentricity as he displayed in every other aspect of his life, there is no evidence that he was anything other than sincere. In *The Speckled Bird*, Yeats has his 'Count Sobrinski' protest—in response to discussion of 'magical symbols'—'Magic is forbidden by the Church, and I, at any rate, am perfectly orthodox' (William Butler Yeats 1976, 78). Despite this claim, however, Ernest Rhys writes of a bequest left to him by Stenbock of 'some of his favourite books, *Rosicrucian* and romantic, with his fantastic serpentine bookmark' (italics mine) (Rhys 1940, 162–163). The apparent ease with which

Stenbock combined his Roman Catholicism with ad hoc forms of idolatry (for example, his shrine of an 'eternal' flame flanked by a bust of Shelley and a statue of Buddha) does raise the question of whether his morbid discomfort with his sexuality was entirely motivated by his faith, which if flexible enough to accommodate his idolatry and occult interests might surely have also accommodated other similarly forbidden practices. Regardless of the coherence or otherwise of his religious convictions, he was certainly critical of scientific materialism: 'Many people have attempted to destroy the Devil from Punch to Professor Huxley. They have hardly succeeded in doing so' (C. S. E. Stenbock 1999, 12–13).

Stenbock is certainly a nebulous figure in terms of his impact, his few books having 'almost dematerialized and grown to be extreme bibliographical rarities' (Reed 1995, 5). Symons described Stenbock as—oxymoronically—'conspicuous' in his 'failures in life and in art which leave no traces behind them, save some faint drift in one's memory' (Symons 1969, 94). Symons's remark should be taken in spirit rather than literally: there are at least traces. Like both Machen and Shiel, Stenbock dabbled in translation and his 1890 rendering (with William Wilson) of a collection of short stories by Balzac generated some praise from the *Review of Reviews*, which enthused that 'Balzac is so much neglected in this country that a popular volume of this kind is to be heartily welcomed' (*Review of Reviews* 1890, 618). Stenbock's second volume of poetry was at least acknowledged in the *Athenaeum*'s review of 'English Literature in 1893', albeit cursorily: 'Count Stenbock, in *The Shadow of Death*, has succeeded, here and there, in giving expression to curiously morbid sensations' (*Athenaeum* 1894, 18).

According to John Adlard, Stenbock submitted a piece called 'La Mazurka des Revenants' to the *Yellow Book* which was rejected in September 1894 (Adlard 1969, 84). His single volume of short fiction, *Studies in Death: Romantic Tales*, received very little attention on its publication that same year and has subsequently been reprinted once in 1984 and then in a small press edition of 300 copies in 1996 (C. S. E. Stenbock 1984; E. Stenbock 1996). The *Glasgow Herald* seems to have been unique in affording the title a review, and was cautiously positive if condescending in its appraisal, also noting its unique design:

> On the quaint cover of this little volume we have presented to us, *inter alia*, an avenue of funeral cypresses, a couple of black cranes, a couple of owls (back and front view), a serpent, and (we rather think, but we are not quite sure) a gravestone. Yet, *Studies of Death* is not quite so depressing as it looks.

It is true that in most of the little stories it contains people die; but, then, heroes and heroines die in novels, whatever may be printed on the title-page, and even without black crows, cypresses, and serpents on the cover. Count Stenbock's style, if it is really that of a foreigner, is remarkably good; an injudicious appreciation of the most objectionable feature of Kipling's writing—viz., oaths, is probably responsible for the language which soils the otherwise pretty tale of 'The Egg of the Albatross'. 'Narcissus' perhaps shows the truest fancy. Amid much that is merely 'precious' in this fantastic volume, we think we discern a writer of ability; at all events, the book is 'curious'. (*Glasgow Herald* 1895, 7)

Studies of Death is a collection of weird tales shot through with a palpable melancholy and desolation, although tempered by touches of cynical wit and irony. The two stories by Stenbock most frequently (albeit that infrequently) anthologized in subsequent collections both concern traditional supernatural tropes: 'The Other Side' is a 'macabre [werewolf] legend with most powerful and haunting effect' first published under the editorship of Alfred Douglas in the June 1893 edition of *The Spirit Lamp*, the Oxford 'Aesthetic, Literary, and Critical Magazine', which also featured contributions from Wilde and John Addington Symonds, as well as Max Beerbohm's print debut, in that same issue (Summers 1928, 324). The second is 'The True Story of a Vampire', one of the constituent tales of *Studies of Death*.

Inconveniently for arguments that fin-de-siècle weird fiction is identifiable by its abandonment of such folkloric tropes, Stenbock's two most popular stories exploit two of the most familiar ones, albeit with considerable subtlety. In the first, a fairy-tale atmosphere is developed in which the human world of an isolated village is separated from an oneiric woodland realm in which the protagonist Gabriel, a young innocent boy, is somehow transformed into a wolf and subjected to the nefarious influence of the 'wolf keeper [...] whose face was veiled in eternal shadow' (Stenbock [sic] 1893, 67). Contrastingly, in 'The True Story of a Vampire', Stenbock immediately deflates any reader expectations suggested by the subject matter with some urbane and subtle humour, anticipating the sardonic tone of Saki:

> Vampire stories are generally located in Styria; mine is also. Styria is by no means the romantic kind of place described by those who have certainly never been there. It is a flat, uninteresting country, only celebrated for its turkeys, its capons, and the stupidity of its inhabitants. Vampires generally

arrive at night, in carriages drawn by two black horses. Our Vampire arrived by the commonplace means of the railway train, and in the afternoon. (Stenbock 1894, 120)

The ensuing narrative describes the fatal influence exerted on a young boy (also named Gabriel) by one of his father's friends, an interloper in the household with a keen interest in the occult. Despite there being a clear pederastic subtext, the tale's narrator (the victim's sister) takes pains to point out that her use of the term 'vampire' is a specific one: 'No, I am quite serious. The Vampire of whom I am speaking, who laid waste our hearth and home, was a real vampire' (120). It is of course possible that Stenbock was distancing himself from his own troubling impulses by making them other and monstrous. Accordingly, Francis King suggests that Stenbock 'made an attempt to understand his homosexuality in terms of traditional occultism, eventually coming to view his condition as an aspect of vampirism and lycanthropy' (King 2004, 18). Stenbock is ever careful in the majority of his fiction to imply nefarious supernatural agency rather than make it directly manifest, and a sinister atmosphere of 'weird insanity' is often communicated in combination with a resigned, dry wit, a technique explicitly advocated by Stenbock: 'I have been purposefully treating this subject in a light vein, in order to accentuate its intense horror' (Symons 1969, 93).

As well as being the subject of an essay by Arthur Symons ('A Study in the Fantastic', circa 1920), Stenbock has been the subject of a single volume of critical biography: John Adlard's *Yeats, Stenbock and the Nineties* (1969). The title is misleading, however, as there are only passing references to Yeats in the volume. Author Mark Valentine, who was acquainted with Adlard (1929–1993), has stated that Adlard added Yeats's name to the title purely to ensure the book's acquisition by libraries, which he felt would otherwise ignore it due to Stenbock's obscurity.[5] The contemporary artist and musician David Tibet has published occasional and very limited small press limited editions of Stenbock's fiction, poetry, and miscellanea since the 1990s, and at the time of writing is about to publish a volume of Stenbock's complete works, including previously unpublished material from the Stenbock archive housed in the Harvard Centre for Renaissance Studies near Florence, Italy.

---

[5] Mark Valentine, personal communication, Brighton, 2 November 2013.

For the connoisseur, then, Stenbock perhaps comes close to fulfilling, both in person and in print, Baudrillard's 'law' that 'an object only acquires its exceptional value *by dint of being absent*', a suggestion reinforced by the title of one of the very few critical works dedicated to him, the privately printed *One Hundred Years of Disappearance: Count Eric Stenbock* (1995) (Baudrillard 1994, 13; Reed 1995). This same span is, perhaps not entirely coincidentally, given between Max Beerbohm's fictional account of another 'forgotten' author of the 1890s, 'Enoch Soames' (1916). Like Stenbock, Soames's poetry owes 'something to the young Parisian decadents, or to the young English ones who owe something to *them*' and his 1893 collection *Fungoids* sells a total of three copies and is all but ignored by his contemporaries (Beerbohm 1919, 15, 18). Also like Stenbock, Soames is a 'Catholic Diabolist', and Beerbohm's account has him in 1897 making a pact with the devil to visit the British Library a century hence (in 1997) in the hope of finding confirmation of his posthumous reputation as a significant literary figure of the period (14, 29). 'Enoch Soames' is in part a satire of what Beerbohm identifies as a 1890s tendency to pretentious self-regard in the insistence on privileging artistic purity over the production of mere 'copy' by the literary 'tradesman' (36, 18). However, it seems likely—even inevitable—that had *Fungoids* existed it would by now be a highly sought-after item not only due to its rarity but precisely because of its obscurity:

> The quintessential creation of the fin de siècle was a slim volume of decadent verse. The attraction of the period to many aesthetes and bibliophiles is the appearance of a few exquisitely-produced books of poems in severely limited editions of a few hundred or less. They bear refulgent titles—*Orchids, Opals, Phantasmagoria, The Shadow of Death*—and the verse within is swooning, either with the perfumed languor of the hothouse or with the lilied scent of decay. (Valentine 2014, 7)

These are the opening sentences of a contemporary literary production that achieves a meta-level manifestation of this impulse, demonstrating its continuing potency: Mark Valentine's essay on 1890s poets whose work is actually nonexistent, the oblique traces of which are instead gleaned from memoirs of the period, is itself a slim, sumptuously produced and hand-sewn volume produced in a limited edition of 106, sold out in advance of publication.

Though certainly foregrounded, this impulse is not of course unique to weird or Decadent fiction. John Gross describes a similar phenomenon which he identifies with the wider literary culture of the later nineteenth century:

> What incensed [Frederic Harrison] most of all, however, was the spread of bibliomania, the passion for resurrecting forgotten texts and dredging up minor curiosities. If there was one literary type of the period whom he thoroughly despised it was the 'book-trotter', whom he depicted wandering aimlessly from shelf to shelf and then finally settling down to write *Half-Hours with Obscure Authors*. (Gross 1973, 129)

However, and regardless of Harrison's disdain for the enterprise, as applied particularly to the 1890s, such bibliomania or (perhaps) cryptobibliomania has been described as 'weird' in itself. In her *Guardian* obituary of Father Brocard Sewell (1912–2000), the 'brilliant connoisseur of 1890s decadence', Fiona McCarthy concludes thus:

> Father Brocard's reclamation of forgotten, esoteric writers of the 1890s was his major literary life's work. Gray and Raffalovich; Arthur Machen; Frederick Rolfe, Baron Corvo; Olive Custance, the poet, Lord Alfred Douglas's wife; the dubious demonologist, the Rev Montague Summers. It has been a weird and marvellous pursuit. (*Guardian* 2000)

Stenbock's particular value as a forgotten or 'absent' quantity is implicitly acknowledged by the (alleged) existence, quasi-existence, or conceit of a 'Count Stenbock Society', whose membership is by invitation only, and which prides itself in the infrequency of its activity ("Thomas Ligotti Online" n.d.). It is also indicative of the potency of the Stenbock mythology that his Wikipedia entry contains (at the time of writing) an unsourced and likely inaccurate assertion that '*Studies of Death* [… was …] good enough to be the subject of favourable comment by H. P. Lovecraft' ('Eric Stenbock' 2013). In fact, Lovecraft refers to 'Stenbock' [sic] only once in his voluminous correspondence, in response to Richard E. Morse's inquiry as to whether Lovecraft was familiar with him:

> No—I never heard the name of Count Eric Stenbock [sic] until I encountered it in the pages of your letter. What you say of him & his work captures my interest most profoundly, & I surely hope that I may encounter his book—or some of his isolated pieces—in the course of time.[6]

Despite this, the assertion that Lovecraft was an admirer of Stenbock's work has proliferated across other websites, perhaps as an act of subconscious wish fulfilment, the two writers' eccentricities making them a particularly

---

[6] Lovecraft, letter to Richard E. Morse, 16 November 1932.

good 'fit' and Lovecraft's 'endorsement' even further enhancing Stenbock's cache, at least among Lovecraft enthusiasts.

Timothy D'Arch Smith has framed Stenbock as a peripheral 'Uranian' poet and associated his work with that of a movement given impetus by

> the prevailing decadence of the nineties when 'new sins' were de rigueur and [… the …] rather heady hermaphroditism, so clear in Beardsley's drawings and in the pages of *The Picture of Dorian Gray*, set off a flood of paederastic material in the form of verse, prose, and paintings. (D'Arch Smith 1970, 2)

According to D'Arch Smith, the Uranian poets and artists were united in their interest in the aesthetic appreciation of male adolescents rather than representations of overt homoeroticism (xx). Much of Stenbock's poetry articulates the irresolvable, morbid conflict between his attraction to the male physique and his conviction of the eternal damnation that awaits him should he succumb to temptation. The tensions resulting from this irreconcilable quandary are further heightened by his apparent thanatophilia. Imagery of dead children and dead or dying young men litters both his prose and his poetry, where his 'musical lyrics sigh for sleep and for self-immolation' (Eng 1981, 419). In this respect, Stenbock joins contemporaries, such as Ernest Dowson and Lionel Johnson, who share a similarly modest status as contributors to the literary canon (perhaps Stenbock most of all in this respect) and whose reputations, Hilary Laird argues, have been overshadowed by their obsession with suicide and death (Laird 2005, 69–100). Stenbock holds a tenuous foothold in the ranks of those 1890s poets whose work has 'long been associated with such epithets as "tragic", "weak", "minor", "failed", "melancholic", "self-destructive", and "feminine"' (Laird 2005, 70).

It is perhaps possible to speculate that the physically perfect adolescent boy, dying prematurely, is a desperate act of imaginary wish fulfilment of Stenbock's, allowing expression of his Uranian pederasty full flight without the possibility that either he or the object of his affections lives long enough to risk perpetual hellfire should he act on his impulses (E. Stenbock 2001, 21):

> I dreamed your soft warm limbs, my love,
> Burnt with Hell's furious fire;
> And demons laughed, and said, This is
> The end of your desire.

He sought escape from these, clearly profound, anxieties through recourse to alcohol and opiates, and his consumption of both was prodigious. Jeremy Reed claims that Stenbock's heavy use of opiates is reflected in the unique quality of his weird fiction, arguing that

> [Stenbock's] fascination [... with the ...] whole vocabulary of the night and oneiric underworld were not just derivations of his readings of Beckford, Poe, and Le Fanu, but a state of mind in part generated by drug abuse, and in part imaginative function. (Reed 1995, 6)

D'Arch Smith argues that Stenbock's engagement with this 'oneiric underworld' was more than 'a literary toying with an ancient legend', being rather a 'serious self-comparison with the vampire legends of his childhood to which he had linked his own lust for young boys and his morbid desire for death as a release from psychological distress' (D'Arch Smith 1970, 37).

As suggested above, even a life lived at the extremes does not prevent further gratuitous biographical embellishment from subsequent commentators. Reed's insistence that Stenbock was an openly practising transvestite who travelled London omnibuses dressed in woman's clothing seems to be nothing more than an extrapolation from unconnected observations that Stenbock both curled and dyed his hair, and regularly travelled by omnibus. Surviving sketches and photographic portraits of Stenbock (including a caricature by Max Beerbohm) all show him soberly attired in black morning dress typical of the time[7] (Fig. 3.1).

The publisher Ernest Rhys (who went on to initiate the Everyman imprint) discusses his acquaintance with Stenbock, with whom he at one point lodged, in some detail in two volumes of memoirs as well as his collected correspondence, and although he mentions the striking impression made upon him by Stenbock's 'most unusual' features, his 'flaxen curls' and 'china-blue eyes', he doesn't mention any predilection for public transvestism (Rhys 1940, 76, 1931, 15). Similarly, his alleged 'zoöphilia' (a term used by both Reed and Cevasco) seems to be an intentional and speculative eroticization of the available anecdotal evidence of his practice of keeping menageries of animals in his homes. It also seems likely that Reed and Cevasco may have employed the term in relation to Stenbock *à propos* Adlard's observation that 'zoöphilia' is one of the items on Nordau's extensive list of the 'stigmata' of degeneration:

---

[7] See, for example, the frontispiece illustration by Max Beerbohm to Mary Costelloe 1980.

Fig. 3.1 Portrait of Eric, Count Stenbock, circa 1886

The stigmata of degeneracy known as Zoöphilia, or excessive love for animals, is strongly shown in [the degenerate]. When he wishes particularly to edify himself he runs 'to contemplate the beautiful eyes of the seal, and to distress himself over the mysterious sufferings of these tender-hearted animals'.[8]

Whereas Adlard uses this excerpt from *Degeneration* in order to suggest that if Nordau ever encountered Stenbock he would have 'a label ready', the specific word 'zoöphilia' is applied to Stenbock by subsequent commentators without explication of Nordau's pejorative employment of the term, and Stenbock's interest in animals is imbued for posterity with the totally spurious suggestion of depravity. Indeed, Adlard is at pains to point out that several of Stenbock's near contemporaries, including Frank Cadogan Cowper, William Michael Rossetti, and Kenneth Grahame, also kept 'strange menageries', although they were spared accusations of similar enormities (Adlard 1969, 45).

[8] Maurice Barrès, qtd in Nordau, p. 315.

Likewise, many of the wilder eccentricities for which he is now remembered (when he is remembered at all)—such as regularly travelling in the company of a life-sized doll, which he claimed was his son and paid a clearly unscrupulous Jesuit priest to educate—seem to be manifestations of his rapidly declining mental and physical health towards the end of his life as much as a contrivance to shock the bourgeoisie. That his attitude with regard to the latter was not ideologically hostile or confrontational can be gleaned from an account by the 'evangelist and religious writer' Hannah Whitall Smith of his attendance and evident interest in a temperance movement tea party (Milligan 2004):

> [Stenbock] seems to like me to have labor [sic] with him about this [opium] habit and the other day I took him out with me to a Temperance Garden Party at Knotts Green, Gurney Barclay's beautiful place at Leyton. […] It was the very first Temperance Meeting Count Stenbock had ever attended in his life and I think he was quite impressed. (Mary Costelloe 1980, 25)

Such humanizing glimpses undermine Symons's mythologized 'monstrous' Stenbock, whose preposterous extravagances of personality and behaviour have contributed so much to his status as a cryptobibliographical fetish of weird fiction connoisseurs. Stenbock's texts themselves, according to this reading, become reliquaries for a cult of personality rather than being valorized for their intrinsic properties.

Smith knew Stenbock through her daughter, Mary Costelloe (sister to Alys, the first wife of Bertrand Russell), who, together with her husband Frank Costelloe, had travelled with Stenbock in Russia and Estonia in the winter of 1886, spending Christmas at his family home in Kolk:

> It is an immense old castle or villa in a rather Italian style, with the Stenbock arms over the entrance and fascinating idiot gargoyles to carry off the rain. It has hundreds of rooms and secret stairs and passages and dark closets without end—there are two family ghosts. (19)

Stenbock's chambers in Kolk were decorated in a 'most aesthetic style', and varied accounts exist of his extravagance in this respect (19). His rooms displayed all the detailed orientalism and cluttered aestheticism necessary to establish the *haute*-Decadent *bricolage* described by Nordau as yet another stigma of degeneration and predicated on the aesthetic template for interior design ideated by Huysmans in *A rebours* (1884), a paradigm-establishing text iconicized by Wilde's citing of the book in his trial.

In long, florid passages, Nordau itemizes the 'bric-à-brac' which constitutes the 'feverish and infernal' style of the degenerate: 'Kurd carpets, Bedouin chests, Circassian narghilehs, and Indian lacquered caskets' and so on for many long, astonishingly detailed paragraphs: 'the walls are either hung with worm-eaten Gobelin tapestry [...] or covered with Morris draperies, on which strange birds flit amongst crazily ramping branches, and blowzy flowers coquet with vain butterflies'; '[i]n a corner a sort of temple is erected to a squatting or a standing Buddha'; 'lamps of the stature of a man illumine these rooms with light both subdued and tinted by sprawling shades, red, yellow or green of hue'; and so on (Nordau 1895, 10–11).

Count Stenbock might have used these passages from *Degeneration* as a manual for his own adventures in interior decoration:

> [Stenbock's bedroom] was painted peacock-blue. Over the marble chimneypiece a great altar had been erected, tricked out with Oriental shawls, peacock feathers, lamps and rosaries. In the middle stood a green bronze statue of Eros. There was a little flame that burned unceasingly, and resin in a copper bowl that scented the air. The floor was covered with thick Smyrna carpets, and [...] he would lie smoking opium, watched by a swinging parrot, a cageful of doves and a smelly monkey perched on some piece of furniture. Tortoises crawled, mice raced, around the bed where their master lay in a dream too marvellous even to be summarized. (Adlard 1969, 37)

Here Stenbock becomes almost indistinguishable from Shiel's Decadent detective Prince Zaleski, who first appeared in the Keynotes series in 1895, the year of Stenbock's death. Zaleski occupies chambers of 'barbaric gorgeousness', the air heavy with 'the fumes of the narcotic cannabis sativa—the base of the bhang of the Mohammedans' (M. P. Shiel 1895, 4). The mixture of curiosities on display contributes to an effect of 'a *bizarrerie* of half-weird sheen and gloom' (4). Reviewing *Zaleski* upon publication for the *Academy*, James Stanley Little was already treating this *mise-en-scène* as a tiresomely familiar one, dismissively describing the prince as being 'environed in the usual assortment of *bric-a-brac*—Graeco-Etruscan vases, Memphitic mummies, Hindu gods—an old curiosity shop, in fact' (Little 1895, 312).

Like Nordau and Huysmans, the prolixity of the cumulative detail employed by Shiel threatens to overwhelm and stagger the senses, replicating the intense effect of heightened aestheticism. Pater's influence can also be felt in this privileging of the *object* over eternalist certainties in aesthetics—when one does away with the notions of the Ideal, the specific instance of the object itself is made paramount in aesthetic contemplation. This adds to the subversiveness of Shiel's conceit in his second Keynotes offering, *Shapes in the Fire* (1896): in the episode 'The Master and Maker', Shiel audaciously decorates the Prime Minister's own rooms along aesthetic lines, envisioning *haute*-Decadent contingencies infecting even Downing Street with 'crystal, porcelain, mirrors, stuffs of Mecca, shawls of India, and a profusion of cushions; the tapestries being panelled in coloured velvets embroidered with sentences from the poet Sadi' (M. P. Shiel 1896a, 127). 'His Lordship' himself wears 'a dressing-gown of crocus satin, widely-cylindrical pantaloons of cerulean silk, slippers which curled high at the toes, and a close gold-wrought cap for calpac and turban', taking 'occasional lazy sips' from his 'hookah' (127).

Here Shiel seems to anticipate and play on Nordau's hysterical dread of 'effeminizing' orientalism in a ludic performance of degeneration and Decadence engendering its rot in the heart of the establishment itself. That this notion was a resonant one is further indicated by E. T. Reed's 1895 Punch cartoon 'Britannia à la Beardsley', which depicted the national iconography of the nation corrupted by the sinister oriental stylization typical of Beardsley. Indicative of the potency of such anxieties is the fact that Arthur Balfour, the *actual* Prime Minister between 1902 and 1905, thought Decadence still topical enough in 1908 to deliver a lecture on the subject (Balfour 1908).

Zaleski's main chamber of repose is 'not a large one, but lofty'. Shiel (the represented narrator who shares the author's surname) goes on to observe that even in

> the semi-darkness of the very faint greenish lustre radiated from an open censerlike *lampas* of fretted gold in the centre of the domed encausted roof, a certain incongruity of barbaric gorgeousness in the furnishing filled me with amazement. (M. P. Shiel 1895, 3–4)

He could be describing Lord Leighton's two-storey 'Arab Hall', constructed between 1877 and 1879 (Sweetman 1987, 190). Indeed, the 'Arab Room' was an 'arresting phenomenon of the last quarter of the nineteenth century and the opening years of the next', associated with an 'association of Islamic style with ideas of recreation and relaxation' extant from at least the eighteenth century (189). By the late nineteenth century, an 'Arab Room' might be a consideration when house planning, to serve as a venue, like the billiard room or the gun room, for male withdrawal and smoking, the latter being especially associated with aesthetic styles redolent of 'the pipe-smoking Muslim and the hookah' (189). The trend for donning a smoking jacket and ornately embroidered smoking cap before relaxing with a pipe or cigar was a perhaps more achievable manifestation of the more ostentatious fin-de-siècle expressions of this association.

Little's allusion to the 'usual [...] old curiosity shop' perhaps indicates (aside from the obvious reference to Dickens) the ubiquity of the nineteenth-century enthusiasm for what Roger Luckhurst calls 'immersive-exotic spaces': private 'Egyptian rooms', public places of entertainment, and the 'oriental rooms' and 'bazaars' of West End shopping emporiums (Luckhurst 2012, 87–118). James Willsher cites the publication of the first English translation of *The Thousand and One Nights* (as *Arabian Nights Entertainment*) in 1704 as the catalyst for a 'fascination with all things oriental', which 'rendered European imaginations delirious with tales of the seraglio, evil viziers and the jinnee' (Willsher 2004, 14).

Weird Orientalism

Edward Said offers some clues on how to parse this appropriation, or rather all out plundering, of exotica in his influential and controversial study *Orientalism* (1978), where he argues that 'words such as "Orient" and "Occident" correspond to no stable reality that exists as a natural fact' and that 'all such geographical designations are an odd combination of the empirical and the imaginative' (Said 2003, 331). Said argues that it is possible to trace this conceit back to Aeschylus and Euripides, who both articulated the Orient with 'the prerogative [...] of a genuine creator, whose life giving power represents, animates, constitutes the otherwise silent and dangerous space beyond familiar boundaries' (57). It is a fictive space where 'rationality is undermined by Eastern excesses' (57). Said's conclusion here is that these 'Oriental mysteries [...] challenge the Western mind to new exercises of its enduring ambition and power' (57). In the context of the texts discussed in this chapter at least, while there seems no doubt that, for example, Shiel, Machen, and Stenbock, like many of their contemporaries, used the Orient as an imaginative space, the claim that they were doing so in order to shore up any notions of occidental primacy seems misplaced.[9] I will argue below that the use of Orientalism in weird fiction is, rather, often a liberation strategy, and one that revels in Said's 'dangerous space beyond familiar boundaries' which undermines the rational.

It is also one that challenges the fin-de-siècle stereotype of Oriental sensuous languor: Wells's Time Traveller boasts that he is 'too Occidental for a long vigil' and that while he 'could work at a problem for years [...] to wait inactive for twenty-four hours—that is another matter' (Wells 2008, 32). This association of the orient with lassitude is strikingly at odds with Machen's styling of London (after Stevenson) as 'the New Baghdad', a conceit which imbues the city and its teeming occupants with manifold dynamism rather than lassitude:

> The infinite varieties of London and its life were, little by little, brought home to me, and the lesson was made plain by R. L. Stevenson's *New Arabian Nights*. From that time forth I thought of the great town as a sailor may think of the ocean or an Arab of the desert; as an object always to be studied and explored, but never known fully, as a region of perpetual surprises and discoveries and adventures of the spirit [...] When I think in more general terms of the pleasures and advantages of London, I think of this Arabian quality that it possesses in such a supereminent degree. (Machen 1914)

Machen's orientalism is intertextual rather than actual, and is demonstrative more of his reading than his interest in the reality of the Arab world. Or, as Derek Trotter puts it in relation to a story by Machen set in America, 'the authenticating detail in "The Novel of the Dark Valley" owes its authenticity not to Machen's knowledge of Nebraska, but to his knowledge of Stevenson' (Trotter 1995, xix).

Similarly, when considered outside of the explicitly colonial and beyond merely the superficial appropriation of material culture, the weird-decadent milieu of Stenbock and his fictional counterpart Zaleski is better understood as an exploration of an imaginative space rather than a serious attempt at empirical cross-cultural engagement: 'The Orient provided a theatre for the decadent imaginations of the Occident' (Willsher 2004, 14). It is a 'fantastic European dream' rather than a reality (Warner 2012, 20). Appropriately,

---

[9] Shiel would later in his career produce novels like *The Yellow Danger* (1898) which almost demand accommodation within Said's argument here, and Christopher Frayling's *The Yellow Peril* (2014) has recently done just that.

Baudrillard also orientalizes *the act of collection itself*: 'Surrounded by objects he possesses, the collector is pre-eminently the sultan of a secret seraglio' (Baudrillard 1994, 10). The dialogue is between the Decadent-performer and the imaginative spaces represented in literature rather than the cultural reality, perhaps analogous to the orientalist visual artists' use of 'the alien and mysterious qualities of Middle Eastern life' as a 'welcome extension of the traditional subject areas of European painting [...] evoking a degree of fantasy in a period of growing materialism' (Sweetman 1987, 190). Similarly, Said writes of the 'literary work of the sort produced by Gautier [...], Swinburne, Baudelaire, and Huysmans' that it displayed a 'fascination with the macabre, with the notion of a Fatal Woman, with secrecy and occultism' and that Nerval's Arabian tales demonstrate a 'quintessential Oriental world of uncertain, fluid dreams infinitely multiplying themselves past resolution, definiteness, materiality' (Said 2003, 180, 183).

This fervid imaginative space had already been established in the writing of Thomas De Quincey, who devotes the 'May 1818' paragraphs of the 'Pains of Opium' section of his *Confessions of an English Opium Eater* (1821) to detailing his 'Asiatic' visions, which commingled 'Oriental imagery and mythological horrors'. In his narcotized contemplations, De Quincey is troubled by the multifariousness and unconscionable dimensions of the Orient, the impossibility of grasping its antiquity and vastness, and its unaccountable populousness as 'part of the earth most swarming with human life'. A febrile confusion of Eastern myth and religious imagery is distorted and contorted by his opium ingestion into a weird phantasmagoria:

> Under the connecting feeling of tropical heat and vertical sunlights I brought together all creatures, birds, beasts, reptiles, all trees and plants, usages and appearances, that are found in all tropical regions, and assembled them together in China or Indostan. From kindred feelings, I soon brought Egypt and all her gods under the same law. I was stared at, hooted at, grinned at, chattered at, by monkeys, by parroquets, by cockatoos. I ran into pagodas, and was fixed for centuries at the summit or in secret rooms: I was the idol; I was the priest; I was worshipped; I was sacrificed. I fled from the wrath of Brama through all the forests of Asia: Vishnu hated me: Seeva laid wait for me. I came suddenly upon Isis and Osiris: I had done a deed, they said, which the ibis and the crocodile trembled at. I was buried for a thousand years in stone coffins, with mummies and sphynxes, in narrow chambers at the heart of eternal pyramids. I was kissed, with cancerous kisses, by crocodiles; and laid, confounded with all unutterable slimy things, amongst reeds and Nilotic mud. (De Quincey 1821, 375–376)

De Quincey's horror is attenuated by 'a further sublimity to the feelings associated with all Oriental names or images' and his visions fill him 'with such amazement at the monstrous scenery that horror seemed absorbed for a while in sheer astonishment' (375, 376).

De Quincey's anticipation of Poe in these passages is perhaps obliquely referred to by Lovecraft when Lovecraft acknowledges (in passing) De Quincey's 'revels in grotesque and arabesque terrors' in *Supernatural Horror in Literature* (Lovecraft 1985, 449–450).[10] L. Moffitt Cecil has demonstrated in detail how Poe used the term 'arabesque' to distinguish his 'serious' tales from his 'humorous and satiric stories' (his 'grotesques') (Cecil 1966). Cecil argues that 'arabesque' as a critical term has three distinct meanings, all of which are employed by Poe: of 'Arabian, Arabic' origin, 'Arabian or Moorish in ornamental design', and a 'figurative sense' of 'strangely mixed, fantastic' (57). Geographically, Poe's 'Arabia' (like Decadence's later conceits) is a fluid, amorphous space, 'embracing Egypt, Arabia, Syria, Persia, Palestine, Turkey, and Greece', whose pantheon of supernatural beings is an incoherent jumble of Christian, Mohammedan, Hebrew, and Greek divinities as well as 'assorted houri, demons, magi, and genii' (58).

Poe's interiors anticipate and directly influence the *haute*-Decadent 'bric-à-brac' discussed above, and Cecil lists a series of instances in Poe's texts the cumulative effect of which is also comparable to those examples. Poe's prototype is, of course, also *The Thousand and One Nights* which he possibly originally encountered in the French translation of Antoine Galland during his boyhood tenure in England, and whose tales he later supplemented with his own 'The Thousand and Second Tale of Scheherezade' (62). Poe was also a keen admirer of William Beckford's Gothic fantasia *Vathek* (1786). Beckford—a 'crucial figure in the history of the *Nights*' reception' in Europe—tested sexual and social boundaries with his 'many weird and violent *Arabian Nights* stories' (Frank 1997, 36; Warner 2012, 270).

As already mentioned above, *The Thousand and One Nights* was, together with and through Poe, a recurring reference point in both the interpretation and creation of writing in the weird mode towards the end of the nineteenth century. Marina Warner notes the relatively low cultural

---

[10] Considering the debt owed by Lovecraft to De Quincey evident in, especially, Lovecraft's short story 'Under the Pyramids' (1924), Lovecraft's dismissal of De Quincey as having 'a desultoriness and learned pomp which deny him the rank of specialist [in the weird]' is perhaps surprising (450).

status afforded the tales in their 'cultures of origin' compared with Europe, describing them as 'beneath the attention of proper literati' and even as 'pulp fiction [...] excluded from the classical Arabic canon' (8). This latter comparison of course resonates with the argument being made here that the influence of the tales was a central one on the 'high phase' of weird fiction, which culminated in the pulp magazines of the 1920s and 1930s.

In her account of the history of *The Thousand and One Nights* in translation ('almost as tangled as the tales themselves'), Warner notes that the 'Victorian and *fin-de-siècle* editions [...] excited heady orientalist fantasists to add their own material', and describes Sir Richard Burton's 1885 effort as 'prolix and rococo' and a 'weird performance'; therefore, perhaps, also an anticipation of Decadence proper (18). Frustratingly for the purposes of this thesis, Warner fails to expand on an exact conception of the latter phrase; despite this, I will appropriate it as a suggestive one. Warner identifies as a culmination of this imbrication of Decadence with the *Nights* the '*Yellow Book* prose' of the 1923 translation by Powys Mathers of the 'lengthy and flamboyant French translation of J. C. V. Mardrus [...] a *fin-de-siècle* aesthete' who contributed his own stories of a 'decidedly decadent and Symbolist character' to the text (18–19). The relationship of *The Thousand and One Nights* to European letters should not, therefore, be considered as being one of the straightforward influence of the former on the latter, but rather a symbiotic literary development. The translations of *The Thousand and One Nights* created a feedback loop, an ongoing process reflecting its influence on European literature and the influence of trends in European literature on concurrent translations of and elaborations on *The Thousand and One Nights*.

Both the original and Stevenson's *New Arabian Nights* were integral to the development of the short story form itself, and directly and indirectly evoked in the form and content of Machen's and Shiel's Keynotes contributions the orientalist turn in Decadence, which was subsequently entrenched in the ensuing development of weird fiction—perhaps most definitively in Lovecraft's enduringly popular creation, the 'Necronomicon', a fictional work of dangerous occult lore written by a 'mad poet of Sanaá, in Yemen', Abdul Alhazred, a character originally created by Lovecraft upon reading *The Thousand and One Nights* when still a young child (Lovecraft 2011, 1; Harms 2003, 7). Indeed, it is perhaps possible to identify the influence of the *Nights* in one of Lovecraft's most famous creations, the cyclopean alien entity 'Cthulhu', who, like the similarly proportioned rebel afrit Dahesh in the 'City of Brass' episode of *The Thousand*

and One Nights, is also imprisoned in a 'living tomb' of black stone, a 'half-living half-dead thing' which 'tests the limits of animate life' (Warner 2012, 55, 59).

As well as the arabesque, the 'Necronomicon' also evidences Lovecraft's debt to *fin-de-siècle* Decadence by being inspired by Robert W. Chambers' *The King in Yellow*, a collection containing several stories concerning a fictional play, 'The King in Yellow', which Chambers describes as being largely suppressed due to its baleful, corrupting, and sanity-shattering effect on those who read it or see it performed. Chambers's 'The King in Yellow' was a heightened, supernatural fictionalization of the 1890s notion of 'dangerous' texts such as Wilde's controversial and banned *Salome* (1893) and Maeterlinck's Symbolist play *Pelléas and Mélisande* (1893), as such anticipating and imitated by later horror texts that similarly employed what John Clute has discussed as 'the motif of harmful sensation' (Clute 2006, 103–104). Discussing *The King in Yellow* in the *Academy* in 1897, William Sharp claims that it demonstrates[11]

> an imagination in fantasy as strange and vivid as that of Stevenson in his *New Arabian Nights*, though more sombre in quality; so touched, indeed, with the contagion of horror akin to madness that one instinctively wondered if the author of 'The Fall of the House of Usher' were reincarnate in this new disciple of 'The Grotesque and Arabesque'. (Sharp 1897, 72)

Cecil's analysis of what he identifies as four differentia between Poe's 'arabesques' (or 'Arabian Tales') and his 'grotesques' are worth exploring in detail for the light they shed on the subsequent tradition they establish. Cecil cites as the 'most obvious' predicate of the Arabian Tale 'the one certified by the name Entertainments', a 'designation which acknowledges that the primary purpose of fiction is to entertain' rather than impart 'a possible moral' (a commitment also valorized by John Buchan: see Chap. 4) (Cecil 1966, 63). Cecil's definition of what constitutes entertainment is a broad one and includes the excitation of 'wonder, or terror, or laughter' (63). An entertainment along these lines also 'might transport one beyond the bounds of the known world as in the story of Sinbad' (63). This dovetails with both the 1890s weird tale's function as short form published in periodicals, whose principal function was profitable entertainment rather than the moral didacticism of the Mudie-controlled three-decker, and also

---

[11] William Sharp (1855–1905) 'maintained a kind of literary split personality, writing sober critical works and poetry under his own name while producing wild tales and fantasies under the female pseudonym Fiona MacLeod' (Joshi 1999, vi).

its frequent engagement with the depiction of liminal spaces at the borderlands of the quotidian.

Cecil identifies a 'characteristic narrative point of view' as being the 'second distinguishing feature of the Arabian tales': 'most [...] are in the first person, told by casually identified narrators' (63). Feddersen posits the same narrative strategy as being a defining characteristic emergent in the early development of the short story, arguing that when 'Washington Irving was transplanting German folktales into the new American soil [... he also ...] moved the folktale into a particular mode of telling in which the dramatized narrator becomes a subjective presence—a particular consciousness through which the tale filters' (Feddersen 2001, xvii).

John Clute suggests that by the fin de siècle, the represented narrator became the definitive narrative form, which he terms the 'Club Story' (Clute 2011, 128). The narrowest definition of the Club Story involves the represented narrator relating an allegedly autobiographical experience to his fellow club members (usually male), either precipitated by something raised in preceding general discussion which triggers a specific memory; to fulfil the expectation of the auditors (who may regularly gather for that specific purpose); or offered by way of simple entertainment to ameliorate an otherwise dull evening. Examples in weird fiction include the 'Jorkens' stories of Lord Dunsany, some of John Buchan's 'Runegates Club' stories, and William Hope Hodgson's 'Carnacki' stories. A typical example is F. Marion Crawford's 'The Upper Berth' (1894) which begins thus:

> Somebody asked for the cigars. We had talked long, and the conversation was beginning to languish; the tobacco smoke had got into the heavy curtains, the wine had got into those brains which were liable to become heavy, and it was already perfectly evident that, unless somebody did something to rouse our oppressed spirits, the meeting would soon come to its natural conclusion, and we, the guests, would speedily go home to bed, and most certainly to sleep. (Crawford 2008, 43)

Before the story is related an atmosphere of contemplative expectation is usually established, and the quotidian concerns of the audience are suspended for the duration of the narrative. The distance placed between the actual reader and the embedded story by the represented narrator further facilitates a rationalizable suspension of disbelief in the face of the unusual or supernatural events being recounted: we are hearing a story the veracity of which we are free to question, rather than immersing ourselves in a mimetic fiction which we are implicitly asked to accept as credible.

Clute cites *The Thousand and One Nights* as one of the 'precursor versions' of the Club Story, and argues that the Club Story 'flourished for half a century or so after Robert Louis Stevenson published *New Arabian Nights*' (Clute 2011, 128). He also implicitly acknowledges one of its key functions as entertainment by observing that the Club Story became 'more and more popular as new magazines like the *Strand* found that the form attracted a continuing readership' (128). The Club Story

> is a tale or tales that the reader is to imagine being recounted orally to a group of listeners foregathered in a venue safe from interruption. Its structure is normally twofold: there is a tale told, and encompassing that there is a frame which introduces the teller of the tale—who may well claim to have himself lived the story he's telling—along with its auditors and the venue (which need not literally be a club). At its most primitive, the Club Story usefully frames Tall Tales in a way that eases our suspension of disbelief during the duration of the telling [...] but then surrender[s] the tale to the judgement of the world once it has been heard. At all levels of sophistication, the Club Story form enforces our understanding that *a tale has been told*. (129)

As well as explicitly linking the Club Story to *The Thousand and One Nights*, Clute argues that the 1890s produced four exemplars of the Club Story, also claiming that they are 'the four greatest novellas published during that period' (129): Wells's *The Time Machine* (1895), James's 'The Turn of the Screw' (1898), Conrad's *Heart of Darkness* (1899), and Machen's 'The Great God Pan' (1894). The latter he describes as a 'recomplicated example of the form'—if he considered it of equal worth to 'Pan', Clute might have as appositely chosen *The Three Impostors*, the eponymous 'Impostors' of which explicitly perform the role of the 'teller of tall tales', thereby considerably increasing the readers' uncertainly over not only the content of the tales themselves, but also over the implications their imposture has for how we are to understand the framing narrative (129).

Stevenson had performed this same sleight of hand before Machen in *The New Arabian Nights* (1882) and, especially, in *More New Arabian Nights: The Dynamiter* (1885) (co-authored with his wife, Fanny Van de Grift Stevenson), where the ingénue terrorist Clara Luxmore adopts various aliases with which to manipulate the male protagonists into assisting her in a sequence of nefarious plots and schemes under the misapprehension that they are being chivalrous. Although Machen owes a huge debt to the omniferous universe conjured up by Stevenson, the latter's embedded stories all avoid supernatural tropes, and Machen therefore considerably ups the ante with the weird incursions and irruptions of the constituent 'novels' of *The Three Impostors*. Another difference is that Stevenson resolves his framing narrative. Stevenson's imposter Luxmore ultimately discards her masks and contritely abandons her political activism and narrative agency for marriage:

> 'What? Are you married?' cried Somerset.
> 'Oh yes,' said Harry, 'quite a long time: a month at least.'
> 'Money?' asked Challoner.
> 'That's the worst of it,' Desborough admitted. 'We are deadly hard up. But [...] Mr Godall is going to do something for us. That is what brings us here.'
> 'Who was Mrs Desborough?' said Challoner, in the tone of a man of society.
> 'She was a Miss Luxmore,' returned Harry. 'You fellows will be sure to like her, for she is much cleverer than I. She tells wonderful stories, too; better than a book.'
> And just then the door opened, and Mrs Desborough entered. Somerset cried out aloud to recognize the young lady of the Superfluous Mansion, and Challoner fell back a step and dropped his cigar as he beheld the sorceress of Chelsea. (Robert Louis Stevenson and Stevenson 1885, 201)

Luxmore, who in some ways anticipates the mercurial fin-de-siècle 'New Woman', is thus tamed and readmitted into patriarchal society, voluntarily resubmitting to male control. In distinct contrast, Machen's *The Three Impostors* ends in failure, fire, and gore, with the three titular antagonists unaccounted for and the status of their testimonies still far from certain.

It should also be acknowledged, however, that in many instances the employment of variations of the framed narrative or Club Story form is also simply a convenient way of repackaging periodical material for potentially quick and easy republication in book form. This was certainly the case with Stevenson's *New Arabian Nights* (the constituent stories of which were previously published in magazines between 1877 and 1880) and also Machen's *The Three Impostors*, the framing narrative of which was composed specifically to create a rationale for connecting the constituent 'novels', only one of which—'The Novel of the Black Seal'—was an original composition, written to replace an earlier, unpublished werewolf story that Machen felt at the last minute to be subpar (Gawsworth 2013, 127). It is perhaps worth noting that, as with the first chapter of 'The Great God Pan', here is an explicit example of Machen rejecting a traditional supernatural trope—concerning a 'benevolent city man' who 'at the full moon, turned into a werewolf'—for a more contemporary theme:

> The theory of ectoplasm at the time was attracting scientists—particularly Sir Oliver Lodge—and using it Machen created a weird story which he added to [*The Three Impostors*]. (127)

It is perhaps not too extravagant a speculation to suggest that had Machen settled for the original werewolf tale, and not replaced it instead with 'The Novel of the Black Seal', his subsequent influence and reputation would not approach what it is. The latter tale, which introduces Machen's theme of the survival of a prehuman atavistic race in the Welsh mountains and elaborates on the notion of hybridity and mutation only hinted at by traditional fairy lore previously explored in 'Pan', exerted a considerable influence not only on H. P. Lovecraft but his 'circle' of *Weird Tales* writers and subsequently much twentieth-century horror fiction and weird fiction. The basic iteration of the Club Story motif, however, had become so ubiquitous by 1924 that Lovecraft was criticizing the overuse of 'the clubroom with well-groomed men around the fire' in the pages of *Weird Tales* as 'hackneyed stuff' (Machin 2015).

The contingency of portmanteau works like Machen's *The Three Impostors* doesn't devalue the interesting new narrative and formal contortions thrown up by these arguably *ad hoc* rather than artistically contrived publishing strategies. In fact, *The Thousand and One Nights* is itself very much a portmanteau compendium of traditional folklore: 'a hybrid, formed through cross-fertilization over time between Europe, Asia, and the Middle East' given an artificial coherence by imposition of the metastructure of the Scheherazade framing narrative (Warner 2012, 20). The expediency of the framing narrative in giving structure to disparate shorter narratives is also to be found in canonical works like Boccaccio's *The Decameron* and Chaucer's *Canterbury Tales,* and perhaps reaches its most complicated and dazzlingly sophisticated expression in Potocki's *The*

Manuscript Found in Saragossa (pub. 1847, written ca. 1790–1815). However, this latter 'novel of frames' also contains stories which were initially printed separately in various contexts before the whole was posthumously published (Maclean 1995, xiii–xiv). It has also been plundered by subsequent anthologizers: for example, the episode titled 'The Story of the Demoniac Pacheco' is used by Italo Calvino to open his anthology *Fantastic Tales* (1997). Considered by Potocki to be a 'Gothic novel "*à la* Radcliffe"', the tortuous hazing and repeated disorientation of the main protagonist, Van Woden, in the face of horrors and wonders of consistently unresolved ontological status (including hallucinations, dreams, antagonistic human manipulation and misdirection, and the genuinely supernatural) goes someway beyond Radcliffe's rather more straightforward 'explained supernatural' (xiv). Introducing the tale, Calvino describes Potocki as 'an ideal prelude to the century of Hoffmann and Poe' (Calvino 2001, 3). As well as tales of 'the macabre, sinister, ghastly, and horrific', *Manuscript Found in Saragossa* also makes by turns ludic and troubling use of the occidental encounter with the orient, its Spain representing a sort of liminal imaginative space between these two mutually fascinated and suspicious cultures (Maclean 1995, xiv).

The third 'distinguishing feature' of the Arabian Tale identified by Cecil is 'their characteristic Oriental view of man and his world' (Cecil 1966, 64). The represented narrator 'postulates an omniferous universe' within which the 'supernatural, ordinarily hidden from us, might at any moment crowd miraculously over into the sphere of the senses' (64). Lovecraft's later definition of the weird tale as one which evokes 'outer, unknown forces' threatening the 'fixed laws of nature' which 'are our only safeguard against [...] the daemons of unplumbed space' is a commensurable (albeit specifically more horrific) postulation of this same 'omniferous universe' (Lovecraft 1985, 426). Cecil usefully links this notion of irruption into another facet of the 'Oriental view of man and his world', the idea that

> [the] charted segment of the earth we inhabit is surrounded by vast unexplored realms differing in kind as well as in degree from the narrow world we know. Out yonder one might expect to find in substantial fact all of the strange, wonderful, terrible figments of man's wildest imaginings. (Cecil 1966, 64)

An alternative to, or consequence of, the (usually supernatural) incursions into the quotidian is the journey beyond the threshold of the known and into weird, unpredictable topographies beyond. An example of the former might be any number of Victorian ghost stories, as well as the weirder irruptions to be found in Machen's work. The fiction of Kipling, Haggard, and Lord Dunsany provide numerous examples of the latter. As indicated by Clute, this topos isn't exclusive to weird fiction, and Conrad's *Heart of Darkness* not only has an explicit concern with Marlowe's transgression into an area of the world not shaded pink on the map, but within the plot anticipates this exploration of the unknown with ominous irruptions into the familiar (for example, the European city in which Marlowe receives his commission is presented as a sinister 'whited sepulchre' (Conrad 1899, 199)). By including the latter story in his list of exemplar Club Stories, Clute perhaps implies that the novella's place in the context of imaginative fiction (or adventure romance) is underexplored.

Cecil's fourth defining characteristic of the Arabian Tale is one that dovetails nearly with my discussion in the Introduction of the original application of the word 'weird'. He observes that the 'world of the Arabian tales is dominated by fate rather than by reason'. In support of this assertion, he quotes the following lines from one of the voyages of Sinbad:

> 'I have made seven voyages,' said Sinbad, 'by each of which hangeth a marvelous tale, such as confoundeth the reason, and all this came to pass by doom of fortune and fate; for from what destiny doth write there is neither refuge nor flight.' (Winterich 1955, I:98)

The neatness with which these four 'generic characteristics' of the arabesque tale dovetail with weird fiction is, considering Poe's generative position in the mode, far from coincidental.

In the above discussion of the arabesque—in terms of both literary form and its wider valences—I have already alluded to Machen and his work. I will now turn to a fuller discussion of Machen (the fourth of Stableford's 'intensely lurid products of English Decadence'), and what his work and reputation can reveal about weird fiction.

Arthur Machen and the Weird Connoisseurs

If Stenbock and Gilchrist are genuinely obscure, minor writers of the 1890s (Shiel less so thanks to his wider genre legacies), Arthur Machen occupies the more complicated position of still being frequently discussed as a 'lost' writer whose work is hard to obtain, while never having been more accessible. In the following section I will first make an argument that contrary to the regularly posited notion of Machen as a 'lost' writer, this narrative has been accorded to him in an intertextual, semi-fictional, and ideated process of mythologization of his life and work, where the connoisseur's privileging of rarity manifests itself in an interest in perpetuating such myths (consciously or no) and therefore maintaining that part of Machen's value that lies in his alleged obscurity. In this analysis I will draw from Bourdieu's concept of cultural distinction in an attempt to understand how his work has been variously de- and revalorized both within his own lifetime and posthumously.

It is problematic to argue convincingly that Machen ever was or is a 'lost writer', although some commentators insist on positioning him as such, citing the alleged difficulty of accessing his work or simply arguing that he is 'little read': the 'forgotten father of weird fiction'.[12] Within recent years, widely available publications include the Creation edition of 'The Great God Pan' (1993, and sold through the Virgin Megastore chain), an Everyman edition of *The Three Impostors* (1995), the inclusion of 'The Great God Pan' in the Oxford World Classics anthology *Late Victorian Gothic Tales* (2005), a Dover omnibus of 'The Great God Pan' and *The Hill of Dreams* (2006), the Library of Wales editions of *The Great God Pan* (2010, a collection) and *The Hill of Dreams* (2010), and the Penguin Classics collection *The White People and Other Weird Stories* published in 2011 (Machen 1993, 1995, 2005, 2006, 2010, 2011a, b). At the time of writing, a new Oxford World Classics collection has just been published (Machen 2018). From 1998, in order to access rarities and other ephemera without recourse to the archive, one could join the Friends of Arthur Machen and receive its journal *Faunus*, which reprints such material on a biannual basis. In 2013, a Delphi Masterworks eBook of Machen's complete works (including collected correspondence and two volumes of autobiography) became available for £1.99, while digital archive sources such as Project Gutenberg and The Internet Archive have also opened up a considerable quantity of material from his long life in letters.

Beyond publishing, in 2012 Machen featured in a British Library exhibition '*Writing Britain*: Wastelands to Wonderlands' and was the subject of an accompanying souvenir postcard. In 2011, several Machen-themed walks were organized under the auspices of the Museum of London. As

---

[12] 'BBC Radio 3—Night Waves, Shame', *BBC* http://www.bbc.co.uk/programmes/b018ssnp [accessed 15 January 2014]; Damien G. Walter, 'Machen Is the Forgotten Father of Weird Fiction', *Guardian* http://www.theguardian.com/books/booksblog/2009/sep/29/arthur-Machen-tartarus-press [accessed 22 January 2014].

mentioned previously, his writing is promoted by internationally recognized mainstream cultural figures like Guillermo del Toro and Stephen King, while more high-brow approval has been bestowed upon Machen from figures including, and as diverse as, writer and film maker Iain Sinclair, philosopher and commentator John Gray, comedian and writer Stewart Lee, and the former Archbishop of Canterbury Reverend Rowan Williams (Sinclair 2013; Gray 2013a, b; "BBC Four—The Review Show, 04/11/2011, Stewart Lee's Bookshelf" n.d.). His impact on writers associated with the New Weird movement has been alluded to above, particularly with regard to the work of M. John Harrison. Machen is perhaps therefore only just behind Lovecraft in terms of his ubiquitous peripherality, and, paradoxically, this perceived peripherality ensures the valorization of the ongoing critical and fan-based attention given to him, as will be argued in more detail below.

Nor has this been a uniquely recent rehabilitation: Machen spent the overwhelming majority of his working life very much in the public eye—a Fleet Street regular whose name appeared in the by-lines of many national newspapers and who had been at the centre of (and inadvertently the creator of) the 'Angels of Mons' controversy of 1916 (see below). Between 1911 and 1916 he was considered to be enough of an establishment figure to become the subject of 'a minor vendetta' pursued by A. R. Orage's modernist magazine *The New Age*, precipitated by Machen's guilt by association with Lord Northcliffe through his employment at the *Evening News* (Valentine 2012, 11). The composer John Ireland dedicated his piece for piano and orchestra *Legend* to Machen, Jorge Luis Borges selected *The Three Impostors* for a list of his favourite books, as did Henry Miller with *The Hill of Dreams*. John Betjeman was unequivocally enthusiastic about his work. Even at the nadir of his literary reputation in the 1960s, Mick Jagger discussed his interest in Machen in an interview with Andy Warhol; other admirers from the field of popular music include The Fall's Mark E. Smith and Current 93's David Tibet.[13]

Machen's cultural footprint far exceeds that outlined above, and his most popular work has consistently *remained* in print, although often not in the form that Machen connoisseurs would necessarily approve of, and would even perhaps wilfully disregard: editions from the 1960s and 1970s tended to be cheap paperbacks from mass-market imprints such as Pinnacle and Panther with cover illustrations that emphasized lurid sex and violence

---

[13] These and other endorsements of Machen are detailed in Games 2007.

largely absent from the stories themselves (Machen 1963, 1975a, b). They were, however, unarguably available.

Machen's reputation as a 'lost writer' can perhaps, however, be explained by the distinction made between these trade paperback reprints and the genuinely rare second-hand volumes of work by Machen entirely unsuitable for repackaging as horror. There is an implicit value placed on works such as *The Secret Glory* (1922) and *The London Adventure* (1924) by emphasizing the rarity of these books and ignoring the ready availability of Panther's two-volume *Tales of Horror and the Supernatural*, or, more recently, Flame Tree Publishing's budget collection *The Three Impostors and Other Creepy Stories* (2014). Most privileged by rarity is the poem *Eleusinia*, a self-published piece of juvenilia of which just one copy out of the original 100 is known to exist, held in the Beinecke Rare Book and Manuscript Library at Yale University, a second-generation copy based on this one being held at Newport Library, Wales:

> [*Eleusinia*] has been the subject of bibliomaniacal fascination ever since the 1920s, when American and British collectors went to great lengths in hunting it. This appeal has spilled over into fiction, with Peter Vincent's story 'Completion' recounting the experiences of one collector's quest to secure a copy of *Eleusinia*, while Mark Samuels vividly describes in 'The Man Who Collected Machen' a sinister collector who has a copy but is not satisfied. (Games 2013, 29)

While acknowledging that there has been a process of 'fetishization of the books because they were missing', Stewart Lee has argued that Machen's mainstreaming is problematic for a writer who should properly remain located in the margins, also speculating that new readers drawn to the Penguin Classics edition by its endorsement from del Toro and '1970s-heavy-metal-album-cover satyr' might be disappointed with gently oblique and subtle stories such as *A Fragment of Life*', replete as it is with the mundane detail of the suburban lives of its protagonists ("BBC Radio 3—Night Waves, Shame" 2012). This resonates with the—perhaps extreme—response of one J. H. Hobbs of a century earlier, detailed in a 1916 letter to the *Academy*; Hobbs felt that this story, then recently anthologized in *The House of Souls* (1906), was so contaminated by its association with Machen's more horrific texts that he 'had taken the liberty of separating "A Fragment of Life" from its companions and binding it up by itself (in a beautiful green cover)' (Hobbs 1916). Lee's concern that the front cover of the Penguin Classics collection, like the 1960s and 1970s trade paperbacks before it, codes Machen's writing as horror, and therefore mis-sells it, carries with it an implicit yet clear distinction between the horror audience and the hypothetical reader who may more appreciate Machen's sophistication.

Although Lee is careful to avoid making any explicit value distinction between the two, it is difficult not to read one in his anxiety over Penguin's marketing strategy; there is a suggestion that Machen's writing is perhaps better suited to an audience with the appropriate 'cultural competence' to appreciate it: in other words, not the average horror fan (Bourdieu 1984, 2). This distinction can be parsed through what Bourdieu has described as the operation of sociological codes by which hierarchies of 'cultural nobility' and cultural 'consecration' are recognized and perpetuated, a process which runs contrary to the traditional notion of the 'pure gaze' mentioned earlier (2–3). McDonald, applying Bourdieu's sociological ideas to the literary field of the fin de siècle, bifurcates that field into two intersecting 'communication circuits': firstly, that of mercantile and business practice, and, secondly, that of cultural capital: the social mechanism through which artistic legitimacy is conferred or withheld. Those operating in the latter circuit measure

> value primarily, if not exclusively, in aesthetic terms; they concern themselves chiefly with the particular demands, traditions, and excellences of their craft; they respect only the opinion of peers or accredited connoisseurs and critics; and they deem legitimate only those rewards, like peer recognition, which affect one's status within the field itself. (McDonald 2002, 13)

McDonald goes on to analyse the ways in which writers of the fin de siècle attempted to negotiate and reconcile these two circuits:

> Of course, in practice, things are not as neat as this idealized opposition between the purists and profiteers makes out. Between these two extremes there are any number of positions which combine the two perspectives in various degrees. (14)

I will discuss Machen's own manoeuvring in this respect below, but when considering his posthumous reputation, it is also evident that the same opposition is idealized, and that there exists an ongoing process of positioning Machen's work between the 'two extremes' negotiated by publishers, marketers, critics, academics, general readers, and connoisseurs.

In *The Pleasures of Horror* (2005) Matt Hills observes with regard to the 'multi-stranded struggles over horror and cultural distinction' that within them '"connoisseurship" emerges as *the* master trope in fan struggles against other "inauthentic" consumers and policing authorities'. For Hills, therefore, the 'pleasures of connoisseurship are thus pleasures of social and cultural distinction/belonging' (Hills 2005, 74). Hills goes on to argue that the horror connoisseur differentiates between 'disturbing' and 'disgusting' horror that privileges the former in a distinct value hierarchy:

> 'Disturbing' horror appears to be discursively constructed by these [online horror] fans as a textual aesthetics that deals with extreme and unsettling representations, without necessarily showing gore (hence it is not 'disgusting' horror) or necessarily scaring a fan. To be disturbed is hence figured as an imaginative, conceptual response; horror is once again treated here as at least partially non-affective or disembodied. It is contextualized and valorized as a 'mind genre' of aesthetic extremes and devices rather than an a priori 'body genre' that possesses any sensationalist or literalist effectivity. (82)

This distinction can also apply when differentiating the type of weird fiction valued by the connoisseur from commercial horror fiction, as demonstrated by Lee's concerns over the cover of the Penguin Classics Machen collection. Aaron Worth has made the analogous argument that if Machen is 'now widely accepted as a foundational figure—for some the foundational figure—in the development of modern horror fiction', it is 'by aristocratic consensus', the 'aristocrats' here meaning the author-connoisseurs subsequently influenced by Machen: 'Machen is, as Dante said of Aristotle, a "maestro di color che sanno"—a master of those who know, a high priest retroactively canonized by later practitioners of his weird art' (Worth 2018, xi). Worth goes on to cite Lovecraft's analysis of Machen in 'Supernatural Horror in Literature' as the first example of this canonization.

Commensurate with this argument is the fact that when the small press imprint Tartarus began republishing Machen's work in the 1990s, they did so using designs based on 1920s editions evocative of those that a book collector or connoisseur would value. Instead of using perhaps more commercially expedient cover illustrations to sell Machen as a straightforward horror writer, Tartarus presents him as a minority-interest 'lost' writer of exquisitely crafted weird fiction:

> The first proper Tartarus Press books were styled on some of the special editions published in the 1920s. Specifically, we looked at the style and design of books like Machen's large paper, limited edition *The Secret Glory*. We rarely laminate our jackets, although it does make them liable to damage. Lamination makes them too shiny and modern looking. Ideally we'd like them all to look like they were published in the 1920s. (*A Mild Case of Bibliomania* 2011)

The haptic materiality of the books produced by Tartarus is therefore an embodiment of the distinctions valued by connoisseurship, including rarity and antiquity, whose 'simple elegance of [...] presentation, hand-stitched hardback bindings jacketed in uniform cream covers with only minimal decoration, recall an earlier age when books were as rare and treasured as jewels' (Walter 2009). Tartarus has been described as presenting its books as 'rarities which remain hidden unless sought out' (ibid.). As well as Machen, the authors republished by Tartarus all accord with those values to varying degrees, M. P. Shiel, William Hope Hodgson, and Robert Aickman being good examples. The living authors published by Tartarus all either produce self-conscious homages to these predecessors or emulate the same distinctions, creating something which 'taken as a whole form a secret library, a catalogue of weird fiction from its roots in Victorian Britain through to the modern day' (ibid.). The selection of material presented by Tartarus accords with Hills's observation that

> contra many theorists' text-derived focus on horror as 'scary', cognitively challenging, or 'uncanny', [...] fans' expressed pleasures typically appear to be those of connoisseurship rather than fear, disgust, intellectual hesitation or ideological subversion/reaffirmation. (Hills 2005, 76)

That Tartarus engages in such an emphasis with conscious reflexivity is explicitly demonstrated in its three volumes of stories by Mark Valentine and John Howard that feature 'The Connoisseur—aesthetical detective extraordinaire [...] following in the footsteps of M. P. Shiel's exotic savant Prince Zaleski and Arthur Machen's Mr Dyson' ("The Collected Connoisseur by Mark Valentine and John Howard, Published by Tartarus Press" n.d.).

It should be readily acknowledged, however, that this value placed on the recondite in literature, as demonstrated in connoisseur culture, carries no presumption of a concomitant interest in preserving the obscurity of any of the works or authors concerned. One key endeavour of connoisseur culture is that of critical recovery, and challenging the canonical literary mainstream, with its traditional emphasis on social realism, by arguing for the artistic value of work that lies outside this critical remit and has therefore been marginalized. One can assume, in other words, that Tartarus republishes work by Machen because they want him to be more widely read, rather than to maintain his obscurity. Similarly, the stated objective of the Friends of Arthur Machen is to promote Machen's work; it is not a secret society dedicated to the preservation of Machen as an esoteric footnote in literary history, the preserve of initiates.

The biographical Machen and the ideated Machen bifurcated perhaps at the moment of his brief American renaissance in the 1920s, when a US audience unfamiliar with his journalism, was instead presented as a revenant of febrile 1890s decadence: 'the flower-tunicked priest of nightmare' whose 'uncompromising dedication to his craft' resulted only in 'critical disdain' and 'the philistinism of publishers' and subsequent neglect (Dobson 1988, 6). The actual Machen was rendered largely indistinguishable from Lucian Taylor, the protagonist of *The Hill of Dreams*, and mutable versions of this narrative have gained currency ever since. Collectors and bibliophiles would ignore the garish, pulpy paperback editions and enjoy the grander mythopoeic narrative of a great writer languishing in obscurity in his lifetime, who bequeathed rare bibliographical treasures to a dedicated and dogged cognoscenti: narratives that can and do slip between and obfuscate the borders of fact and fiction.

It is of course not only Machen who is now a fully accessible writer thanks to the digital archives. The digital age is a distinct and increasing threat to the continuation of Baudrillard's concept of the connoisseur as being one who values rarity above all things, at least in regard to texts rather than material books. In a recent interview, R. B. Russell of the Tartarus Press expressed disappointment that online marketplaces like abebooks.com have sounded the death knell for his type of book collecting:

> I'm not sure that I collect anything now. With Arthur Machen and Sylvia Townsend Warner I did want to have everything that they'd ever published, and I pretty much succeeded with just a few exceptions. Some of the fun went out of it when the internet came along. I could go to my computer right now and order those last few items to finalize the set, as long as I can stump up the cash. [...] I don't want to collect the books simply for the sake of collecting any more. (*A Mild Case of Bibliomania* 2011)

This sentiment is echoed in a 2010 article by Godfrey Brangham, secretary of the Friends of Arthur Machen, under the subtitle 'A Lament', concerning the death of the antiquarian book trade at the hands of the 'internet victorious' (Brangham 2012, 52). Such testimonies articulate a sense of impersonal digital transactions extinguishing the romance of haunting obscure bookshops for lost tomes, an activity celebrated as a weird adventure in its own right. For example, in his 1998 reminiscence 'Have You Any Books by Arthur Machen?', an episode in Brangham's early adventures as a Machen collector is presented in a form that intentionally resonates with a recognizable trope of weird fiction, that of the discovery of rare and baleful, occult and occulted tomes in an obscure corner of an out-of-the-way bookshop, complete with the sinister bookseller acting as a 'gatekeeper' to forbidden knowledge:

> [It was a] small, well-hidden book shop slightly off the beaten track down a narrow winding lane. [...] I plucked up enough courage to ask if he had any Arthur Machen books in stock. For a few seconds he regarded me in silence, then frowned and finally said: 'Why do you want to read Arthur Machen?' He escorted me to an alcove which was screened off from general view by a heavy embroidered curtain. With a rather theatrical sweep of his arm, he pulled back the curtain to reveal an entire shelf full of Machen books! ... With trembling hands, I picked off the shelves, in increasingly rapid succession, first editions ... [some] signed. (Brangham 1998, 45)

A similar, though fully fictionalized narrative, exaggerated for effect, is to be found in Mark Samuels's 2010 short story 'The Man Who Collected Machen'. Possibly to sidestep the problematic issue of the contemporary availability of Machen's work, the story is set in the 1960s, when the represented narrator, Lundwick (reminiscing years later) is a Machen enthusiast regularly indulging this pastime at the British Library. Lundwick takes pains to distance himself from orthodox scholarship, using language typical of the connoisseur's hostile suspicion of their enthusiasms falling into the purview of (perceived) academic sciolism and disdain for genre:

> I had long ago determined I would devote my life to literary scholarship. Not, let me emphasize, the dry-as-dust scholarship of academe, the crushing orthodoxy to be found in universities, but rather the recondite scholarship that is a journey into the unknown. I refer, chiefly, to those dead authors whose works savour of the uncanny and the marvellous, authors whose unique perspectives are beyond the self-stultifying purview of the modern critical mania for so-called realism. (Samuels 2010, 297)

Here Samuels neatly articulates the connoisseur's resistance to reductive academic readings that 'explain away' and therefore neuter the potency of weird fiction, and also the hierarchical privileging of literary realism.

Appropriately, the volumes most of interest to Lundwick are the 'fugitive items' listed in a Machen bibliography but not contained in the library. Lundwick is observed in his endeavours by one Aloysius Condor:

> [Condor] wore a crimson and paisley cravat rather than a necktie around his throat. With his natty little moustache he looked like an out of work actor. But for all his sartorial flamboyance, it was obvious that he was a very ill man. His skin was almost the colour of cigarette ash. [...] It had occurred to me that the man might be a homosexual. (339)

With his extravagant name (again, evocative of Waugh's Sebastian Flyte), 'sartorial flamboyance', unhealthiness, seediness, and possible homosexuality, Condor is an unmistakably decadent, Stenbockian figure, another embodiment of ideated degeneracy reanimating the 1890s. Condor is a bibliophile and connoisseur who owns 'hundreds of books by Machen, as well as directly-related titles by other authors'. He has entire shelves dedicated to 'varying editions of *The Secret Glory* [... and ...] *The Hill of Dreams*' and an almost limitless library (385). However, whether Condor owns the contemporaneous pulp editions of Machen's work then in print remains undiscussed. 'The Man Who Collected Machen' draws to its conclusion with the increasingly sinister Condor welcoming Lundwick into the 'Lost Club' (the title of one of Machen's earliest published short stories) and, making his excuses, the unnerved Lundwick debouches into the London streets only to discover that they have undergone a subtle 'transmutation', 'transmutation' being a Machenian trope immediately recognizable to enthusiasts. Samuels's prose becomes more and more imitative of Machen's until it is virtually indistinguishable. Employing yet another Machen motif, it is finally revealed that Lundwick is making his testimony in one of the apparently limitless 'stucco-fronted villas' that line the endless streets he has become stranded in. Presumably now forever lost in Machen's 'grey soul of London', he has become the 'Man Who Believed Machen'.

As indicated above, Samuels's story runs in suggestive parallel to the oft-blurred boundaries between Machen and his fictions: 'The Man Who Collected Machen' fictionalizes a historical tendency to wilfully blur these boundaries to add potency to the readings of the texts themselves. In the next section I shall attempt to strip away some of this obfuscation to differentiate Machen's life and work from that of his mythopoeic avatar.

Arthur Machen: Between Eleusis and New Grub Street

That the mythology surrounding Decadence promoted by Yeats and dismantled by MacLeod is still very much prevalent is evidenced by A. N. Wilson's treatment of Decadence and Machen in *The Victorians* (2002). He discusses the movement as an almost exclusively aristocratic high-art phenomenon, and alights upon Machen as a contrasting example to prove this 'rule'. Machen is presented as a middle-class aspirational Decadent; a Pooterish suburbanite outsider artist dreaming up louche and exotic fantasies amusingly at odds with his shabby-gentile anonymity (Wilson 2003, 556). Buying into the narrative of Decadence-as-upper class perhaps makes such clumsy glosses inevitable, although in this instance the misreading is considerably conflated by the author's obvious lack of acquaintance with Machen's biography, which results in his account ignoring—among several other things—Machen's shared background with many of the 'Tragic Generation' as a middle-class son of a clergyman, his initial commercial success, and acquaintance and friendship with many of the leading literary figures of the time—decadent or not—including Wilde, Jerome K. Jerome, George Egerton, and Yeats.

Wilson also propagates the common misreading of Machen's *The Hill of Dreams* as autobiographical reportage from the mid-decade. Although the Wilde trial ('the disaster' as Machen referred to it) certainly cut short in the most dramatic fashion Machen's initial commercial success, the 1890s were years of relative prosperity for him thanks to a timely inheritance (Machen 1994, 18). It was this relative freedom from commercial pressure that perhaps allowed him to move away from the more explicitly commercial Stevensonian style of *The Great God Pan* and *The Three Impostors* to the production of his far more self-consciously artistically ambitious works of the second half of the decade—*The Hill of Dreams* and *Ornaments in Jade*—which due to the post-'disaster' publishing climate, didn't see light of day until the mid-1900s. These biographical details also run contrary to the argument that the Wilde trial saw a wholesale and frantic scramble of writers tripping over themselves to distance themselves from the movement.

Machen's notebook from the period clearly demonstrates—through his preparatory sketches for ideas that would subsequently develop into *The Hill of Dreams* and *Ornaments in Jade*—that the Wilde trial had no chastening or cautionary effect of dissuading him and others from

Decadence. His record of his reading in the year 1896 also reminds us that Decadent fiction was still being published, reviewed, and read after the Wilde trial, and evidently feeding directly into Machen's own work. Titles recorded by Machen include the following:

- *The Tides Ebb Out to the Night* (1896), 'edited' by Hugh Langley, which presents itself as the 'the journal of a young man, Basil Brooke' (Machen 2016, 98). The *Athenaeum* disparagingly reviewed it as 'a diagnosis of the diseased, self-interested personality of a youth' and 'a record of the "views" and woes of a young Decadent'. (*Athenaeum* 1896b, 713)
- *A Fool and his Heart*, by F. Norreys Connell (pseudonym of the Irish novelist Conal O'Riordan, 1896), a semi-autobiographical work that 'runs from Dublin to the literary "Bohemias" of London and the Continent'. (Machen 2016, 80; *Athenaeum* 1896a, 156)
- *Aphrodite* (1896) by Pierre Louÿs, the French writer and associate of Wilde (Machen 2016, 99). The book was described by J. E. Hodder Williams in the pages of the *Speaker* as 'probably the most inexcusably revolting piece of fiction published in any country during the last ten years' (Williams 1897, 110). Williams goes on to lament that the novel 'met with enormous success, and the market is now deluged with stories of a similar nature' and adds that 'there can be no possible excuse for the author who writes, for the publisher who produces, or the bookseller who sells such nauseating pornography'.

Machen's reading and literary production in this period gives an indication that contrary to some accounts, literary Decadence was extant if not thriving in the aftermath of the Wilde trial.

Machen began his career at the unforgiving coal face of publishing portrayed so vividly by Gissing in *New Grub Street*, and struggled for several years translating, cataloguing, engaged in temporary clerical work, and producing loss-making pastiches and romances before finding some commercial success with his two contributions to the Keynotes series, *The Great God Pan and The Inmost Light* (1894)—containing the two eponymous short stories—and *The Three Impostors* (1895), a portmanteau of short stories (some previously published) contained within a framing narrative. Both are now widely regarded as being both indicative of the decade in which they were published and influential classics of weird fiction. Gissing in fact anticipates Machen's story 'The Great God Pan' in the episode in *New Grub Street* when, in an attempt to ensure some commercial success for struggling literary 'artist' Reardon, the careerist and practical Milvain suggests a suitably sensationalist title for Reardon's next project:

> 'How would this do: "The Weird Sisters"? Devilish good, eh? Suggests all sorts of things, both to the vulgar and the educated. Nothing brutally claptrap about it, you know.'
> 'But—what does it suggest to you?'
> 'Oh, witch-like, mysterious girls or women. Think it over.' (Gissing 2007, 117)

Machen's 'The Great God Pan' certainly has nothing 'brutally clap-trap' about it, but also might have appealed to the 'vulgar' as well as the 'educated', with its sensational plot hinging on a 'witch-like, mysterious' woman presented in intelligent and sophisticated modern prose.

As previously discussed, after his initial success Machen pursued a more consciously purist course with his next novel *The Hill of Dreams*, having found himself loath to 'recook that cabbage which was already boiled to death', feeling he had exhausted the Stevensonian experiments in horror of his Keynotes books (Machen 1923c, 101). As McDonald points out, the desire of writers of fiction to access the new periodical market by tailoring their work to specific commercial demands shouldn't necessarily be confused with cynical careerism, although it can certainly be differentiated from 'high art' ideals then becoming entrenched in that coterie of 'purist' writers who appointed themselves as guardians of culture in the face of the new populist mass market. As previously discussed, McDonald has also demonstrated that these purist defenders and constructors of 'high art' could not be understood as occupying identical or even similar political or social ground.

MacLeod has reinforced this point with her deconstruction of the myth of the independently wealthy, aristocratic Decadent writer who in their art and life remained unsullied by the tawdry concerns of the marketplace. It is at least partly because of these obfuscations and partly by his association with John Lane that Machen has come to be regarded as an exemplar Decadent despite his own subsequent attempts to maintain a distance from a movement to which he was never an intentional adherent, but to which he was perhaps happy to hitch his wagon when expedient. Machen's immediate successor in the Keynotes series, M. P. Shiel, held Poe in a similarly high regard to Machen (who regarded Poe as no less than 'one of the most important figures in the whole history of the fine art of letters'), although also admitted that he consciously attempted to write work in 'the modern style' to succeed in making sales (Machen 2002, 55; Matthew Phipps Shiel 1950, 20). It is impossible to guess with any specificity Shiel's own definition of this 'modern style', but it might be reasonable to equate it with McDonald's impressionistic purism, as described in some detail in his discussion of the dogged manoeuvring engaged in by Joseph Conrad to secure the 'correct' sort of literary reputation and acceptance.

When, facilitated by MacLeod, we dispense with the face-value acceptance that Decadent writing operates at a single gear—normally the rarefied meditations of the effete dandy (or its inverse cliché, the care-free penniless bohemian) shunning the vulgar herd in pursuit of 'art for art's sake'—and reintroduce the notion of commerce and market-led artistic decisions, embedded in a literary milieu of writers being excited by the artistic possibilities of 'the new style', and publishers being excited about the commercial possibilities of 'the new style', the motivations behind the balancing act that Machen performs in his two Keynotes volumes becomes clearer. We can perhaps adumbrate an ambitious young writer pitching his work at the market by employing what Lovecraft disparagingly refers to as the 'jaunty Stevenson manner', while using the *mise-en-scène* of Decadence to give the work the contemporary *frisson* and relevance that John Lane was looking to exploit commercially.

Indeed, it is difficult to imagine a stylistic epithet more incommensurate with 'true' Decadence than 'jaunty'. In the same year that John Lane published *The Great God Pan and The Inmost Light*, Hubert Crackanthorpe wrote a defence of the Decadent movement against the 'jaunty courage of ignorance' that emboldened its critics and contrasted the current zeitgeist with the 'old jaunty spirit' which can never return (Crackanthorpe 1894, 10). Similarly, Shiel, who subsequently never expressed any interest in what is now defined as Decadence, and instead (like Machen) identified with canonical and far less controversial writers of fiction and nonfiction (typically Dickens, Shakespeare, Cervantes, Carlyle, and Johnson), was happy to approximate 'the new style' in his work to secure initial publication, while at the same time not holding it in particular regard, implying an osmotic process rather than an active one. Despite his comparably conservative taste in literature, Machen was also an enthusiastic consumer of popular magazines, reminiscing in his memoirs about spending evenings 'with a bound volume of *Chambers's Journal*, *All the Year Round*, *Cornhill* [where he would likely have first encountered Stevenson's short fiction], or *The Welcome Guest*', and describing these magazines as 'always a great resource', presumably for his own writing (Machen 1923c, 35). Not all English writers associated with Decadence, therefore, were 'still obviously learning from their French masters' (Thornton 1980, 20).

That some of those published in the Keynotes series were ignorant of any explicit agenda of presenting the reading public with a construct of British Decadence is evidenced by Machen's suggestion, in a letter to John Lane of November 1895, that he consider M. R. James for a book in the series: 'Have you seen "The Scrap Book of Canon Alberic" in the *National Review* by M. R. James? He should write a 'Keynotes' (Brangham 2007, 14). It is difficult to imagine a figure more challenging to position as a Decadent than the fustian and donnish M. R. James. Machen's suggestion in this respect implies that he saw the Keynotes series as a venue for *risqué* writing of a generally 'unhealthy' kind rather than of that having a specifically Decadent influence. As previously suggested, Machen's own commensurability with Decadence is arguably based largely on the influence of Poe and even Stevenson, both of whom influenced (most notably the former) the course of French literature in the second half of the nineteenth century. Machen's 'Decadence' was a manifestation of a shared inheritance of Poe rather than a direct one imbibed from the heady cup of French Symbolism. That the latter assumption is incorrect is indicated by a footnote in a eulogizing pamphlet on Machen's work titled *Arthur Machen: A Novelist of Ecstasy and Sin* (1918), in which its author Vincent Starrett retracts the assertion made within the text of a Baudelarian influence on Machen's writing, having been corrected by Machen himself: 'Mr. Machen writes me that I am in error. "I never read a line of Baudelaire," he says, "but I have read deeply in Poe"', from whom (Machen goes on to say) he believes Baudelaire largely derives (Starrett 1918, 19).

Reflecting on the 1890s in a piece written for the Christmas 1936 edition of the *Radio Times*, Holbrook Jackson took pains to disentangle that decade from Decadence, and *vice versa*:

> George Moore, A. E. Housman, W. B. Yeats, H. G. Wells, Israel Zangwill, Joseph Conrad, George Gissing, Arthur Machen, Alice Meynell, Bernard Shaw, and Rudyard Kipling [...] all of whom belonged to the decade but not to what is called decadence. All the originality of the decade was not decadent any more than all that was called decadent was disastrous. (Jackson 1913, 5)

In Machen's work of this period the literary tensions of the age are arguably perceptible in the hesitancy or equipoise of his writing, which could fairly be argued to be evidence of a lack of conviction as to which of the prevailing and conflicting streams of literary culture he should plunge into, instead tentatively dipping his toes into several to see which is the most comfortable. Perhaps a fairer summation, however, is that *The Three Impostors* is rather the product of the irreconcilable oppositions in the wider literary discourses of literature at the time, and keenly felt commercial demands to be both subversive and popular—a balancing act demanded by circumstances evident across the field of cultural production in the 1890s.

However, accommodating commercial concerns in stylistic choices shouldn't be confused with emotional and intellectual disconnect from one's work. The desire of writers of fiction to access the new periodical market by tailoring their work to specific commercial demands doesn't necessitate any cynical careerism, although it can certainly be differentiated from ideals then becoming entrenched in that coterie of 'purist' writers who appointed themselves as guardians of culture in the face of the new populist mass market. Machen fought against changes to his text suggested by John Lane with a vigour that reveals no dispassion on his part. For example, despite a fraught correspondence, Lane eventually backed down on his request that Machen rewrite one specific word in the closing pages of *The Three Impostors*, after Machen presented a robust defence against the suggested edit:

> I have been thinking a good deal over our conversation of a fortnight ago: I mean so far as it has affected my literary reputation, performances etc. [...] I have made up my mind on the point. I do not propose to alter or soften down *The Three Impostors* in any way whatsoever. In short I am not going to be 'quiltered' in any manner whatsoever. (Brangham 2007, 10)

Godfrey Brangham identifies Machen's coining of the word 'quiltered' here as a reference to an article by Quilter previously cited by Machen in his correspondence. The article concerned, which appeared in the *Contemporary Review* in June 1895, was titled 'The Gospel of Intensity' and within it Quilter launched various broadsides against not only Machen, but many of his contemporaries associated with the Keynotes series. Quilter, who Oscar Wilde described as 'the apostle of the middle classes', certainly had previous form when it came to robust confrontation with aspects of the cultural avant-garde with which he disapproved (Wilde 1886). He had been involved in several long-running feuds since the 1870s, including one with the American-born painter James Abbott McNeill Whistler, prominent exponent of the 'art for art's sake' school anathema to Quilter, which culminated in Quilter purchasing Whistler's former home and enraging him by stripping out his painstakingly created aesthetic interior decoration (Roberts 2004).

In 'The Gospel of Intensity' Quilter argues that there exists a conspiracy of writers and critics endeavouring to debase contemporary letters with venal disregard for the ensuing damaging impact on society. As previously mentioned, Quilter even co-opts the unimpeachably respectable (despite his acquaintance with Wilde) Arthur Conan Doyle into the plot, quite incorrectly citing Doyle's 1894 novelette 'The Parasite' as a Keynotes book. The 'monstrous creations' issuing from Machen's 'diseased brain' are delineated as being not only a moral threat to the reading public, but a physical one—the loathsomeness of the texts charged with potentially having a tangibly deleterious effect on the health and sanity of the reading public (concerns resonating with R. W. Chambers's baleful creation 'The King in Yellow', also published that year). According to Quilter, Machen's stories will 'in all human probability […] do a great deal of harm' (Quilter 1895, 774)

Quilter's convictions in this respect clearly did not stay his hand from quoting great swathes of 'Pan' in constructing his case for the prosecution. He argues for a curtailment of 'blasphemy, indecency and disease' in the arts although pleads innocent of seeking to stem the tide of 'progress' (762). Quilter's disingenuousness is indicated by the following transparently oxymoronic comment about Wilde: 'It is not my business to cast a stone at him, nor have I any wish or intention to dwell upon a subject so unpleasant' (763). The argument Quilter makes is one against 'realism', 'suggestiveness', 'immorality' as represented in recent 'degrading art'. He goes so far as to claim that it is no more acceptable for an editor of a periodical to commission or publish representations of 'what is coarse and degrading' than it would be for him to 'pay men to commit acts of a like character' (766). Here, Quilter reveals his moral essentialism: 'degrading' art is 'degrading' in *actuality*; therefore the representation and the act are morally equivalent.

Given this view, it is little wonder that Quilter found Machen's 'Pan' so reprehensible. 'Pan', Quilter claims, is a 'perfectly abominable story, in which the author has spared no endeavour to suggest loathsomeness and horror which he describes as beyond the reach of words' (772). Wilfully ignoring his earlier assertion that the representation is as bad as the deed, he then quotes in full the most explicit final passages from 'The Great God Pan' (the antiheroine Helen Vaughan's protoplasmic collapse), including the line 'I saw the form waver from sex to sex'. Sexual ambiguity and polymorphous androgyny seem to be of specific interest to Quilter, as not only does he finish his attack on 'Pan' with a disparaging remark about the 'nasty little naked figure of dubious sex and humanity with which Mr Aubrey Beardsley has prefaced the story', he raises the same concern in several different contexts throughout the article. He concludes his attack on Machen by asking the following questions:

> Why should we allow a novelist to describe abortions, moral and physical, which in reality would fill us with horror and disgust? What conceivable right have two men, author and publisher, to collaborate together for the purpose of writing, printing, and distributing stories which [...] in all probability, will do a great deal of harm? [...] Why should [Machen] be allowed, for the sake of a few miserable pounds, to cast into our midst these monstrous creations of his diseased brain? (773–774)

Here Quilter squarely apportions equal responsibility on author and publisher both for the alleged enormities of the Keynotes series. Although the only immediate impact Quilter's *ad hominem* castigation of Machen seemed to have on his subsequent attitude to his work was the previously mentioned argument Machen had with John Lane over whether to include the word 'entrails' in *The Three Impostors*, the longer-term impact of Machen's 'quilterization' is harder to ascertain. Although resistant to any immediate efforts to censor his work, Machen was clearly still feeling the pressure being brought to bear on him and his contemporaries, for he was in 'great anxiety' about the possibility of being named in a suit brought against the publishers of his recent translation of Casanova's *Memoirs*, presumably on charges of obscenity (Brangham 2007, 8).

Machen's response to the implications of the new atmosphere represented by Quilter's piece was neither a knee-jerk dismissal of its commercial implications for his career or an immediate submission to Lane's demands, which might indicate a privileging of the commercial potential of his work over his interest in its artistic integrity. Instead, Machen's reaction was one of considered refusal to cooperate in the dilution of his work to ameliorate post-Wilde trial anxieties. His resolve in this was perhaps toughened by the experience of negative and frequently hostile reviews to both *The Great God Pan and the Inmost Light* and *The Three Impostors*. Machen's brief mention of the affair in his second volume of memoirs, *Things Near and Far* (1923), certainly does not exhibit any residual ill feeling on his part. He recalls that he wrote 'a temperate letter' to Quilter, not to take him to task for writing such a rancorously *ad hominem* attack, but merely to point out that, contrary to Quilter's allegation of conspiracy, Machen simply did not move in the rarefied literary circles necessary to effect such a scheme (Machen 1923c, 97). In a subsequent letter, he also noted that neither did *The Great God Pan and The Inmost Light* actually receive the overwhelmingly positive notices upon which Quilter's argument is predicated (Machen 2000, 39). Machen challenges the factual inaccuracies of which Quilter has 'no knowledge', while fully concedes Quilter's right as a critic to opine on the contents of the book itself (Machen 2000, 39).

Quilter does not clearly distinguish Machen's book from the rest of the Keynotes series thus far published, beyond including 'imaginary devilries' as one of his list of accusations alongside 'sketches of prostitution' and 'loathsome eccentricity'. As discussed above, as recently as 1968, no formal distinction was being made between Machen's weird fiction and the very different realist work of some of his Keynotes contemporaries. However, in 1907 Machen was being differentiated from 'novelists' as a writer of romances in the pages of the *Academy* by its editor, Lord Alfred Douglas, himself a prominent figure in the cultural battles of the 1890s (when he was better known as Wilde's 'Bosie'). Douglas seems sympathetic to Machen's already apparent critical neglect in his response to a correspondent who has questioned Machen's absence from an article in the previous issue discussing the country's preeminent living novelists. The correspondent, Arthur Milbank, is enthusiastic enough about Machen to put him 'at the head of all our living novelists, with the exception of Mr Meredith and Mr Hardy'. Lord Douglas responds by pleading a category error rather than questioning Milbank's judgement regarding Machen's cultural value:

> [We] would be inclined to class Mr Machen rather as a writer of romances as distinct from novels than as a novelist; and we are under the impression that Mr Machen himself would not describe himself as a novelist. As a writer of romances Mr Machen does stand high among contemporary writers, he stands, as far as we are able to judge, alone. The difference between a writer of romances and a writer of novels is a subject on which we invite correspondence. (Milbank 1907, 148–149)

Inconveniently for this thesis, the invited correspondence failed to ensue. Admittedly, a privileging of the artistic value of the novel over the romance could be read into Douglas's judgement, but the tone certainly seems to suggest a genuine admiration for Machen as a writer. The latter interpretation is also supported by the fact that Machen was at that time frequently contributing to the *Academy*, which had recently serialized his satirical critique of puritanism, *Dr. Stiggins: His Views and Principles*.[14]

Writing in 1882, Stevenson had made the distinction that 'Drama is the poetry of conduct, romance the poetry of circumstance' (R. L. Stevenson 1882, 70). This remark, at once succinct and comprehensive, and suggesting the emphasis on manners, social interaction, and social negotiations in the former and action and/or 'event' in the latter, anticipates Andrew Lang's robust defence of the romance over realism, and the increasingly muddied waters of 1890s literary discourse investigated by McDonald (I further discuss the fortunes of the romance at the fin de siècle and in the early twentieth century in Chap. 4). Machen himself continued to resist being considered as a 'novelist' into the 1930s, not simply as an expression of the wilful antiquarianism demonstrated in his employment of the term 'novel' for 'short story' or 'tale' in *The Three Impostors*, but also to claim some of the nuance of the term 'romance' for his work: 'I am no novelist. I do not like to see *The Hill of Dreams* or *The Secret Glory* discussed as novels. They are, or they are meant to be, Romances: tales of adventure of the spirit' (Machen 1988, 237). Typically of Machen, his addition here of 'of the spirit' both complicates and helps reveal the ambiguous position of his writing between the popular and the more hermetic cultural streams of his age.

As discussed above, Machen's choice of Poe as a model for potentially commercial fiction could reasonably be seen as an obvious one. Poe was a master and innovator of the new short story form and there could be few better models for an aspiring author upon which to base one's work, and his skill at imbricating content and style to a unified 'totality' of effect was more often than not predicated upon employment of the supernatural and horrific (Poe 1984, 586). Machen's reading of Poe was sufficiently close for him to take issue with the reading matter Poe chose to ascribe to Roderick Usher in 'The Fall of the House of Usher' (according to Machen,

---

[14] Arthur Machen, 'Dr. Stiggins: His Views and Principles', *Academy and Literature*, 12 October 1907, 11–14; 19 October 1907, 35–39; 26 October 1907, 60–63; 2 November 1907, 89–93; 9 November 1907, 119–23.

'one of the finest stories that has ever been written') (Machen 2002). Machen argued that the volumes that furnish Usher's bookshelf, which Poe employed as examples of Usher's 'singularly morbid' reading material, in fact only serve to reveal Poe's unfamiliarity with the works he cites beyond their suitably evocative titles. Machen observes that the content of the named volumes (for example, Pomponius Mela's *De Situ Orbis*) 'to which the hero of this weird tale was vastly addicted' was 'not in the least mysterious or awe-inspiring', and that 'for a person with a taste in occult literature, the ancient geographers would prove but dull reading' (Gawsworth 2013, 70–71).

Machen made these criticisms in 1887 correspondence in the *Walford's Antiquarian*, while employed as a clerk by the publisher George Redway at the age of 24 and yet to make any attempt at writing in the vein of Poe, which he here describes using the specific term 'weird tale'. His use of the term seems in fact to be unique to this instance, and he is perhaps employing it as an archaism: inconveniently for this thesis, Machen subsequently tends to use the phrase 'occult literature' for supernatural fiction.

Apart from his innate mystical bent, Machen's period of employment as a cataloguer of an occult library provided him with plenty of similar grist for his imaginative mill when it came to producing weird fiction. His business acumen was at least enough to see that to sell a story to a late nineteenth-century audience, the old folkloric prototypes incommensurate with the modern age were no longer adequate, hence his use of science and pseudoscience to create the inciting incident of a narrative:

> [We] must link our wonders to some scientific or pseudo-scientific fact, or basis, or method. If Stevenson had written his great masterpiece about 1590–1650, Dr Jekyll would have made a compact with the devil; in 1886 Dr Jekyll sends to the Bond Street chemists for some rare drugs. (Machen 1988, 73)

Ever consistent, Nordau identified the trend of writers presenting 'ghost-stories [...] in scientific disguise' as yet another symptom of degeneration, contrasting with Machen's own simpler explanation that it was simply a method of 'selling' an otherwise outré plot to a contemporary audience (Nordau 1895, 13).

In a reversal of this strategy, Machen's fellow Keynotes contributor Grant Allen's first foray into fiction was his presentation of a scientific argument in the form of a weird tale (briefly discussed above). However, and in sharp contrast to Allen, Machen's interest in science itself was a superficial and rebarbative one. As an essayist, he regularly lambasted scientific materialism and what he saw as one of its most pernicious cultural manifestations: literary realism. He predicated the entire thesis of *Hieroglyphics* (1902) and the larger part of his published literary criticism upon the failures he perceived in such literature, claiming by way of analogy that there was 'all the difference in the world between a landscape by Turner and the best photograph of the same scene':

> In the order of nature there were masses of earth and water and the growth of trees; on the canvas these things have become sacrament and symbol. Hence it follows that all great art is profoundly 'realist'. It is time that this word with its ancient and honourable philosophical associations should be definitely rescued from the intolerable degradation into which it has now fallen. (Machen 1908, 109–110)

Machen's use of scientific motifs has perhaps therefore been taken too much at face value in some discourses; there is little indication of any serious knowledge of, or indeed interest in, the subject on his part, and occasional slips reveal surprising levels of ignorance: for example, Machen was still claiming in 1923 that 'very early man most probably did see dragons—known to science as pterodactyls' (Machen 1923c, 79).

His hostility to science could also occasionally be extreme: 'It is monstrous that science, shown to be mad in the abstract, should presume to dictate to us in the concrete' (Machen 1924, 146). He regarded science as a 'great bully', which 'for the last sixty or seventy years […] has been bragging and blustering and pretending to know everything […] and committing the most tremendous howlers on every possible subject' (148–149). Machen's definition of science was broad enough to include 'Scripture History' and anthropology as represented by James Frazer's *The Golden Bough*. Machen dispatches the former with the observation that contemporary Biblical criticism disputed the existence of writing in the Abrahamic period 'before certain inscribed tablets were found in Tel-el Amarna' and proved otherwise, and the latter for supposing that 'the Holy Grail was a saucepan used for cooking spring cabbage', before concluding that 'it seems the province of science to give fools their meat in due season' (149–150).

Although it is clear Machen was willing to press contemporary scientific (and pseudoscientific) ideas to his own ends when in search of up-to-date material for his weird tales, such statements do not sit comfortably with the reading of Machen as a deeply engaged cogitator and interpreter of contemporary scientific discourse and accompanying neuroses surrounding evolution and degeneration. Susan Navarettte's assertion that 'Machen's notion of cultural decadence was shaped in part by his awareness of contemporary emphases in evolutionary biology, which in [... 'The Great God Pan' ...] are sensationalized' is not (as Navarette certainly concedes) a comprehensive account of his fiction and therefore leaves room for and perhaps demands other approaches to parsing his work (Navarette 1993, 101).

Machen's responses to science and specifically materialism betray an exasperation with a (to his mind) misplaced emphasis on the represented rather than the ineffable 'mystery' and 'ecstasy' accessible only through art and religion, sometimes expressed in terms explicitly disdainful of Huxley and Darwin, which—as suggested—considerably problematizes the relationship of the texts to the 'standard' fin-de-siècle degeneration debates:

> [If I declared] that I experienced [...] a delight in the spectacle of a desolate, smoking marsh, where a red sun sinks from a world of shivering reeds, I suppose I should hear that some remote ancestor of mine had found in some such place 'pterodactyls plentiful and strong on the wing'. And if I like the woods, it was because a monkey sat at the root of my family tree, and if I love an ancient garden it is because I am 'second cousin to the worm'. (Machen 1923b, 159)

Despite 'The Great God Pan' having been posited explicitly as 'an aesthetic response to Huxley's theory of protoplasm', Christopher Josiffe has argued that one of the most celebrated examples of Machen's alleged demonstrations of a kind of 'perfect storm' of fin-de-siècle anxieties (the reverse evolution and physical degeneration of the sexually predatory new woman Helen Vaughan) was actually inspired by a specific alchemical treatise Machen encountered during his tenure 'cataloguing books on magic and alchemy and the secret arts in general':

> Clearly, this is no mere decay or decomposition; rather, it is a reversion or reduction to 'first matter'. Very likely the name of Helen Vaughan was suggested by that of the alchemist Thomas Vaughan, whose *Lumen de Lumine* (held in high regard by Machen) speaks of this first matter as being slime, a 'horrible, inexpressible darkness'. (MacLeod 1998, 217; Machen 1923c, 36; Josiffe 2009, 30)

According to Herbert Silberer, anyone who 'makes a thorough study of the alchemistic literature must be struck with the religious seriousness that prevails in the writings of the more important authors' (Silberer 1971, 146), and works like Mary Ann Atwood's *A Suggestive Inquiry into the Hermetic Mystery* (1850) place a clear emphasis on the centrality of moral regeneration to the alchemical project; indeed, arguing that spiritual refinement *is* the alchemical project:

> [Far from alchemy] having its origin in the application of a mystical doctrine to physical things, physical Alchemy has been the result and by-product of the original doctrine; an after-growth and to some extent a perversion of it, an adaptation [...] to inorganic material of a principle originally applied exclusively to the spiritual nature of *man*. (Atwood 1850, 59)

Machen's erudition and interest in alchemy was informed early in life by his employment in 1885 to catalogue a library of antiquarian works on 'occultism and archaeology' for the publisher John Redway in preparation for sale (Gawsworth 2013, 57). The depth of his interest is evident from the fact that his last novel, *The Green Round* (1933) still includes various discourses on the subject, and also on Machen's suspicion of scientific materialism, five decades on (Machen 1968).

Understanding the spiritual symbolism of Helen Vaughan's protoplasmic collapse and its employment of the alchemical notion of the *prima materia* is, therefore, more commensurate with both Machen's interest not only in alchemy, but in quiddity and numinosity (and their evocation in his understanding of 'realism' of literature), and his relative ignorance of and outright hostility to science. Bearing in mind that the male protagonist of 'The Novel of the White Powder' suffers a similar climactic disintegration to that of Helen Vaughan, this interpretation of the latter's doom may also absolve Machen of occasional charges of misogyny that are made against him.

Specifically, 'The Great God Pan' has attracted several casual and uninterrogated references to 'the text's misogyny', a perhaps inevitable result of Machen's narrative technique of avoiding direct representation of suggested horrors (Smith 2012, 225). The absence of a direct representation of Helen Vaughan in the text can therefore be interpreted as a denial of female agency, although one would have to isolate her absence from the many other narrative occlusions to do so. An interesting comparator in this respect is Vernon Lee's 'Dionea', which, first published in 1890, anticipates and perhaps influenced Machen's narrative strategy with 'The Great God Pan' (Lee 1906). The story of the eponymous foundling, strongly hinted to be at least semi-divine, is related obliquely through an epistolary structure which, like 'The Great God Pan', reveals the history of Dionea and her baleful influence on the small Italian community in which she resides, without ever directly representing the character. Her motives remain inscrutable and inaccessible to the reader, intensifying the mystery central to the tale.

It would seem self-evidently ridiculous to level any accusation of misogyny against Vernon Lee for constructing the story in this manner. Machen, on the other hand, by having the audacity to cast a woman as the principle antagonist, has invited suggestions that 'The Great God Pan' should be read as a representation of late Victorian patriarchal animus against the increasing profile of the 'New Woman' in the public sphere. Consequently, whereas the protoplasmic disintegration of the male protagonist of Machen's 'The Novel of the White Powder' (published the year after 'The Great God Pan') hardly raises an eyebrow, the almost identical fate of Helen Vaughan at the end of 'Pan' is a 'grotesque snuff-murder', adduced as evidence of Machen's 'prurient misogyny' (Miéville 2009, 513). This misreading of Machen is implicitly underwritten by Joshi's insistence on parsing 'The Great God Pan' as symptomatic of Machen's 'horror of aberrant sexuality', a horror evidenced by 'The Great God Pan' (Joshi 2012, 2:362). This circular argument is in fact, as Joshi fully acknowledges, appropriated from Lovecraft's own criticisms of Machen's 'horror of sex', which arguably reveals more about Lovecraft than it does Machen.

The point is worth dwelling on since, beyond the simple expedient of correcting a misunderstanding of Machen's character in this respect, such assumptions also lead to procrustean readings that attempt to fit Machen and his work too neatly into off-the-peg fin-de-siècle critical frames. The circumstantial evidence against Machen's alleged 'horror of sex' is formidable and even insurmountable, unless one is singularly committed to a specific parsing of the finale of 'The Great God Pan' as a synecdoche for some otherwise unperceivable animus of its author, an approach criticized by Todorov. Précising Peter Penzoldt's position that 'a certain neurotic writer will project his symptoms into his work', Todorov goes on to point out that 'these tendencies are not always distinctly manifest outside their work' (Todorov 1975, 152):

No sooner has [Penzoldt] said that Machen's education explains his work than he finds himself obliged to add, 'fortunately, the man Machen was quite different from the writer Machen. ... Thus Machen lived the life of a normal man, whereas part of his work became the expression of a terrible neurosis'.

Again, we are left with a circular argument that, contrary to all other available evidence, 'The Great God Pan' demonstrates Machen's 'misogyny' simply because we are able to read it this way. Although such specious assertions serve to demonstrate the political virtue of the critic, they do a genuine disservice to the author as an individual. Machen's first wife Amy Hogg was described by Jerome K Jerome as a 'pioneer' who 'lived by herself [...] frequented restaurants [...] and had many men friends: all of which was considered very shocking in those days' (Brangham 2006, 37). Machen's second wife, the actress Dorothy Purefoy Machen, was described by A. E. Waite as an absinthe drinker and smoker who 'has no conventions and requires none' (Gilbert 2017, xxi). Dr Raymond's impatient dismissal of the relevancy of Mary's virginal status in the opening pages of 'The Great God Pan' ('That is nonsense. I assure you') could be read as the author's own attempt to remove prurience from the reader's mind from the outset (Machen 2006, 12). As an essayist, Machen dedicated a considerable amount of energy to combating puritanism wherever he found it, but particularly in letters. He began his career by translating the *Memoirs* of Casanova and the renaissance 'amatory tales' of *The Heptameron* by Marguerite, Queen of Navarre, before going on to compose his own ribald Rabelaisian fantasy *The Chronicle of Clemendy* (Casanova 1894; Valentine 1995, 19; Queen of Navarre 1886; Machen 1888). He produced *Dr Stiggins*, the above-mentioned satire and condemnation of puritanism, at around the time he completed a stint as a strolling player in the Benson Company. All in all, a peculiar career trajectory for a blushing, neurotic prude.

Approaching the climax of 'The Great God Pan' through the spagyric frame discussed above is simply more commensurate with Machen's own declared interests than with the speculative allegation of misogyny. The influence of the seventeenth-century alchemist and natural philosopher Thomas Vaughan on Machen's fiction also expresses itself through his employment of the motif of 'the veil' in order to describe the liminal barrier preventing ordinary access to the occulted quiddity of nature. In *Lumen de Lumine* (1651), Vaughan considers the 'fabric of the world' as 'a series, a link or chain, which is extended from [...] that which is beneath all apprehension to that which is above all apprehension' (Vaughan 1910, 35). He posits a hierarchy of noumenal being, inaccessible to ordinary intelligence: that which is 'beneath all degrees of sense is a certain horrible, inexpressible darkness', and that which is 'above all degree of intelligence is a certain infinite, inaccessible fire of light', the latter called by Dionysius 'Divine Obscurity' (35). Here is a metaphysical framework for much of Machen's subsequent fiction and an anticipation of his anxiety regarding his 'horrific' work: 'I translated awe, at worst awfulness, into evil; again, I say, one dreams in fire and works in clay' (Machen 1923a, 127). Machen's fiction progresses along Vaughan's 'scale', which 'doth reach from Tartarus to the First Fire, from the subternatural [sic] darkness to the supernatural fire' (36). Between these two ordinarily inaccessible realms lies the quotidian 'substance or chain [...] which we commonly call Nature' (36).

In Machen's more overtly horrific fiction, such as 'Pan', the revelation is of the adumbral numinous, the 'subternatural darkness'. In his later, visionary work, such as *The Secret Glory* (1922) and *A Fragment of Life* (1904), the encounter is with the 'Divine Obscurity'. Although the analogue isn't a perfect one (Machen often used the imagery of fire and light rather than darkness to evoke an impression of diabolic irruptions into the mundane world), his early and continuing advocacy of Vaughan, and the specific textual similarities to be found by comparing Machen's fiction with Vaughan's discourse on the 'First Matter' offer evidence of his close reading of the latter. Vaughan argues that the 'Divine Obscurity' (analogous to the cabalistic notion of 'Ain') is 'pure Deity, having no veil' and that its emanation into 'that which we commonly call Nature' is effected through the operation of 'a certain water', called the 'First Matter' (36). His description of the 'First Matter' defines it in alchemical terms as an 'animated mass [...] the union of masculine and feminine spirits', and discusses it in chemical terms as liquid Mercury.

> I conclude that the Mosaical earth was the virgin Sulpher, which is an earth without form, for it hath no determinated figure. It is a laxative, unstable, uncomposed substance of a porous, empty *crasis*, like sponge or soot. In a word I have seen it, and it is impossible to describe it. (46)

A comparable incidence of protoplasmic eruption (or perhaps irruption) can be found in 'The Novel of the Black Seal' episode in *The Three*

Impostors. In an isolated manor house in the middle of the Welsh mountains, a young country boy is suspected by an anthropologist of being the progeny of the sinister 'little folk' whose actuality gave rise to fairy lore. He displays evidence of this alleged provenance one night by producing a pseudopod from his abdomen, leaving a sticky residue on a statue on the top shelf of the Professor's office.

Although it is difficult to read the episode without immediately being struck by its apparently obvious implications of emergent sexuality in a pubescent teenager, Machen claims that it was in fact inspired by his reading of the then nascent trend in spiritualism of producing 'ectoplasm' at séances and of crediting this substance with the production of various associated phenomena:

> [Sir Oliver Lodge] advanced the striking hypothesis that the piano was played and the objects fetched from the sideboard by a kind of extension of the medium's body. I forget whether the distinguished Professor used the instance but I know that the impression conveyed to my mind was that something happened similar to the protrusion and withdrawal of a snail's horns: Eusapia's [Palladino, the Italian medium] arm became twice or thrice its usual length, performed the required feat [...] and then shrank back to normal size. (Machen 1923c, 107)

Machen goes on to describe the theory as 'in all probability [...] a pack of nonsense', but it provided him with a grotesque and striking image that could perhaps add value to the affect, and therefore success, of his story.

Machen, whose son Hilary was unequivocal in describing him as 'never anything but a High Church Tory', failed to display evidence of any doubt or anxiety in his faith over the course of his life, unless one interprets his brief dalliance with the Order of the Golden Dawn as evidence of such a crisis. One could also treat stories like 'The Great God Pan' as expressions of a sublimated fear or anxiety regarding the 'quiddity' of the universe: a negative, adumbral shadow of the 'Holy' numinous reality that formed the basis of his mysticism. Such readings raise similar problems to those involved in making the accusation of misogyny discussed above, however. However, in some respects Machen's anti-materialism was commensurate with the 'new' awareness of humanity's limited knowledge of possibly unknowable 'reality', except that instead of precipitating despair, he revelled in the 'fire and mystery'. His dogma was based on the symbolic value of the Church (especially the pre-Reformation 'Catholic' church) of making the existence of this mystery in some way intelligible, even if the mystery itself was forever ineffable. Although he disapproved of what he considered to be his friend A. E. Waite's 'Pantheism', he was sympathetic to Waite's enthusiasm for Roman Catholicism 'as a great system of symbolism', perhaps meaning that it was an aesthetically pleasing language with which to approach the quiddity of things. Machen was certainly among those who 'seize avidly on the loopholes of the materialistic system and regard each loophole found as an affirmation of man's spiritual life', but despite this he still reached a similar conclusion to the most rigorous sceptics of the age: that the world is essentially unknowable (Lester 1968, 37).

In the above chapter, I have discussed the weird fiction of Gilchrist, Stenbock, Shiel, and Machen, primarily in terms of both content and cultural history. By the close of the 1890s, Stenbock was dead, a victim of his own addictions and neuroses, and Gilchrist had largely abandoned writing in this vein and turned his attention to producing Peak District guidebooks. Shiel and Machen continued prolific careers, both diversifying and undergoing mixed critical and commercial fortunes until their deaths in the mid-1940s. While these British exponents largely abandoned the stylistic excesses of Decadence with the close of the 1890s, that decade's influence persisted on the other side of the Atlantic and its literary productions were to be enthusiastically absorbed and curated by the American pulp magazines of the 1920s and 1930s, a subject I will return to in Chap. 5.

In this chapter I have focused on minor writers who have nevertheless persisted as cult figures thanks to their influence on wider genre literature of the twentieth and twenty-first centuries. In the next I will take a different approach, looking instead at a successful and mainstream presence who nevertheless regularly turned his hand to weird fiction, John Buchan, and will attempt to glean further understanding of weird fiction by investigating why he did so.

Works Cited

"A List of New Books & Announcements of Methuen and Company Publishers". 1893. In. Methuen.
A Mild Case of Bibliomania. 2011. https://youtu.be/7h7-aIZRhhs.
Academy. 1899. Mr. R Murray Gilchrist, December 9.

Adlard, John. 1969. *Stenbock, Yeats and the Nineties*. London: Cecil & Amelia Woolf.
Aickman, Robert. 1967. Introduction. In *The 4th Fontana Book of Great Ghost Stories*, 7–10. Glasgow: Fontana.
Athenaeum. 1894. English Literature in 1893, January 6.
———. 1896a. The Fool and His Heart, August 1.
———. 1896b. The Tides Ebb Out to the Night, November 21.
Atwood, Mary Anne. 1850. *A Suggestive Inquiry into the Hermetic Mystery*. London: Trelawney Saunders.
Balfour, Arthur James. 1908. *Decadence*. Cambridge: Cambridge University Press.
Baudrillard, Jean. 1994. The System of Collecting. In *The Cultures of Collecting*, ed. John Elsner and Roger Cardinal, Trans. Roger Cardinal, 7–24. London: Reaktion.
BBC Four—The Review Show, 04/11/2011, Stewart Lee's Bookshelf. n.d. http://www.bbc.co.uk/programmes/p00lmyhd. Accessed 21 Jan 2014.
BBC Radio 3 — Night Waves, Shame. 2012. *BBC*. http://www.bbc.co.uk/programmes/b018ssnp. Accessed 15 Jan 2014.
Beerbohm, Max. 1919. Enoch Soames. In *Seven Men*, 3–48. London: William Heinemann.
Billings, Harold. 2010. *M. P. Shiel: The Middle Years*. Austin: Roger Beacham.
Bourdieu, Pierre. 1984. *Distinction: A Social Critique of the Judgement of Taste*. Trans. Richard Nice. Cambridge: Harvard.
Brangham, Godfrey. 1998. Have You Any Books by Arthur Machen? *Faunus: The Journal of the Friends of Arthur Machen*, Spring.
———. 2006. Fate and the Shepherdess. *Faunus: The Journal of the Friends of Arthur Machen*, Summer.
———. 2007. John Lane and Arthur Machen: A Correspondence. *Faunus: The Journal of the Friends of Arthur Machen*, Summer.
———. 2012. Rambling After Machen. *Faunus: The Journal of the Friends of Arthur Machen*, Autumn.
Bristow, Joseph, ed. 2005. *The Fin-de-Siècle Poem: English Literary Culture and the 1890s*. Athens: Ohio University Press.
Bush, Laurence. 2010. The Weird Majesty of R. Murray Gilchrist. *Weird Fiction Review* 1: 32–37.
Caine, Hall. 1890. The New Watchwords of Fiction. *Contemporary Review*, April.
Calvino, Italo. 2001. *Fantastic Tales*. London: Penguin.
Carey, John. 1992. *The Intellectuals and the Masses*. London: Faber.
Casanova, Jacques. 1894. *The Memoirs of Casanova*. Trans. Arthur Machen. 12 vols. London: Privately Printed.
Cecil, L. Moffitt. 1966. Poe's 'Arabesque. *Comparative Literature* 18 (1): 55–70. https://doi.org/10.2307/1769598.

Clute, John. 2006. *The Darkening Garden: A Short Lexicon of Horror*. Cauheegan: Payseur & Schmidt.
———. 2011. *Pardon This Intrusion: Fantastika in the World Storm*. Essex: Beccon.
Conrad, Joseph. 1899. The Heart of Darkness. *Blackwood's Edinburgh Magazine*, February.
Costelloe, Mary. 1980. *Christmas with Count Stenbock*. Ed. John Adlard. London: Enitharmon.
Count Stenbock | Home. n.d. http://www.countstenbock.com/. Accessed 6 Oct 2013.
Crackanthorpe, Hubert. 1894. Reticence in Literature Some Roundabout Remarks. *Yellow Book*, July.
Crawford, F. Marion. 2008. The Upper Berth. In *The Witch of Prague & Other Tales*, 43–61. Ware: Wordsworth.
D'Arch Smith, Timothy. 1970. *Love in Earnest: Some Notes on the Lives and Writings of English Uranian Poets from 1889 to 1930*. London: Routledge.
De Quincey, Thomas. 1821. Confessions of an English Opium-Eater: Being an Extract from the Life of a Scholar. *London Magazine*, October.
Dobson, Roger. 1988. Preface. In *Arthur Machen: Selected Letters*, ed. Roger Dobson, Godfrey Brangham, and R.A. Gilbert, 5–8. Wellingborough: Aquarian.
Eng, Steve. 1981. Supernatural Verse in English. In *Horror Literature: A Core Collection and Reference Guide*, 401–452. New York/London: Bowker.
Eric Stenbock. 2013. *Wikipedia, the Free Encyclopedia*. http://en.wikipedia.org/w/index.php?title=Eric_Stenbock&oldid=577730776.
Feddersen, R.C. 2001. Introduction: A Glance at the History of the Short Story in English. In *A Reader's Companion to the Short Story in English*, xv–xxxiv. Chicago: Fitzroy Dearborn.
Fiction. 1896. *Speaker* 14 (December): 701–702.
Frank, Frederick S. 1997. *The Poe Encyclopedia*. Westport: Greenwood Publishing Group.
Frayling, Christopher. 2014. *The Yellow Peril: Dr Fu Manchu & The Rise of Chinaphobia*. London: Thames & Hudson.
Freeman, Nicholas. 2014. *1895: Drama, Disaster and Disgrace in Late Victorian Britain*. Edinburgh: Edinburgh University Press.
Games, Gwilym, ed. 2007. *Machenology: Tributes to the Master of Mysteries*. Croydon: The Friends of Arthur Machen.
———. 2013. 'Before the Greyness of the World Had Come': The Origins and Significance of Eleusinia. In *Eleusinia*, ed. Jonathan Preece, 29–34. Croydon: The Friends of Arthur Machen.
Gawsworth, John. 2013. *The Life of Arthur Machen*. Leyburn: Tartarus.

Gilbert, R.A. 2017. Introduction. In *The House of the Hidden Light*, ed. Arthur Machen and A.E. Waite, v–xxv. Leyburn: Tartarus.
Gilchrist, R. Murray. 2006. *A Night on the Moor & Other Tales of Dread*. Ware: Wordsworth.
Gissing, George. 2007. *New Grub Street*, ed. Stephen Arata. Peterborough: Broadview.
Glasgow Herald. 1895. Literature, January 17.
Gray, John. 2013a. *BBC News*—A Point of View: The Doors of Perception. http://www.bbc.co.uk/news/magazine-22648328. Accessed 21 Jan 2014.
———. 2013b. *The Kefahuchi Tract Trilogy: A Future Without Nostalgia*. http://www.newstatesman.com/2013/10/future-without-nostalgia. Accessed 4 Dec 2013.
Gross, John. 1973. *The Rise and Fall of the Man of Letters*. London: Penguin.
Guardian. 2000. Father Brocard Sewell, April 4, sec. News. http://www.theguardian.com/news/2000/apr/04/guardianobituaries.
Harms, Daniel. 2003. *The Encyclopedia Cthulhiana: A Guide to Lovecraftian Horror*. Oakland: Chaosium.
Hills, Matt. 2005. *The Pleasures of Horror*. London: Continuum.
Hobbs, J.H. 1916. Zangwill and Machen. *Academy and Literature*, September 1.
Hueffer, Francis, ed. 1878. Current Literature and Current Criticism. *New Quarterly* 10 (20): 432–460.
Jackson, Holbrook. 1913. *The Eighteen Nineties: A Review of Art and Ideas at the Close of the Nineteenth Century*. London: Grant Richards.
Joshi, S.T. 1999. Introduction. In *Great Weird Tales*, v–xi. Mineola: Dover.
———. 2012. *Unutterable Horror: A History of Supernatural Fiction*. Vol. 2. Hornsea: PS Publishing.
Josiffe, Christopher. 2009. Trafficking with Elementals: Kenneth Grant and Arthur Machen. *Faunus: The Journal of the Friends of Arthur Machen* 20: 25–36.
King, Francis. 2004. *Megatherion: The Magical World of Aleister Crowley*. London: Creation Books.
Laird, Hilary. 2005. The Death of the Author by Suicide: Fin-de-Siècle Poets and the Construction of Identity. In *The Fin-de-Siècle Poem: English Literary Culture and the 1890s*, ed. Joseph Bristow, 69–100. Athens: Ohio University Press.
Lamb, Hugh. 1977. *Victorian Nightmares*. New York: Taplinger.
Lee, Vernon. 1906. Dionea. In *Hauntings; Fantastic Stories*, 61–103. London: John Lane.
Lester, John Ashby. 1968. *Journey Through Despair, 1880–1914: Transformations in British Literary Culture*. Princeton: Princeton University Press.
Little, Jas Stanley. 1895. New Novels. *Academy*, April 13.

Lorre, Christine. 2006. The Canon as Dialectical Process: A Study of Three Recent Chinese American Narratives. *Revue Française d'études Américaines* 110 (December): 78–96.

Lovecraft, H.P. 1985. Supernatural Horror in Literature. In *Dagon and Other Macabre Tales*, 421–512. London: Panther.

———. 2011. A History of the Necronomicon. In *Eldritch Tales*, 1–3. London: Gollancz.

Luckhurst, Roger, ed. 2005. Introduction. In *Late Victorian Gothic Tales*. Oxford: Oxford University Press.

———. 2012. *The Mummy's Curse*. Oxford: Oxford University Press.

Machen, Arthur. 1888. *The Chronicle of Clemendy*. London: Carbonek.

———. 1907a. Dr. Stiggins: His Views and Principles. *Academy and Literature*, October 12.

———. 1907b. Dr. Stiggins: His Views and Principles. *Academy and Literature*, October 19.

———. 1907c. Dr. Stiggins: His Views and Principles. *Academy and Literature*, October 26.

———. 1907d. Dr. Stiggins: His Views and Principles. *Academy and Literature*, November 2.

———. 1907e. Dr. Stiggins: His Views and Principles. *Academy and Literature*, November 9.

———. 1908. Realism and Symbol. *Academy and Literature*, August 1.

———. 1914. The Joy of London. *The Evening News*, January.

———. 1923a. *Far Off Things*. London: Martin Secker.

———. 1923b. *Hieroglyphics*. London: Martin Secker.

———. 1923c. *Things Near and Far*. London: Secker.

———. 1924. *Dog and Duck*. London: Jonathan Cape.

———. 1963. *Tales of Horror and the Supernatural*. London: Hamilton.

———. 1968. *The Green Round*. Sauk City: Arkham House.

———. 1975a. *Tales of Horror and the Supernatural: Volume I*. Frogmore: Panther.

———. 1975b. *Tales of Horror and the Supernatural: Volume II*. Frogmore: Panther.

———. 1988. *Selected Letters*. Eds. Roger Dobson, Godfrey Brangham, and R.A Gilbert. Wellingborough: Aquarian.

———. 1993. *The Great God Pan*. London: Creation.

———. 1994. *Arthur Machen & Montgomery Evans: Letters of a Literary Friendship, 1923–1947*. Kent: Kent State University Press.

———. 1995. *The Three Impostors*. Ed. David Trotter. London: Everyman.

———. 2000. A Letter to Harry Quilter. *Faunus: The Journal of the Friends of Arthur Machen*, Autumn.

———. 2002. Poe the Enchanter. *Faunus: The Journal of the Friends of Arthur Machen*, Autumn.

———. 2005. The Great God Pan. In *Late Victorian Gothic Tales (Oxford World Classics)*, ed. Roger Luckhurst, 183–233. Oxford: Oxford University Press.

———. 2006. *The Great God Pan and The Hill of Dreams*. New York: Dover.

———. 2010. *The Hill of Dreams*. Swansea: Parthian.

———. 2011a. *The Great God Pan*. Swansea: Parthian.

———. 2011b. *The White People and Other Weird Stories*. Ed. S.T. Joshi. London: Penguin.

———. 2016. *Arthur Machen's 1890s Notebook*. Ed. The Friends of Arthur Machen. Leyburn: Tartarus.

———. 2018. *The Great God Pan and Other Horror Stories*. Ed. Aaron Worth. Oxford: Oxford University Press.

Machin, James. 2015. Fellows Find: H. P. Lovecraft Letter Sheds Light on Pivotal Moment in His Career. *Cultural Compass* (blog). http://blog.hrc.utexas.edu/2015/01/27/fellows-find-h-p-lovecraft-letter/. Accessed 26 Jan 2016.

Maclean, Ian. 1995. Introduction. In *The Manuscript Found in Saragossa*, ed. Jan Potocki. London: Penguin.

MacLeod, Kirsten. 1998. Review of: The Shape of Fear: Horror and the Fin de Siècle Culture of Decadence by Susan J. Navarette. *Victorian Review* 24 (2): 215–218. https://doi.org/10.2307/27794914.

———. 2004. Romps with Ransom's King: Fans, Collectors, Academics, and the M. P. Shiel Archives. *ESC: English Studies in Canada* 30 (1): 117–136.

———. 2006. *Fictions of British Decadence: High Art, Popular Writing and the Fin De Siècle*. New York: Palgrave Macmillan.

———. 2008. M. P. Shiel and the Love of Pubescent Girls: The Other 'Love That Dare Not Speak Its Name'. *English Literature in Transition, 1880–1920* 51 (4): 355–380. https://doi.org/10.2487/elt.51.4(2008)0028.

McDonald, Peter D. 2002. *British Literary Culture and Publishing Practice, 1880–1914*. Cambridge: Cambridge University Press.

Miéville, China. 2009. Weird Fiction. In *The Routledge Companion to Science Fiction*, ed. Mark Bould, Adam Roberts, Andrew M. Butler, and Sherryl Vint, 510–515. London: Routledge.

Milbank, Arthur. 1907. Mr. Machen's Place Among Contemporary Writers. *Academy and Literature*, November 16.

Milligan, Edward H. 2004. Oxford DNB Article: Smith, Hannah. https://doi.org/10.1093/ref:odnb/47062. Accessed 18 Sept 2013.

National Observer. 1895. The Yellow Book, August 10.

Navarette, Susan J. 1993. The Soul of the Plot: The Aesthetics of Fin de Siècle Literature of Horror. In *Styles of Creation: Aesthetic Techniques*, ed. George Edgar Slusser and Eric S. Rabkin, 88–113. Athens: University of Georgia Press.

Nordau, Max Simon. 1895. *Degeneration*. New York: Appleton.

Poe, Edgar Allan. 1984. Reviews of American Authors: Nathaniel Hawthorne. In *Poe Essays and Reviews*, ed. G.R. Thompson, 568–588. New York: Library of America.
Queen of Navarre, Marguerite. 1886. *The Heptameron*. Trans. Arthur Machen. London: Redway.
Quilter, Harry. 1895. The Gospel of Intensity. *Contemporary Review*, June.
Reed, Jeremy. 1995. *A Hundred Years of Disappearance: Count Eric Stenbock*. Privately Printed.
Review of Reviews. 1890. Gift Books for Adults, December.
———. 1895. Our Monthly Parcel of Books, March.
Rhys, Ernest. 1931. *Everyman Remembers*. London: Dent.
———. 1940. *Wales England Wed: An Autobiography*. London: Dent.
Robert Murray Gilchrist (1868–1917): Lost among Genres and Genders. 2011. http://www.victorianweb.org/authors/gilchrist/intro.html.
Roberts, William. 2004. Oxford DNB Article: Quilter, Harry. https://doi.org/10.1093/ref:odnb/35641. Accessed 6 Jan 2014.
Rogers, E. 1899. Mr. Murray Gilchrist's Earlier Work. *Academy*, November 4.
Rose, Jonathan. 2002. *The Intellectual Life of the British Working Classes*. New Haven: Yale University Press.
Said, Edward W. 2003. *Orientalism*. New York: Vintage Books.
Samuels, Mark. 2010. The Man Who Collected Machen. In *The Man Who Collected Machen [EBook]*, Kindle Locations, 291–491. Richmond: Chômu.
Saturday Review. 1894. Some Every-Day Folks, April 21.
———. 1896. Fiction, July 25.
———. 1897. Fiction, March 13.
Sharp, William. 1897. Robert W. Chambers. *Academy*, January 16.
Shiel, M.P. 1894. The Eagle's Crag. *Strand Magazine*.
———. 1895. The Race of Orven. In *Prince Zaleski*, 1–59. London: John Lane.
———. 1896a. *Shapes in the Fire*. London: John Lane.
———. 1896b. *The Rajah's Sapphire*. London: Ward Lock.
———. 1950. *Science, Life, and Literature*. London: Williams & Norgate.
———. 2012. *The Purple Cloud*. Ed. John Sutherland. London: Penguin Classics.
Silberer, Herbert. 1971. *Hidden Symbolism of Alchemy and the Occult Arts*. Trans. Smith Ely Jelliffe. New York: Dover.
Sinclair, Iain. 2013. *Our Unknown Everywhere: Arthur Machen as Presence*. Talybont: Three Impostors.
Smith, Andrew. 2012. *The Victorian Gothic: An Edinburgh Companion*. Edinburgh: Edinburgh University Press.
Stableford, Brian M., ed. 1993. Introduction. In *The Dedalus Book of Decadence (Moral Ruins)*. Sawtry: Dedalus.
Stableford, Brian. 2009. *Jaunting on the Scoriac Tempests and Other Essays on Fantastic Literature*. San Bernardino: Borgo.

Starrett, Vincent. 1918. *Arthur Machen: A Novelist of Ecstasy and Sin*. Chicago: Hill.
Stenbock, Eric Count. 1894. The True Story of a Vampire. In *Studies of Death*, 120–147. London: David Nutt.
Stenbock, Count Stanislaus Eric. 1984. *The Shadow of Death/Studies of Death*. New York: Garland.
———. 1999. *The Myth of Punch*. Ed. David Tibet. London: Durtro.
Stenbock, Eric. 1893. The Other Side: A Breton Legend. *The Spirit Lamp*, June.
———. 1996. *Studies of Death*. London: Durtro.
———. 2001. *The Collected Poems of Eric, Count Stenbock*. Ed. David Tibet. London: Durto.
Stevenson, Robert Louis. 1882. A Gossip on Romance. *Longman's Magazine, 1882–1905* 1 (1): 69–79.
———. 1888. *New Arabian Nights*. New York: Charles Scribner's Sons.
Stevenson, Robert Louis, and Fanny Van de Grift Stevenson. 1885. *More New Arabian Nights: The Dynamiter*. London: Longmans.
Summers, Montague. 1928. *The Vampire: His Kith and Kin*. London: Kegan Paul & Co..
Sutherland, John. 2012. Introduction. In *The Purple Cloud*, ed. M.P. Shiel, xiii–xxxviii. London: Penguin Classics.
Sweetman, John. 1987. *The Oriental Obsession: Islamic Inspiration in British and American Art and Architecture 1500–1920*. Cambridge: Cambridge University Press.
Symons, Arthur, ed. 1896. Advertisement. *Savoy*, no. 8 (December): 93–104.
———. 1969. A Study in the Fantastic. In *Stenbock, Yeats and the Nineties*, ed. John Adlard. London: Cecil & Amelia Woolf.
The Collected Connoisseur by Mark Valentine and John Howard, Published by Tartarus Press. n.d. http://www.tartaruspress.com/collectedconnoisseur.htm. Accessed 21 Jan 2014.
Thomas Ligotti Online. n.d. http://www.ligotti.net/showthread.php?t=3811. Accessed 7 May 2016.
Thornton, R.K.R. 1980. 'Decadence' in Later Nineteenth-Century England. In *Decadence and the 1890s*, ed. Ian Fletcher, 15–30. London: Holmes & Meier.
Todorov, Tsvetan. 1975. *The Fantastic: A Structural Approach to a Literary Genre*. Trans. Richard Howard and Robert Scholes. Fourth Printing edition. Ithaca: Cornell University Press.
Trotter, David. 1995. Introduction. In *The Three Imposters*, ed. Arthur Machen, xvii–xxxi. London: Everyman.
Valentine, Mark. 1995. *Arthur Machen*. Bridgend: Seren.
———. 2012. 'The Cackling Old Gander': The New Age and Arthur Machen. *Faunus: The Journal of the Friends of Arthur Machen*, Autumn.

———. 2014. Wraiths. In *Wraiths and What Became of Dr Ludovicus*, 7–17. Düsseldorf: Zagava.
Vaughan, Thomas. 1910. *Lumen de Lumine; or, A New Magical Light*. London: Watkins.
Walter, Damien G. 2009. Machen Is the Forgotten Father of Weird Fiction. *Guardian*. http://www.theguardian.com/books/booksblog/2009/sep/29/arthur-Machen-tartarus-press. Accessed 22 Jan 2014.
Warner, Marina. 2012. *Stranger Magic*. London: Vintage.
Wells, H.G. 2008. *The Time Machine*. Ed. Stephen Arata. New York: Norton.
White, Hayden. 1982. Method and Ideology in Intellectual History: The Case of Henry Adams. In *Modern European Intellectual History: Reappraisals and New Perspectives*, ed. Dominick LaCapra and Steven L. Kaplan, 280–310. Ithaca: Cornell University Press.
Wilde, Oscar. 1886. A 'Jolly' Art Critic. *Pall Mall Gazette*, November 18.
Williams, J.E. Hodder. 1897. New French Fiction. *The Speaker* 16 (July): 109–110.
Willsher, James. 2004. Introduction. In *The Dedalus Book of English Decadence: Vile Emperors and Elegant Degenerates*, 11–35. Cambs: Dedalus.
Wilson, A.N. 2003. *The Victorians*. London: Arrow.
Winterich, John T., ed. 1955. *The Arabian Nights Entertainments*. Vol. I. New York: Heritage.
Worth, Aaron. 2018. Introduction. In *The Great God Pan and Other Horror Stories*, Oxford World Classics, ed. Arthur Machen, ix–xxxvi. New York: Oxford University Press.
Yeats, William Butler, ed. 1936. *The Oxford Book of Modern Verse, 1892–1935: Chosen by W. B. Yeats*. Oxford: Clarendon Press.
———. 1976. *The Speckled Bird*. Toronto: Mcclelland and Stewart.

CHAPTER 4

Buchan

John Gross and others have argued that Arnold Bennett's reputation as an epitome of the 'gaudiest notion of literary success' is one that still unfairly obscures his literary achievements (Gross 1973, 230).[1] Gross in part ascribes the 'easy acceptance' of Ezra Pound's 'lampoon' of Bennett, in Pound's poem *Hugh Selwyn Mauberley* (1920), to

> our need to construct a literary mythology, in which writers act out exemplary roles. It is as though we required symbolic sacrifices on the altar of artistic integrity, authors weighed down with all the sins of lusting after wealth and fame which we are anxious to disown in ourselves. (Gross 1973, 230–231)

'At the opposite mythological extreme', Gross continues, 'are the martyrs.' In the previous chapter, I have concentrated on these 'martyrs', non-canonical writers whose weird fiction has arguably contributed to their minor status. In this chapter I will look at the weird fiction, and other relevant aspects of the literary career, of one of—as I will argue—these 'symbolic sacrifices on the altar of artistic integrity': John Buchan, 'first Baron Tweedsmuir (1875–1940), author, publisher, and governor-general of Canada' (Matthew 2004).

[1] For further discussion of Bennett's literary reputation, see Peter D. McDonald, *British Literary Culture and Publishing Practice, 1880-1914* (Cambridge University Press, 2002) and (Carey 1992).

In terms of the overall arc of my argument, if Machen, Stenbock, Shiel, and Gilchrist represent weird fiction's provenance within the Poe tradition valorized at the fin de siècle, both in terms of form (the commercial viability of the short story) and content (Decadence), then Buchan represents a comingling of this tradition with the (more popular) colonial weird of Haggard and Kipling. I will argue in the final section of this thesis that the content of *Weird Tales* was iterative of the genre tensions thrown up by its accommodation of these two traditions. I will look at how Buchan anticipates these tensions, between the psychological horrors of introspective Decadence and the more outward-facing engagement with colonial liminalities. I will examine relevant aspects of Buchan's life and posthumous reputation, Buchan and his relationship with Decadence, and Buchan as a writer and critic of weird fiction. I will also posit Paganism as a key commonality working across Buchan's weird and other fiction, one which ties together—through the notion of 'backsliding'—the Decadent and the colonial, and also serves to situate his weird fiction more firmly within the same tradition as that of the 'martyr' writers discussed in previous chapters.

First of all, however, and since it is not how Buchan's work is usually perceived, it is necessary to present some initial explanation of Buchan's presence in a thesis about weird fiction. Buchan's lasting reputation as an author is almost solely due to his series of 'shockers' (to use his own term) featuring the character Richard Hannay, the first and still most famous of which, *The Thirty-Nine Steps*, was published in 1915 in the opening years of the Great War (Lownie 1995, 119). However, previous to his success with *The Thirty-Nine Steps*, Buchan had enjoyed an already considerable career in print since his university days, his early precocity in letters earning him an entry in *Who's Who* by his early twenties, 'possibly the only person in the 1898 volume whose occupation was "undergraduate"' (Adam Smith 1985a, 61). Although, at the time of writing, there is no edition of his weird or supernatural tales in print (the last trade paperback anthology was published in 1997), by 1902 he had a considerable reputation as a writer of 'tales of the weird and uncanny', largely based on his work for *Blackwood's Magazine* (Buchan 1997a; "Fiction" 1902, 490).

I have so far identified two contributory factors to the obscurity of Buchan's weird fiction: the eclipsing effect of the Richard Hannay thrillers' rapid ascent to iconic status on most other valences of Buchan's career; and the debarment of Buchan, resulting from this and other successes, from the ranks of Gross's literary 'martyrs'. Another obfuscation of his work in the mode results from the subtlety of his deployment of it, which while indicative of how the mode operates, means that it has never since been easily accommodated into Buchan's corpus. While Buchan engaged with and evoked the supernatural he rarely if ever fulfilled the necessary criteria to enable easy classification into, for example, the neat generic parameters of the Ghost Story or Gothic horror/romance. He certainly never indulged in the type of horror fiction that Lovecraft disparaged as 'sordid, sanguinary gruesomeness [...] bloody axe murders and sadistic morbidities', in a 1924 letter to J. C. Henneberger (J. Machin 2015).

In other words, Buchan's ambiguity and reticence in this respect make him an exemplary exponent of the weird mode, according to the argument I set out in my introduction. Buchan's reader's reports for John Lane, discussed below, clearly indicate that his avoidance of genre cliché was intentional, and contrasts with his contrived exploitation of genre cliché in his thriller writing. Because this aspect of his fiction doesn't neatly dovetail with his image as an establishment figure and author of jingoistic adventure novels, it is—again—usually sidelined or simply ignored within the context of wider literary scholarship. For instance, his entry in the *Oxford Companion to Edwardian Literature* makes no mention of this aspect of his writing, and neither does his *Oxford Dictionary of National Biography* entry, unless one reads an awful lot into the laconic description of his short story 'The Grove of Ashtaroth' (1912) as 'remarkable' (Kemp et al. 2002a, 47–48; Matthew 2004).

In terms of specialist genre and fan culture, if Buchan's weird fiction has not been entirely ignored, its difficulty to situate in genre has resulted in reactions from hesitancy to outright frustration. In a brief obituary published in the seminal British science fiction fanzine *The Futurian*, although it is acknowledged that 'fantasy enthusiasts, in common with the larger world interested in literature generally, have much to mourn in the sudden passing of Lord Tweedsmuir, whom we know better as John Buchan,' most of the space is given to puzzling over Buchan's place in genre:

> In his long writing career John Buchan touched on fantasy many times; but did not adventure into a full-blooded fantasy at all. Probably the only story we fans admit into our collections, is *The Gap in the Curtain* [...] which deals with an attempt to pierce the veil of the future and, like all his works is most competently written. One or two assortments of short stories might perhaps scrape in, because of odd tales wherein appear supernormal forces or curious conjectures. ("Jemini" 1940)

It is possible to read in this a certain testiness or impatience with Buchan's failure to produce more straightforwardly classifiable genre fiction. The phrase 'full-blooded fantasy' suggests a robustly delineated genre, and there is also perhaps an implication that Buchan's failure to commit to such a genre opens his writing up to the charge of being too adulterated (an antonym of 'full-blooded' being 'hybrid'). It is also possible to glean, particularly from the comment that some of Buchan's short stories might only 'scrape in' to genre consideration, a further sense of the slipperiness and resistance to classification presented by some of Buchan's work. For a high-profile writer working in the mode during the 'high phase' of weird fiction, and especially for one so enthusiastically endorsed by H. P. Lovecraft (see below), Buchan is noticeable by his absence from both anthologies of weird fiction from the period and also from contemporary critical work in the field. Paul Benedict Grant describes what he calls Buchan's 'supernatural fiction' as 'one of the most critically underworked aspects of his literary legacy' (Grant 2009, 192). One reason for this could be Buchan's particular resistance to Gothic cliché and the obviously horrific, meaning that his weird fiction is difficult to place within such traditions. Rather, it is perhaps more comfortably positioned within his own wider oeuvre. Juanita Kruse's comment that Buchan's 'best fiction contains a sense of an uncanny world beneath the veneer of civilization—a world both fascinating and terrifying'—is not aimed at his weird fiction only (Kruse 1989, 7:7). Similarly, Christopher Hitchens observed, referring to Buchan's writing generally rather than his supernatural fiction specifically, that 'the occult [...] provides a continual undertone of fascination, attractive and repulsive in almost equal degrees' and that generally Buchan's 'writing shows an attraction [...] to the exotic and the numinous' (Hitchens 2004).

Buchan's weird fiction has a particular focus on that 'sense of the uncanny' that, while less immediately obvious, still underpins his other writing, and his entire worldview. John Clute's term 'equipoise' is a particularly useful referent when considering the operation of this worldview on the interplay between the quotidian and supernatural in Buchan's fiction:

> Equipoise describes [...] a very loose category of stories which—rather than 'failing' to achieve generic closure, or 'failing' to give birth phoenix-like to some new form of genre—can be seen as taking their nature precisely from their refusal of closure. (Clute 2006, 63)

Clute goes on to explicitly define 'equipoise' against Todorov's 'duration of uncertainty', arguing that, contrary to Todorov's focus on the reader's anticipation of the narrative commitment to ultimately decide between the marvellous and the 'merely' uncanny (Todorov 1975, 25), equipoise 'does not describe a decision point' (Clute 2006, 63). These 'decision points' are almost entirely absent from Buchan's weird oeuvre (the short story 'Skule Skerry' (1928) being a counterexample), and his focus on liminal narrative spaces is a definitive feature of such work. Equipoisal writing credits the reader with the wherewithal to deal with not only a 'duration of uncertainty' but with uncertainty itself, and the resulting frisson and/or jolt is the reader's reward, not, necessarily, the narrative conclusion. Contrary to Buchan's enduring reputation, 'full-blooded' and 'healthy' it is not.

As with his work in the thriller genre, Buchan 'wrote in generic forms but [...] was not unduly constrained by generic conventions' (Waddell 2009, 3). When introducing his chapter on Buchan's 'supernatural' fiction in a recent critical anthology, it is indicative that Paul Benedict Grant finds Lovecraft's notion of weird fiction a 'useful theoretical model' with which to parse such otherwise tricky material (Grant 2009, 183). Buchan continued to write in this generically ambiguous vein right up to and including his final novel, *Sick Heart River*, published posthumously in 1941. *Sick Heart River* was still provoking some head-scratching in 2000: 'While some [have] suggested [... *Sick Heart River* ...] is a borderline supernatural work, its themes are more metaphysical than macabre ghostly' (Wilson 2000, 113). It is telling that this prevarication did not preclude the novel from inclusion in the *Guide to Supernatural Fiction* from which the remark originates.

Buchan's Life and Posthumous Reputation

John Buchan was born in Perth in 1875, the son of a Free Church of Scotland Minister, a 'lively character, an enthusiast for border ballads and other Scots songs' (Matthew 2004). His mother's comparative seriousness and religious strictness counterbalanced this, and although Buchan 'remained a Presbyterian', he was a 'liberal Calvinist with distinctly ecumenical leanings', perhaps reflecting the relative benignity of the atmosphere in which he was raised (Greig 2009, 7). While the household was imbued with religion, it was not 'carried to the harsh and rigid extremes against which so many Victorian children rebelled in later life' (Kruse

1989, 7:7). From what was a fairly modest middle-class beginning, he worked his way through grammar school, Glasgow University, and ultimately Oxford on a series of scholarships and bursaries, supplementing his finances with his earnings as a writer and publisher's reader.

By the early 1900s, he was a qualified barrister, had experience in South Africa working as an administrator in the aftermath of the Boer War, was an editor and columnist for the *Spectator*, and worked for publisher (and friend) Thomas Nelson. He sought political office in 1911, becoming the MP for Peeblesshire and Selkirk. Aged 39, he was deemed unfit for service in 1914 due to a stomach ulcer, a 'psychological blow from which he perhaps never fully recovered' (Matthew 2004). He instead threw his considerable energies into working in government intelligence and propaganda. After the war, and now a well-known public figure and a successful author of the spy thrillers for which he is now most often remembered, he continued writing and working in publishing alongside his political career: 'His every leisure moment was devoted to writing, with an output of novels, biographies, and histories that amounted to graphomania' (Hitchens 2004). In 1935 he was appointed governor-general of Canada, a role in which he 'set a pace and range of activity which his successors were unable to match' and was to remain in until his death in 1940 at the age of 64 (Matthew 2004).

Although Buchan enjoyed enormous success and popularity as a writer, his posthumous reputation increasingly suffered as political attitudes changed and developed over the course of the twentieth century.[2] Writing in 1960, Gertrude Himmelfarb summed up his critical standing as follows:

> What makes Buchan, and the ethos with which he is identified, so unpalatable today is not one or another cause for distaste: the idea that the good life is a matter of cold baths, rousing games, and indifferent sex; the apparent philistinism that put a high premium on success and a low premium on intelligence; an unseemly preoccupation with race and class; and a still more unseemly glorification of nation and empire. It is each of these and more: the sense of a temperament and mentality that is inimical to the prevailing 'liberal imagination'. (Himmelfarb 1995, 271)

However, a proper interrogation of Buchan's life and work seriously undermines this still widely held view, and while his writing certainly provides a

---

[2] Despite this historical neglect, the considerable dearth of serious academic engagement with Buchan's work has now begun to be addressed with the recent publication of three critical works: *Modern John Buchan: A Critical Introduction* (2009), *Reassessing John Buchan* (2009), and *John Buchan and the Idea of Modernity* (2013).

fecund source of evidence in support of each individual claim, it also frequently problematizes and subverts any crude political glossing.

Failing to acknowledge this ambiguity sometimes results in serious misrepresentation or straightforward sneering: the *Oxford Companion to Edwardian Fiction* bluntly describes Buchan's imperialism as being a 'serious handicap' in his writing (Kemp et al. 2002a, 49). While Buchan's fiction is damned *because* of its imperialism, in the same volume Haggard's is afforded critical respectability *in spite of* its imperialism:

> By the time of [Haggard's] death, and for years afterwards, his fiction was derided as escapist, imperialist schoolboy fantasy. However, more recently Haggard's novels have been the object of much critical attention, as prejudices against the supernatural and the imperial elements have both faded, and it has been again possible to appreciate the power with which the plots image the anxieties of the period. (Kemp et al. 2002b, 167)

A possible explanation for this difference in treatment is that Buchan's imperialism was often expressed more reflexively and unequivocally in his work—for example, discussed by characters more explicitly—than in Haggard's most popular romances (or, at least, *King Solomon's Mines* and *She*), in which imperial concerns tend to be implicit subtexts and so more amenable to variegated scholarly interpretation. In other words, Haggard's best known work lends itself to more charitable postcolonial readings than Buchan's, despite the fact that Haggard in old age was 'a disillusioned imperialist with authoritarian, racist leanings' whose 'ranting' diatribes against Jews and Indian nationalists were expunged from his published diaries (Cohen 2004).

Buchan, although a similarly disillusioned imperialist by the end of his life, bitterly regretted that the word 'Empire' had been 'sadly tarnished' by its identification with 'callous racial arrogance': 'Our creed was not based on antagonism to any other people. It was humanitarian and international; we believed that we were laying the basis of a federation of the world' (Buchan 1941, 124). In this respect too, Buchan evades neat categorization, both in terms of genre and politics:

> For the most part, Buchan's protagonists were, for adventure heroes, singularly law-abiding and unbloodthirsty. In some ways Buchan might be seen as a transitional figure—far less violent than older men like Rider Haggard or G. A. Henty but never willing entirely to renounce the use of force for imperial defence as were younger men like John Galsworthy and E. M. Forster. (Kruse 1989, 7:19)

A good deal of confusion is also caused by reading the Hannay novels, especially *The Thirty-Nine Steps*, as representative of a monolithic political worldview, rather than wartime propaganda and morale-boosting popular entertainment, and in isolation from the rest of Buchan's fiction.

Buchan's more populist exercises in fictional 'derring-do, of British heroism and triumphs in distant parts of the world' now eclipse other work which is far more nuanced in its concerns with the fragile contingency of Christian civilization (discussed in further detail below) (Eldridge 1996, 57). Buchan's weird fiction is on the whole a more sophisticated venue for his anxieties regarding the fragility of civilization and modernity than the more reductive propagandizing of the work for which he is more well known, and which was often written with explicitly that agenda. Like much adventure fiction of the time, Buchan's casual racism and imperialist flag-waving make it difficult if not impossible for the contemporary reader to engage with it other than at arm's length. Buchan's weird fiction, however, is often free from explicit and problematic politicking and it has been argued that 'Buchan perhaps revealed more of himself in apparently ephemeral magazine fiction than in the works by which he was best known during his lifetime' (Freeman 2008, 25). The 'thinness' of civilization with which many of these stories is concerned is more an existential anxiety than a political one, relating to human vulnerability in a chaotic and hostile cosmos.

In his weird fiction, this concern of Buchan's slips easily into outright horror, and what he identified in Poe's work as the revelation of 'the shadowy domain of the back-world, and behind our smug complacency the shrieking horror of the unknown' (Buchan 1911, 7). Although it is his adventure fiction which has been described as being based upon the notion of 'something familiar, reliable, and dearly loved threatened by the unknown and the incomprehensible,' this theme is addressed even more explicitly in his weird fiction, and I will argue this in more detail in what follows (Kemp et al. 2002a, 48).

High/Middlebrow

As a writer, Buchan has been accused of defying 'the naturalism, realism, and concern for the inner life of characters which predominate in the early twentieth-century novelists' and are commonly accepted (without further interrogation) as key indicators of literature 'proper' (47). Buchan is, then, a critical casualty of these demarcations of literature emergent at the time, although his problematic status was surely exacerbated by the fact that he engaged in popular forms of writing as well as more self-consciously literary pieces (47). Commenting in 1975, Tim Heald was also of the view that the 'range of [Buchan's] interest and the extent of his output, astonishing though they are, have tended [...] to diminish his reputation' (Heald 1975). This echoes Janet Adam Smith's comment that Buchan 'bothers critics, many of whom are uneasy at the variety of his achievement yet irritated that the achievement was not greater' (Adam Smith 1985a, 8). In other words, there is a sense of frustration that he did not apply his inarguably generous talents to more purist literary ends.

What John Carey writes of Arnold Bennett could equally apply to Buchan in this respect: 'Bennett did not renounce art, of course, but he did not expect others to keep him while he produced it' (Carey 1992, 154). Buchan's unapologetic lack of discomfort with the commerce of literary production perhaps stems from the fact that his earliest forays into publishing were undertaken for the specific purpose of paying his way through university. Although keenly engaged with the literary debates of the day, he was equally involved with the mercantile side of publishing, detailing a business plan for his writing in his Glasgow University commonplace book, which shows that 'he aspired to publish books of essays and criticism with Chatto and Windus, novels with Longmans [... and ...] poetry with Elkin Matthews and John Lane' (Adam Smith 1985a, 51). Buchan's modest beginnings and stubborn determination that the expense of his education should not be a burden to his family (who could ill afford to provide for him) resulted in an organized and largely successful strategy of applying for scholarships in tandem with generating income from writing fiction. Fiction was always a mercantile exercise for Buchan as much as an artistic one, although the two are of course not mutually exclusive.

Later, more concerted efforts at producing popular genre fiction were in part inspired by the same emergent pulp magazine market in the United States that saw the establishment of *Weird Tales* in 1923. Kate Macdonald has identified a hiatus, a handful of short stories aside, in Buchan's literary output between 1901 and 1909 and Patrick Scott Belk (after MacDonald) argues that it was Buchan's exposure, through his work with Thomas Nelson, to the American pulp magazines that gave him 'the renewed impetus to write his own fiction again' (Belk 2013, 156; Macdonald 2010, 33):

> At a time when British popular fiction writers were in vogue with editors of American magazines, Buchan occupied a strategic position at the centre of the London literary establishment. His professional obligations to Thomas

Nelson & Sons from 1907, and his long-standing ties with the A. P. Watt literary agency, afforded him routine access to important contacts within the international export market for British popular fiction. (Belk 2013, 156)

Buchan's exposure to the new genres being forged in the pulps, as well as the thrillers of E. Phillips Oppenheim (recommended to Buchan by Arthur Balfour), influenced his decision to write—and the stylistic choices made in—what is considered his first genre work proper, *The Power-House*, published in *Blackwood's* in 1913, a year before he had his breakthrough commercial success with *The Thirty-Nine Steps* (Adam Smith 1985a, 192; Belk 2013, 156–157). However, it has been argued that Buchan's subsequent reputation and critical treatment as a populist, middlebrow writer is predicated on 'serious distortions of both his own life and his literary practice' (Waddell 2009, 3). In the introduction to a recent critical anthology, Macdonald and Nathan Waddell reinforce this view, arguing that Buchan's writing 'steered a course through middlebrow cultures' but, like his 'modernist peers', was 'fundamentally attuned to the moral, political, religious, socio-cultural, philosophical, and racial ambiguities of his time' (Waddell and Macdonald 2013). This assertion, albeit irrefutable, resonates with Miéville's claim regarding weird fiction and Modernism discussed in the Introduction, and arguably demonstrates the same desire to legitimize material previously held to be déclassé.

According to the *Oxford English Dictionary*, the term 'middlebrow' emerged in the 1920s as a pejorative for consumers of culture 'regarded as intellectually unchallenging or of limited intellectual or cultural value', although the corollary of this was that such material tended to be popular and commercially successful, in contrast to minority-interest, recondite, and often inaccessible 'highbrow' culture ("Middlebrow, n. and Adj." n.d.). Lawrence S. Rainey places the first use of the term earlier: 'In 1906 [...] the first appearance is reported of the word *middlebrow*, a term that acknowledges not just increasing stratification but also increasing interchanges among different cultural sectors' (Rainey 1998, 3). Buchan, who in his publishing capacity also served as a functionary at these interchanges, seems to have been blithely resigned to his degraded critical status: Andrew Lownie records that in 'a speech in February 1939 [Buchan] claimed that if there were six categories "from highbrow to solid ivory" he placed himself in the third—"high-lowbrow"' (Lownie 1995).

One particular aspect of Buchan's fiction which precluded him from the 'highbrow' was that 'he never rejected the adventure story as a medium for his fiction, even for his more serious works' (Kruse 1989, 7:6). Even at university in the 1890s, Asquith had 'chaffed' Buchan over his 'crude passion for romance' (Buchan 1941). Although some, like Machen, clung on to the idea that they were producing 'romances' rather than 'novels' (see Chap. 3), by the early twentieth century this could be an act of wilful contrariness: despite Andrew Lang's best efforts, the romance—whose 'trespass on realism' had been questioned since the late eighteenth century—became a hopelessly devalued critical quantity and has remained so to this day (Baxter 2010, 6).

The fact that Joseph Conrad's and Ford Madox Ford's 1906 collaborative novel *Romance* was so titled gave it an air of overt commercialism and a 'perceived lack of realism' that led to its dismissal by critics then as it continues to now (Baxter 2010, 56). Rainey remarks that

> by the decade 1900–1910, the later years of Henry James and the period when Joseph Conrad most acutely felt the tension between the claims of his art and the imperatives of the marketplace, the polarization between 'high' and 'low' literature had firmly crystallized, and the modernist project issued its claim to aesthetic dignity by repudiating that Victorian literature, above all fiction, that sold itself to a mass reading public. (Rainey 1998, 2)

Romance, as an exemplarily populist genre, was an immediately visible target for this purge. G. H. Powell (1856–1924), writing in 1912, complained that literary discourse had become an 'obscurantist intellectual jungle of anti-romanticism', with 'strange chatterations of simian contortionists ensconced up more or less inaccessible trees' (Powell 1912, 164). By the time Conrad's *The Rescue* was published in 1920, its author could lament that it was the 'swan song of romance' (Baxter 2010, 15).

Powell's complaint resonates with John Carey's argument that 'highbrow' literary Modernism was to some extent predicated on differentiating itself from middlebrow culture and 'can be seen as a hostile reaction to the unprecedentedly large reading public created by late nineteenth-century educational reforms' (Carey 1992, Preface). Although Buchan undoubtedly regarded this 'large reading public' as his audience, there is—again—a serious risk of misrepresentation if one regards this as straightforward populism. Buchan's commercial success needs to be seen in the context of his development as a writer during the 1890s and 1900s. In the following section I shall examine Buchan's pre–*Thirty-Nine Steps* literary career, partly to reclaim this aspect of his output from comparative disregard, and also to look at how Buchan's weird fiction tracks a course—both stylistically and in terms of publishing history—between the 1890s and the Modernist period. Buchan was not only a transitional figure in terms of this imperialism, but also between the literary cultures of the 'yellow nineties' and the age of pulp modernism. As I shall argue in the Conclusion and with specific regard to *Weird Tales*, these two ostensibly very different cultures were in fact intractably entangled, especially through and with regard to weird fiction.

Buchan and Decadence

Buchan's relationship with Aestheticism and Decadence was far more nuanced than the subsequent stereotypes of his more famous works would suggest. Based on the Hannay novels alone, it might seem reasonable to assume that Buchan was firmly in the 'healthy' Lang-approved school of vigorous, inspiring Romance and imperialist propaganda, the antithesis of the louche ennui and artificial poise of Decadence. However, Buchan's engagement with the cultural climate of the 1890s had many more valences, often eclipsed by his subsequent commercial success.

Buchan's pragmatically business-like approach to his literary affairs from his earliest forays as a student did not preclude him being a committed acolyte of 'the high-priest of aesthetic prose-style' Walter Pater (Richards 1976, 40). His decision to apply (successfully) for an undergraduate place at Brasenose 'was due partly to Buchan's enthusiasm for Pater, who was a Fellow at that college' (Adam Smith 1985a, 41, 52):

> Brasenose as the home of Walter Pater had a special fascination for me, and, though he had died in the spring before I sat for a scholarship, I was glad to go to a college where he had lectured on Plato, and which was full of his friends. (Buchan 1941, 47)

Buchan may at first glance seem a rather unlikely Paterian, but, writing on Buchan's 'aesthetic consciousness', Bernard Richards notes that Buchan certainly wasn't unique in this regard, observing that 'a surprising variety of people at the end of the Victorian era were impressed with Pater, ranging from Wilde and Raffalovich to Field Marshal Earl Haig' (Richards 1976, 40). However, Richards also avers that while 'in some cases the admiration may not have been more than skin deep, in Buchan's case it was profound,' arguing that his admiration 'helps us notice and identify some traits in Buchan which are a little surprising when one thinks of that composite image derived from the "shockers" and the photographs of the tweedy English country gentleman born in Scotland' (40).

At Brasenose, Buchan identified with the 'scholars' rather than the 'rowdies' (Adam Smith 1985a, 41, 52). He also established a coterie of close friends at Balliol, including those, like Raymond Asquith who had about them an air of 'pre-war dandyism, that over-ripeness and weary elegance, that only the Scotsman in the group could resist' (Green 1977, 76–77). This observation that Buchan's stance was one of resistance to, rather than rejection of, Decadent culture is a perspicacious one: his subsequent criticism of Decadence was that of a cautious associate rather than an outsider.

At least partly in reaction to the philistine culture associated with groups like the Freshman's Wine Club, Buchan and some like-minded individuals formed the Ibsen Society 'to read and discuss the dramas of the Master' (Adam Smith 1985a, 52). The Ibsen Society quickly 'degenerated' and abandoned Ibsen for '*Cymbeline, The Dolly Dialogues*, Kenneth Grahame's *Golden Age*, till they came to Rudyard Kipling and stayed there' (52). Under its new incarnation as the Crocodile Club, works read and discussed included 'Kipling's *Life's Handicap*, R. L. Stevenson's *Island Night Entertainments*, Austin Dobson's *Old World Idylls*, and Arthur Machen's *The Great God Pan*', Machen's subsequent influence on Buchan being 'noticeable in Buchan's early writing' and (I will argue) some of his later (Lownie 1995, 41). The weird fiction under discussion by the society not only included Machen, therefore, but also Kipling, whose collection *Life's Handicap* (1891) included short stories that—setting a precedent that Buchan would later emulate—ambiguously engaged the supernatural and reflected the unsettling comingling of 'knowledge and superstition' of the colonial encounter, ultimately offering no easy resolutions for the reader: 'At the End of the Passage', 'The Mark of the Beast', and 'The Return of Imray' (Luckhurst 2005, xxiv).

Within his first year at Brasenose, Buchan gained an introduction to John Lane through the artist D. Y. Cameron, rather breathlessly writing to a friend in Glasgow:

> I will tell you a great secret, which you must not mention to a soul. I am to be exalted to the post of literary adviser to the great firm of Lane *vice* Le Gallienne sacked. That is a joke of course, but he is going to send me manuscripts to read for him, for which I shall be paid. (Adam Smith 1985a, 51)

In fact, as revealed by the reader's reports in the John Lane Business Records archive, Buchan's tenure as a reader for John Lane coincided with that of Le Gallienne for much of the rest of the decade, both readers regularly reporting to Lane on the same manuscripts submitted to the publisher for consideration.[3]

This trajectory of literary interest, taking in Pater, Ibsen, Machen, the John Lane imprint, and a professional association with Le Gallienne, would seem to firmly embed the young John Buchan within the Decadence of the time. In terms of personal literary taste, he was antipathetic to the stylistic excesses frequently associated with the movement: 'another [belief] was a certain austerity—I disliked writing which was luscious and overripe' (Buchan 1941, 200). However, his essay 'Nonconformity in Literature' published in the 2 November 1895, edition of the *Glasgow Herald*, during his first term at Brasenose, also displays an unambiguous hostility to some of the (post-Wilde trial) popularly demonized valences of the contemporary literary scene:

> In a time when [...] no writers of surpassing greatness are among us, it is no more than natural that the heart of the people should go after strange gods, and our younger writers vie with one another in seeking for the odd, and, when found, proclaiming its magnitude. [...] Of all the forms of this non-conformity the most oppressive and obvious to-day [sic] is that cult of the decadent and sickly which claims so many votaries. (Buchan 1895)

Buchan continues in this vein, reminiscent of Harry Quilter in the June 1895 article discussed in Chap. 3:

> Their distinguishing feature is a sort of disdain for the things which common men think great and good, and an affected seeking after esoteric beauties and virtues. From Baudelaire down to, let us say, Mr Arthur Symons and his comrades, their work is one long string of indelicate indelicacies, virtues so cloaked as to be irrecognisable, and vices with a touch of paint and a coating of sugar. (4)

As was the case with Henley's public denunciation of Wilde in the pages of the *National Observer* (see Chap. 2), such grandstanding in print could be a more accurate reflection of a particular editorial policy rather than an individual writer's deeply held conviction. Nevertheless, Buchan's article

---

[3] Austin, HRC, John Lane Company Records, Box 64, Reader's reports 1894–1899.

is unequivocal in decrying subject matter which is 'openly vicious, dealing with the seamier side of life'.

Curiously for someone who at the time had been involved in convening an Ibsen Society, Buchan then expresses disdain for 'terrible spectacled men and women [...] with a Norwegian dictionary and a slight knowledge of the English tongue'. However, an explanation is forthcoming:

> It is one of the worst emanations from the prevalent admiration for Ibsen, and, much as we prize the work of the Norwegian dramatist, we cannot but think that this message-bearing is at once a silliness and a presumption. (4)

While Buchan 'prizes' the work of Ibsen itself, he is less approving of its influence with regard to 'message-bearing' literature. He similarly excuses Kipling's 'indelicacies' due to his 'frank disavowal of any ethical or didactic purpose'. This is perhaps the point at which the agendas of the romance writers and the Decadents are most in alignment: they are equally disdainful of moral didactics, the former through its privileging of story above all else, and the latter in its engagement with notions of relativity and subjectivity.

Perhaps due to the common influence of Pater, Buchan is here in accord with Wilde's famous remark in the preface of *The Picture of Dorian Gray* that 'All art is quite useless', but rather than interpret Wilde's diktat as a Paterian abandonment of subjective certainties and moral didacticism in literature, Buchan's not incommensurable argument is that 'message-bearing' simply gets in the way of good writing and storytelling:

> The writer of modern times who seems to us most like the 'simple great ones gone,' Robert Louis Stevenson, owes much of his excellence to his modesty in being subject to restraint and his good sense in burdening himself with no partial doctrines to expound. (4)

It is possible to speculate that this article reflects a position arrived at as a result of Buchan's experience at Brasenose and his involvement with the Ibsen Society, and the Society's discussion of the work of the Norwegian dramatist and his influence on English letters: Ibsen was later described by Richard Le Gallienne, in his retrospective of the 1890s, as 'perhaps the figure of most sinister portent' to have emerged in that decade (Le Gallienne 1925, 67). Sally Ledger observes that, emerging in the 1880s and 1890s, 'Ibsenism' was a 'political and cultural formation consisting of

Marxists, socialists, Fabians and feminists, who jointly hailed Ibsen as a spokesman for their various causes' (Ledger 2008, 2–3). As well as his natural political antipathy, Buchan's critique of 'Ibsenism' may also have reflected his frustration at the 'degeneration' of the Ibsen Society at Brasenose referred to above. Despite this, Buchan remains enthusiastic for Ibsen's work, but hostile to what he clearly views as manipulation of Ibsen's influence for explicitly doctrinaire political ends.

As discussed in Chap. 2, although at the epicentre of British Decadence in publishing terms, John Lane himself was at least as concerned with quotidian business matters as contemporary literary debates. Despite Buchan's equivocation on the prominence of his role at the Bodley Head, by the following year, Arnold Bennett remarked of Buchan in his diary that Buchan was 'now principal "reader" to the Bodley Head' going on to say that 'already—he cannot be more than 23 [in fact he was 20]—he is a favourite of publishers, who actually seek after him' (Adam Smith 1985a, 56). Indeed, as well as John Lane, Buchan had by then received overtures from Blackwood and Fisher Unwin (who published Buchan's first novel *Sir Quixote of the Moors* in October 1895 when the author was 19) and had been singled out for praise by the *Bookman* in their 'New Writers' column of December 1895 for a 'precocious literary record' that was 'extraordinary and interesting' (Adam Smith 1985a, 30; *Bookman* 1895).

By 1896, the 20-year-old undergraduate John Buchan, enthusiastic reader of Pater and Ibsen, albeit hostile critic of the 'cult of the decadent and sickly' from 'Baudelaire down to [...] Arthur Symons', was helping—as both a reader for John Lane and a contributor—to steer the imprint and the *Yellow Book* into its post-Wilde and Beardsley incarnation. As Richards succinctly observes, 'one is taken aback rather if one's image of Buchan in the 90s is based on the famous cartoon of a young tyke brandishing a club [...] and then encounters an early book of his—*The Scholar Gipsies* [sic: actually *Scholar Gipsies*] (1896a), dolled up in aesthetic binding designed by an imitator of Aubrey Beardsley and published by the effete firm of John Lane' (Richards 1976, 40–41) (Fig. 4.1).

Adam Smith accounts for Buchan's ambiguous relationship with—and often inconsistent attitude to—contemporaneous literary culture by arguing that Buchan's distrust of the influence of Decadence shouldn't be confused with a lack of enthusiasm for at least some of the writers associated with Decadence. Regardless of his reservations about Decadence, the

Fig. 4.1 Cover design for John Buchan's *Scholar Gipsies* (1896a) (image courtesy of Kenneth Hillier)

insipidness of the prevailing 'Kailyard School of Novelists', then dominating Scottish letters with 'their parochialism and their smugness', had somewhat forced his hand: if 'Scottish literary culture meant the Kailyarders, then […] he preferred London and the *Yellow Book*' (Adam

Smith 1985a, 87).[4] Adam Smith's assertion in this respect is certainly borne out by Buchan's reader's reports for Lane in which he uses the term 'Kailyarder' as a pejorative:

> This is a specimen of rather a poor variety of 'Kailyard' novel—the kind, I mean, where the plot is one of the stock ones, and we have long pieces of dialogue between people in the village sandwiched between the acts of the story.[5]

And 'This is an amiable, foolish work—a sort of Devonshire "Kailyarder".'[6]

Nevertheless, writing to Katherine Lyon Mix in the 1930s regarding the *Yellow Book*, Buchan confessed that 'I always thought it a very odd medium for work of mine to appear in' (Mix 1960, 197). The overall impression created is of a writer who is more interested in good writing than correct writing, whether deemed artistically correct by the belletrist literary elite or correctly decent by the apocryphal Mrs Grundy and others of the self-appointed moral guardians of the reading public. Writing of his literary career in the immediate aftermath of the war, Buchan remarks that 'as an author I was a link to the past, for in my extreme youth in the 'nineties I had contributed to the old *Yellow Book*' (Buchan 1941, 193)—he was clearly conscious of the persisting baggage of his involvement with a title so closely identified with its age.

Further information on Buchan's attitude to Decadence can be gleaned from two later novels, *Mr. Standfast* (1919) and *The Dancing Floor* (1926). In the wartime thriller *Mr. Standfast*, Richard Hannay is recalled from the front to undertake an undercover intelligence operation within the British pacifist movement to identify and neutralize German infiltration. Hannay is far from comfortable with the bohemian *milieu* he finds himself in, and his tone veers between gently mocking and sneeringly hostile:

> Several were pointed out to me as artists who had gone one better than anybody else, and a vast billowy creature was described as the leader of the new Orientalism. I noticed that these people, according to Jimson, were all 'great', and that they all dabbled in something 'new'. (Buchan 1919, 32)

---

[4] According to Ian Ousby, *The Cambridge Paperback Guide to Literature in English* (Cambridge University Press, 1996), 212, the Kailyard School was 'a group of nineteenth-century Scottish writers who wrote [...] about homespun topics and promoted a sentimental image of small-town life. "Kailyard", meaning "cabbage patch".'

[5] Austin, HRC, John Lane Company Records, Box 64, Reader's reports 1894–1899, 15 July 1896.

[6] Austin, HRC, John Lane Company Records, Box 64, Reader's reports 1894–1899, 17 February 1897.

It is difficult to clearly ascertain here whether Buchan is using the term 'new Orientalism' in the sense of that associated with the 1890s (i.e., 'new' in terms of recent decades) or that of a new Modernist Orientalism. A third interpretation, entirely possible, is that Buchan did not (without the benefit of hindsight and ensuing neat, retroactive periodization) distinguish Modernism from Decadence.

Hannay reserves special scorn for Launcelot Wake, a 'tallish, lean fellow of round about thirty years. [...] His thin face was sallow as if from living indoors, and he had rather more hair on his head than most of us' (21). Hannay's fellow spy and love interest Mary Lamington later cautions him that his work will involve tolerating people like Wake who are 'half-baked' and occupy 'gimcrack little "arty" houses': 'You will hear everything you regard as sacred laughed at and condemned, and every kind of nauseous folly acclaimed, and you must hold your tongue and pretend to agree' (28). Feebleness, pretension, and artifice go hand in hand with the failure to pitch in with the war effort, as does an interest in modern French art:

> The walls and the ceiling were covered with a dead-black satiny paper on which hung the most monstrous pictures in large dull-gold frames. I could only see them dimly, but they seemed to be a mere riot of ugly colour. The young man nodded towards them. 'I see you have got the Dégousses hung at last,' he said. (22)

Christoph Ehlund has compared Buchan's presentation of the pacifist community infiltrated by Hannay to 'the spoiled yet pitifully naïve Eloi in H. G. Wells's *The Time Machine* (1895)' (Kerr 2013, 120). Despite his initial hostility, as the novel unfolds, Hannay is forced to revise his opinion and overcome his own prejudices as Wake reveals himself to be, despite his pacifism and idealism, a man of integrity and bravery, who ultimately dies a heroic death as a noncombatant messenger on the front. However, Hannay's ultimate admiration for Wake is predicated specifically on Wake's decision to 'come down from his pedestal and become one of the crowd' (Buchan 1919, 367). If Buchan was no philistine, by the First World War he also had no time for art for art's sake, as his role as a propagandist demonstrated.

Similarly, the bohemianism of Koré Arabin, a central character in *The Dancing Floor* (1926)—which according to Mary Butts was 'one of the first novels to owe its origin to [J. G. Frazer's] *The Golden Bough*'—is initially presented very unsympathetically (Butts 1933, 433). Edward Leithen is at first appalled by her and finds her seeming contempt for convention 'detestable' and representative of a postwar generation for whom 'Apollo has been ousted by Dionysos' (Buchan 1946, 77, 67). The name 'Koré Arabin' evokes an exotic otherness at odds with her British identity, most directly through the fact that she is named after the maiden figure from Greek mythology (the 'daughter of Zeus and Demeter, known as Persephone when she married Hades') and the associated representations in Greek art, the 'statue of a draped maiden' ("Kore, N." n.d.). The name also suggests 'Kôr', the name of the mysterious city that is home to H. Rider Haggard's immortal African queen in *She* (1887). Leithen imagines (presumptuously, as it turns out) that she lives in a 'slovenly place full of cushions and French novels and hot-house flowers', his references remaining the stereotypical and by then dated *Yellow Book*/Huysmans bricolage (Buchan 1946, 107).

Koré Arabin's bohemianism is explained by her provenance as well as her explicitly Orientalist name: she is the granddaughter of a man who was 'an intimate of all the poets of that time—Byron, Shelley' and 'called his son after Shelley' (58). Shelley Arabin, Koré's father, is given the biography of an *Ur*-Decadent, so comprehensive in delineating the clichés of the movement as to be worth quoting almost in full:

> They were Catholics of course. All his boyhood he spent in that island among the peasants and the kind of raffish company that his father invited to the house. What kind of company? Well, I should say all the varieties of humbug that Europe produces—soldiers of fortune, and bad poets, and the gentry who have made their native countries too hot for them. [...] Ultimately the boy was packed off to Cambridge, where he arrived speaking English a generation out of date, and with the tastes of a Turkish pasha, but with the most beautiful manners. Tom, when he wasn't in a passion, had the graciousness of a king, and Shelley was a young prince in air and feature. He was terribly good-looking in a way no man has a right to be, and that prejudiced him in the eyes of his young contemporaries. [...] There was a scandal—rather a bad one, I fancy—and he left under the blackest kind of cloud. [...] I suppose a lawyer does not concern himself with poetry, but I can assure you that Shelley Arabin made quite a name for himself in the late eighties. I believe bibliophiles still collect his first editions. [...] And there were his love sonnets, beautiful languid things, quite phosphorescent with decay. He carried Swinburne and Baudelaire a stage further. Well, that mood has gone from the world, and Shelley Arabin's reputation with it, but at one time sober critics felt obliged to praise him even when they detested him. (59–60)

Shelley Arabin is rendered here as an amalgam of Lord Byron, 'a thinly-veiled Aleister Crowley', Dorian Gray, and Count Stenbock (Freeman 2008, 27). The language of the 1890s is explicitly evoked (Arabin's sonnets are 'beautiful languid things, quite phosphorescent with decay') and the idea of his collectability as a poet alluded to, with his sought-after first editions.

Buchan had previously also given the antagonist of a Richard Hannay novel, *The Three Hostages* (1924), a history of publishing poetry: the MP Dominic Medina, who uses nefarious oriental techniques of hypnotism to coerce others into villainy, is introduced as 'a mixture of Byron and Sir Richard Burton and the young political highbrow' (Buchan 1992, 696). Again, Buchan's own contradictory enthusiasms and anxieties are revealed: '[Medina will] advance in his glorious career, and may become Prime Minister—or Viceroy of India—what a chance the second would be for him!—and publish exquisite little poetry books, as finished and melancholy as *The* [sic] *Shropshire Lad* [A. E. Housman, 1896]' (784). By projecting a career for one of his villains that is remarkably similar to his own eventual one (Buchan was a lifelong poet as well as fiction writer) he again reveals an implicit anxiety over the incommensurability of the 1890s artistic impulse with his public service and developing political ambitions.

While Leithen radically revises his initial impression of Koré over the course of the narrative of *The Dancing Floor*, this is in spite of rather than because of Shelley Arabin's enormities, which are so grotesque as to be only hinted at rather than detailed. He is, of course, a 'connoisseur and high priest of the uttermost evil' and Vernon Milburne, breaking into the Arabin house on the fictional Greek island of Plakos, is confronted by not only the usual bric-à-brac of Decadence ('Oriental rugs [...] and a litter of Chinese vases and antique silver lamps') but transgressive pagan pornography:

> The background was a mountain glade, and on the lawns and beside the pools of a stream figures were engaged in wild dances. Pan and his satyrs were there, and a bevy of nymphs, and strange figures half animal, half human. The thing was done with immense skill—the slanted eyes of the fauns, the leer in a contorted satyr face, the mingled lust and terror of the nymphs, the horrid obscenity of the movements. It was a carnival of bestiality that stared from the four walls. The man who conceived it had worshipped darker gods even than Priapus. There were other things which Vernon noted in the jumble of the room. A head of Aphrodite, for instance—Pandemos, not Urania. A broken statuette of a boy which made him sick. A

group of little figures which were a miracle in the imaginative degradation of the human form. Not the worst relics from the lupanars of Pompeii compared with these in sheer subtlety of filth. And all this in a shuttered room stifling with mould and disuse. (Buchan 1946, 223–24)

Here, then, Arabin's Decadence outstrips that of Rome's decline and anything remotely conscionable for Leithen who (as discussed in Chap. 2) admits to being given a 'distaste for the fantastic' by 'four years' hard campaigning' (a distaste shared by critics in light of literary Modernism as well as the war). There is also a clear articulation of the potential for corruption or obscenity latent in Paganism, the shuttered room serving as a Freudian metaphor for the suppression of the troubling, psychologically and morally destabilizing, aspects of the Classical world that are the flipside to its spiritually enriching numinosity and the noble and ennobling Paterian aspiration for the 'perfect life' (see below).

As mentioned, Shelley Arabin is analogous to and perhaps inspired by Crowley, who established his 'Abbey of Thelema' in Sicily in 1920 and whose 'activities served mainly to intensify the element of revulsion in horror stories which transformed Decadent sensibilities and Decadent ambitions into a stereotype of misguided evil' (Stableford 1998, 122). According to Douglas Kerr, the history of the Arabin family is one of 'romanticism turned in on itself, and become diseased, septic, decadent' (Kerr 2013, 151). As suggested previously, this again might be an expression of Buchan's anxiety over his reactions to Decadence and Paganism: fascination and repulsion in equal measure, and a palpable sense of psychological, as well as social, threat.

This same admixture is situated in a colonial context—informed by Buchan's familiarity with the South African landscape—in 'The Grove of Ashtaroth'. Despite the remoteness of the story's setting from Vigo Street, Buchan's preoccupation with Decadence and 1890s aestheticism remains a reference point. The story is presented as an account by a represented narrator of his friend Lawson—'one of those fellows who are born Colonial'—and his efforts to establish a permanent residence ('a civilised house') in a particular range of isolated country 'some thirty miles north of a place called Taqui' (Buchan 1910, 805). While Lawson is immediately smitten with the spot, the narrator is perturbed by one feature of the landscape:

It was no Christian wood. It was not a copse, but a 'grove,'—one such as Artemis may have flitted through in the moonlight. It was small, forty or fifty yards in diameter, and there was a dark something at the heart of it which for a second I thought was a house. (805)

The 'little conical tower, ancient and lichened' at the centre of the grove reminds the narrator of 'the famous Conical Temple at Zimbabwe' and his disquiet intensifies as they approach: 'I felt as if I were penetrating the temenos of some strange and lovely divinity, the goddess of this pleasant vale. There was a spell in the air, it seemed, and an odd dead silence' (805–06). James C. G. Grieg has identified the notion of the *temenos* as one of several categories into which Buchan's supernatural tales can be divided, noting his regular use of the sacred grove motif in his short stories (for example 'No-Man's-Land') and more explicitly in the *The Dancing Floor*. The temenos is a space dedicated to ritual and which has a function identical to that of the magic circle which 'delimits a boundary between law and transgression, the legitimate and illegitimate, the sacred and profane' (Thacker 2011, 57). This concept resonates with a childhood conceit of Buchan's which persisted into adulthood:

> I came to identify abstractions with special localities. The Soul, a shining cylindrical thing, was linked with a particular patch of bent and heather, and in that theatre its struggles took place, while Sin, a horrid substance like black salt, was intimately connected with a certain thicket of brambles and spotted toadstools. This odd habit long remained with me. (Buchan 1941, 16–17)

This childhood imposition of an imaginary narrative on the countryside, cast as a 'theatre' in which 'struggles took place', would develop into more sophisticated fictions like *The Dancing Floor*, *Witch Wood* (1927), and 'The Grove of Ashtaroth'.

In 'The Grove of Ashtaroth', the eponymous *temenos* acts as a catalyst for both the narrator's mysticism and—more acutely—for Lawson's suppressed Jewish heritage. The protagonist is aware of rumours concerning Lawson's ancestry. Ostensibly of Scottish border stock, there are insinuations of 'a grandfather who sold antiques in a back street at Brighton [who] had not changed his name, and still frequented the synagogue' (Buchan 1910, 803). Lawson's physical features confirm these suspicions to the narrator. His eyes are 'large and brown and mysterious, and the light of another race was in their odd depths' (803). Moreover, the narrator asserts that this Semitic influence results in an essential duality in Lawson's character: 'The two races were very clear in him—the one desiring gorgeousness, the other athirst for the soothing spaces of the North' (804).

As well as (according to Buchan) being indicative of his Jewish heritage, that Lawson desires 'gorgeousness' is also framed in the story in terms of

Lawson's predilection for the trappings of Decadence. Lawson's tastes in art and décor are also brought to bear as evidence of his atavistic impulses, and their dissonance with his ostensibly robust, Northern European colonial mind. In the anthologized version, the story establishes this tone by opening with a quote from 'Grotesques' by Paul Verlaine, from *Poèmes saturniens* (1866), in which the exemplar Decadent laments 'Des vieux morts et des anciens dieux!' [the old dead and the ancient gods!] (Buchan 1912, 141). The narrator is bemused by Lawson's intention to decorate his projected new home with 'Ming pots' and other extravagancies:

> He talked for a good hour of what he would do, and his dream grew richer as he talked, till by the time we went to bed he had sketched something liker a palace than a country-house. Lawson was by no means a luxurious man. At present he was well content with a Wolseley valise, and shaved cheerfully out of a tin mug. It struck me as odd that a man so simple in his habits should have so sumptuous a taste in bric-à-brac. I told myself, as I turned in, that the Saxon mother from the Midlands had done little to dilute the strong wine of the East. (Buchan 1910, 804)

When, years later, the narrator returns to visit Lawson in the now realized estate, the 'bric-à-brac' has failed to materialize. However, their absence is the result of Lawson discovering the wellspring of the 'strong wine of East' itself rather than its mere representation in decorative appurtenances. Regardless, when the narrator seeks a book to read to pass an evening, he finds a 'French' novel, Paul Bourget's *Cruelle Énigme* (1885).

Bourget was 'one of the most prestigious contemporary critics to dignify Decadent art with serious consideration and tentative approval' and provided the 'first formal "explanation" of what the writers of the Decadent Movement were doing, and why it was culturally significant' (Stableford 1998, 64). Buchan's choice of author here is therefore significant, despite the fact that as literary adviser to Nelson's selection of reprints for their French series, Buchan reassured the publisher that Bourget was 'both first-class and quite proper' (Adam Smith 1979, 52). Such references litter his later work and represent a continuing preoccupation with, and anxiety regarding, the cultural mood of the decade in which he established himself as a writer.

One particular aspect of this mood which persisted into the twentieth century with Buchan is paganism. Before further exploring manifestations of paganism and Buchan's attitude to paganism, a central trope of his weird fiction, I will first position Buchan more firmly as both a writer and a critic of (and without implying any stable or definite application of the term) weird fiction; that is, a writer who was perceived by his contemporaries as, among other things, an author of 'tales of the weird and uncanny' ("Fiction" 1902, 490).

BUCHAN AS A WRITER AND CRITIC OF WEIRD FICTION

Despite and because of Buchan's prominence as an individual, the difficulty in placing his weird fiction has resulted in it being all but forgotten. It is as obscure in its own way as Stenbock's, and if not that then certainly less read or discussed than Machen's. Only a decade after his death, genre fans expressed surprise upon discovering this aspect of his writing: in a letter in the February 1950 edition of *Famous Fantastic Mysteries*, a reader confesses to being 'greatly surprised to discover John Buchan in F.F.M.' (*Famous Fantastic Mysteries* 1950a, 114). Another reader is similarly bemused, remarking '"No-Man's-Land" by John Buchan was very, very good, and if it were not for the fact that Messrs. Merritt [A. Merritt (1884–1943), regular *Weird Tales* contributor] & Lovecraft are no longer living, I'd suspect that this was a probable collaboration between both of these great authors' (*Famous Fantastic Mysteries* 1950b, 118).

Contrastingly, a sense of Buchan's pre-war reputation as a writer can be gleaned from a *Punch* review of Buchan's 1912 anthology *The Moon Endureth*, published only three years before *The Thirty-Nine Steps*:

> His title [*The Moon Endureth*], which is not very happily chosen, refers really not to the promise of the Psalmist, but to the belief of St Francis that the moon stands for the dominion of all strange things in water or air. In that region of mystery and horror Mr Buchan is always at home. (*Punch* 1912, 379)

Ten years earlier, Buchan's work was being similarly described in the *Academy*, which said of his first anthology of short fiction, *The Watcher by the Threshold* (1902), that the stories therein

> [d]eal with shadows, ideas, possessions, sometimes supernatural, sometimes born only of the imagination, but always having a touch of mystery or dread. (*Academy and Literature* 1902, 553)

Reviewing the same collection, the *Speaker* argued that the discipline necessitated by the short story results in superior work:

> In his tales of the weird and uncanny [...] Buchan has done some of the best work we have yet seen from his pen. The necessities of the short story form prohibit much of the diffuse and apparently aimless writing which disfigured some of his longer novels. ("Fiction" 1902, 490)

It has similarly been argued more recently that Buchan 'tended to relegate his most profound epiphanies to his short fiction' (Freeman 2008, 25). It is interesting that the novels to which the reviewer is favourably comparing the anthology would have been the historical romance *John Barnet of Barnes* and the melodrama *The Half-Hearted*—in other words, works in a more mimetic and realistic vein than his weird fiction.

Although John Wylie Griffith makes explicit the shared thematic concerns of 'No-Man's-Land' and 'Heart of Darkness' (see below), he is evidently reticent about acknowledging the fact that Buchan's story is not an example of literary realism. Drawing on Machen, the lost race stories of Haggard, as well as the 'Turanian pygmy' theory of Scottish folklorist David MacRitchie (1851–1925), who argued that fairy lore was folkloric memory, the 'primitivism' of Buchan's text is represented by an actual relict population of prehuman hominins lurking in the Pentland Hills (Fergus 2015).[7] Although they are depicted as a far more unequivocally physical presence than Machen's mercurial and ontologically ambiguous 'little people' of Wales, this central narrative device is firmly of a different order to Conrad's text (and oeuvre). It would be presumptuous to do more than suggest that it is at least possible that Griffith obscures this aspect of the story through embarrassment, using it to evidence his wider argument while being coy about its possibly déclassé nature.

Regardless, at the time of publication, 'No-Man's-Land' was unequivocally regarded by its publisher as first-rate literature:

> In September 1898 William [Blackwood ...] entertained at Gogar Mount a twenty-three year old Scotsman, John Buchan, who had sent him some short stories from Brasenose College. In December William sent him a cheque for £40 and told him that his 'striking and powerful story "No-Man's-Land" would be given the place of honour in the January "Maga"'. 'I hope you will like the company your first contribution to "Maga" is in', he wrote. 'The story reads very well in print, and has a freshness and a real grasp of literary power which is very pleasing to an oldish editor to find in a new young contributor'. (Tredrey 1954, 184)

[7] A later, comparable example of a similar trope is E. F. Benson's 1922 story 'The Horror Horn', set in the Swiss Alps.

Conrad was certainly aware of Buchan's work although was more cautious in his appraisal of Buchan's skills as a writer, only conceding to William Blackwood that 'The Far Islands' was 'grammatically written' (Kerr 2009, 143). Douglas Kerr has detailed how in the same letter Conrad 'unleashes [the] missile' that Buchan had plagiarized the story from Kipling's 'The Finest Story in the World': 'Its idea, its feeling, its suggestion and even *the most subtly significant details* have been wrenched alive out of Kipling's tale' (Kerr 2009, 143). Kerr argues that Conrad's wrath was misplaced and possibly more a reflection of his own insecurities and Buchan's parvenu status than an actual instance of plagiarism: while superficially similar in their subject matter, the stories are wildly different in both tone and execution.

Kerr also recognizes that Kipling had no claim on the mutual theme of both tales, that of the reassertion of ancient ancestral memories in the lives of the protagonists:

> The trope of a recovered memory of earlier incarnations was not original to either story. [...] Ancestral memory is quite frequently encountered in late Victorian fiction, and accompanies the epoch's fascination with all kinds of inheritance—the cultural inheritance explored in the anthropology of myth and folklore, the narratives of physical inheritance for which Darwin had provided an explanation, and the psychic legacies assumed in the idea of tendencies—to crime, for example—transmitted with physiological features from one generation to the next within a family or a people. (Kerr 2009, 144)

As I will discuss in more detail below, Buchan was no exception, frequently weaving all of these concerns into a single narrative.

When H. P. Lovecraft extensively revised his essay 'Supernatural Horror in Literature' for serialization in the *Fantasy Fan* in 1933 (it had been originally published in the *Recluse* in 1927), he included a new paragraph on Buchan after encountering his work during 'an extensive course of rereading and analysing the weird classics in an attempt to revive what Lovecraft believed to be his flagging creative powers' (Joshi 2013, 2:861). In his commonplace book he made extensive notes on 'Weird Story Plots', and thought sufficiently of Buchan, evidently a recent discovery, to include him among such luminaries of the mode as 'Poe, Machen, Blackwood, de la Mare, M. R. James, Dunsany, E. F. Benson [and] Robert W. Chambers' (861). The three stories summarized by Lovecraft are 'The Green Wildebeeste' (1927), 'The Wind in the Portico' (1928), and 'Skule Skerry'

(1928), an identical choice to the three stories mentioned in the revised 'Supernatural Horror in Literature', which suggests that Lovecraft's access to Buchan was limited to a single anthology, *The Runagates Club* (Houghton Mifflin: Boston & New York, 1928)—consisting of club stories originally published in the *London Pall Mall Magazine*, September 1927 to July 1928—and the novel *Witch Wood* (Houghton Mifflin: Boston, 1927):

> In the novel *Witch Wood* John Buchan depicts with tremendous force a survival of the evil Sabbat in a lonely district of Scotland. The description of the black forest with the evil stone, and of the terrible cosmic adumbrations when the horror is finally extirpated, will repay one for wading through the very gradual action and plethora of Scottish dialect. Some of Mr. Buchan's short stories are also extremely vivid in their spectral intimations; 'The Green Wildebeest' [sic], a tale of African witchcraft, 'The Wind in the Portico, with its awakening of dead Britanno-Roman horrors, and 'Skule Skerry', with its touches of sub-arctic fright, being especially remarkable. (Lovecraft 1985, 486)

In his commonplace book, Lovecraft noted that 'The Green Wildebeeste' (which features Richard Hannay as the represented narrator) had an 'impressive atmosphere' and that 'ultimate explanations are left to reader'; that 'The Wind in the Portico' is set in an 'odd region of Shropshire where ancient influences subtly linger'; and that in 'Skule Skerry', the visitor to the eponymous islet 'acquires a strange, weird sensation of loneliness—of being at the very edge of things and close to the Abyss that contains only death' (Lovecraft 2004, 165). Lovecraft's selection suggests that he wasn't familiar with *The Moon Endureth: Tales and Fancies* (New York: Sturgis and Walton, 1912), as his failure to similarly enthuse about 'No-Man's-Land', 'Space', 'The Grove of Ashtaroth', or 'The Kings of Orion' is difficult to otherwise account for.

Lovecraft's phrase 'spectral intimations' here is a telling one, and resonates with Grant's application of Lovecraft's theoretical model of 'weird fiction' to Buchan to resolve the problem of using the term 'supernatural fiction' for stories that have no explicit supernatural content, but do possess, rather, 'spectral intimations' or to use John Clute's broader term, 'equipoise', analogous to Buchan's own 'sense of indefinable mystery' upon which great art was predicated.[8] In a BBC radio programme of

---

[8] (Grant 2009, 183); Austin, HRC, John Lane Company Records, Box 64, Reader's reports 1894–1899, 2 July 1896.

2014, *The Thirty-Nine Steps* and Buchan's other thrillers are identified as also being, to some extent, reflections on the 'wider mysteries of existence and the limits of rational inquiry' and also an acknowledgement that the 'world is essentially unknowable' (this resonating with the orientalist notion of the 'omniferous' universe and Machen's foundational positioning of immanent mystery discussed in Chap. 3). Michael Redley argues that the nebulous conspiracies at their heart remain mysterious in a way that reveals 'an element in [Buchan's] prose of mysticism' ("The Thirty-Nine Steps and World War I" 2014).

In *A Lodge in the Wilderness* (1906), one of the characters defines Imperialism, somewhat startlingly for the modern reader, as 'an enlarged sense of the beauty and mystery of the world' (Buchan 1906, 28). As with Machen, in Buchan's weird fiction, these concerns and uncertainties are foregrounded to become the central preoccupation, in many cases, of the text. Again, Clute's term 'equipoise' is a useful tool to understanding this: 'all stories are to some inherent degree—some stories being conspicuously so—not only signposts that tell you where you are, but also crossroads: hoverings of the liminal' (Clute 2006, 82). In *Mr. Standfast* (1919) Richard Hannay listens to an account of an uncanny encounter in wartime France and is given the following explanation: 'I just struck a crack in the old universe and pushed my head outside' (Buchan 1919, 202). Buchan feels it necessary for Hannay, his represented narrator in *Mr. Standfast*, to alert the reader to a weird episode in an otherwise worldly and down-to-earth spy thriller by flagging it up with references to both M. R. James's ghost stories and Hannay's own *Runagates Club* episode 'The Green Wildebeeste':

> One man had been reading a book called the Ghost Stories of an Antiquary, and the talk turned on the unexplainable things that happen to everybody once or twice in a lifetime. I contributed a yarn about the men who went to look for Kruger's treasure in the bushveld and got scared by a green wildebeeste. (200)

Clute's 'equipoise' is doubled in both the content and the form of weird fiction: both its liminal generic status and the liminality of the 'spectral intimations', bordering the known and the unknown, the mimetic and the fantastic. Eugene Thacker has delineated a difference between the 'supernatural' as employed by weird fiction and that which 'is so often confirmed within the labyrinths of Scholastic theology', which is useful when considering

Buchan's weird fiction: 'in the horror genre the supernatural is duplicitous; it is the name for something that is indistinct and yet omnipresent, something that defies easy categorization and that is, nevertheless, inscribed by a kind of logic' (Thacker 2015, 113–114).

As previously argued, that consideration of Buchan's weird fiction is a lacuna in contemporary critical treatment of his work is hardly surprising given that academic attention to his entire corpus has been sparse, and tends to focus on the most commercially and culturally impactful valences of his writing, that is, his 'shockers'. As previously discussed, before *The Thirty-Nine Steps* Buchan was certainly identified as a writer specializing in weird, supernaturally tinged fiction by contemporaries, as evidenced by the contemporary reviewers already quoted above, and also the *Bookman*:

> It may be confidently asserted that what Mr. Buchan set out to do he has done with a large measure of success. His is not a cheerful intention. Indeed, persons who demand cheerful literature should keep the book far from them; for it is the 'back-world of Scotland' he tries to describe, 'the land behind the mist, and over the seven bens,' the land where linger old terrors, which is haunted by ancient cruelties and a paganism so outworn as to be quite reasonable called inhuman. In 'No-Man's-Land' he tells of a folk beside whom the Celts are *parvenus*. 'The Watcher by the Threshold' is a terrible tale of possession of a modern man in the grip of an ancient, over powering personality. In 'The Far Away [sic] Islands', the haunter is an idea, a dream, that generation after generation draws a son of an old house to his doom. However, unlike in plot, vague terror of an unrecognised reality, the survival of an unkindly time, is in them all, to shake our smug content with the triumphs of civilization, and to stir forgotten depths, from which rise wars against our comfort. The book is one to shudder over; but through it run veins of genuine beauty. (*The Bookman* 1902)

As well as reading for John Lane, Buchan published with the firm, including in 1896 two short stories in issues 8 and 9 of the *Yellow Book* and an anthology of essays titled *Scholar Gipsies* (mainly composed of work that had previously seen print in *Macmillan's* magazine), all of which reveal to varying degrees an interest in supernatural themes (Buchan 1896a, b, c). 'A Captain of Salvation', concerns a Salvation Army captain who, on a patrol in the East End, is tempted to abandon the straight and narrow by the recursions in various guises representing his dissolute past. It was criticized by the *National Observer* for its 'touch of unrealism' which 'spoiled' a 'good story in the making' (*National Observer* 1896a). The trope of temptation by the Devil is repeated in 'A Journey of Little Profit', although this time with a more successful Scott-influenced historical Borders setting. The overall tone is humorous, but despite this there are some authentically sinister descriptions of the lone shepherd attempting to successfully navigate his herd to market across a desolate marsh.

As the above suggests, Buchan's output in the 1890s, both in terms of his novels and short fiction, occasionally displayed 'touches of unrealism' rather than examples of weird fiction proper, and it was not until 1899 that he produced his first story that can indisputably be considered an example of writing in the mode, 'No-Man's-Land' (Buchan 1899). However, his reader's reports for John Lane provide clear evidence that when he had occasion to, he gave serious consideration to it. His lack of employment of the specific term 'weird fiction' can perhaps be ascribed to the word's far more specific meaning in Scottish dialect, as discussed in the Introduction. In *The Dancing Floor*, the first-person narrator Leithen further delineates the word: 'I have heard stories of inherited obsessions and premonitions—what they call a "weird" in Scotland' (Buchan 1946, 33). Several of Buchan's stories concern the trope of 'inherited obsessions'— for example, 'The Far Islands' (1899), 'The Watcher by the Threshold' (1900), 'The Kings of Orion' (1906), 'The Grove of Ashtaroth', to name four of arguably many more.

As a reader for John Lane in the 1890s, Buchan demonstrated well-developed and clearly articulated beliefs on what sort of supernatural fiction was credible for the modern reader, using these distinctions as the basis for his advice to Lane as to whether to accept or decline manuscript submissions for publication. Advising Lane to decline a manuscript titled *Miss Crump* by a C. H. Campbell, Buchan acknowledges that as 'a ghost-story this book is quite well-done' and that 'the mystery is kept up till quite the end, and the explanation is most credible'.[9] However, one of the grounds upon which Buchan advises against publication is that 'the ghosts, though well-done, are a little out-of-date', adding that 'we want something a little more recondite nowadays than sheeted monks, vaults, iron chests and missing marriage certificates'. He concludes that the interest of the novel is 'narrow, conventional and [again] out-of-date' and would therefore 'not be successful'.

---

[9] Austin, HRC, John Lane Company Records, Box 64, Reader's reports 1894–1899, 28 July 1896.

It is clear from this judgement that Buchan regards the traditional tropes of the Gothic, and of the Ghost Story, as no longer being credible devices for supernatural fiction, and his emphasis on 'something a little more recondite' is commensurable with both his own weird fiction and subsequent accounts of the rise of weird fiction in the late-Victorian and Edwardian periods. He, perhaps reflexively, uses this delineation to narrative effect in *The Dancing Floor*. The novel is an expanded (and considerably improved upon) version of Buchan's own 1914 short story for *Blackwoods*, 'Basilissa', which effectively serves as an introductory episode firmly in the realm of the Northern European Gothic.

After a hill-walking mishap, Edward Leithen (often regarded as the Buchan character most clearly a proxy for its author) seeks refuge in the country estate of a young acquaintance, Vernon Milburne. At the beginning of the novel, Milburne—based on Buchan's university friend Raymond Asquith—strikes a classically Gothic figure (Green 1977, 78). Milburne is the last of his race, isolated within the echoing stone walls of his rambling ancestral home whose architecture is the 'worst kind of Victorian Gothic', decorated with 'sham-medieval upholstered magnificence' (Buchan 1946, 17). Leithen goes so far as to describe it as being 'Gothic with every merit of Gothic left out' and pities Milburne as 'a boy of nineteen alone in this Gothic mausoleum' (17–18). In what is in effect a prologue to the narrative proper, Buchan appears to entertain the trappings of Gothic horror while simultaneously acknowledging that this *milieu* is an ersatz one, necessary to establish the correct circumstances for Milburne to relate a troubling secret, which he describes as a 'thing like a ghost story' (23). Leithen agrees and, as tradition demands, it is only later that evening when they are ensconced by the fireplace that suitable conditions are met for Milburne to begin his 'ghost story', which transpires to be an annually recurring nightmare.

Again, the Gothic is very much evoked in the nature of this fervid persecution. Milburne finds himself in a bedroom, similar to his actual one yet lacking any windows and only accessible by a single door facing the bed. Finding himself in an oneiric version of one of Piranesi's similarly inspired *Carceri* prints, he knows that beyond the door is a room identical to the one he is presently in, and beyond that, another identical room, and so on, until there is formed a sort of endless corridor:

> There seemed to the boy to be no end to this fantastic suite. He thought of it as a great snake of masonry, winding up hill and down dale away to the fells or the sea. (27)

The conceit is a potent example of both the Gothic's preoccupation with the sublime affect of infinite recession and spatial disorientation, and weird fiction's distortion of architectural space. Moreover, Milburne is aware that a terrible presence is somewhere advancing inexorably towards him:

> Somewhere far away in one of the rooms was a terror waiting on him, or, as he feared, coming towards him. Even now it might be flitting from room to room, every minute bringing its soft tread nearer to the chamber of the wood fire. About this time of his life the dream was an unmitigated horror. (27–28)

Here again, the language used is unmistakably that of the Gothic, and of the traditional ghost story: the 'soft tread' approaching the 'chamber of the wood fire'. Buchan's deployment of what he had previously suggested as out-of-date and conventional language of horror works here because of the sudden gear change after this episode, where the main narrative of the novel begins in earnest.

From this northern Gothic beginning, the action abruptly shifts to a Greek island and a discussion of pre-Olympian paganism, of satyrs, pan pipes, and Attic mysteries. Milburne and Leithen are now on a yachting holiday some time later and alight on a small, obscure island. Both are immediately affected by some quality of the landscape and Milburne launches into a lengthy disquisition on the origins of Catholicism in antique paganism, thus establishing the subsequent tone of the narrative. However effective the atmosphere created by the notion of an inexorable doom steadily approaching through an impossibly arranged series of rooms may be, Buchan's use of traditional Gothic tropes at the outset of the novel lulls the reader into a false sense of familiarity, resulting in the novel being all the more effective for being not really 'a thing like a ghost story' at all.

His function as an adviser to a leading publisher also demonstrates that the move away from the traditional Gothic was in some respects a market-driven as well as a purely aesthetic choice—Buchan's advice not to publish comes down to the fact that the novel 'would not be successful'. Buchan's parameters for successful supernatural fiction are not simply confined to novelty, however. He ruminates in detail on the difficulty differentiating between 'mere horror [… and …] legitimate art' when reporting on a manuscript titled *The Fratricide* by the Anglo-Canadian writer Ernest G. Henham.[10] He defines 'legitimate art' again in explicitly commercial

---

[10] Austin, HRC, John Lane Company Records, Box 64, Reader's reports 1894–1899, 2 July 1896.

terms: 'I use the word *legitimate* merely from the commercial point of view, as equivalent to what is read and tolerated by readers of fiction.' Once again, however, he emphasizes the importance of the recondite: 'In a book of horrors we demand that the absorbing interest does not lie in the horrors themselves, but in some mystery, intrigue, or some human passion of love or sacrifice.' Buchan regards Henham's tale as a failure in at least this respect, although he does acknowledge that 'the book is ably written and in parts very powerful'.

The Fratricide concerns a murderer who 'has always had a horror of spiders': 'to his diseased mind his sin takes the shape of a great black spider which threatens to clutch at his face' until at last he 'stabs himself to escape from it' (ibid.). Buchan negatively compares Henham's execution of the story with three writers who, in the context of this thesis, are by now familiar names: Stevenson, Poe, and Machen:

> Take *Dr. Jekyll*. What made that book a great work of art was the sense of indefinable mystery which hung over it to the very end, as also the genuine romantic quality of contrast between the horror and the humdrum life around. Take Poe's better tales. All have some plot, mystery, tragic adventure, as the framework on which their web of horrors is woven. Take Arthur Machen's *Great God Pan*. There is the romantic element, the feeling of impossible adventure, which gives credence to the horror and makes the book tolerable to the reader.

Buchan concludes his analysis by stating unequivocally that a text which is no more than an 'exclusive analysis of madness and horrible nightmare is an offence against art and the ordinary interests of men'. His strength of feeling is also suggested by his statement that he 'cannot recommend any alterations, for the error seems to [...] lie very deep', regardless that 'the author has genuine talents'. Buchan is not interested in, and actively dislikes, prurient depictions of the horrific for their own sake, but accepts the horrific if it is employed towards a larger end of evoking a 'sense of indefinable mystery' which 'hangs over [...] to the very end'; in other words, the unresolved equipoise typical of weird fiction. Buchan's theorizing here is subsequently put into practice in his own later output in this vein, as discussed above and in further detail below.

The Fratricide was evidently declined by John Lane on Buchan's advice, as well as that of Le Gallienne, whose more laconic, though commensurate, response concludes that Henham 'attempts the sublimely horrible and achieves the unpleasantly ridiculous' and that Le Gallienne does not 'think it would have any chance of success'.[11] Buchan also mentions that 'there is something of a reaction against such books at the present moment', perhaps referring to the newly censorious post-Wilde trial mood, although he adds that 'this book would be unpopular at any time'. Nevertheless, a version of *The Fratricide* was eventually published under the title *Tenebrae* in 1898 by Skeffington (Henham 1898). The reviews *Tenebrae* received certainly agree with Buchan's and Le Gallienne's negative appraisal of the manuscript. According to the *Athenaeum*, *Tenebrae* 'teems with horrors, more or less badly described. [...] Mania, madness, murder, and suicide are a few of the less-important subjects of the story, which is, in fact, a hopeless jumble of atrocities' (*Athenaeum* 1898). According to the *Saturday Review*:

> *Tenebrae* (Skeffington) by Ernest Henham is an unpleasant but not particularly terrifying nightmare in 329 pages. The author is not a master of the horror that comes at a word or the hint of a word. His only resource is to pile up descriptions of blood, big spiders and madness, and then more descriptions of madness and blood and big spiders. It is rather nasty sometimes, certainly, but all the big spiders in the world could not make it impressive. We began more than one conscientious shudder, but it always ended in the ordinary yawn of everyday reading. (*Saturday Review* 1898)

The *Academy* is equally damning, and in a rather mean-spirited fashion concludes its desultorily brief review by presenting Henham's own words without further comment: 'The doctor who supplies an elucidatory appendix says of the madman's MS: "The closing pages are most awful. The very paper seems to scream with torture"' (*Academy* 1898). *Tenebrae* certainly didn't trouble the bestseller listings of the *Bookman*'s 'Monthly Reports on the Wholesale Book Trade' for that year and the original edition has since become a rare and valuable collector's item: at the time of writing a single copy is available on www.abebooks.com priced at £1200 (*Bookman* 1898; "Tenebrae by Henham, Ernest G, First Edition - AbeBooks" n.d.). Under the pen name of John Trevena, Henham went on to produce naturalistic novels that received favourable comparison to Hardy, and these are now again receiving some 'serious critical recognition', although *Tenebrae* remains obscured beneath its 'cloak of Gothicism's extreme psychopathic imagery' (Monsman 2015, 241, 252).

---

[11] Austin, HRC, John Lane Company Records, Box 64, Reader's reports 1894–1899, undated, *circa* July 1896.

One work that succeeded in meeting Buchan's criteria for successful supernatural fiction while he was a reader for Lane was *'Twixt Dog and Wolf* by C. F. Keary (1848–1917), submitted to Lane for consideration in 1897. Charles Francis Keary is described in the *Oxford Dictionary of National Biography* as a 'numismatist and writer', which gives only an indication of the polymath range of his career ("Oxford DNB Article: Keary, Charles Francis" 2004). He was, additionally, a scholar and antiquarian, a spiritualist, he worked in the Department of Coins at the British Museum, and was a reasonably successful novelist, as such described by the *Academy* as one whose failures were 'more interesting than the successes of most people' (*Academy* 1899, 689).

The variety of Keary's literary output is suggested by the titles of two volumes from the early 1890s: *The Vikings in Western Christendom A.D. 789 to A.D. 888* (1891) and *A Mariage de Convenance* (1893) (Charles Francis Keary 1893, C. F. Keary 1891). His *Times* obituary says of Keary's novels that they aim 'at depicting life, after the manner of the great Russian writers, in its chaotic reality and avoiding conventional selection and arrangement', adding that while they 'never had a large popular circulation' they were 'very highly thought of within the limited literary set' (*The Times* 1917). He was also, however, a writer of short fiction for the periodical market and, in the 1890s, produced several stories that, in distinct contrast to his novels—exercises in what the *Speaker* described as 'the modern political and social sphere' of fiction—were unmistakably tinged with the yellow hue of the era, and expertly evoked an oneiric, vesperal realm of disconcerting shadows and dark forces moving unseen, yet tangible, in tandem with our own (O 1902, 623).

Both Buchan and Le Gallienne were voluble in their praise in their reader's reports for the anthology of short stories and sketches submitted by Keary to John Lane in 1897 under the title *'Twixt Dog and Wolf*.[12] At least some of the contents of the anthology were already familiar to both since they had already appeared in the *New Review* (under Henley's editorship) and *Macmillan's*, some only very recently (C. F. Keary 1892, 1896a, b, 1897a, b, c). Buchan had 'read some of them in the *New Review* and admired them greatly' while Le Gallienne knew of Keary at least by reputation: 'I happen to know that Mr Henley thought ["Elizabeth"] an extraordinarily fine piece of work.' As well as short stories, the volume

---

[12] Austin, HRC, John Lane Company Records, Box 64, Reader's reports 1894–1899, 2 April 1897.

contained some prose poems or fables ('Phantasies'), of which Le Galliene opined, 'some are very pretty and quasi-symbolical, some are weird and horrible—all are worth reprinting'.[13] Despite their enthusiasm, the book was not published by John Lane and did not see publication at all until 1901, described in 1911 by *The Times* as 'a series of short sketches in the weird and *macabre* [...] excellently done' (*The Times* 1917). However, it is now, like its author, all but forgotten.[14]

It is possible to reasonably speculate that Lane's decision not to publish in 1897 was a consequence of the same post-Wilde trial mood that imposed a similar lacuna on Machen's published output and which Buchan referred to in his report on Henham's manuscript quoted above, although it could of course have simply been the result of a failure to meet terms. Certainly, in comparison with the majority of readers' reports filed by Lane and Le Gallienne in the 1890s, the feedback on *'Twixt Dog and Wolf* by both is exceptional in its enthusiasm and even more anomalous in the unequivocalness of that enthusiasm. Le Gallienne writes:

> I do not think you need have any hesitation in publishing this book. It is a collection of stories—in the case of "phantasies" of course something slighter—each with an element of the weird, the uncanny, the mystical. Such an element, well managed, will always attract readers, and Mr. Keary's management of it is one of the best I have ever seen.[15]

Buchan's estimation of the quality of Keary's work is fully commensurate with Le Gallienne's:

> He writes carefully and exquisitely, without the vice of artifice which spoils so much of modern work. His sketches are stories of *diablerie* of the strange sights and sounds which follow on the twilight, between the dog barking and the appearance of the grey wolf. The first is a tale of the conflict between the ordinary Greek religion and the old wild nature worship—of Pan and the nymphs—which it displaced. The second *Elizabeth* is a story of medieval

---

[13] Austin, HRC, John Lane Company Records, Box 64, Reader's reports 1894–1899, undated (*circa* April 1896).

[14] James Joyce mentions Keary in a letter *circa* 24 September 1905, to his brother Stanislaus, and in a footnote the editors of the *Selected Letters* suggest that *'Twixt Dog and Wolf* is 'probably meant'. However, Keary's 'novel of Bloomsbury life' *Bloomsbury* (1905) seems a far more likely candidate. See (Joyce 1957, II:111).

[15] Austin, HRC, John Lane Company Records, Box 64, Reader's reports 1894–1899, undated (*circa* April 1896).

Germany—one of the finest witch-tales I know. The *Four Students* is a tale of the Paris of the Revolution. *Phantasies* are slightly different: I am not sure that I always catch Keary's meaning; but they seem to me in the whole to be nearly as good work in metaphysics as Stevenson's *Fables*.

Mr Keary has wide knowledge, a great gift of style, and a wonderful power of suggesting vague mystery. His work is in every way admirable and I gladly recommend you to take the book.[16]

The strength of the impression made on Buchan by *'Twixt Dog and Wolf* is also evident in Buchan's own subsequent career as an author. As mentioned above, a trope frequently employed by Buchan in his weird fiction was that of sacred grove, or *temenos*. This is anticipated and explored in Keary's 'The Four Students', in which Keary makes the chilling geographical association between the site of the mass executions of the Terror and that of the hideous rites of antique pagan ritual, suggesting that the influence of the same maleficent *genius loci* is responsible for both. Both this theme and Keary's 'witch-tale' 'Elizabeth' clearly resonates with, and perhaps directly influenced, Buchan's own novel of seventeenth-century '*diablerie*', *Witch Wood* (1927), arguably the template for the 1970s 'folk horror' films *Blood on Satan's Claw* (1970) and *The Wicker Man* (1973). The structural theme common to both Keary's work and Buchan's is the conflict between pre-Classical paganism and modern religion, a theme which underpins so much of Buchan's weird and other fiction that it demands to be examined in further detail.

Weird Pagan Survivals

> Christianity is generally supposed to have annihilated heathenism. [...] In reality it merely smoothed over and swallowed its victim, and the contour of its prey, as in the case of the boa-constrictor, can be distinctly traced under the glistening colours of its beautiful skin. Paganism still exists, it is merely inside instead of outside. (Wood-Martin 1902, I: viii)

The Dancing Floor culminates in a very literal resurgence of Greece's Classical Pagan past. The islanders, some of whom, it is darkly hinted, had first-hand experience of Shelley Arabin's depravity, have long since designated Koré Arabin a witch and the cause of all their woes, the most recent

---

[16] Austin, HRC, John Lane Company Records, Box 64, Reader's reports 1894–1899, 2 April 1896.

of which is a harsh and unforgiving winter, resulting in widespread hunger and despair. The island priest warns Leithen that church attendance has nearly dropped off altogether and that he fears that a desperate reversion to forbidden pagan practices is imminent in the face of the crisis, with Koré Arabin inevitably serving as the scapegoat:

> The insistence that Christianity wins out over the older faiths it supplanted in truth suggests not that it has conquered them outright but that the island is a form of spiritual palimpsest where the Christian overlays and partially obscures something far more ancient and perhaps more powerful. (Freeman 2008, 30)

While at Brasenose, Buchan had discussed the possibility of the survival of such 'ancient cults' with his tutor, Dr F. W. Bussell, college chaplain and erstwhile friend of Pater (Richards 1976, 41).

The 'dancing floor' of the title is the venue for these grim proceedings and the mysteries enacted at the narrative climax: a sacred pasture in which ancient rites are once again rehearsed by moonlight:

> The place was no more the Valley of the Shadow of Life, but Life itself—a surge of dæmonic energy out of the deeps of the past. It was wild and yet ordered, savage and yet sacramental, the home of an ancient knowledge which shattered for me the modern world and left me gasping like a caveman before his mysteries. The magic smote on my brain, though I struggled against it. The passionless moonlight and the passionate torches—that, I think, was the final miracle—a marrying of the eternal cycle of nature with the fantasies of man. (Buchan 1946, 191–192)

This 'shattering' of the modern world by ancient mysteries is, in this instance, a purely subjective experience for Leithen, and, typically of the equipoise of Buchan's writing of this type, there is no conclusively supernatural manifestation. The work remains generically slippery: not quite a thriller, certainly not realism in the widely understood sense, but also lacking a tangible representation of the supernatural, only the perception by the represented narrator of some immanence which 'smites the brain', and, in Lovecraft's words, a 'breathless and unexplainable dread of outer, unknown forces', a facility for which Buchan demonstrated time and again in his fiction.

The survival of the pagan and its threat to modernity was a concern sustained by Buchan over the course of his writing career, informed by his family background, his education, and his wider experiences as a colonial administrator. Buchan's upbringing in a Calvinist household, the son of a minister of the Free Church of Scotland, was tempered by his enthusiastic interest and education in the Classics, including works of late Roman pagan philosophy: he described the 'Latin and Greek classics' as his 'first real intellectual interest' (Buchan 1941, 39). This interest was nurtured under the tutelage of Gilbert Murray, 'then a young man in his middle twenties and [...] known only by his Oxford reputation', who left an indelible impression on Buchan at Glasgow University:

> To me his lectures were, in Wordsworth's phrase, like 'kindlings of the morning.' Men are by nature Greeks or Romans, Hellenists or Latinists. Murray was essentially a Greek; my own predilection has always been for Rome; but I owe it to him that I was able to understand something of the Greek spirit and still more to come under the spell of the classic discipline in letters and life. (34)

Buchan's enthusiasm for Pater's *Marius the Epicurean*, a work considered remarkable in the 'seriousness with which it handles Roman religion' (Kemp et al. 2002a, 47; *Saturday Review* 1885, 351):

> I think I was born with the same temperament as the Platonists of the early seventeenth century, who had what Walter Pater has called 'a sensuous love of the unseen,' or, to put it more exactly, who combined a passion for the unseen and the eternal with a delight in the seen and the temporal. (Buchan 1941, 39)

Buchan's fin-de-siècle Paganism was learned in schoolrooms and lecture theatres rather than in occult lodges and Bohemian salons, and, far from instilling in him any antiestablishment animus or moral incontinence, inculcated him with 'classic discipline':

> This preoccupation with the classics was the happiest thing that could have befallen me. It gave me a standard of values. [...] The classics enjoined humility. The spectacle of such magnificence was a corrective to youthful immodesty, and, like Dr. Johnson, I lived 'entirely without my own approbation.' Again, they corrected a young man's passion for rhetoric. This was in the 'nineties, when the Corinthian manner was more in vogue than the Attic. Faulty though my own practice has always been, I learned sound doctrine—the virtue of a clean bare style, of simplicity, of a hard substance and an austere pattern. (35)

It was his study of classical philosophy at Glasgow University that led him to adopt for a while 'the demeanour of the Platonic, dressing soberly and striving to order his life "according to the rules of philosophy"' (Kruse 1989, 7:14). Although Buchan found this 'classic discipline in letters and life' to be commensurate with his Calvinism, it was regarded by others, including Yeats, as a tradition threatened by the waxing of Christianity: 'Odor of blood when Christ was slain | Made all Platonic tolerance vain | And vain all Doric discipline' (Yeats 1928, 48). In *The Decline and Fall of the Roman Empire* (1776–88), Gibbon had regarded the 'conversion of the crumbling empire to the new religion simply as one more stage in its decline' from 'an altogether admirable ideal' (Stableford 1998, 7). In terms of 'letters' rather than 'life', the phrase 'classic discipline' implied 'qualities of form, grace, and dignity in the use of language, and the literature of our people' based on the classical ideal, an aesthetic principle as well as a practical one (F. M. F. 1918, 18). One corollary of this valorization of classical culture in the British education system, however, was that it exposed young minds to ideas, philosophies, and religious practices distinctly antithetical to Christianity.

Throughout his corpus, many of Buchan's characters reveal a pragmatic loyalty to Christianity while regularly being tempted or part-seduced by the dark glamour of paganism. Despite the fact that his upbringing was not blighted by the grim repression experienced by, for example, Algernon Blackwood, and often associated with Calvinism's sometimes dour doctrine of predestination, Buchan's sustained occupation with this dissonance between his faith and his fascination with Roman antiquity demonstrates that it was clearly on some level a troublesome one for him. He was certainly not alone in his preoccupations, however, and although not usually a figure one would associate with the 'pagan revival' of the 1890s, his weird fiction expresses similar concerns, albeit from the establishment point of view rather than the bohemian one. For Buchan there was no disputing either Paganism's dark seductive power nor the vigilance against which that power must be resisted if modernity is to remain civilized. His attitude in this respect informed the equivocalness of his view of literary Decadence and resonated with contemporary concerns discussed in previous chapters. Buchan's discomfort with valences of contemporary culture that he thought resulted from dangerous atavism informed his fiction for decades into the twentieth century.

As already suggested, the term 'Pagan' would have evoked a complicated set of resonances for Buchan and many of his contemporaries. The education of many was built upon the valorization of the historical pagan culture of the Classical age as a model for an Empire partly justified by its attempts to eradicate paganism from the territories it controlled. Although often discussed only in terms of bohemian 'occulture', in actuality Classical Paganism was as much of an intellectual and philosophical bedrock of the establishment Right as Christianity: every eager public-school boy being groomed for imperial and public service would have been weaned on Homer and Virgil and known his Greek and Latin tags. Buchan, no public-school boy, nevertheless found his Calvinism to be 'confirmed' by his study of the Classics.

The florid, sensuous paganism of the Victorian occult underground and associated with societies like the Golden Dawn and its predecessor, the Isis-Urania Temple, would have been anathema to Buchan in practice, and, indeed, the association of fin-de-siècle occult activity with Paganism is sometimes overstated: while there was certainly a vogue for Buddhism and Eastern mysticism, the rituals of the Golden Dawn were largely based on Jewish kabbalist texts, broadly commensurate with and certainly not antithetical to Christianity—occasionally explicitly Christian (The Golden Dawn's 'Cromlech' temple, for example)—and when Egyptian ritual was practised, the actual content tended to be derived from Freemasonry rather than authentic ancient pagan practices (J. Machin 2013).

Aleister Crowley rebelled against his dourly repressive Plymouth Brethren upbringing by embracing Isis-Urania/Golden Dawn ritualism with every fibre of his being (ibid.). Perhaps Buchan wore his Calvinism too lightly for there to be any similar transgressive appeal in abandoning it to pursue esoteric, Catholic-leaning branches of Christian ritualism. Buchan's interest in Classical paganism was, therefore, in no way an indication of any predisposal to involve himself in any of the occult societies flourishing at the time. Contrarily, he argues that

> above all the Calvinism of my boyhood was broadened, mellowed, and also confirmed. For if the classics widened my sense of the joy of life they also taught its littleness and transience; if they exalted the dignity of human nature they insisted upon its frailties and the aidos with which the temporal must regard the eternal. I lost then any chance of being a rebel, for I became profoundly conscious of the dominion of unalterable law. Prometheus might be a fine fellow in his way, but Zeus was king of gods and men. (Buchan 1941, 35–36)

It is indicative of his attitude to Paganism that he fabricated a quote from 'Donisarius, Monk of Padua' to open one of his earliest published stories, 'A Captain of Salvation', which appeared in the *Yellow Book* in 1896. In the passage ascribed to him by Buchan, this fictional 'Donisarius' acknowledges the variegated virtues and noble attributes of various Roman divinities, but he nevertheless negatively compares them to what he deems to be superior Christian analogues:

> Nor is it any matter of sorrow to us that the gods of the Pagans are no more. For whatsoever virtue was theirs is embodied in our most blessed faith. For whereas Apollo was the most noble of men in appearance and seemed to his devotees the incarnation [...] of the beauty of the male, we have learned to apprehend a higher beauty of the Spirit, as in our blessed Saints. And whereas Jupiter was the king of the world, we have another and more excellent King, even God the Father, the holy Trinity. And whereas Mars was the god of war, the strongest and most warlike of beings, we have the great soldier of our cause, even the Captain of our Salvation. And whereas the most lovely of women was Venus, beautiful alike in spirit and body, to wit our Blessed Lady. So it is seen that whatever delights are carnal and of the flesh, such are met by greater delights of Christ and His Church. (Buchan 1896b, 143)

Buchan's attitude to paganism can be contextualized within a wider establishment resistance to the appropriation of Classical paganism by what the *Saturday Review* described as '*les jeunes*'. These two competing 'Paganisms', new and old, were already recognized by the *Saturday Review* in 1892:

> There can be no better cure for the errors of Neo-paganism than a study of the old pagans: HOMER, SOPHOCLES, VIRGIL. They, not M. PAUL VERLAINE, not even Mr. GEORGE MEREDITH, not even BAUDELAIRE (as the *Pagan Review* calls that author, who himself smote the Neo-Pagans in a memorable essay) are the guides to follow. (*Saturday Review of Politics, Literature, Science and Art* 1892, 269)

This disparagement was a response to William Sharp's one-issue journal the *Pagan Review*, in which, under an editorial alias of W. H. Brooks (Fiona MacLeod later becoming his better-known pen name), Sharp attempted to 'present a range of historical, mythological, and spiritual perspectives of paganism as a living, global phenomenon' (Denisoff 2012). Despite the grand scale of this vision, however, the *Saturday Review* clearly regarded what it called the 'Neo-pagan' as a literary phenomenon rather than a holistic lifestyle choice. Moreover, and anticipating the wider criticism of Decadence only two or three years later, it criticized Neo-pagan style as fussy and overcomplicated: 'the art of writing well is not the trick of laying on adjectives with a palette-knife' (*Saturday Review of Politics, Literature, Science and Art* 1892, 269). It also makes an early identification of the conflicting currents of paganism operating through the culture, one establishment and reactionary, the other an attempt at artistic and philosophical radicalism: 'Real paganism to the modern Neo-Pagan would have seemed Tory in politics, bald in art, and unadventurous in morals' (269).

This 1892 manifestation of literary 'Neo-paganism', which elides so easily into Decadence, was superseded by others. In June 1896, the *National Observer* wrote a witheringly antipathetic account of the latest Parisian 'neo-Paganism' apropos of Pierre Louÿs's *Aphrodite*:

> A person sorely dissatisfied with the existing order of things as to be reduced to the extremity of becoming a Pagan naturally has but a slight respect for the institutions he desires to see superseded, and the Frenchman, when disposed to be disrespectful, is in the habit of allowing himself the utmost licence of expression. [...] In conclusion we are asked to believe that these and all the other ills of contemporary existence would vanish were we to revert to the customs and resume the worship of the deities of the ancient world. (*National Observer* 1896b, 180)

It also delineates a specific 'neo-Pagan' ethos or animus, which it then attacks as simply an attempt to give debauchery the respectable sheen of religion:

> The book [*Aphrodite*] which has aroused this enthusiasm endeavours to make good the thesis that the perfect life was the life led by the ancient Greeks at the crowning epoch of their history. [...] M. Pierre Louÿs has a mighty fine air, but at bottom he is merely the apologist of all manner of unclean things. (181)

It is clear from these attempts to distinguish 'good' Paganism from 'bad' Paganism that Buchan's conflicted attitude to the Classical and pre-Classical past was shared by others. The concern of the writer in the *National Observer* is specifically that Paganism is simply an excuse for indulging in 'all manner of unclean things', and, indeed, this alleged corollary of Paganism is still one often assumed today.

However, operating alongside the suspicions and outright accusations that Paganism was merely 'gilt on the gingerbread of lechery', was the 'respectable' Paganism and the religious seriousness of Pater, the cultural bedrock of 'HOMER, SOPHOCLES, VIRGIL', and the vigorous defences of other commentators like Machen against the charge of licentiousness (Machen 1924, 8):

> There is another error of comparison between Christianity and Paganism; an error [...] almost deserving to be placed on the Academic List of Vulgar Errors. This latter misconception is to the effect that, whereas good Christians are obliged to live very strict lives, good pagans could do exactly as they pleased. [...] I suppose many people think of paganism as of one long revel; of the faithful pagans as continually engaged in their religious duties of crowning themselves—and everything—with roses, of singing odes in honour of the Nymphs and the Graces, of drinking Falernian wine, and of—well—enjoying themselves in other agreeable fashions. The pagan world is imagined as a vast Abbey of Thelema, where everybody did exactly as he liked, where there were no morals and no rules, and no such words as 'no' or 'you musn't' were ever heard. [...] I believe that there was very little difference between the average 'morals' of an average Greek village in the fifth century before Christ and the average 'morals' of an English village of to-day. (Machen 1908, 206)

In making this remark Machen is, albeit perhaps inadvertently, undermining the entire project of the British Empire. Machen goes on to ascribe 'periods of corruption and decay' in the Classical world rather to 'practical atheism' and complains that it is 'really difficult to conceive how this utterly nonsensical idea of universal libertinism can have arisen' (207). Buchan the Paterian and classical scholar would no doubt have sympathized with Machen's criticism of the popular view of pagan worship as inherently debauched and orgiastic, a practice 'in which men [... did ...] what they would, devoid of morals altogether' with 'no law to restrain you, from within or from without' (Machen 1924, 7). This possibly tempered Buchan's view of native religions and stayed his hand from condemning non-Abrahamic faiths as crudely and stridently as some of his fellow colonialists.

Buchan's emphasis on the role of Greek culture in inculcating him with 'the classic discipline' is one that the *Saturday Review* would have approved of as the correct message to take from paganism. Buchan was not immune, however, from the more romantic and visionary strains of neo-paganism then ascendant:

> A quarter of my blood was Highland and in that I developed a new pride, for it was a time when people talked of the 'Celtic twilight,' and Mr. Yeats had just published his *Wind Among the Reeds*. (Buchan 1941, 81)

In fact, his response was a productive one: he imaginatively restaged classical culture in his native landscape:

> If Gilbert Murray was the principal influence in shaping my interests, another was the Border country, which I regarded as my proper home. [...] Tweeddale [had] an aura of classical convention, and 'Pan playing on his aiten reed' has never ceased to be a denizen of its green valleys. There is a graciousness there, a mellow habitable charm, unlike the harsh Gothic of most of the Scots landscape. I got it into my head that here was the appropriate setting for pastoral, for the shepherds of Theocritus and Virgil, for the lyrists of the Greek Anthology, and for Horace's Sabine farm. [...] My fancy had its uses, for I never read classical poetry with such gusto as in my Border holidays, and it served as a link between my gipsy childhood and the new world of scholarship into which I was seeking entrance. (34–35)

Although there seems little evidence from such reflections that Buchan felt any particular compromise or tension between these paganisms, or between his bucolic romanticism and his Christianity, just as Machen was already contorting this gentle pastoral Classicism into far more sinister shapes, Buchan too would follow suit in his own weird fiction. Several of Buchan's tales explore the potential for horror in pagan imminences in the landscape and our psychological heritage. Once again, Smith's notion of 'Caledonian Antisyzygy' can be invoked here, which identifies in Scottish writing a tendency to be 'fundamentally bipolar, oscillating between extremes of [...] civilised urbanity and savage rusticity' (Goldie 2012, 190).

In Buchan's 1928 story 'The Wind in the Portico' (one of the 'Runagates Club' stories originally published in the *Pall Mall* magazine), the reclusive Shropshire squire Dubellay might look 'exactly like the city solicitors you see dining in the Junior Carlton' but his lonely obsession with pagan antiquity proves his undoing. The 'Runagates Club' tales are, unsurprisingly, presented explicitly as Club Stories. The Runagates includes Buchan-regular Richard Hannay among its members and it is a comment of his which occasions the telling of this particular tale:

> Hannay was talking about his Cotswold house, which was on the Fosse Way, and saying that it always puzzled him how so elaborate a civilisation as Roman Britain could have been destroyed utterly and left no mark on the

national history beyond a few roads and ruins and place-names. Peckwether, the historian, demurred, and had a good deal to say about how much the Roman tradition was woven into the Saxon culture. 'Rome only sleeps,' he said; 'she never dies.' Nightingale nodded. 'Sometimes she dreams in her sleep and talks. Once she scared me out of my senses.' (Buchan 1997b, 195–196)

Hannay's assumption that the Roman influence has long been erased from the British psyche is challenged by Nightingale, a scholar. Nightingale's account of the disastrous and mysterious chain of events precipitated by Dubellay's discovery of a Roman altar in the wooded hills surrounding his estate not only contradicts Hannay's remark, but suggests that it is dangerous complacency to assume that Christianity has expunged Classical paganism, which, while for the most part dormant, is still worryingly potent.

The inciting incident of the story is, therefore, Dubellay's intentional act of transgression in reactivating this latent Pagan animus: 'I couldn't leave the altar on the hillside. [...] I had to make a place for it, so I turned the old front of the house into a sort of temple' (205–06). Typically of Buchan's reticence in lurid or unambiguous representations of the supernatural, the altar's power manifests itself as a mysteriously occurring strong current of hot air running through the portico. On the ritually significant date of midsummer's eve, Dubellay pays for his transgression with his life:

> From the altar a great tongue of flame seemed to shoot upwards and lick the roof, and from its pediment ran flaming streams. In front of it lay a body—Dubellay's—a naked body, already charred and black. There was nothing else, except that the Gorgon's head in the wall seemed to glow like a sun in hell. (216)

Nightingale, the narrator of the story, states that when discussing his discovery of the Roman altar, Dubellay's face takes 'on a new look—not of fear but of secrecy, a kind of secret excitement' (205–06). Buchan makes no attempt to conceal the appeal of paganism, but by the same token the entire narrative is cautionary against succumbing to that appeal.

Buchan's presentation of the dangerous, destructive potential of Roman mysteries here is certainly far removed from the popular view of Classical paganism as 'an elegant and poetic Bank Holiday, a perpetual riot, a rosy debauch' (Machen 1924, 9). The Paterian seriousness with which Buchan approached Classical paganism was informed by and informed his experience of contemporary pagan cultures. Like other writers of his age, Buchan's position regarding the cultures of modernity and his anxieties over the dangers of pagan recidivism were reinforced by his first-hand experiences as a colonial. In 1900 he took a job on Lord Milner's staff as a colonial administrator in South Africa. His role was 'hands on' and he spent much of his time travelling on horseback and personally overseeing Lord Milner's efforts to ameliorate the worst effects of the Boer War, specifically the disastrous sanitation situations in the concentration camps (Adam Smith 1985b). He was keenly aware of the vulnerable attenuation of the colonial presence in some areas and saw this in terms of a conflict between 'civilization' and 'savagery'.

Janet Adam Smith identifies the central conflict of Buchan's 1910 colonial adventure novel *Prester John* (1910) as being 'not between black and white; it is between civilization [...] and savagery' (Adam Smith 1985a, 144). In *The Power-House* (1913) the main antagonist Andrew Lumley opines at length on the contingency of civilization, arguing that its 'tenure' is 'precarious':

> 'You think that a wall as solid as the earth separates civilisation from barbarism. I tell you the division is a thread, a sheet of glass. A touch here, a push there, and you bring back the reign of Saturn.' (Buchan 1913, 731)

Furthermore, the fragility of civilization is actually exacerbated by modernity: 'Consider how delicate the machine is growing. As life grows more complex, the machinery grows more intricate, and therefore more vulnerable.' While Lumley sees this increased vulnerability precipitated by industrial modernity as a weakness to be exploited, Leithen is of the view that it is his responsibility to do everything in his (and by implication, the reader's) power to safeguard civilization's survival. Adam Smith draws a line between Buchan's alarum at civilization's fragility in *The Power-House*, written immediately before the Great War, and his earlier Classical interests as evident in 'The Watcher by the Threshold', where the bust of Justinian which obsesses one of the main characters has an expression suggestive of 'the intangible mystery of culture on the verge of savagery', Constantine being a liminal Janus figure between the Classical and Christian eras (Adam Smith 1985a, 253). In fact, Adam Smith asserts categorically that 'in all the tales there is a stress on the thinness of civilization' (103).

This concern was of course far from unique to Buchan, and shared by at least some of his contemporaries. Joseph Conrad, for example, begins 'Heart of Darkness' by foregrounding Britain's pagan past and the contingency of its Imperial dream with Marlowe's account of the Roman soldier 'in some inland post [feeling] the savagery, the utter savagery, had closed around him' (Conrad 1899, 195–196). The first part of 'Heart of Darkness' was published in *Blackwood's* (as 'The Heart of Darkness') the month after it concluded Buchan's 'No-Man's-Land', in which Buchan speculated on the survival of pre-Roman 'savagery' into the present day. Described by Griffith as a 'parallel journey into the remote anthropological past' to that of 'Heart of Darkness', 'No-Man's-Land' elaborates on the 'images of British barbarism at the beginning of Conrad's novella' (Griffith 1995, 118). Griffith regards the tale as 'an interesting example of the Victorian fascination with their own culture's past savagery, and, by implication, with the latent savagery still existing in some dark corner of their own mind' (Griffith 1995, 119). Although Griffith makes explicit the shared thematic concerns of 'No-Man's-Land' and 'Heart of Darkness', he is evidently reticent about acknowledging the fact that Buchan's story is unarguably weird where Conrad is realist, Buchan drawing heavily on Machen, the lost race stories of Rider Haggard, as well as the 'Turanian pygmy' theory of Scottish folklorist David MacRitchie (1851–1925), who argued that fairy lore was folkloric memory: the 'primitivism' of Buchan's text is represented by an actual relict population of prehuman hominins lurking in the Pentland Hills (Fergus 2015).

I have remarked above that Buchan's weird tales are best parsed as examples of him applying a particular focus to an aspect of his wider worldview: the notion (comparable to Lovecraft's) of civilization and modernity as a contingent 'island' surrounded by incomprehensible forces of chaos and irrationality. This 'island' can be seen as psychological as well as geographical: the integrity of the mind is threatened as much as the parameters of Empire. A through-line from the 'omniferous' universe of *The Thousand and One Nights* discussed in the previous chapter to colonial adventure fiction operates throughout these texts.

THE WEIRD MIND OF IMPERIALISM

In this chapter I have sketched out two fin-de-siècle contexts that provoked and informed the weird mode in Buchan's fiction: paganism and imperialism. The former obtrudes into Buchan's fiction, often destabilizing an otherwise ordered and stable establishment figure's life (Buchan's protagonists are predominantly politicians, aristocrats, soldiers, or a mix of all three). This destabilization can also occur in an imperial context, where the stakes are arguably higher since it calls into question the integrity of what Robinson and Gallagher called 'the official mind of imperialism'. This 'official mind' was the fardel of 'beliefs about morals and politics, about the duties of government, the ordering of society and international relations' (Robinson et al. 1981, 20).

Buchan may have been a participant in as well as a theorist of the British Empire (in, for example, *The African Colony* (1903) and *A Lodge in the Wilderness*), but his weird fiction was, in effect, a subversive challenge to the idea that the Victorian imperial psyche was unassailably, or even particularly, robust (Buchan 1903, 1906). On a fundamental level, it is confirmation that 'stereotypes of "colonialists" or similar convenient groupings are as superficial as stereotypes of nations' (N. Machin 1998). One of the characters in *A Lodge in the Wilderness*—a fictionalized discourse on the state of the British Empire in the aftermath of the landslide Liberal victory at the 1906 general election—argues that 'Imperialism, if we regard it properly, is not a creed or a principle, but an attitude of mind' (Buchan 1906, 77). Although much of Buchan's fiction and nonfiction celebrates this 'attitude of mind' as a strong and unhesitant force for good in the world, short stories like 'The Watcher by the Threshold' (1900), 'The Kings of Orion' (1906), 'The Grove of Ashtaroth' (1912), or '*Tendebant Manaus*' (1926) conversely present the reader with characters whose psyches are vulnerable, damaged, and fragile.

An associated trope frequently employed by Buchan in his weird fiction was that of competing *daemons* or personalities, often framed in terms of different (alleged) racial characteristics competing for dominance in an individual. In this respect (and others), Buchan demonstrates a trait of Scottish literature identified by G. Gregory Smith, and described by him as 'Caledonian Antisyzygy', a 'combination of opposites' and 'the contrasts which the Scot shows at every turn' in his literature (Smith 1919, 4). Like his contemporary and probable acquaintance Algernon Blackwood, one of Buchan's personal terrors was that of losing one's identity:[17] Buchan was 'never much frightened' by anything he read as a child apart from

---

[17] For a discussion of this aspect of Blackwood's fiction, see my 'Algernon Blackwood' for *Weird Fiction Review*, 2013 (http://weirdfictionreview.com/2013/01/wfrs-101-weird-writers-19-algernon-blackwood/).

Alice in Wonderland, Alice's 'loss of identity haunt[ing] him like a nightmare' (Adam Smith 1985a, 15). Perhaps an inevitable corollary of privileging a racial and cultural ideal, and predicating one's identity upon it, is that this identity is then immediately under threat of compromise from both internal decadence and external alien aggression, infiltration, or corruption. A desperate vigilance is entailed in sustaining such a construct. Lovecraft would later demonstrate—to a still unrivalled degree of shrill, hysterical, and hallucinatory intensity—that weird fiction can be the vehicle for expression of this vulnerability and ensuing angst.

Buchan's expression of such anxieties in this regard may be quieter and more sober-headed, but they are still very much indicative of this particular valence of the mode. Like many of his characters, Buchan's reputation as a doughty servant of the Empire—dispensing solid good sense and Christian benevolence in his political office, and healthy invigorating diversion as a popular author—operated in tandem with a 'fey' aspect to his nature, which occasionally expressed itself in his fiction as both a visionary strain of mysticism and the troublesome nightmares and fever dreams of the otherwise stolid imperial mind. The claim that Conrad's fiction 'calls into question the rationalities that govern concepts of race, geography and history' applies equally well to Buchan in this respect (Baxter 2010, 14).

One typically Protestant, and arguably Scottish (the earliest attribution in the *Oxford English Dictionary* is to John Knox), word used by Buchan is 'backsliding': 'One who backslides or falls away from an adopted course, esp. of religious faith or practice; an apostate, renegade' ("Backsliding, N." n.d.). This concept can limn a through-line in his work. In *Witch Wood*, a historical novel set in early seventeenth-century Scotland, the protagonist is David Semphill, a clergyman set against his own flock when he becomes aware of a general 'backsliding' into pagan practices when he stumbles across an orgiastic rite in the wood. In 'The Wind in the Portico' and 'The Watcher by the Threshold', Buchan broadens the application of the word to include the 'backsliding' of an individual psyche from modernity into pre-Christian and prerational practices and states of consciousness.

In 'The Grove of Ashtaroth', this is framed along explicitly colonial, racial, and orientalist lines: Lawson's Semitic heritage is drawn as a latent weakness, decadence, or predisposition to backsliding, catalysed at the colonial frontier, where mysterious pagan forces hold sway and he is free from the stabilizing effects of European civilization. As a child, Buchan had already rehearsed such narratives in the Scottish countryside:

Israel warred in the woods, Israelitish prophets kennelled in the shale of the burns, backsliding Judah built altars to Baal on some knoll under the pines. I knew exactly what a heathenish 'grove' was: it was a cluster of self-sown beeches on a certain 'high place.' The imagery of the Psalms haunted every sylvan corner. (Buchan 1941, 16)

Buchan's anxiety about backsliding is, as I have argued, the result of the tension resulting from the opposition of fascination with pagan culture, his 'fey', mystical tendencies, and their iterations in 1890s literary culture, to his firm conviction in the superiority of Christianity and his commitment to the 'official mind' of Empire. In this respect, 'The Far Islands' (see discussion above) might be seen as autobiographical, with Raden's smooth path into the upper echelons of the establishment subtly self-sabotaged by obtrusions of destabilizing visionary mysticism.

Buchan's weird tales can be seen as an exercise in caution against imbalance, arguably what he feared as his own potential for imbalance in reconciling his imaginative life with his public life. When discussing the 'official thinking' of the oligarchy that controlled the British Empire, Robinson and Gallagher emphasize the importance of considering the wider beliefs and moral structures underpinning the 'mechanical choices and expedients' of colonialists: 'England's rulers shared an esoteric view of desirable and undesirable trends stretching from the past and present to the future' (Robinson et al. 1981, 21). Buchan's weird fiction demonstrates this argument well beyond its immediate and intended scope and application. Buchan's sense of the past was one that encompassed not just British imperial history but Old Testament lore and pre-Christian gods, and he saw the Empire as a contingency operating within this macroscopic context, with nebulous pagan forces and revenants from antiquity both pressing upon and latent within the modern mind; the civilized mind that must remain ever-vigilant against their potential to reassert themselves and destroy it utterly.

WORKS CITED

Academy. 1898. The Newest Fiction, March 12.
———. 1899. Mr. C. F. Keary, December 9.
Academy and Literature. 1902. The Watcher by the Threshold, May 31.
Adam Smith, Janet. 1979. *John Buchan and His World.* London: Thames & Hudson.
———. 1985a. *John Buchan: A Biography.* Oxford: Oxford University Press.

———. 1985b. 'Milner's Young Man: 1901–1903. In *John Buchan: A Biography*, 106–145. Oxford: Oxford University Press.
Athenaeum. 1898. Tenebrae, April 2.
Backsliding, N. n.d. *OED Online*. Oxford University Press. http://www.oed.com/view/entry/14453. Accessed 7 Sept 2015.
Baxter, Katherine Isobel. 2010. *Joseph Conrad and the Swan Song of Romance*. Farnham: Ashgate.
Belk, Patrick Scott. 2013. John Buchan and the American Pulp Magazines. In *John Buchan and the Idea of Modernity*, ed. Nathan Waddell and Kate Macdonald, 1st ed., 155–168. London: Pickering & Chatto Publishers.
Bookman. 1895. New Writers: Mr. John Buchan, December.
———. 1898. Monthly Report of the Wholesale Book Trade, December.
Buchan, John. 1895. Nonconformity in Literature. *Glasgow Herald*, November 2.
———. 1896a. *Scholar Gipsies*. London: John Lane/The Bodley Head.
———. 1896b. A Captain of Salvation. *Yellow Book*, January.
———. 1896c. A Journey of Little Profit. *Yellow Book*, April.
———. 1899. No-Man's-Land. *Blackwood's Edinburgh Magazine*, January.
———. 1903. *The African Colony: Studies in the Reconstruction*. Edinburgh/London: Blackwood.
———. 1906. *A Lodge in the Wilderness*. Edinburgh and London: Blackwood.
———. 1910. The Grove of Ashtaroth. *Blackwood's Edinburgh Magazine*, June.
———. 1911. Introduction. In *Tales of Mystery and Imagination*, ed. Edgar Allan Poe, 1–9. London: Nelson.
———. 1912. The Grove of Ashtaroth. In *The Moon Endureth*, 141–171. London: Hodder & Stoughton.
———. 1913. The Power-House. *Blackwood's Edinburgh Magazine*, December.
———. 1919. *Mr. Standfast*. New York: Doran.
———. 1941. *Memory Hold the Door*. London: Hodder & Stoughton.
———. 1946. *The Dancing Floor*. London: Thomas Nelson.
———. 1992. The Three Hostages. In *The Complete Richard Hannay*, 657–928. London: Penguin.
———. 1997a. *Supernatural Tales*. Ed. David Daniell. Edinburgh: Black and White Publishing.
———. 1997b. The Wind in the Portico. In *Supernatural Tales*, ed. David Daniell, 195–217. Edinburgh: Black and White Publishing.
Butts, Mary. 1933. 'Ghosties and Ghoulies'—continued. *Bookman*, February.
Carey, John. 1992. *The Intellectuals and the Masses*. London: Faber.
Clute, John. 2006. *The Darkening Garden: A Short Lexicon of Horror*. Cauheegan: Payseur & Schmidt.

Cohen, Morton N. 2004. Oxford DNB Article: Haggard, Sir (Henry) Rider. https://doi.org/10.1093/ref:odnb/33632. Accessed 3 July 2015.
Conrad, Joseph. 1899. The Heart of Darkness. *Blackwood's Edinburgh Magazine*, February.
Denisoff, Dennis. 2012. The Pagan Review: Introduction to Volume 1 (August 1892). http://www.1890s.ca/HTML.aspx?s=PRV1_Intro.html. Accessed 1 June 2015.
Eldridge, C.C. 1996. *The Imperial Experience: From Carlyle to Forster*. Houndmills, Basingstoke, Hampshire: Palgrave Macmillan.
F. M. F. 1918. The Head Master and Art. *Athenaeum*, January.
Famous Fantastic Mysteries. 1950a. February.
———. 1950b. April.
Fergus, Emily. 2015. 'A Wilder Reality': Euhemerism and Arthur Machen's 'Little People'. *Faunus: The Journal of the Friends of Arthur Machen*, Autumn.
"Fiction." 1902. *The Speaker*, August, 489–490.
Freeman, Nick. 2008. A Country for the Savant: Paganism, Popular Fiction and the Invention of Greece, 1914–1966. *Pomegranate: The International Journal of Pagan Studies* 10 (1): 21–40. https://doi.org/10.1558/pome.v10i1.21.
Goldie, David. 2012. Popular Fiction. In *The Cambridge Companion to Scottish Literature*, ed. Gerard Carruthers and Liam MacIlvanney, 188–202. Cambridge: Cambridge University Press.
Grant, Paul Benedict. 2009. Buchan's Supernatural Fiction. In *Reassessing John Buchane: Beyond the Thirty-Nine Steps*, ed. Kate Macdonald, 183–192. London: Pickering & Chatto.
Green, Martin. 1977. *Children of the Sun: A Narrative of 'Decadence' in England after 1918*. London: Constable.
Greig, The Rev. James C. G. 2009. John Buchan and Calvinism. In *Reassessing John Buchan: Beyond the Thirty-Nine Steps*, ed. Kate Macdonald, 7–16. London: Pickering & Chatto.
Griffith, John Wylie. 1995. *Joseph Conrad and the Anthropological Dilemma: 'Bewildered Traveller'*. New York: Oxford University Press.
Gross, John. 1973. *The Rise and Fall of the Man of Letters*. London: Penguin.
Heald, Tim. 1975. Standfast and Look at Buchan! *The Times*, August 25.
Henham, Ernest George. 1898. *Tenebrae*. London: Skeffington & Son.
Himmelfarb, Gertrude. 1995. *Victorian Minds*. London: Rowman & Littlefield.
Hitchens, Christopher. 2004. Great Scot. *Atlantic*, March. http://www.theatlantic.com/magazine/archive/2004/03/great-scot/302897/.
"Jemini". 1940. In Memoriam. *The Futurian*, Winter.
Joshi, S.T. 2013. *I Am Providence: The Life and Times of H. P. Lovecraft*. Vol. 2. 2 vols. New York: Hippocampus Press.
Joyce, James. 1957. *Letters of James Joyce*. Eds. Richard Ellmann and Stuart Gilbert. Vol. II. 3 vols. London: Faber and Faber.

Keary, C.F. 1891. *The Vikings in Western Christendom A.D. 789 to A.D. 888*. London: Fisher Unwin.
———. 1892. The Four Students. *Macmillan's*, January.
———. 1896a. Elizabeth. *New Review*, September.
———. 1896b. Elizabeth. *New Review*, October.
———. 1897a. Phantasies. *New Review*, January.
———. 1897b. Phantasies. *New Review*, March.
———. 1897c. Phantasies. *The New Review*, April.
———. 1893. *A Mariage de Convenance*. London: Fisher Unwin.
———. 1901. *'Twixt Dog and Wolf*. London: R. Brimley Johnson.
Kemp, Sandra, Charlotte Mitchell, and David Trotter, eds. 2002a. *Oxford Companion to Edwardian Fiction*. Oxford: Oxford University Press.
———. 2002b. *Oxford Companion to Edwardian Fiction 1900–14: New Voices in the Age of Uncertainty*. Oxford: Oxford University Press.
Kerr, Douglas. 2009. 'A Fraud Called John Buchan': Buchan, Joseph Conrad and Literary Theft. In *Reassessing John Buchan: Beyond the Thirty-Nine Steps*, ed. Kate Macdonald, 141–152. London: Pickering & Chatto.
———. 2013. John Buchan, Myth and Modernism. In *John Buchan and the Idea of Modernity*, ed. Kate Macdonald and Nathan Waddell, 141–153. London: Pickering & Chatto.
Kore, N. n.d. *OED Online*. Oxford University Press. http://www.oed.com/view/Entry/104362. Accessed 5 Apr 2015.
Kruse, Juanita. 1989. *John Buchan and the Idea of Empire*, Studies in British History. Vol. 7. Lewiston/Queenston/Lampeter: The Edwin Mellen Press.
Le Gallienne, Richard. 1925. *The Romantic '90s*. Garden City: Doubleday.
Ledger, Sally. 2008. *Henrik Ibsen*. Tavistock: Northcote House.
Lovecraft, H.P. 1985. Supernatural Horror in Literature. In *Dagon and Other Macabre Tales*, 421–512. London: Panther.
———. 2004. *Collected Essays 2: Literary Criticism*. Ed. S.T. Joshi. New York: Hippocampus Press.
Lownie, Andrew. 1995. *John Buchan: The Presbyterian Cavalier*. Edinburgh: Canongate.
Luckhurst, Roger, ed. 2005. Introduction. In *Late Victorian Gothic Tales*. Oxford: Oxford University Press.
Macdonald, Kate. 2010. John Buchan's Breakthrough: The Conjunction of Experience, Markets and Forms That Made The Thirty-Nine Steps. *Publishing History* 68 (3): 25–107.
Machen, Arthur. 1908. Paganism. *Academy*, August 29.
———. 1924. Preface. In *Afterglow; Pastels of Greek Egypt, 69 B.C.*, ed. Mitchell S. Buck, 7–19. New York: N. L. Brown.
Machin, James. 2013. Towards a Golden Dawn: Esoteric Christianity and the Development of Nineteenth-Century British Occultism. *The Victorian* 1 (1). http://journals.sfu.ca/vict/index.php/vict/article/view/32.

———. 2015. Fellows Find: H. P. Lovecraft Letter Sheds Light on Pivotal Moment in His Career. *Cultural Compass* (blog). http://blog.hrc.utexas.edu/2015/01/27/fellows-find-h-p-lovecraft-letter/. Accessed 26 Jan 2016.

Machin, Noel. 1998. Government Anthropologist: A Life of R. S. Rattray. http://lucy.ukc.ac.uk/machin/machin_1.html#Section1.

Matthew, H.C.G. 2004. Oxford DNB Article: Buchan, John. http://www.oxforddnb.com/view/article/32145.

McDonald, Peter D. 2002. *British Literary Culture and Publishing Practice, 1880–1914*. Cambridge: Cambridge University Press.

"Middlebrow, n. and Adj." n.d. *OED Online*. Oxford University Press. http://www.oed.com/view/Entry/252048. Accessed 29 July 2014.

Mix, Katherine Lyon. 1960. *A Study in Yellow: The Yellow Book and Its Contributors*. Constable: Kansas University Press.

Monsman, Gerald. 2015. The Emergence of John Trevena: A Case Study of a Pseudonym. *English Literature in Transition, 1880–1920* 58 (2): 241–256.

National Observer. 1896a. The Yellow Book, February 8.

———. 1896b. Neo-Paganism in Paris, June 27.

O. 1902. A Dream of Lost Gods. *Speaker* 5 (126): 623–624.

Ousby, Ian. 1996. *The Cambridge Paperback Guide to Literature in English*. Cambridge: Cambridge University Press.

Oxford DNB Article: Keary, Charles Francis. 2004. https://doi.org/10.1093/ref:odnb/61037. Accessed 16 Sept 2014.

Powell, G.H. 1912. Romance Versus Reality. *Fortnightly Review* 92 (547): 155–164.

Punch. 1912. Our Booking-Office, May 15.

Rainey, Lawrence S. 1998. *Institutions of Modernism*. New Haven/London: Yale.

Richards, Bernard. 1976. John Buchan's Aesthetic Consciousness. *Brazen Nose* XVI (2): 40–42.

Robinson, Ronald, John Gallagher, and Alice Denny. 1981. *Africa and the Victorians: The Official Mind of Imperialism*. London: Macmillan.

Saturday Review. 1885. Marius the Epicurean, March 14.

———. 1898. Fiction, March 26.

Saturday Review of Politics, Literature, Science and Art. 1892. The Pagan Review, September 3.

Smith, G. Gregory. 1919. *Scottish Literature, Character & Influence*. London: Macmillan.

Stableford, Brian M. 1998. *Glorious Perversity: The Decline and Fall of Literary Decadence*. San Bernardino: Borgo Press.

"Tenebrae by Henham, Ernest G, First Edition—AbeBooks." n.d. http://bit.ly/1ZsP7n4. Accessed 17 Sept 2014.

Thacker, Eugene. 2011. *In the Dust of This Planet: Horror of Philosophy* Vol. 1. Winchester: Zero Books.

———. 2015. *Tentacles Longer Than Night: Horror of Philosophy*. Vol. 3. Winchester: Zero Books.
The Bookman. 1902. The Watcher by the Threshold, and Other Tales, June.
The Thirty-Nine Steps and World War I. 2014. *BBC Radio 3*. http://www.bbc.co.uk/programmes/b047bs5z.
The Times. 1917. Obituary: Mr. C. F. Keary, October 27.
Todorov, Tsvetan. 1975. *The Fantastic: A Structural Approach to a Literary Genre*. Trans. Richard Howard and Robert Scholes. Fourth Printing edition. Ithaca: Cornell University Press.
Tredrey, F.D. 1954. *The House of Blackwood, 1804–1954: The History of a Publishing Firm*. Edinburgh: Blackwood.
Waddell, Nathan. 2009. *Modern John Buchan: A Critical Introduction*. Newcastle: Cambridge Scholars.
Waddell, Nathan, and Kate Macdonald. 2013. *John Buchan and the Idea of Modernity*. 1st ed. London: Pickering & Chatto Publishers.
Wilson, Neil. 2000. *Shadows in the Attic: A Guide to British Supernatural Fiction, 1820–1950*. Boston Spa: British Library.
Wood-Martin, W.G. 1902. *Traces of the Elder Faiths of Ireland; a Folklore Sketch; a Handbook of Irish Pre-Christian Traditions*. Vol. I. 2 vols. London: Longmans, Green.
Yeats, William Butler. 1928. *The Tower*. London: Macmillan & Co.

CHAPTER 5

Weird Tales and Pulp Decadence

Although there is a view that literary Decadence was a precursor to and a striving towards what became Modernism, it was not extinguished entirely by this more impactful and valorized successor, which for some still represents the apotheosis of literature as a purist art form. The United States has been described as 'the last place on earth to provide fertile soil for literary Decadence', but despite this it was in the United States that Decadence had an afterlife distinct from Modernism, maintaining something of its original aesthetic identity in the face of highbrow literary tastes (Stableford 1998, 130). The American revival of interest in Arthur Machen, and his styling as 'The Flower-Tunicked Priest of Nightmare'—a propagation of a distinctly Decadent identity rather at odds with the Johnsonian figure he was by then cutting on Fleet Street—has been discussed in Chap. 3. Brian Stableford has identified a recognizable American lineage of East-Coast Decadence which he traces from Ambrose Bierce, Robert W. Chambers, and George Sterling to Clark Ashton Smith and H. P. Lovecraft. He describes the latter as making 'extravagant, if belated, use of such Decadent tropes as hereditary degeneracy, ultimately formulating a strange cosmic perspective which made such degeneracy a condition of the universe' (132). Lovecraft and Smith were frequent contributors to *Weird Tales* (hereafter *WT*), which, I will argue below, brought Decadence, often undiluted, from the salons of fin-de-siècle Europe to the bustling newsstands of 1920s America.

The 'Weird Story Reprint'

When looking through editions of *WT* from the 1920s and 1930s, as well as its associated fanzine *The Fantasy Fan*, it is clear that the touchstones of British weird fiction canonized by Lovecraft in *Supernatural Horror in Literature* remained constant. The 'favorite weird tale' lists published by *The Fantasy Fan* demonstrate an unwavering regard for the British weird fiction discussed in the previous chapters of this study. Clark Ashton Smith's choices in 1934 include, for example, Blackwood's 'The Willows', M. R. James's 'A View from a Hill', Machen's 'The Novel of the White Powder', and Shiel's 'The House of Sounds' ("The Favorite Weird Stories of Clark Ashton Smith" 1934). Lovecraft's choices similarly include 'The Willows', 'The Novel of the White Powder', and 'The House of Sounds', as well as Machen's 'The Novel of the Black Seal' and M. R. James's 'Count Magnus' ("The Favorite Weird Stories of H. P. Lovecraft" 1934). August Derleth's selection in the June 1934 edition is similar, and also includes de la Mare's 'Seaton's Aunt' ("The Favorite Weird Tales of August W. Derleth" 1934). Within the letters pages of *WT* throughout the preceding decade, the readers and contributors consistently use these writers as benchmarks for weird fiction, regularly citing them as negative and positive comparators to the stories published in *WT*. Despite this regard and influence, and one story by Machen aside ('The Bowmen' in the July 1928 edition), no fiction—new or reprinted—by these writers actually appeared in the pages of *WT* (Fig. 5.1). All were still active in the period and specific transatlantic rights and other issues may have been an insurmountable financial obstacle. Author and editor Stefan Dziemianowicz also speculates that Farnsworth Wright, 'for all of his *apparent* editorial shortcomings, was extremely attentive to the tastes of his readers' and that James, Blackwood, Shiel, and (the high-profile story 'The Bowmen' aside) Machen might not have appealed to a core readership that 'couldn't get enough of Seabury Quinn's Jules de Grandin stories, which in the 1920s/1930s were significant financial props to a magazine in terminally desperate financial straits'.[1]

However, *WT* did not only publish new work by writers working in what they self-identified as a weird tradition. In its 'Weird Story Reprints' section it recycled a combination of popular stories from its own archive, as well as other previously published fiction and poetry that fell within its

---

[1] Stefan Dziemianowicz, personal communication, 21 February 2018.

Fig. 5.1 July 1928 edition of *Weird Tales*, featuring 'The Bowmen' by Arthur Machen (image courtesy of Alamy)

purview. As well as, predictably, many tales by Poe, the following work—including poetry—by writers normally associated with Decadence or Symbolism rather than pulp adventure was readily available to the magazine's readers in early twentieth-century America. Below are examples from the 1920s, *WT*'s first decade of existence:

Weird Tales issue:	*Work (inc. original publication date. 'ss' = short story, 'p' = poem):*
November 1925	'The Young King' (ss, 1891) by Oscar Wilde
February 1926	'The White Dog' (ss, 1908) by Theodor Sologub
February 1926	'Spleen' (p, 1869) by Charles Baudelaire, new translation of poem for WT by Clark Ashton Smith
April 1926	'The Mummy's Foot' (ss, 1840) by Théophile Gautier
May 1926	'Horreur Sympathique' (p, 1861) by Charles Baudelaire, new translation of poem from the second edition of *Fleurs du Mal* for WT by Clark Ashton Smith
March 1927	'Lazarus' (ss, 1906) by Leonid Andreyev
February 1928	'Clarimonde' (ss, 1836) by Théophile Gautier, translated by Lafcadio Hearn
February 1928	'The Three Witches' (p, 1899) by Ernest Dowson
March 1928	'Epigraphe Pour Un Livre Condamné' (p, 1868) by Charles Baudelaire, new translation of poem from the third (posthumous) edition of *Fleurs du Mal* for WT by Clark Ashton Smith
August 1928	'The Demoiselle d'Ys' (ss, 1895) by Robert W. Chambers
August 1928	'Three Poems in Prose': 'L'Irréparable' (p, 1861), 'Les Sept Vieillards' (p, 1861), 'Une Charogne' (p, 1857) by Charles Baudelaire, new translations of poems from *Fleurs du Mal* for WT by Clark Ashton Smith
May 1929	'Le Revenant' (p, 1857) by Charles Baudelaire, new translation of poem from the first edition of *Fleurs du Mal* for WT by Clark Ashton Smith

In addition to this Decadent material, the 'Weird Story Reprints' section included work from a variety of canonical sources and—again—material not generally associated with the pulp market: Alphonse Daudet (the

July 1925 issue), Keats (August 1925), Alexander Pushkin (August 1927), Ivan Turgenev (June 1927), Gustave Flaubert (April 1928), William Morris (November 1929), W. E. Henley (December 1929), Guy de Maupassant (February 1930 and February/March 1931), Charles Dickens (April 1930 and August 1930), and Balzac (December 1936). This was in addition (despite the omissions noted above) to reprints of work by authors one might expect to see in the magazine, such as Sheridan Le Fanu, Arthur Machen, H. G. Wells, Arthur Conan Doyle, and E. F. Benson.

This bewildering variety of content challenges received notions of pulp magazines as solely 'lowbrow' venues for bad or crudely generic writing. In Chap. 4 I discussed the perception that literary Modernism involved a sloughing off of populist literary forms. In the case of *WT* at least, no equivalent, reciprocal distinction was made: canonical, highbrow work was presented alongside original genre work by contemporary authors. Arguably, among at least some of these authors—Lovecraft and Smith being good examples—these two strands were imbricated in new fiction which demonstrated a distinct Decadent lineage as well as displaying and sometimes pioneering genre trappings associated with the twentieth-century: science fiction, fantasy, and horror.

The range of material in *WT* could at first glance be interpreted as evidencing a lack of ostensibly coherent or carefully delineated generic boundaries, beyond the criterion of being arguably 'weird' enough—in other words, an editorial carelessness or indifference to both content and genre. An anecdote provided by *WT* contributor E. Hoffmann Price (1898–1988) in his memoir seems to refute this, however:

> Wright [Farnsworth, editor of *WT*] had scarcely found me a chair when he repeated, in effect, what he'd written from Indianapolis, May 1926: 'Permit me to thank you for the latest story, "The Peacock's Shadow". It has all the exotic witchery in its imagery that one would expect to find only in Gautier. I would be false to our readers were I to reject it, for it will give tone to *Weird Tales*—in fact, I think it would give tone to *Blackwood's*, or to *Century* or *Harper's*. (Price 2001, 10)

Here Wright clearly articulates both a valorization of Decadence (Gautier's 'exotic witchery') and an aspiration to the high(er)brow literary respectability of the upmarket 'slicks'. Both the *WT* editorials and the letters pages further evidence that content and genre (and how they interrelate), as well as purist distinctions regarding literary merit, dominated the discourse of the editor and readers alike.

Although, as detailed below, there were ongoing attempts at 'setting out a stall' in terms of genre, there was no particularly stable delineation of weird fiction established and throughout the first two decades (at least) of the title's existence, the matter of 'what was weird enough' to warrant inclusion was one of prolonged, occasionally fraught, and never-resolved discussion among the readership, editor, and contributors:

> With *WT* a discourse community was formed, made up of editors, authors, readers, and fans who celebrated the nonrealist, extra-mainstream nature of speculative fiction in the early twentieth century, even as that community took apart that fiction and reassembled it into taxonomic categories—often in heated epistolary exchanges. (Everett and Shanks 2015, ix)

This 'discourse community' undertook detailed discussion and analysis, demonstrating reflexivity and often considerable anxiety, in the editorial and letters pages over what constituted appropriate content for *WT*. Over the course of nearly two decades, the same conflicts of opinion arose again and again, as well as regular editorial opinion pieces, manifestos on the subject of what sort of magazine *WT* should be.

The subset of the *WT* discourse community especially pertinent to this thesis is that which, occurring after the birth of literary Modernism, acted as an aesthetic connoisseur 'cercle' identifying those valences of *WT*'s content that it could use to distinguish 'literary' weird fiction from 'mere' pulp offerings. Lovecraft was central to this discourse, which—together with his own fiction—explains his persisting, and some have argued (see Introduction) disproportionate influence, on the discourse ever since. As discussed in the Introduction, in 'Supernatural Horror in Literature', Lovecraft in fact defines 'the weird in fiction' in such a way that it allows him to use it as just such a mark of distinction. 'Supernatural Horror in Literature' was revised by Lovecraft for publication in the *Fantasy Fan* (*FF*), the amateur weird fiction journal (or fanzine) which ran for 18 issues between 1933 and 1934. Dedicated to discussion relating to *WT*, the *FF* further expanded the *WT* discourse community, and was recommended by the editor of *WT* as an appropriate venue for more detailed discussion of weird fiction:

> From time to time we are importuned by our readers to devote several pages of *WT* each month to a forum in which the lovers of fantastic fiction can exchange views. We are asked to have articles on weird fiction generally, information about our authors, debates between the fans. It has been suggested that we expand the Eyrie for this purpose, and make it a battleground for the conflicts of the weird fiction fans. [...] Instead of reducing our story space to make room for such a department, we suggest that you write to Charles D. Hornig, editor of *The Fantasy Fan*. [...] We have been receiving *The Fantasy Fan* for several months, and we think it is just the forum you want—that is, those of you who make weird fiction your hobby. (*Weird Tales* 1934, 394)

The *FF* essentially functioned as a fanzine for *WT* readers, and even greater depth of argument and reflexive analysis on weird fiction was undertaken through correspondence and reader-generated opinion pieces. As discussed in more detail below, the *FF* threw into sharper relief schisms that were already evident in the letters pages of *WT*, partly through its rather more bruising style of debate, in which civility often fell victim to robust presentation of opinion. In some ways the journal anticipates the notoriously fractious nature of contemporary online fan discourse: the equivalent of *WT*'s 'The Eyrie' in the *FF* was appropriately dubbed 'The Boiling Point'.

Tracking this long conversation, undertaken by the *WT* discourse community across both *WT* and the *FF*, it becomes clear that *WT* in effect operated as two magazines in one: sex, violence, and formulaic space opera for the readers who wanted easy escapism, and a more purist form of weird fiction for the coterie of connoisseurs who lobbied for, and aspired to the status of, 'real literature' and valorized what they regarded as more cerebral contributions from writers like Lovecraft and Smith, logrolling for each other as well as aiming brickbats at the more formulaic pulp writing that appeared in the magazine. This is an argument that has never since been resolved over the ensuing history of genre in the twentieth century and into the twenty-first.

'THE WEIRDER THE BETTER'

In the editorial for the July 1927 issue, there is an anomalous example of a confident parsing of the word 'weird' in its literary context, and it is (once again) Poe whose name is invoked:

If one were asked to name the author whose genius made the weird tale popular, the instant answer would be Edgar Allan Poe. We owe not only the weird tale to Poe, but we are also indebted to him from the word itself. Poe was not the creator of the word 'weird', but he rescued it from oblivion and made it popular, so that now the word is understood and used by everyone. (*Weird Tales* 1927c, 138)

Evidence for this assertion is provided by recourse to quoting Lafcadio Hearn (1850–1904) on Poe's poetry, worth transcribing in full here (as it was in the magazine) as it both serves as a précis of the Introduction and also demonstrates that *WT* claimed a lineage and tradition dating back to at least the nineteenth century:

> When you read in [Tennyson's] the 'Idyls [sic] of the King' such phrases as 'The weirdly sculptured gate,' perhaps you have never suspected that this use of the adverb weirdly was derived from the study of the American poet. There were two words used by the Saxons of a very powerful kind; one referring to destiny or fate, the other to supernatural terror. 'Weird' is a later form of the Anglo-Saxon word meaning fate. The northern mythology, like the Greek, had its Fates, who devised the life histories of men.
>
> Later the word came also to be used in relation to the future of the man himself; the ancient writers spoke of 'his weird,' 'her weird.' Still later the term came to mean simply supernatural influence of a mysterious kind. Poe found it so used, and made it into a living adjective, after it had become almost forgotten, by using it very cleverly in his poems and stories. As he used it, it means ghostly, or ghostly looking, or suggesting the supernatural and the occult. Hundreds of writers imitated Poe in this respect; and now it is so much the rule, that the word must be used very sparingly. It is the mark of a very young writer to use it often. (Hearn 1915a, 2:158)

The book from which this extract was taken, *Interpretations of Literature*, was published posthumously in 1915 and is a collection of lectures delivered by Hearn when he 'held the chair of English literature in the University of Tokyo from 1896 to 1902' (Hearn 1915b, 1:v).

Hearn's comment regarding what he considers to be the word's overuse suggests that by the time he was delivering the lecture, it was sufficiently ubiquitous to be at risk of being the sort of lazy shorthand typical of the novice author. Grant Allen's use of the term in his 1892 story 'Pallinghurst Barrow' (according to Wells, 'not free from touches of slipshod writing which spoil so much of the clever fiction of [Allen]') is perhaps an example of what Hearn was criticizing (*Saturday Review* 1893, 612). Although arguably in keeping with the narrative voice, in which a supernatural incident is being related 'scientifically', Allen repetitively deploys the word 'weird' in lieu of taking the trouble to convey any more nuanced evocation of atmosphere: 'There was something about that sunset and the lights on the bracken—something weird and unearthly' (Grant Allen 1892, 12); 'a very weird yet definite feeling' (12); 'A weird and awful feeling' (12); and, desultory to the point of being risible, 'he felt a weird and creepy sense of mystery and the supernatural' (17).

However, such clumsy precedents did not deter Hearn from translating the Japanese term in the title of his final book, *Kwaidan: Stories and Studies of Strange Things* (1904), as 'Weird Tales' in his preface (Hearn 1904, iii). Hearn had, from the outset of his authorial career, been a writer attracted to the supernatural, and anticipated the Decadence and orientalism of the 1890s in his treatment of such material:

> His first stabs at literature [...] were lurid and over-coloured, such as his translation of Gautier, entitled *Cleopatra's Nights and other Fantastic Romances* (1882), and his original volumes of short stories, *Stray Leaves from Strange Literature* (1884) and *Some Chinese Ghosts* (1887). (Chubbuck 2004)

In this last volume, Hearn in his introduction specifies that 'in preparing the legends I sought especially for *weird beauty*' [italics in original] (Hearn 1887, iii). He goes on to cite a remark by Sir Walter Scott as a template for effective treatment of such material: 'The supernatural, though appealing to certain powerful emotions very widely and deeply sown amongst the human race, is, nevertheless, *a spring which is peculiarly apt to lose its elasticity by being too much pressed upon*' (iii, italics in original). Here again is evidence of a link between the weird mode (or a certain type of writing in the mode) and an ambiguity or at least hesitancy in representations of the explicitly supernatural. 'The value of the word [weird]', argued Hearn elsewhere, 'really lies in its vagueness' (Hearn 1915a, 2:159). Lovecraft, who 'owned [...] Hearn's translation of [Gautier's] *One of Cleopatra's Nights and Other Fantastic Romances* (1882)', endorsed Hearn as 'strange, wandering, and exotic' (Joshi 2013, 2:500):

> His *Fantastics*, written in America, contains some of the most impressive ghoulishness in all literature; whilst his *Kwaidan*, written in Japan, crystallises with matchless skill and delicacy the eerie lore and whispered legends of that

richly colourful nation. Still more of Hearn's weird wizardry of language is shewn in some of his translations from the French, especially from Gautier and Flaubert. (H. P. Lovecraft 1985, 483)

Hearn himself confessed in a letter of 1884 to being 'terribly ignorant of classic English literature' and claimed to have at some stage consciously circumvented the canon—and implicitly the desire for canonicity—or at least admitted to only using the canon sparingly and instrumentally in pursuit of his chosen specialism:

> Not having studied [classic English literature] much when at college, I now find life too short to study it, except for style. When I want to clear mine—as coffee is cleared by the white of an egg,—I pour a little quaint English into my brain-cup, and the Oriental extravagances are gradually precipitated. But I think a man must devote himself to one thing in order to succeed: so I have pledged me to the worship of the Odd, the Queer, the Strange, the Exotic, the Monstrous. It quite suits my temperament. (Hearn and Bisland 1907a, 1:326)

Elizabeth Bisland argued that Hearn's taste for 'the grotesque, the fantastic, the bizarre' was a result of him falling 'under the spell of the French Romantic [i.e., Decadent] school' and his subsequent early attempts at translation:

> The works of Théophile Gautier were his daily companions, in which he saturated his mind with fantasies of the Orient, Spain, and Egypt, refreshing himself after the dull routine of the day's work with endeavours to transliterate [sic] into English the strange and monstrous tales of his model, those abnormal imaginations whose alien aroma almost defied transference into a less supple tongue. (61)

There are obvious resonances here with not only Decadence but also the weird orientalism and valorization of obscurity discussed in Chap. 3.

However, despite his professions of intentional pursuit of the outré, Hearn still had no hesitation in distinguishing 'literature' from lowbrow mass culture, which in 1902 he perceived as having all but extinguished highbrow literary culture in the United States:

> What a nice little paper *Euterpe* is! Long ago we used to have good papers like that—real literary papers, in nearly the same format—in America. The taste for good literature in America is practically dead: vulgar fiction has

killed the higher fictions; 'sensationalism' and blatant cheap journalism have murdered the magazines; and poetry is silent. (II, 472)

As unequivocal as this assertion is, it should not be implied that Hearn saw any contradiction in his chosen specialism and highbrow, 'good literature', the latter predicated on notions of neither canonicity nor genre. In fact, writing in 1890, he claimed that at one point he planned writing an essay arguing that 'ghostliness' was an inherent quality shared by all 'fine art' (Hearn and Bisland 1907b, 2:19). Writing in 1923, Lovecraft adduced Hearn for his own conceit of a nineteenth-century tradition at odds with, peripheral to, but preferable to, that advocated by 'those critics who are hurling the English nineteenth century in our faces with so much gusto, finality, and drollery' (H. P. Lovecraft 2004, 71):

> Without wishing to emulate their own fetching pageantry of mighty names across the learned page, [I] would bid them consider such titans as Walter Pater, Lafcadio Hearn, Arthur Symons, Arthur Machen, Wilde, Gautier, Flaubert, Baudelaire, Verlaine, Rimbaud, Mallarmé, Laforgue, D'Annunzio, or Croce.

Although it would seem perfectly fitting for *WT* to appropriate such a figure as Hearn to explicate the content it sought to fulfil its function as 'the unique magazine', the fact that he is given such a prominent position further complicates reductive generalizations about pulp magazines, their readership, and their content.

The suggestion by Hearn that 'weird' was a literary cliché did not, evidently, dissuade the publisher J. C. Henneberger from using the word for his new vehicle for stories in the Poe tradition that didn't quite fit anywhere else. Although it is (as I have detailed in the Introduction) now regarded as a mercurial mode almost defined by its very indefinability, there seemed to be little hesitancy implicit in the title chosen by J. C. Henneberger, although there is some ambiguity evident in its subtitle: 'the unique magazine'. Henneberger envisioned *WT* as a venue for stories 'of the unconventional type' which would be difficult to place elsewhere, and the decision to position Poe as the exemplar author met with majority approval from the readership, including William Bolitho (of whom more later): 'Where do you think Poe and E. T. A. Hoffmann would take their stuff if they were alive today? *Weird Tales* of course!' (*Weird Tales* 1930c, 580).

In the May 1927 issue there was also a corollary implication that weird fiction was perceived as a neglected mode that was being revived, rather than innovated, by *WT*, which the editorial suggests represents 'the *return* of weird fiction to the news stands' [italics mine] (*Weird Tales* 1927b, 711). A reader signing themselves L. L. S. in a letter in the July 1929 issue explained:

> I have been reading *Weird Tales* since 1923. At that time I had exhausted all of Poe's works that I could lay my hands on, and had come to the conclusion that as far as further exploitation of the weird and gruesome in literature was concerned 'there just wasn't any more'. Then I discovered *Weird Tales*. (*Weird Tales* 1929a, 275)

As will be discussed in more detail, the readership of *WT* overwhelmingly interpreted Henneberger's founding formulation for *WT* as meaning fiction and poetry dealing with themes, principally of supernatural horror, that avoided sanguinary extremes and romantic melodrama, and that strained against generic constraints. In his editorial for the April 1926 issue, Farnsworth Wright asserted that, unlike *WT*, 'other magazines put up bars against stories that *wander very far*' [italics mine] (*Weird Tales* 1926a, 566). This ideal translated into writers being free, most of all, from the generic constraints normally imposed on more formal pulp genres of, for example, the adventure story, the detective story, the Western, and so on. It also meant freedom from the constraints of realism but with retention of the ambition of achieving 'great literature': 'I must confess', Henneberger wrote, 'that the main motive in establishing *Weird Tales* was to give the writer free rein to express his innermost feelings in a manner befitting great literature' (Robert E. Weinberg 1977, 3). One only has to point to the cover of the first issue of *WT*—featuring an encounter with the eponymous protoplasmic antagonist of the story 'Ooze'—in order to pillory such ambition as absurd pretension. As detailed above, however, and establishing a pattern and ongoing tension that defined *Weird Tales* in at least its first incarnation, as well as crude pulp exuberance, there was what by any ordinary, uncontentious definition amounted to genuine literature to be found within its pages.

This is perhaps the obverse of the contemporaneous situation of Modernism. Andreas Huyssen's position in 1988 was that 'ever since the mid-19th century [...] Modernism constituted itself through a conscious strategy of exclusion, an anxiety of contamination by its other: an increasingly consuming and engulfing mass culture' (Huyssen 1988, 7). However, Catherine Turner has argued that the received wisdom that 'modernism generated its tradition outside of the commodity culture that surrounded it' has been undermined by subsequent scholarship (Turner 2003, 2). She suggests it has been demonstrated that 'modernism developed its tradition by becoming deeply embedded in the commercial market' and that subsequently 'we cannot take for granted that modern novels, even those of the avant-garde, were somehow significantly different from other literary commodities at the time' (2–3). Just as far removed from Theodor Adorno's conception of mass culture as 'modern art's commodified "other"' is Mark Morrisson's suggestion that as (Cook 1996, 106).

> British and American modernists tried to find ways to use the new institutions of culture of the period to create a prominent public role for their art and literature, they felt that the mass market was the key to restoring the central cultural position of aesthetic experiment. (Morrisson 2001, 7)

If not identical in intent, it is difficult to identify a difference in practice between this version of Modernism and Henneberger's and Wright's aspirations for *WT*. Baudelaire, identified by Huyssen as an exemplar of mid-nineteenth-century Modernism, may have, in his lifetime, engaged in 'conscious strategies of exclusion' but posthumously found a mass-market American audience through *WT*.

Despite this, *WT*'s striving after literary legitimacy remains obscured by the general understanding of pulp magazine publishing as an explicitly, solely commercial enterprise. Different avant-gardes (as a cultural impulse distinct from, but imbricated with, Modernism as a movement) have sometimes been defined in opposition to 'the mass-produced object' in which 'the creative individuality of the producer is negated' (Bürger and Shaw 1985, 29). Peter Bürger and Michael Shaw adumbrate 'avant-garde' by invoking pulp literature culture as a delineating apotheosis (or perhaps nadir) of Adornian soma culture:

> Aestheticism is, among other things, a response to the total tailoring of production to the socially produced 'false' needs of recipients, a phenomenon that is typical of pulp literature. Aestheticism seeks to realize the unity of producer and recipient without surrendering the claim to a realization of creative individuality. But this necessarily entails a shrinkage of the attainable public to a small circle of connoisseurs so that the fact that works change nothing whatever in the real world becomes the very criterion of their value.

> Aestheticism can create the unity of producer and recipient only if it reduces a potentially all-inclusive public to the dimensions of a 'cercle' which takes in just a few individuals. (30)

Although the term 'aestheticism' here isn't used specifically with reference to the late nineteenth-century cultural movement, the fact that *WT* reprinted decadent and aesthetic fiction and poetry, and printed new work directly influenced by such, seems to at least complicate Bürger's and Shaw's argument. However, as I will go on to argue, the *WT* discourse community was keenly aware of this tension between aesthetic ideal and the reality of *WT* as it appeared at the newsstands.

Despite his attempts to secure a privileged position for high culture, Adorno also recognized what has been described as an 'interdependency' between high art and mass culture, and perhaps *WT* is best seen as an iteration of this interdependency rather than a simple exercise in the 'total tailoring of production' to the masses, with the pejorative implications of that assumption in terms of both the content and the audience such a judgement entails, in regard to the former presupposing a functionary cynicism in the cultural producer, whose agency is diminished and who is relegated to the position of a mere hack distanced and alienated from his or her creation. Once more, we return to a concern that there is a basic 'incommensurability of high modern art and the culture industry' or 'more utilitarian art dependent on industrial production' (Cook 1996, 106). Originating in his discussion of 'light and serious music' (105), Adorno subsequently expanded his conceit of high and low culture as 'torn halves' of a whole, arguing that a critical immanence in both as a totality was pre-conditional to any critical transcendence (the latter analogous to Bourdieu's irrealizable 'pure gaze' discussed in Chap. 3) (Young 1996, 27). If the torn halves are a condition of capitalism and a manifestation of its 'antagonistic structure', there is an essential paradox in the position of the critic:

> If culture consists of torn halves that do not add up, then so too must the practice of cultural criticism be one of sameness and difference. As Tzvetan Todorov puts it, 'being outside is an advantage only if one is at the same time completely inside'. (27)

There is an implicit 'top down' perspective for the critic assumed in this entire argument, but the *WT* discourse community and Lovecraft in particular demonstrate that the symbiosis of and interdependency between high and low culture were—in this case at least—just as keenly felt by those 'looking up'.

In the May 1930 *WT* it was reported with some excitement that 'an authority on contemporary literature' had singled out *WT* for praise in the pages of the *New York World*, with the relevant piece reprinted almost in its entirety in that issue's 'Eyrie'. In fact, South African–born William Bolitho (1891–1930) was more celebrated for his journalism than as a literary critic, although he wrote one posthumously published novel (1931's *Twelve Against the Gods*) and certainly moved in literary circles; he was a friend of Hemingway's and Noël Coward wrote the preface for his nonfiction anthology *Camera Obscura* (1931) (Lynn 1995, 184). In his article on 'Pulp Magazines', Bolitho recognized in *WT* both the sporadic attainment of 'literariness'—which Bolitho tellingly describes as an 'unjust standard'—and the vitality of its discourse community:

> I know as well as anyone, that they are in a certain proportion, as large as you like, the product of hack writers. What does that matter? The strange thing in these circles is that criticism is much more remorseless and sincere than in the more pretentious. For hack or not, whatever the pay, each of the pulp magazine authors has to produce interest; he has to hold his readers, not merely to show how clever he is, or he is lost. And the standard, the unjust literary standard itself, is surprisingly satisfied often with them. Make no mistake about that. (*Weird Tales* 1930c, 582)

Bolitho also recognized *Weird Tales* as a mass-market venue for poetry, remarking, '[m]editate on that [...] there are still poets here of the pure Poe school who sell and are printed for a vast public' (582). Lovecraft took a concomitant approach of carefully selecting specific stories and poems in *WT* for valorization as satisfying his literary standard (or containing elements which did so), with the editor of *WT* not only unhesitatingly accepting but acting upon his judgement:

> H. P. Lovecraft writes that he has gone through his file of *Weird Tales* from the beginning and has picked out the following stories as having the greatest amount of truly cosmic horror and macabre convincingness: 'Beyond the Door' by Paul Suter, 'The Floor Above' by M. L. Humphreys, 'The Night Wire' by H. F. Arnold [subsequently included in *The Weird: A Compendium of Strange and Dark Stories*], 'The Canal' by Everil Worrell, 'Bells of Oceana' by Arthur J. Burks, and 'In Amundsen's Tent' by John Martin Leahy. All or most of these will be used later as Weird Story Reprints. (*Weird Tales* 1930d, 12)

Lovecraft undertook this function in public while in private correspondence unambiguously identifying the pulps as low culture, sometimes in extremely caustic terms:

> As I've been trying to make clear, the popular magazine world is essentially an *underworld* or caricature-imitation world so far as serious writing is concerned. Absolutely nothing about it is worthy of mature consideration or permanent preservation. That is why I am so absolutely unwilling to make any concessions to its standards, & so much disposed to repudiate it entirely in an effort to achieve real aesthetic expression even on the humblest plane. (Howard Phillips Lovecraft 1971, 3:416)

Here, Lovecraft derides the context of his writing—languishing in the 'humblest plane'—but also claims that through his commitment to 'real aesthetic expression' he is surpassing its limitations. On occasion, Lovecraft's views elide almost seamlessly with Adorno's condemnation of early twentieth-century mass culture as a manipulated reinforcement of false consciousness:

> The popular tastes and perspectives are all false things of the surface unworthy of a sober thinker's attention, and [...] the proportionate importance of the different factors in life is never even approximated by romantic popular literature with its artificial, catchpenny standards based on the dull comprehension of the brainless majority. Learn to lose interest in the tawdry and tinsel things exalted by cheap novelists, and to gain interest in the only two things worthy of a high-grade adult mind—*truth and beauty*. (Howard Phillips Lovecraft 1968, 2:326–327)

However, it is worth noting that Lovecraft was himself working within the pulp market and therefore (if one is to accept that Lovecraft deserves his current canonical status) refuting his own argument by his practice as a writer.

Lovecraft's acute self-consciousness regarding the lowly status of *WT* did not translate into a sustained attempt to place his writing with a mainstream publishing house. The frustration of his biographer is palpable as he describes Lovecraft's self-sabotaging response to an approach from Allen G. Ullman, an editor at Knopf, in 1933 (Joshi 2013, 2:855–856). Ullman was alerted to Lovecraft's writing by a mutual acquaintance and at Ullman's request Lovecraft sent him seven stories. Ullman expressed enthusiasm but when Lovecraft sent him a further 18 stories, he did so accompanied by a lengthy letter masochistically detailing their various shortcomings and failures. Needless to say, Ullman decided against adding Lovecraft to Knopf's roster, although Joshi suggests that (despite Lovecraft's subsequent 'self-recrimination') Farnsworth Wright's failure to guarantee a sale of 1000 copies of such a volume through *WT* was at least just as responsible for Ullman's reticence (856). It is interesting to note that Lovecraft's abortive, but at one point very credible, attempt to move into 'legitimate' publishing was, when it came down to it, still firmly situated within and dependent upon the marketing paradigm of *WT*; with Knopf apparently rather more interested in 'tapping in' to *WT*'s customer base than conferring literary respectability onto one of *WT*'s writers.

If Lovecraft took an austerely critical stance regarding *WT* and his own work, he was just as rigorous in his treatment of highbrow literature and Modernism; and if his criticism of the pulp magazines was by no means predicated on an un-interrogated assumption of the superiority of the highbrow, neither was he wholly dismissive. Despite lampooning 'The Waste Land' in his parodic 'Waste Paper' (1923), he attended a reading by Eliot in Providence in 1933 and found it 'interesting if not quite explicable' (926). He was similarly equivocal in his responses to Lawrence, Joyce, and Hemingway, enthusiastic about Conrad, and reserved his most unconditional praise for Proust and for continental fiction generally: 'The French are the real masters [...]—Balzac, Gautier, Flaubert, de Maupassant, Stendhal, Proust. ... Nobody can beat them unless it is the 19th century Russians—Dostoievsky [sic], Chekhov, Turgeniev' (924). As a reader, then, Lovecraft was as discriminating and critical in his responses to the highbrow as he was to *WT*. He also indicated on at least one occasion that his specialism was the result not of choice but of necessity:

> When I say I can write nothing but weird fiction, I am not trying to exalt that medium but am merely confessing my own weakness. The reason I can't write other kinds is not that I don't value and respect them, but merely that my slender set of endowments does not enable me to extract a compellingly acute personal sense of interest and drama from the natural phenomena of life [...] an art based on them is greater than any which fantasy could evoke—but I'm simply not big enough to react to them in the sensitive way necessary for artistic response and literary use. [...] I'd certainly be glad enough to be a Shakespeare or Balzac or Turgeniev *if I could!* [italics in original] (Howard Phillips Lovecraft 1976, 4:267–68)

But, as evidenced above, this occasional inferiority complex did not deter Lovecraft from his commitment to achieving 'literariness' in weird fiction against what he regarded as the lowbrow grain of the pulps:

> Above *everything else* comes good literature. And of course a concomitant to all this would be a complete swearing-off of the cinema and of cheap magazines. You can't bury that stuff too deeply out of sight and memory for your own artistic good!! (Howard Phillips Lovecraft 1971, 3:14–15)

Throughout the first two decades of its existence, this seemingly irresolvable conflict between literary ambition and a desire for literary legitimacy—or, to borrow Rainey's term, the 'claim to aesthetic dignity'—on the one hand and the pulp reality on the other was also discussed with a great deal of reflexivity by the wider *WT* discourse community (Rainey 1998, 2). The latter often consisted of communications from *WT* contributors like Lovecraft, Howard, and Smith, discussing their conceptual notions of weird fiction and the shortcomings of its actuality. Many readers also contributed to this ongoing discussion. I will outline below what amounts to an argument between enthusiasts for crude genre cliché, who relished unchallenging escapist fantasy, and a connoisseur group urging that such populism be jettisoned in favour of their conception of a 'literary' weird. I have previously expanded upon the notion that weird fiction is at least partly distinguished from other, ostensibly 'lowbrow' genres in the Introduction, and in Chap. 3 discussed in more detail the persisting connoisseur culture associated with weird fiction and its use of the term to make this distinction.

Here again, the invocation of the term is used as an indicator of distinction. The conversations undertaken by the *WT* discourse community referred to not only the stories within the pages of the magazine, but also the cover art and illustrations, which were repeatedly criticized for using sex to sell the title while misrepresenting its contents: 'The appearance of nude females gives the impression that *Weird Tales* is sexy and trashy, in my opinion, whereas its stories are anything but that' (*Weird Tales* 1933c, 516). There were two main, interrelated, through-lines to the correspondence: first, the attempt to classify weird fiction and distinguish it from other genres and implicitly from genre itself, discussed above. Second, the activity of petitioning for the best weird fiction to be considered 'great literature' and occasionally arguing its superiority to realism. The arguments ranged from clumsy and risible to sophisticated, although the nature of the debate and its platform will be enough for some to consider it inescapably déclassé. Regardless, what it does unequivocally demonstrate is literary aspiration (or—to put it less charitably—pretension).

'Real Literature' v 'Scienti-Fiction'

As far as distinguishing weird fiction from other genres is concerned, one ongoing controversy in 'The Eyrie' was the appropriateness or otherwise of the inclusion of (what would now be considered) science fiction: 'I don't care much about "Scienti-fiction," but I do like everything else in the magazine—the weirder the better' (*Weird Tales* 1929a, 278); 'I do not see that a *scientific* story belongs in *Weird Tales*' (*Weird Tales* 1928a, 4); 'Be careful not to print too much weird-scientific fiction in a single copy' cautions one reader (*Weird Tales* 1930b, 438); 'I like to collect the weirdest stories that I can find but generally scientific stories don't interest me' (*Weird Tales* 1930g, 586); 'interplanetary stories [...] to my mind they're not weird and have no place in *Weird Tales*' (*Weird Tales* 1931a, 6); 'Science fiction is O.K. but keep it weird' (*Weird Tales* 1932, 414); the intimidatingly purist argument that 'weird scientific stories are not weird' (*Weird Tales* 1933b, 787); 'more weird less science fiction' (*Weird Tales* 1935, 780); and one correspondent expressed preference for the '"pure type" of weird tale (Poe) vs pseudoscience (Verne)' (*Weird Tales* 1926c, 857). Some correspondents demur on the issue, but a distinct minority lobbied that science fiction was tautologically weird—'if interplanetary stories are not weird, then please tell me what is weird'—though more often the argument was that individual 'science' stories can make the grade if they meet certain conditions (*Weird Tales* 1931b, 154): 'Stories must be eery [sic] enough to class as *weird-scientific*' (*Weird Tales* 1933a, 138). This patrolling of genre boundaries was further amplified in *The Fantasy Fan*, where the young Forest J. Ackerman (1916–2008)—who went on to become 'the world's greatest science fiction fan'—took the isolated and unpopular position of criticizing Lovecraft's and Smith's contributions to *WT*, only to be met with what Lovecraft approvingly described as 'a good barrage' from other *The Fantasy Fan* readers (Carlson 2008; *The Fantasy Fan* 1934, 68). Ackerman eventually lamented:

> Being more of a weird fans' magazine, I can't expect many voices on my side from *The Fantasy Fan* readers. [...] As the science fiction fan I am always eager to see stf [sic] in *Weird Tales* and any other magazine. [...] Numerous

Eyrie letters knock stf in *Weird* [sic]. I only did the same, but from the other side of the fence. (*The Fantasy Fan* 1934, 67–68)

The attempt to distance *WT* from science fiction is commensurate with the repeated claims to legitimacy made by invocation of the word 'literary' and its cognates. In support of claims that *WT* has a 'distinct literary quality' that differentiates it from other pulp titles, one correspondent, an 'English teacher', offers the following testimony:

> 'Do you ever get letters from bona fide English teachers?' writes Don C. Hilsinger, of St. Louis, Michigan. 'I am one myself, but am not one of those teachers who believe that no literature was written before or after Shakespeare. Neither do I avow Browning to have been the last real poet. In fact, my favourite poets and authors are not all dead and what is more I defend them against the invectiveness of my professors. On several occasions I have mentioned *Weird Tales* only to have it scorned as only a Ph. D. in English can scorn a magazine. Then one day I saw the list of stories that this Ph. D. was teaching in his short-story class. Ha ha ha! I had read several of them in *Weird Tales* and I told him so. He registered a very operatic expression of surprize [sic] and said, "Is that so?" Then he proceeded to ponder on the subject for a while and finally gave his decision to the effect that if you published in your monthly reprint section such stories as the ones I mentioned, the rest of your stories would have to be good too, or your readers would object to them by comparison.' (*Weird Tales* 1930f, 423)

Hilsinger's excitable testimony serves as a microcosm of some of the genre tensions discussed above and, moreover, presents *WT* as successfully wrong-footing the academy. According to the received wisdom of the 'professors' and 'Ph. D.'s—or, to put it in the Bourdieuan terms employed in Chap. 3, a cultural elite identified by 'its titles of nobility […] awarded by the educational system'—a pulp magazine should be essentially a venue for populist writing of no literary value (Bourdieu 1984, 2). This assumption is challenged by the crossover of material to be found in both *WT* and the syllabus of the 'short-story class': the 'Ph. D' is forced to accommodate *WT* as being of literary worth, not only by virtue of its reprints, but— by implication—for its new fiction. The 'Ph. D.' may have retracted this last pendant to his conclusion had he familiarized himself with *WT* itself: rubbing shoulders with the reprints of work by Dickens and Balzac, and earnest requests for the inclusion of 'more poetry by Matthew Arnold', were new stories about 'killer tables' and 'a Mayan temple and a green snake that could swallow an Elephant'.

Regardless of the unavoidable silliness of some of the content, Wright's self-declared interest in *WT* publishing 'literature' remained not only an editorial concern, but a key aspiration of the discourse community. Stories are praised on the basis of their 'distinct literary quality' (*Weird Tales* 1927a, 275): H. Warner Munn's 'torture' story 'The Chain' is lauded as 'a weird tale that is real literature' (*Weird Tales* 1928b); a poem by Robert E. Howard is enthusiastically declared to be 'literature' (*Weird Tales* 1928c); Lovecraft's 'genius' places him alongside '"real" authors' like Shakespeare and Poe (*Weird Tales* 1929b); *WT* converts an erstwhile 'sceptic of cheap literature' (*Weird Tales* 1930a, 294); Smith's work is distinguished for its 'real literary quality' and he is compared to 'Rabelais and Petronius' (*Weird Tales* 1930d, 8; *Weird Tales* 1932, 414); a reader remarks of 'The End of the Story' by Smith that 'in the publications pretending to culture and sophistication one would look in vain for the writings of anyone of the caliber [sic] of Mr. Smith—a true poet' (*Weird Tales* 1930d, 10); and *WT* generally is considered 'far beyond the pulp-paper "news stand" class' and to achieve a 'high literary standard' unappreciated by the 'simple-minded public' (*Weird Tales* 1930e, 148; *Weird Tales* 1931c, 463; *Weird Tales* 1930h, 724). Indeed, Smith (a protégé of George Sterling) had previously experienced prodigious if transient international success as a teenage poet: his poem 'A Dream of Beauty' had appeared in the *Academy and Literature* in 1911 and his 1912 collection *The Star-Treader and Other Poems* was favourably reviewed by Machen in the London *Evening News* (Smith 1911; Machen 1916).

It is clear from these claims that at least some of *WT*'s readers did not consider themselves a pulp audience and were, rather, making distinctions based on the idea of 'literature' and literary purism. Implicit in this is an assumption that other pulp readerships were more comfortably resigned to the lowbrow status of their chosen titles, as certainly appeared to be the case in Britain: 'In the 1940s Mass Observation surveys confirmed that fans of cheap thrillers commonly acknowledged they were facile and not to be compared with classics' (Rose 2002, 370). Compared to this easy acceptance of the undemanding nature of such material, the *WT* discourse community could appear neurotic and overreaching in its petitioning for highbrow status:

> If you do not believe that bizarre tales offer opportunity for the highest artistry to the literary genius who is endowed with imagination, then read H. P. Lovecraft's story, *The Outsider*, on page 449 of this issue. Where in the

whole realm of literature will you find a more original conception, or more consummate artistry in the workmanship, than in this story? Its every sentence bears the mark of the master literary craftsman; it is a sheer triumph of bizarrerie and outré invention. Not even Poe in his wildest flights of fancy has surpassed the winged beauty of this imaginative weird tale. Truly, when such geniuses as Edgar Allan Poe, Ambrose Bierce, Arthur Machen, Algernon Blackwood and H. P. Lovecraft achieve their best and most artistic results through the medium of the weird tale, then the literary merit of this type of fiction is established beyond dispute or cavil. (*Weird Tales* 1926a, 566)

This letter positions Lovecraft, out of all *WT*'s contributors, as the author most perfectly fulfilling the connoisseur 'cercle' understanding of weird fiction: 'consummate artistry', the 1890s-hued 'bizarrerie and outré invention', and a literary provenance of names (or rather 'geniuses') by now familiar to the reader of this thesis.

Lovecraft's Aesthetic 'Cercle'

The 'master literary craftsman' concerned, Lovecraft, was approached by Henneberger at some point before February 1924 with an invitation to edit *WT*. Lovecraft's response to the proposal resonates (unsurprisingly) with many of the issues and tensions discussed above. The fact that Lovecraft saw them as insurmountable grounds for declining the offer of the editorship is perhaps more surprising, considering what must have been a very tempting proposition for the struggling, unemployed author (although there were other circumstantial explanations for Lovecraft's decision) (Machin 2015). Writing to Henneberger on 2 February 1924, Lovecraft expanded on his reasons for declining in considerable detail, detail which also sheds light on some of the issues discussed above. Lovecraft praises *WT*'s editor at the time, Edwin Baird, remarking of the previous issue, 'that [Baird] could get hold of as many as five perfectly satisfactory yarns is an almost remarkable phenomenon in view of the lack of truly artistic and individual expression among professional fiction-writers'. Lovecraft clearly did not regard the fact that *WT* was a pulp title as an implicit bar to 'artistic and individual expression', but rather the general rarity of these qualities as the obstacle. His explanation for this paucity of literary talent broadens the discussion from pulp publishing to the reading public at large:

Here in America we have a very conventional and half-educated public—a public trained under one phase or another of the Puritan tradition, and almost dulled to aesthetic sensitiveness because of the monotonous and omnipresent overstressing of the ethical element. ("H. P. Lovecraft to J. C. Henneberger" 1924)

This disparagement of the competency of the reading public is remarkably congruent to similar complaints made in Britain 30 years earlier (see Chap. 2).

Acknowledging the commercial pressures facing *WT*, and that pursuing an exclusively purist editorial policy would be unrealistic, Lovecraft continues:

If publishers of general magazines sought and used artistically original types of fiction, they would lose their readers almost to a man. Half of the people wouldn't understand what the tales were about, and the other half would find the characters unsympathetic—because they would think and act like real people.

He then adduces modernity itself as a contributory factor to his pessimism regarding the possibility of producing a magazine of consistently high literary quality:

Added to this, as if by the perversity of a malign fate, is the demand of an overspeeding public for excessive *quantity production* [emphasis in original]. Baldly put, the American people demand more stories per year than the really artistic authors of America could possibly write.

The 'excessive quantity production' demanded by the 'overspeeding public' makes it extremely difficult to meet the conditions for highbrow literary production:

A real artist never works fast, and never turns out large quantities. He can't contract to deliver so many words in such and such a time, but must work slowly, gradually, and by mood; utilising favourable states of mind and refraining from putting down the stuff his brain turns out when it is tired or disinclined to such work.

It is worth emphasizing that Lovecraft's reservations about the tenability of maintaining a high standard (or his definition thereof) of content for *WT* are nothing to do with the pulp market *qua* the pulp market. His criticisms and objections to contemporary publishing and reading practices would apply as much to the high-end 'slick' as they would to the lowliest pulp. There is here of course an implicit criticism of 'overspeeding' modernity itself. Lovecraft was certainly one of the twentieth-century 'hierarchists of culture' and 'disenfranchised' intellectuals described by Clive Bloom, who held a 'fascination born of horror' with 'popular culture and by implication mass-democratic society' (121). However, unlike F. R. Leavis, Lovecraft's keenly felt indignity was that as an author he was slumming it in the pulps.

Although Lovecraft turned down the editorship of *WT*, his role in the magazine—as a contributor and correspondent—developed over the ensuing years such that by the time of his death in 1936, he was one of the most keenly valorized and influential members of the *WT* discourse community. Moreover, he was a key player in the connoisseur faction outlined above, lobbying for the title to focus its attention on their own 'purist' interpretation of weird fiction, and away from science fiction and 'sordid, sanguinary gruesomeness'. In this regard, their activity was, almost to the letter, commensurate with Bürger's and Shaw's dictum that 'Aestheticism can create the unity of producer and recipient only if it reduces a potentially all-inclusive public to the dimensions of a "cercle" which takes in just a few individuals' (Bürger and Shaw 1985, 30). Brian Stableford has argued that Lovecraft's 'peculiar theories of the aesthetics of horror engulfed many of the writers who appeared in *Weird Tales*':

> Lovecraft's aesthetic theories were thoroughly Decadent, and many of his other correspondents, including the poets Samuel Loveman and Vincent Starrett [who did much to renew American enthusiasm for Machen's writing at this time], assiduously turned out Decadent work for which there was no obvious audience at all. (Stableford 1998, 132)

I have attempted to demonstrate above that, arguably contradicting this latter point, *WT* had found such an audience. Rather than louche studio-bound aesthetes, however, this new readership for Decadence was the modern American reader of pulp magazines, who may have been seeking out the cheap thrills disingenuously promised by the lurid cover art, but could just as easily find themselves reading Baudelaire, Gautier, Wilde, or Dowson.

Besides simply serving as a crucible for the talents of the Lovecraft cercle, *WT* and its discourse community undertook the first reflexive performance of the wider and ongoing connoisseur culture—discussed in Chap. 3—that uses 'weird fiction' as a mark of distinction. By this reading, beyond the expediency of using the term to liberate the writer from any obligation to employ increasingly tiresome generic structures and appurtenances, the New Weird of the early twenty-first century (see Introduction) could be accused of misplaced nostalgia. The attempt to use the word 'weird' to gesture back to a putative period (the 'Old Weird' of *WT*) before such distinctions—generic and artistic—ever had to be made is based on a misunderstanding. As I have demonstrated above, the *WT* discourse community was in fact consistently preoccupied with, if not dominated by, discussion of these same distinctions.

WORKS CITED

Allen, Grant. 1892. Pallinghurst Barrow. *Illustrated London News*, November 28.
Bourdieu, Pierre. 1984. *Distinction: A Social Critique of the Judgement of Taste*. Trans. Richard Nice. Cambridge: Harvard.
Bürger, Peter, and Michael Shaw. 1985. The Institution of 'Art' as a Category in the Sociology of Literature. *Cultural Critique* 2: 5–33. https://doi.org/10.2307/1354199.
Carlson, Michael. 2008. Forrest J Ackerman. *Guardian*, December 7, sec. Books. http://www.theguardian.com/books/2008/dec/07/forrest-ackerman-science-fiction-obituary.
Chubbuck, Katherine. 2004. Oxford DNB Article: Hearn, (Patricio) Lafcadio Carlos. https://doi.org/10.1093/ref:odnb/41244. Accessed 25 Jan 2016.
Cook, Deborah. 1996. *The Culture Industry Revisited: Theodor W. Adorno on Mass Culture*. Lanham: Rowman & Littlefield.
Everett, Justin, and Jeffrey H. Shanks. 2015. Introduction: Weird Tales—Discourse Community and Genre Nexus. In *The Unique Legacy of Weird Tales: The Evolution of Modern Fantasy and Horror*, ix–xix. London: Rowman & Littlefield.
Fish, Stanley E. 1976. Interpreting the "Variorum". *Critical Inquiry* 2 (3): 465–485.
"H.P. Lovecraft to J.C. Henneberger." 1924. Letters. Harry Ransom Center, February 2.
Hearn, Lafcadio. 1887. *Some Chinese Ghosts*. Boston: Roberts Brothers.
———. 1904. *Kwaidan*. Boston/New York: Houghton Mifflin.
———. 1915a. *Interpretations of Literature*. Ed. John Erskine. Vol. 2. 2 vols. New York: Dodd, Mead and Co.

———. 1915b. *Interpretations of Literature*. Ed. John Erskine. Vol. 1. 2 vols. New York: Dodd, Mead and Co.
Hearn, Lafcadio, and Elizabeth Bisland. 1907a. *The Life and Letters of Lafcadio Hearn*. Vol. 1. 2 vols. London: Archibald Constable & Co.
———. 1907b. *The Life and Letters of Lafcadio Hearn*. Vol. 2. 2 vols. London: Archibald Constable & Co.
Huyssen, Andreas. 1988. *After the Great Divide: Modernism, Mass Culture and Postmodernism*. Basingstoke: Macmillan.
Joshi, S.T. 2013. *I Am Providence: The Life and Times of H. P. Lovecraft*. Vol. 2. 2 vols. New York: Hippocampus Press.
Lovecraft, H.P. 1985. Supernatural Horror in Literature. In *Dagon and Other Macabre Tales*, 421–512. London: Panther.
———. 2004. In *Collected Essays 2: Literary Criticism*, ed. S.T. Joshi. New York: Hippocampus Press.
Lovecraft, Howard Phillips. 1968. *Selected Letters*. E. August Derleth and Donald Wandrei. Vol. 2. 5 vols. Sauk City: Arkham House.
———. 1971. *Selected Letters*. Ed. August Derleth and Donald Wandrei. Vol. 3. 5 vols. Sauk City: Arkham House.
———. 1976. *Selected Letters*. Ed. August Derleth and James Turner. Vol. 4. 5 vols. Sauk City: Arkham House.
Lynn, Kenneth Schuyler. 1995. *Hemingway*. London: Harvard University Press.
Machen, Arthur. 1916. Books of Today. *Evening News*, February 12.
Machin, James. 2015. Fellows Find: H. P. Lovecraft Letter Sheds Light on Pivotal Moment in His Career. *Cultural Compass* (blog). http://blog.hrc.utexas.edu/2015/01/27/fellows-find-h-p-lovecraft-letter/. Accessed 26 Jan 2016.
Morrisson, Mark S. 2001. *The Public Face of Modernism: Little Magazines, Audiences, and Reception, 1905–1920*. Madison: University of Wisconsin Press.
Price, E. Hoffmann. 2001. *Book of the Dead: Friends of Yesteryear: Fictioneers & Others*. Sauk City: Arkham House Publishers.
Rainey, Lawrence S. 1998. *Institutions of Modernism*. New Haven/London: Yale.
Rose, Jonathan. 2002. *The Intellectual Life of the British Working Classes*. New Haven: Yale University Press.
Saturday Review. 1893. New Books and Reprints, June 3.
Smith, Clark Ashton. 1911. A Dream of Beauty. *Academy and Literature*, August 12.
Sorensen, Leif. 2010. A Weird Modernist Archive: Pulp Fiction, Pseudobiblia, H. P. Lovecraft. *Modernism/Modernity* 17 (3): 501–522.
Stableford, Brian M. 1998. *Glorious Perversity: The Decline and Fall of Literary Decadence*. San Bernardino: Borgo Press.
The Fantasy Fan. 1934. The Boiling Point. January.
———. 1934. "The Favorite Weird Stories of Clark Ashton Smith." December.
———. 1934. "The Favorite Weird Stories of H. P. Lovecraft." October.

———. 1934. "The Favorite Weird Tales of August W. Derleth." June.
Turner, Catherine. 2003. *Marketing Modernism Between the Two World Wars*. Amherst: University of Massachusetts Press.
Weinberg, Robert E. 1977. *The Weird Tales Story*. Oregon: Fax.
Weird Tales. 1924. The Eyrie. March.
———. 1926a. The Eyrie. April.
———. 1926b. The Eyrie. June.
———. 1927a. The Eyrie. February.
———. 1927b. The Eyrie. May.
———. 1927c. The Eyrie. July.
———. 1928a. The Eyrie. January.
———. 1928b. The Eyrie. July.
———. 1928c. The Eyrie. December.
———. 1929a. The Eyrie. February.
———. 1929b. The Eyrie. June.
———. 1930a. The Eyrie. March.
———. 1930b. The Eyrie. April.
———. 1930c. The Eyrie. May.
———. 1930d. The Eyrie. July.
———. 1930e. The Eyrie. August.
———. 1930f. The Eyrie. September.
———. 1930g. The Eyrie. November.
———. 1930h. The Eyrie. December.
———. 1931a. The Eyrie. January.
———. 1931b. The Eyrie. March.
———. 1931c. The Eyrie. July.
———. 1932. The Eyrie. March.
———. 1933a. The Eyrie. January.
———. 1933b. The Eyrie. June.
———. 1933c. The Eyrie. October.
———. 1934. The Eyrie. September.
———. 1935. The Eyrie. December.
Young, Robert. 1996. *Torn Halves: Political Conflict in Literary and Cultural Theory*. Manchester: Manchester University Press.

Afterword

In terms of its use in the early twenty-first century, the term 'weird fiction' is sometimes deployed simply to sidestep the conversation by using 'weird' interchangeably with 'good' (or more specifically 'literary') and particularly as an attempted divestment of the déclassé baggage of horror. As discussed in the Introduction, Simon Strantzas for one has already questioned its use in this regard, arguing that by making such distinctions at all we are only reinforcing the assumption that there are inherently debased genres from which the respectable writer or connoisseur would do well to distance themselves. It seems unlikely, however, that an instinct as ingrained and essentially human as the desire to define one's self against a troubling mass culture could (or should) be blithely abandoned.

As evidenced above, the *WT* discourse community considered itself to be operating within, and contributing to the curation of, a 'weird tradition' rather than pioneering a new generic form calibrated as a response to emergent early twentieth-century discourses (whether literary or wider). The imaginative exuberance of the fin de siècle represented a high watermark of both the critical respectability and commercial value of weird fiction in the Poe tradition. That this tradition fell on the wrong side of the bifurcation of highbrow and lowbrow was an eventuality that contributed to and exacerbated the status anxieties that persist to this day between 'literary' and genre fiction. Attempting to extract weird fiction from this complex historical lineage and give it a progressive Modernist imprimatur is, in itself, a manifestation of that struggle for literary legitimacy. It is part of an ongoing and wider process of jostling for admission into the dominant cultural *prises de position*. However, weird fiction not only represents a reactive negotiation between these various competing claims. It is also a commitment to fashioning a literary space free from the strictures of both generic formula and staid realist respectability, a space which also challenges and provokes interrogation of what is usually regarded as inviolable highbrow doctrine.

Index[1]

A

Ackerman, Forest J., 239
Adam Smith, Janet, 164, 171, 172, 174, 175, 178, 180, 186, 210, 213
Adlard, John, 102, 103, 105, 109, 110, 112
Adorno, Theodor W., 233, 234, 236
Aestheticism, 52, 55, 57, 65, 76, 111, 112, 174, 184, 233, 234, 244
Aickman, Robert, 83, 93, 131
Allen, Grant, 54, 60, 62, 75, 145, 146, 228, 229
  'Pallinghurst Barrow,' 228
  Philistia, 62
  Strange Stories, 62
  Women Who Did, The, 54
Altman, Rick, 12
Anderson, Poul, 32
  Broken Sword, The, 32
Atwood, Mary Anne, 148
  Suggestive Inquiry into the Hermetic Mystery, A, 148

B

'Backsliding,' 164, 213, 214
Balfour, Arthur, 113, 172
Balzac, Honoré de, 103, 225, 237, 240
Barbauld, Anna Laetitia, 26–28
  'Summer Evening's Meditation, A,' 26
Baudelaire, Charles, 66, 73, 87, 100, 116, 139, 176, 178, 182, 224, 231, 233, 244
Baudrillard, Jean, 49, 106, 116, 132
Bayley, John, 69–71
Beardsley, Aubrey, 14, 56, 66, 93–95, 108, 113, 142, 178
Beckford, William, 109, 117
  Vathek, 117
Beerbohm, Max, 58, 66, 74, 104, 106, 109
  'Enoch Soames,' 106
Bennett, Arnold, 62, 163, 163n1, 171, 178

---

[1] Note: Page numbers followed by 'n' refer to notes.

Benson, E. F., 20, 26, 150, 188n7, 189, 225
Bierce, Ambrose, 221, 242
Billings, Harold, 63, 65, 95, 97
Blackwood, Algernon, 11, 12, 19, 20, 38, 178, 203, 212, 212n17, 222, 242
  'Willows, The,' 19, 20, 222
Blackwood's Magazine, 164
Blanchot, Maurice, 70, 71
Blind, Karl, 32, 33
Boer War, 58, 168, 210
Bolitho, William, 231, 235
Bourdieu, Pierre, 14, 39, 50, 51, 126, 129, 234, 240
Brangham, Godfrey, 133, 139, 140, 142, 150
Bristow, Joseph, 102
British Empire
  and colonialism, 212, 214
  imperialism, 212
Buchan, John, 4, 5, 13, 16, 26, 30, 38–40, 64, 80–83, 87, 119, 120, 153, 163–214
  African Colony, The, 212
  'Captain of Salvation, A,' 192, 205
  Dancing Floor, The, 82, 180, 181, 183, 185, 193, 194, 200
  'Far Islands, The,' 189, 193, 214
  'Green Wildebeeste, The,' 189–191
  'Grove of Ashtaroth, The,' 165, 184, 185, 190, 193, 212, 213
  'Journey of Little Profit, A,' 193
  'Kings of Orion, The,' 190, 193, 212
  Lodge in the Wilderness, A, 191, 212
  Mr. Standfast, 180, 191
  'No-Man's-Land,' 64, 185, 187, 188, 190, 192, 193, 211
  Power-House, The, 172, 210
  Prester John, 210
  Scholar Gipsies, 64, 178, 179, 192
  'Shut Door, The,' 80, 82
  Sick Heart River, 167
  Sir Quixote of the Moors, 178
  'Skule Skerry,' 167, 189, 190
  'Tendebant Manaus,' 212
  Thirty-Nine Steps, The, 64, 164, 170, 172, 187, 191, 192
  'Watcher by the Threshold, The,' 187, 192, 193, 210, 212, 213
  'Wind in the Portico, The,' 189, 190, 208, 213
Buddhism, 76, 204
Bulwer-Lytton, Edward, 22, 53n1
  Zanoni, 22
Burke, Edmund, 27
Burton, Sir Richard, 118, 183

C
'Caledonian Antisyzygy,' 208, 212
Calvinism, 203, 204
Calvino, Italo, 124
Campbell, Ramsey, 8
Carey, John, 83, 87, 163n1, 171, 173
Carlyle, Thomas, 98, 138
Catholicism, 195
Cecil, L. Moffitt, 117, 119, 120, 124, 125
Celts, 192
Chambers, Robert W., 72, 119, 141, 189, 221, 224
  King in Yellow, The, 72, 119, 141
Christianity, 200, 201, 203, 204, 207–209, 214
Circulating libraries, 52, 53
Classicism, 208
Club Story, 81, 120–123, 125, 208
Clute, John, 82, 83, 119–121, 125, 166, 167, 190, 191
Coleridge, Samuel Taylor, 36
  Rime of the Ancient Mariner, The, 36

Connoisseurs and 'connoisseur culture,' 4, 13, 39, 49, 98, 102, 106, 107, 111, 125–134, 183, 226, 227, 233, 238, 242, 244, 245
Conrad, Joseph, 69, 75, 121, 125, 138, 139, 173, 188, 189, 211, 213, 237
  Heart of Darkness, 121, 125, 188, 211
  Romance (Conrad and Madox Ford), 173
Cory, Annie Sophie, 54, 55
  Woman Who Didn't, The, 54
Cosmic horror, 3, 26–31, 235
Costelloe, Mary, 111
Crawford, F. Marion, 120
  'Upper Berth, The,' 120
Critchley, Simon, 71
Croft-Cooke, Rupert, 53, 59, 60
Crowe, Catherine, 22
  Night Side of Nature, The, 22
Crowley, Aleister, 183, 184, 204

D

Daemons, 2, 124, 212
Darwin, Charles, 75, 147, 189
Decadence, 38–40, 50, 54–57, 59, 66, 68, 72–80, 84, 87, 93–95, 98–102, 107, 108, 113, 117–119, 125, 132, 135, 136, 138, 139, 147, 153, 164, 174–187, 203, 206, 213, 221–245
de la Mare, Walter, 83–85, 189, 222
  'Recluse, A,' 85
  'Seaton's Aunt,' 84, 85, 222
del Toro, Guillermo, 49, 127, 128
De Quincey, Thomas, 116, 117, 117n10

Confessions of an English Opium Eater, 116
Derleth, August, 222
Dickens, Charles, 18, 19, 22, 35, 53n1, 114, 138, 225, 240
Discourse communities, 226, 227, 234, 235, 238, 241, 244, 245, 249
Douglas, Lord Alfred, ('Bosie'), 55, 104, 107, 143, 144
Dowson, Ernest, 108, 224, 244
Doyle, Sir Arthur Conan, 16, 17, 37, 59, 63–68, 96, 97, 141, 225
  'Parasite, The,' 65, 141
  Sign of Four, The, 65
Dunsany, Lord, 14, 29–31, 38, 120, 125, 189
  Gods of Pegāna, The, 29

E

Education Act, 51
Egerton, George, 56, 60, 75, 135
Eliot, T. S., 237
  'Waste Land, The,' 237

F

Fantasy, 3, 7, 8, 26, 29–32, 38, 82, 84, 97, 98, 116, 119, 119n11, 135, 150, 165, 166, 169, 201, 225, 230, 237, 238
Fantasy Fan, The, 37, 48, 189, 222, 226, 227, 239, 240
Feddersen, R. C., 67, 68, 120
First World War, 80, 82, 181, 191
Fisher, Mark, 10, 11, 30
Frazer, J. G., 146, 181
  Golden Bough, The, 146, 181
Freemasonry, 204
Futurian, The, 165

G

Gaskell, Elizabeth, 35
 'Old Nurse's Story, The,' 35
Gautier, Théophile, 116, 224, 225, 229–231, 237, 244
Geis, 33
Genius loci, 19, 200
Genre, 3–9, 11–32, 38, 39, 48, 49, 60, 62–64, 70, 73, 86, 95, 98, 100, 125, 133, 153, 164–167, 169, 171–173, 187, 192, 225–227, 231, 232, 238–240, 249
Gernsback, Hugo, 28
Ghosts and ghost stories, 8, 17–23, 25, 26, 36, 60, 86, 87, 111, 125, 145, 165, 191, 193–195
Gilchrist, Robert Murray, 26, 39, 78, 80, 93–153, 164
 'Crimson Weaver, The,' 99
 Stone Dragon, The, 78, 99, 100
Gissing, George, 52, 53, 58, 62, 63, 75, 136, 137, 139
 New Grub Street, 63, 75, 136, 137
Gogol, Nikolai, 67
 'Overcoat, The,' 67
Gothic, 3, 7, 14, 16, 17, 22, 27, 37, 38, 47, 48, 68, 72, 117, 165, 166, 194, 195, 208
Grahame, Kenneth, 83, 99, 110, 175
Gray, John, 70, 107, 127
Greek mythology, 182
Gross, John, 53n1, 58, 66, 66n4, 95, 106, 107, 163, 164

H

Haggard, H. Rider, 17, 59, 62–64, 82, 125, 164, 169, 182, 188, 211
 Cetywayo and His White Neighbours, 64
 Dawn, 64
 King Solomon's Mines, 64, 169
 She, 64, 169, 182

Hall Caine, Sir Thomas Henry, 95
Harland, Henry, 65, 100
Harman, Graham, 10, 11
Harrison, Frederic, 58, 66n4, 107
Harrison, M. John, 6, 70, 94, 127
 Course of the Heart, The, 94
Harris, Wendell V., 59, 60, 66, 79
Harte, Bret, 67, 68
Haute Weird, 11, 12, 21, 39, 47
Hawthorne, Nathanial, 36, 67
Hearn, Lafcadio, 36, 224, 228–231
 Interpretations of Literature, 228
 Kwaidan: Stories and Studies of Strange Things, 229
Henley, William Ernest, 57–59, 64, 65, 74, 99, 100, 176, 198, 225
Henneberger, J. C., 165, 231–233, 242, 243
Hermetic Order of the Golden Dawn, 152
Highbrow/middlebrow/lowbrow, 48, 50, 59, 127, 170–174, 183, 221, 225, 230, 231, 237, 238, 241, 243, 249, 250
Hills, Matt, 130, 131
Hobsbawm, Eric, 80
Hodgson, William Hope, 11, 14, 27–29, 31, 31n6, 120, 131
 House on the Borderland, The, 27
 Night Land, The, 27, 31
Hoffmann, E. T. A., 231
Horror, 3, 47, 94, 164, 225, 249
Houellebecq, Michel, 10, 30
Howard, John, 131
Howard, Robert E., 1, 29–31, 241
 'Tower of the Elephant, The,' 31
Huxley, Thomas Henry, 103, 147

I

Ibsen, Henrik, 176–178
Imperialism and colonialism, 57, 169, 174, 191, 207, 211–214

J

Jackson, Holbrook, 55, 56, 58, 69, 139
James, Henry, 18, 26, 64, 86, 99, 121, 173
James, M. R., 18, 21, 26, 38, 139, 189, 191, 222
  'Count Magnus,' 222
  'View from a Hill, A,' 222
Jerome, Jerome K., 62, 64, 135, 150
Johnson, Lionel, 108
Joshi, S. T., 4, 10–13, 16, 17, 20, 21, 29, 30, 37, 38, 47, 149, 189, 229, 236, 237
Josiffe, Christopher, 147

K

Kant, Immanuel, 26, 27, 30
Keating, Peter, 21, 51, 52
Kenealy, Edward, 34, 35
  'Ballad of Gunhild, or the Phantom Ship,' 34
Keynotes, 5, 55, 60, 62–65, 75, 78, 79, 97, 112, 113, 118, 136–143, 145
King, Stephen, 8, 48, 49, 127
Kipling, Rudyard, 16, 17, 37, 62, 64, 69, 104, 125, 139, 164, 175, 177, 189
  'At the End of the Passage,' 69, 175
  Life's Handicap, 175
  'Strange Ride of Morrowbie Jukes, The,' 69

L

Lane, John, 13n4, 40, 53, 54, 56, 59–60, 63–65, 95–98, 137–140, 142, 165, 171, 175, 176, 178, 180, 192, 193, 196, 198, 199
  keynotes, 54, 59, 60, 63, 95
  Vigo Street office, 56
Lang, Andrew, 59, 64, 144, 173
Langley, Hugh, 136
  Tides Ebb Out to the Night, The, 136
Ledger, Sally, 177, 178
Lee, Vernon, 5, 20, 148, 149
  'Dionea,' 20, 148, 149
  Hauntings, 20
Lee, Stewart, 127, 128
Le Gallienne, Richard, 60, 100, 175–177, 196, 198, 199
Leighton, Frederic, Lord, 113
Ligotti, Thomas, 4, 72, 107
Lodge, Sir Oliver, 123, 152
Louÿs, Pierre, 136, 206
  Aphrodite, 136, 206
Lovecraft, H. P., 1–3, 5–7, 9–14, 16, 21, 27–30, 117, 130, 189, 190, 222, 226, 237
  'Call of Cthulhu, The,' 14
  'Shadow Out of Time, The,' 28
  Supernatural Horror in Literature, 2, 9, 117, 130, 189, 190, 222, 226
  'Waste Paper,' 237
  'Whisperer in Darkness, The,' 28
Luckhurst, Roger, 3, 3n2, 10, 16, 28, 97, 98, 114, 175

M

Macbeth, 32, 34
Macdonald, Kate, 171, 172
McDonald, Peter D., 50, 58, 60, 62, 65, 129, 137, 138, 144, 163n1
Machen, Arthur, 2, 5, 11, 12, 14, 26, 39, 49, 57, 60, 63, 78, 83, 87, 93–153, 175, 196, 221–223, 225, 231, 242
  'Bowmen, The,' 222, 223
  Chronicle of Clemendy, The, 150
  Dr. Stiggins: His Views and Principles, 144
  Eleusinia, 128

Machen, Arthur (*cont.*)
  Fragment of Life, A, 83, 87, 94, 128, 151
  Great God Pan and the Inmost Light, The, 60, 78, 136, 143
  'Great God Pan, The,' 57, 63, 83, 94, 175, 196
  Green Round, The, 94, 148
  Hieroglyphics, 4, 146
  Hill of Dreams, The, 14, 126, 127, 132, 134, 135, 137
  House of Souls, The, 14, 128
  London Adventure, The, 128
  'N,' 5
  'Novel of the Black Seal, The,' 123, 151, 222
  'Novel of the White Powder, The,' 148, 149, 222
  Secret Glory, The, 128, 131, 134, 151
  Three Impostors, The, 2, 49, 63, 122, 123, 126, 127, 140, 143
  White People, The, 126
MacLeod, Kirsten, 49, 77, 78, 80, 98, 135, 137, 138, 147, 205
MacRitchie, David, 188, 211
Madox Ford, Ford, 173
Maeterlinck, Maurice, 75
March-Russell, Paul, 67, 68
Martin, George R. R., 32
  Song of Ice and Fire, A, 32
Miéville, China, 1, 6
Miller, Thomas, 34
  'Gray Old Ash Tree, The,' 34
Modernism, 1, 2, 40, 48, 56, 66, 85, 127, 172–174, 181, 184, 221, 225, 226, 232, 233, 237
Moore, Frankfort, 63
  I Forbid the Banns, 63
  Secret of the Court, The, 63
Moore, George, 52
Munn, Walter H., 241
Murdoch, William Garden Blaikie, 54
Murray, Gilbert, 202, 208

N
Necronomicon, 118, 119
Nesbit, E., 21, 22
  'Man-Size in Marble,' 21
New Weird, 6–10, 72, 94, 127, 245
Nordau, Max, 76, 77, 87, 109–113, 145
  Degeneration, 76, 77, 110, 112
Noys, Benjamin, 4, 10, 12

O
Occult, 35, 103, 105, 118, 133, 145, 166, 202, 204, 228
Oliphant, Margaret, 17, 20
Omniferous universe, 4, 82, 122, 124, 191, 211
Onions, Oliver, 20, 26, 83, 85–87
  'Beckoning Fair One, The,' 85, 87
  'Benlian,' 86
  Hic Jacet, 87
  'Io,' 87
  Widdershins, 20, 86, 87
Orage, A. R., 127
Orientalism, 39, 99, 111, 113–125, 180–182, 191, 213, 229, 230
O'Riordan, Conal, 136
  Fool and His Heart, A, 136
O'Sullivan, Vincent, 93
  Book of Bargains, A, 93

P
Paganism, 30, 40, 87, 164, 184, 186, 192, 195, 200, 202–209, 211
  neo-Paganism, 205
Pagan Review, 205
Pall Mall Gazette, 52, 76
Pater, Walter, 73, 74, 77, 174, 178, 201, 202, 207, 231

Renaissance: Studies in Art and Poetry, The, 73
Penzoldt, Peter, 149, 150
Pick, Daniel, 76
Poe, Edgar Allan, 16, 17, 22, 30, 34, 36–38, 49, 50, 63, 65–69, 71, 96, 100, 109, 117, 119, 124, 125, 138, 139, 144, 145, 164, 170, 189, 196, 224, 227, 228, 231, 232, 235, 239, 241, 242, 249
 'Fall of the House of Usher, The,' 119, 144
Potocki, Jan, Count, 123, 124
 Manuscript Found in Saragossa, The, 124

Q

Quilter, Harry, 57, 64, 65, 75, 140–143, 176

R

Radcliffe, Anne, 27, 124
Rainey, Lawrence S., 172, 173, 238
Redway, John, 145
Reynolds, George W. M., 35
 Necromancer: A Romance, The, 35
Rhymers' Club, 66, 77, 78
Rhys, Ernest, 102, 109
Riddell, Charlotte, 17, 20, 23, 38
 'Sandy the Tinker,' 23
 Weird Stories, 17, 23
Roman Catholicism, 102, 103, 153
Romance, 14, 17, 27, 58–60, 63, 64, 66, 70, 97, 125, 133, 136, 143, 144, 165, 169, 173, 174, 177, 188
Rosicrucianism, 102
Russell, R. B., 111, 132

S

Said, Edward, 114–116, 115n9
'Saki', (Hector Hugh Munro), 83, 104
Samuels, Mark, 128, 133, 134
 'Man Who Collected Machen, The,' 128, 133, 134
Schwob, Marcel, 59
Science fiction, 3, 7, 8, 11, 13, 17, 27–29, 28n5, 31, 38, 98, 165, 225, 239, 240, 244
Scott, Sir Walter, 14, 22, 34, 36, 193
 Bridal of Triermain, The, 34
Sewell, Father Brocard, 107
Sharp, William, ('Fiona MacLeod'), 59, 62, 100, 119, 119n11, 205
Shiel, M. P., 26, 39, 48, 63–65, 77–80, 93–153, 164, 222
 'Eagle's Crag, The,' 95
 'House of Sounds, The,' 97, 98, 222
 Prince Zaleski, 78, 95–97, 112, 131
 Purple Cloud, The, 98
 Rajah's Sapphire, The, 96
 Shapes in the Fire, 78, 95, 97, 113
 Yellow Danger, The, 98
Short story, 16, 37–39, 49, 66–72, 78, 84, 93, 94, 99, 100, 117n10, 118, 120, 144, 164, 165, 167, 187, 188, 194, 240
Silberer, Herbert, 148
Sime, Sidney, 14
Sinclair, Iain, 127
Smith, Clark Ashton, 33, 37, 221, 222, 224
Spiritualism, 85, 152
Stableford, Brian, 20, 26, 27, 39, 78–80, 93, 94, 97, 100, 101, 125, 184, 186, 203, 221, 244
Stead, W. T., 53, 96, 97

Stenbock, Eric, 26, 38, 39, 49, 75, 78, 80, 93–153, 164, 183, 187
  Shadow of Death, The, 75, 103, 106
  Studies of Death, 78, 101, 104, 107
  Studies in Death, 103
  'True Story of a Vampire, The,' 104
Sterling, George, 221, 241
Stevenson, Fanny Van de Grift, 121, 122
Stevenson, Robert Louis, 14, 17, 49, 50, 59, 70, 71, 96, 115, 118, 119, 121, 122, 139, 144, 145, 175, 177, 196, 200
  New Arabian Nights, 70, 96, 115, 118, 119, 121, 122
  'Olalla,' 70
  Strange Case of Dr Jekyll and Mr Hyde, 14
  'Thrawn Janet,' 70
Stoker, Bram, 14, 47
  Dracula, 14, 47
Strantzas, Simon, 8, 9, 249
Symbolism, 57, 74, 139, 148, 153, 224
Symonds, John Addington, 104
Symons, Arthur, 56, 57, 74–79, 93, 101, 103, 105, 111, 176, 178, 231

T
Tartarus Press, 94, 131, 132
Temenos, 19, 185, 200
Thacker, Eugene, 3n2, 11, 29, 185, 191, 192
Thousand and One Nights, The, 114, 117, 118, 121, 123, 211
Tibet, David, 105, 127
Todorov, Tzvetan, 10, 10n3, 149, 167, 234

Tolkien, J. R. R., 29–31, 83
  Lord of the Rings, The, 30, 83
True Detective, 72

U
Ullman, Allen G., 236, 237
Uranian poets, 108

V
Valentine, Mark, 105, 106, 127, 131, 150
VanderMeer, Ann, 1, 2, 3n2, 5, 13, 72
  Weird: A Compendium of Strange and Dark Stories, The, 2, 5, 72, 235
VanderMeer, Jeff, 1, 2, 3n2, 5, 6, 12, 72
  Weird: A Compendium of Strange and Dark Stories, The, 2, 5, 72, 235
Vaughan, Thomas, 147, 150, 151
  Lumen de Lumine, 147, 150
Verlaine, Paul, 76, 186, 205
Verne, Jules, 27, 239
Villiers de l'Isle Adam, Auguste, 63
Vizetelly & Co., 53
Vizetelly, Henry, 53

W
Waite, A. E., 150, 153
Warner, Marina, 115, 117–119, 123
Warner, Sylvia Townsend, 132
Weird fiction as a mode, 4, 13
Weird sisters, 32, 37, 137
Weird Tales, 1, 2, 5, 7, 11, 12, 21, 33, 40, 98, 123, 164, 171, 174, 187, 221–245
  'Eyrie, The,' 227, 239

Wells, H. G., 2, 27, 29, 97, 100, 115, 121, 139, 181, 225, 228
  Time Machine, The, 27, 121, 181
Whistler, James Abbott McNeill, 141
Wilde, Oscar, 55–57, 65, 74, 77, 78, 111, 119, 140, 141, 143, 177, 224
  Picture of Dorian Gray, The, 65, 74, 78, 108, 177
Worth, Aaron, 20, 130
Wright, Farnsworth, 222, 225, 232, 233, 237, 241

Y
Yeats, W. B., 57, 77, 78, 102, 105, 135, 139, 203, 208
  Speckled Bird, The, 102
Yellow Book, 40, 53–56, 64, 65, 74, 99, 103, 118, 178–180, 182, 192, 205

Z
Zola, Émile, 53, 59, 75

GPSR Compliance

The European Union's (EU) General Product Safety Regulation (GPSR) is a set of rules that requires consumer products to be safe and our obligations to ensure this.

If you have any concerns about our products, you can contact us on

ProductSafety@springernature.com

In case Publisher is established outside the EU, the EU authorized representative is:

Springer Nature Customer Service Center GmbH
Europaplatz 3
69115 Heidelberg, Germany